CW00959151

ANOTHER HILL

AN AUTOBIOGRAPHICAL NOVEL

MILTON WOLFF

ANOTHER HILL

Introduction & Afterword

by Cary Nelson

University of Illinois Press Urbana & Chicago

Publication

of this book

was supported

by a grant from

the National

Endowment

for the Arts.

First Illinois paperback, 2001

© 1994 by the Board of Trustees

of the University of Illinois

Manufactured in the United States of America

2   3   4   5   6   C   P   6   5   4   3   2

This book is printed on acid-free paper.

Library of Congress

Cataloging-in-Publication Data

Wolff, Milton.

Another hill : an autobiographical novel /

Milton Wolff ; introd. and afterword by Cary Nelson.

p.   cm.

ISBN 0-252-02091-X (alk. paper)

1. Spain—History—Civil War, 1936–39—

Participation, American—Fiction. 2. Americans—

Spain—History—20th century—Fiction.

I. Title.

PS3545.0348A83   1994

813'.54—dc20   93-40189

                                        CIP

Map reprinted from Edwin Rolfe's *The Lincoln Battalion*
(1939) with permission of Mary Rolfe.

Paperback ISBN 978-0-252-06983-3

FRIEDA

And who goeth to warfare at his own cost?

—I Corinthians 9:7

In appreciation:

Cary Nelson, who discovered and

then rescued the manuscript from

the university's archives; and

Karla Huebner, who helped edit

and shape it up.

—MW

INTRODUCTION

CARY NELSON

We had all agreed with Mike's plan to scoop a hollow beside the ancient olive tree and to pitch our pup tent over it. The theory was that digging below the field level would offer us protection from shell or bomb fragments. Jacob Jorgensen, the blond Viking from Canada's forests; Gus Hiesler, the little New York plumber; Leo Kaufman, the bespectacled student from Philadelphia; Mike Pappas, the handsomest Greek in New York's fur industry; and myself, from Brooklyn: we shared the hole beneath the tent below the ancient olive tree, and none of us suspected that it might rain in June in the Morata Valley, behind the lines of Jarama in Spain. We were getting in our last words about this and that, smoking our last cigarette, shifting our bodies around the protruding rocks and roots that made up part of our mattress, when it happened. A flash of lightning, a roll of thunder, and the rain commenced to fall – but definitely. It took us about one minute to realize that the hole we were in *might* have saved us from shell fragments if any had been flying around, but that nothing was going to save us from finding ourselves in a deep pool of water since we had dug a convenient place for the water to come to. We sat there and waited for the hole to fill. There was nothing else for us to do, and fill it did. Listening to the rain and thunder we sat in a huddle, our teeth chattering, muttering feeble curses, when we all became quiet and looked at one another. The storm wasn't responsible for those sharp reports, the whining ending in close explosions, the rattle of machine guns. We had gone to bed fully dressed, so it took us less than a minute to splash our way out of our tent into the rain. We stood in a group, under the dripping olive tree, and faced the west, the lines, five kilometers distant, of Jarama. The lines were in flames. Shells, uninterruptedly, burst along the ridge that was the front, and the town of Morata, below the ridge and closer to us, showed in silhouettes as shells burst in its streets.

The year is 1937; Spain is a divided country, the west held by rebel Nationalist troops, the east controlled by loyalist forces of the Spanish Republic. Milt Wolff, an American volunteer on the side of the Republic, will soon be in the lines, fighting to win back territory and keep the fascists from overrunning the rest of Spain. This passage, from one of two brief memoirs Wolff wrote in the decade following his return to the United States in 1938, never found its way into print. American publishers had little interest in memoirs about Spain then; the three thousand Americans who fought there were officially considered "premature" antifascists. Such stands were not appropriate matters for individual conscience; best to wait for government policy to point the way. Wolff did not wait, neither then nor when World War II began; he acted. But he has waited – and for much longer – to tell his story in full. *Another Hill,* part autobiography and part novel, is his effort to tell that story now. It also brings us the story of the Americans who fought in the Spanish Civil War from a unique perspective – that of their last commander.

When a group of highly conservative army officers organized an armed attempt to overthrow the elected and notably progressive government of Spain in July 1936, it soon became clear that the conflict would focus the deepening worldwide struggle between fascism and democracy. Mussolini and Hitler immediately offered Franco and the other rebel officers extensive support in the form of weapons and troops. The Western democratic countries meanwhile hesitated to become involved. Perhaps a policy of nonintervention would persuade the fascist powers to withdraw their support. Foreign involvement, moreover, might trigger a wider war in Europe. Was Spain really worth that risk? Was even a cautiously progressive government in Spain – with its hints of land reform – in the best interests of conservative economic powers in the democracies? It would not be long before this variously cowardly, reactionary, and ineffective policy extended to further efforts to appease Hitler. Meanwhile, the Spanish people were dying, not only combatants but also civilians in Loyalist cities subjected to the first heavy artillery and air bombardments the world had known.

Around the world, progressive men and women realized that a fascist victory in Spain could put everyone in danger. However divided and unstable the Spanish Republic was, moreover, it represented values worth defending. An early spontaneous effort to aid the Spanish people and their government began to take shape in Britain, Europe, and the United States, as individuals traveled to France and crossed the border into Spain. Before long, the Communist International, at first ambivalent, decided to help recruit and organize volunteers by making arrangements for their travel, formally organizing the International Brigades, and promoting the cause of Loyalist Spain. Meanwhile, an administrative center for the brigades was established in the Spanish city of Albacete and training bases were set up in nearby towns. Some forty thousand people eventually volunteered from fifty-three different countries. The Soviet Union provided some material aid to the Spanish government, including selling arms fairly regularly, but it was not enough to counter the coordinated application of the men and supplies provided by Germany and Italy. Often able to block rebel assaults – as in the dramatic and successful effort to defend the capital city, Madrid, in the opening months of the war – the forces of the Republic were much less successful at holding the ground won in their own offensives. In the Spain of 1938, after nearly two years of war, Nationalist forces broke through to the Mediterranean and cut the Republic in two.

Both because of language differences and because it was desirable to publicize the commitments volunteers from different countries were making, the International Brigades were eventually organized into battalions according to their country of origin. The divisions were not absolute, however, since individual volunteers were often sent where their skills were most needed. Toward the end of the war, moreover, losses were so heavy that the battalions had to be filled out with Spanish volunteers. Nonetheless, a number of Americans were gathered in the Abraham Lincoln and George Washington Battalions, which were later combined.

One of the young Americans who volunteered to fight in Spain was Milton Wolff, a twenty-one-year-old former art student from Brooklyn. After traveling to France on an ocean liner, he hiked across the Pyrenees, trained near Tarazona, and found himself carrying water for a machine gun company. But that was only the beginning of his story. Something latent in his character in the United States took shape in Spain, and the men and

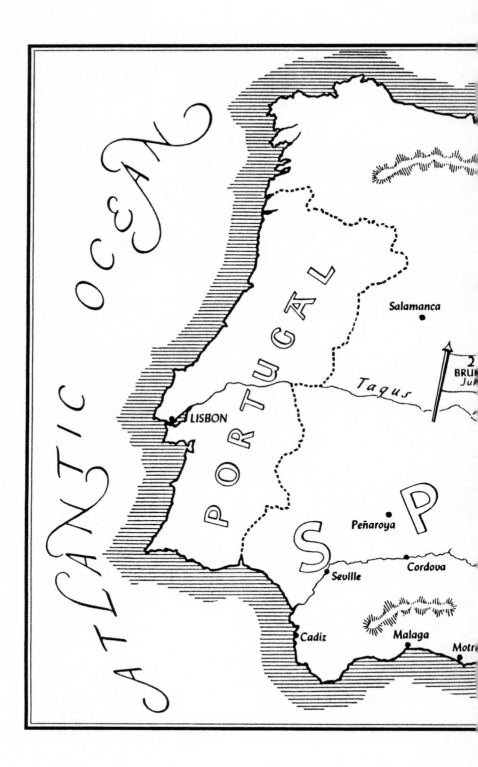

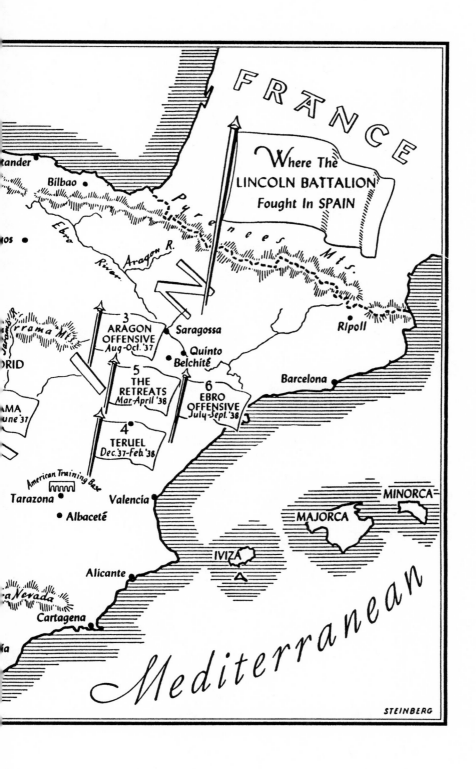

FRANCE

Where The
LINCOLN BATTALION
Fought In SPAIN

ander

Bilbao •

Ebro River   Aragon R.

Pyrenees   Mts.

os •

Ripoll •

rrama Mts

3
ARAGON
OFFENSIVE
Aug.-Oct. '37

Saragossa •

RID

Quinto •
Belchité •

MA
une '37

5
THE
RETREATS
Mar-April '38

6
EBRO
OFFENSIVE
July-Sept. '38

Barcelona •

4
TERUEL
Dec. 37-Feb. '38

American Training Base

Tarazona •

Valencia •

MINORCA

• Albaceté

MAJORCA

IVIZA

Alicante •

aNevada

Cartagena •

Mediterranean

STEINBERG

brigade leaders took note of it. He had a capacity to lead men in battle. He would later command that machine gun company and would finally command the Lincoln Battalion itself. As events unfolded, he would become the battalion's last commander. When an organization called the Veterans of the Abraham Lincoln Brigade was formed after the war, Wolff would become its commander as well.

The bare outlines of Wolff's role in Spain – and something of what people thought of him at the time – are evoked succinctly in a piece Ernest Hemingway wrote in 1938 for *Spanish Portraits*, a booklet of photographs of Jo Davidson's sculptures accompanied by prose tributes to the men and women depicted:

> Nine men commanded the Lincoln and Lincoln-Washington Battalions. There is no space to tell about them here but four are dead and four are wounded and this is the head of the ninth and last commander, Milton Wolff, 23 years old, tall as Lincoln, gaunt as Lincoln, and as brave and as good a soldier as any that commanded battalions at Gettysburg. He is alive and unhit by the same hazard that leaves one tall palm tree standing where a hurricane has passed.
>
> Milt Wolff arrived in Spain March 7, 1937, trained with the Washington Battalion and after reserve service at Jarama fought through the July heat and thirst of the blood bath that was called Bruneté as a machine gunner. In September in the blowing dust of Aragon at the taking of Quinto and the storming of Belchite he was leading a section. In the Fifteenth Brigade's Passchendaele at Fuentes de Ebro he commanded a machine gun company. In the defense of Teruel fighting in the cold and the snow he was captain and adjutant. When Dave Reiss was killed at Belchite he took over the battalion and through the March [1938] retreat led it wisely and heroically. When finally it was surrounded and cut to pieces through no fault of his, outside Gandesa he swam the Ebro with its remnants.
>
> When what was left of the Fifteenth Brigade held at Mora de Ebro Wolff trained and reorganized his battalion and led it in the great offensive across the Ebro that changed the course of the war and saved Valencia. In the high mountains of Sierra Pandols, attacked repeatedly under the heaviest artillery and aviation bombardments of the war, they held their gains and turned them over intact to the Spaniards when the Internationals were withdrawn. He is a retired major now at twenty-three and still alive and pretty soon he will be coming home as other men his age

and rank came home after the peace at Appomattox courthouse long ago. Except the peace was made at Munich now and no good men will be at home for long.

The story of the Americans who fought in Spain has been told several times, most thoroughly in several nonfiction books, including Edwin Rolfe's *The Lincoln Battalion* (1939), Alvah Bessie's *Men in Battle* (1939), Arthur Landis's *The Abraham Lincoln Brigade* (1967), Cecil Eby's *Between the Bullet and the Lie* (1969), Robert Rosenstone's *Crusade of the Left* (1969), and Peter Carroll's *Americans in the Spanish Civil War* (1994). Now Milt Wolff has chosen to tell this story in a strikingly different form – an autobiographical novel. Because this form is more unusual than it may seem to some readers and because the relationship between fact and fiction in *Another Hill* is complex and sometimes potentially deceptive, some prefatory remarks about the book are appropriate.

In effect, because *Another Hill* is both an autobiography and a novel and thus a complexly positioned instance of historical testimony, my job here is necessarily paradoxical. To make the historical record as clear as possible, I must partially restore the line between fact and fiction that the book deliberately blurs. Of course not all readers will come to this book equally disempowered. Those who were in Spain with its author and those who have already read widely about the war will recognize many of the people and events Wolff describes. Thus, although some of the characters in the book have real names and others have fictional names, some readers will be able to recognize real people behind fictional masks and thus give a number of apparently invented characters their real identities. Sorting out the decisions about which people to identify openly and which people to grant fictional identities was often quite difficult for Wolff. Not all participants who are still alive, of course, will be pleased with Wolff's decisions, which continued to change through the novel's various drafts; nor will everyone who was there in Spain be happy with his or her characterization here. Occasionally, it is important to note, Wolff did more than change a name to protect a living person; sometimes a character – based on a real individual who survived the war – does not survive the novel. Strategies like that sometimes make it possible to tell a greater truth while sacrificing a lesser one, an option only honorably available in this hybrid form.

The book has two main characters: Mitch Castle and Leo Rogin, both partly based on real people but given fictional elaboration. As anyone familiar with the American role in Spain will immediately realize, Mitch

Castle is modeled on Milt Wolff himself. Moreover, so much of what Castle sees and does in the book is confirmed, albeit more fragmentarily, by what historians and journalists have written about the Americans in Spain that knowledgeable readers may conclude that *Another Hill* is merely thinly disguised autobiography. Yet that is not the case.

For the most part, Wolff recounts his own role accurately, and thus we are able to get more detailed descriptions than we have ever had of what it was like to fight and to command troops in Spain. Dozens of well-known incidents are given a narrative depth they did not have before. Thus anyone who has read one of the histories of the Lincoln Battalion will know that Wolff was separated from his troops during the retreats in the spring of 1938, that he gradually worked his way through the enemy lines and eventually swam the Ebro River to rejoin his men. What *Another Hill* does is give us a detailed picture of what it was like to spend several days behind enemy lines, almost without food, until Wolff could make it across the Ebro. The last night is spent under cover inside a hollow tree; that too is based on his memory of the events as they took place.

In describing the war now – in a novel written and rewritten over the last twenty-some years – Wolff has tried to tell the truth of Spain as he remembers it, and in the light of what he knew then and has learned since. Both the main lines of the narrative and the major characterizations were established in the first draft, begun in 1968 and completed in 1970. In most of the conversations that take place in the book, Wolff has worked to recreate the kinds of roles people played then. But the words they say here are Wolff's efforts to write plausible dialogue; they are not conversations recorded at the time. He tries, for example, to give characters who appear under their own names – such as Ernest Hemingway, Herbert Matthews, Vincent Sheean, Martha Gellhorn, and Joe North – lines that reflect the arguments they made at the time and speaking styles reasonably close to their own. But the actual dialogue is fictional. Thus Hemingway did show Wolff the manuscript of "The Fifth Column" in Madrid and did let Wolff walk off with the woman he was with at the Cafe Chicote. But the recreation of those events is partly novelistic.

Historical novels with real people as characters are, of course, common enough. Most often, however, the authors were not present at the events they describe. Autobiographical novels are also a well-known form, though they are not commonly peopled at once with characters who retain their real names, with real people whose names have been changed, and with composite characters. The form Wolff has chosen is thus a hybrid; because

the story flows smoothly and, for the most part, seems realistic, it is sometimes difficult to remember that there is a line here – however unstable –
between fiction and reality. Because Wolff's responsibility in the Lincoln
Battalion was a major one and because he has chosen this hybrid form not
merely to write a readable novel but also to tell what he believes to be certain truths about a war that still matters to many people, the book also serves
as important historical testimony. Indeed, there is a deeper sense in which
Wolff stands by everything here – the moments he witnessed, the moments
he describes from other people's accounts, and the moments he invents.
The choice of an autobiographical novel, rather than a pure autobiography,
by which to tell his story was neither accidental nor immediate. In fact
Wolff first made some efforts at writing an autobiography, but he found
himself psychologically constrained by that form. It sometimes seemed that
the people he fought with in Spain stood at his shoulder while he wrote,
arguing with him, urging one interpretation or another on him. The small
but decisive distance provided by autobiographical fiction finally gave him
the space of relative freedom in which to work. Yet Wolff has still been re-
luctant to show the manuscript to other veterans. The result of negotiating
all these difficulties, however, is in many ways a book that has more of the
truth of Spain in it than a book in any other form might have had.

That is not to say, however, that Wolff's Spain was everyone's Spain. Indeed, the parties with an interest in Spain were so diverse that no single
image of the war can be sustained. That is obviously true to some degree of
any war, although the perspective of the losing side is often swept aside by
the stories told by the victors. After the Spanish Civil War came to an end
in 1939, Franco's immediate and later reprisals left thousands more dead.
Survivors – like Wolff – wrote their stories from exile. Yet because the war
was both a fractious internal conflict and an international struggle conducted by vastly different constituencies, its irreducible plurality seems distinctive. The war Franco claimed to be fighting – against atheism and communism – was not the antifascist war many of the internationals fought in; nor
was either of these wars wholly compatible with the interests of all the
Spanish parties to the conflict. For many Spaniards the war remained primarily a national rather than an international issue. The German officers
who saw the war as an opportunity to test new weapons and gauge civilian
reaction to saturation bombing of cities like Guernica were not fighting the
same war as the German volunteers who stood against fascism in the International Brigades. The experienced organizers sent to Spain by various
Communist parties were perhaps not fighting the same war as the ordinary

seamen who went there out of straightforward antifascism or solidarity with Spanish workers. It seems more reasonable to concede that there were numerous Spanish Civil Wars fought simultaneously.

For all these reasons I neither can nor would choose to try to draw thoroughgoing distinctions between what is true and what is fictional in *Another Hill*, nor would I want to suggest that the line between truth and fiction is ever secure. All purportedly objective historical books, for example, have narrative elements that make them partly novelistic. It is impossible to write about Spain, moreover, without taking up distinct political and moral perspectives. Despite all this, however, there are a few crucial differences, a few places where a distinction between fiction and reality can be established.

Like the character of Mitch Castle, the character of Leo Rogin, a troubled volunteer who deserts more than once, is also based upon a real person. Like Milt Wolff, his name has been changed. It is Leo's character, however, that is most heavily fictionalized and Leo's character, moreover, that the novel gives Wolff the greatest freedom to explore. There is no way a historian could enter so fully into the mind of a soldier unable to integrate the self-interested desire to maintain a respectable fiction about his service among those at home, fear for his own survival, and a belated sympathy for the Spanish people. Wolff did not know the person Rogin's character is based on well; he has used other people's comments at the time and his own informed speculation to flesh out Rogin's personality. He combines all of this to give us a picture of a man drawn to the cause but incapacitated on the battlefield, driven to desert repeatedly and yet capable of rationalizing everything to himself so as to retain his dignity. Castle's story, often true, alternates through much of the book with Rogin's, which is, more often than Wolff's, partly fictional.

Some of the scenes Wolff describes in Rogin's chapters, however, are based either on his own experience or on conversations with other veterans. For example, the account of the black market in Barcelona – and of a restaurant Wolff never visited – is grounded both in what Wolff learned at the time and in what other veterans have told him in the years since then. The result, he believes, is quite accurate. The description of Rogin's panic in battle – in which he feigns being wounded and allows himself to be carried to safety – combines speculation about Rogin's state of mind with events observed at the time and reported accurately here. Rogin's relationship with a Spanish woman is fictional but realistic. The story of Rogin's trip to Barcelona with her is a composite of several wartime stories. A number of people in the countryside, including the woman described here, traveled to that hospital in Barcelona to get medical assistance. Wolff learned about her from one of the medical people in Barcelona. A number of deserters headed for Barcelona as well. From such elements Wolff composed a narrative that takes us persuasively into Rogin's feelings and motivations. One of the surprising things about *Another Hill* is that a commander who was notoriously fearless has somehow written sympathetically about a soldier who could not stop himself from being afraid. Indeed, at moments Rogin almost becomes Castle's double – the rogue within the warrior – voicing the doubts Castle learns to suppress in order to survive, maintain his political commitments, and do what he needs to do. Their eventual confrontation is thus not only political but also psychological. Alan Wald has suggested to me that this puts *Another Hill* into a wide modern tradition about doubles, a tradition ranging from Conrad's "The Secret Sharer" to Bellow's *The Victim*.

If one specific forerunner is to be singled out for comparison, however, it would be Hemingway's *For Whom the Bell Tolls*, a book whose portrait of La Pasionaria (Dolores Ibarruri Gomez) and whose failure to distinguish between terrorism and government policy angered Wolff on its publication in 1940. Wolff offers his own portrait of La Pasionaria here and gives an account of how one event that some would call terrorism has to be understood in its context. Although it was not Wolff's chief reason for writing *Another Hill*, the book is, among other things, Wolff's answer to Hemingway, his effort by way of hybrid fiction to tell a more thoroughgoing truth about the Internationals in Spain than Hemingway's novel about Robert Jordan did. Like Jordan, interestingly, both Castle and Rogin have relationships with Spanish women, though hardly in the form of idealized romances behind enemy lines.

In addition to the novel's depiction of Leo Rogin's mental life, one other major element of *Another Hill* is heavily fictionalized. The relationship between Rogin and Castle – from the beginning to the end of the book – is partly a novelistic creation. At various points Wolff did see the character Rogin is based on, and occasionally he interacted with him, probably on the initial trip across the Pyrenees and certainly in training, but a number of the interactions recounted in *Another Hill* did not take place. Contrary to the story the novel tells, Wolff did not talk with the real Rogin in this detail; Wolff was, however, aware of his presence and of the difficulties he was having.

In the case of the dramatic final confrontation between Castle and Rogin, I am honoring Wolff's wish to keep matters ambiguous. Whether or not

Wolff was involved roughly in the way he reports the story here, he has used the novel to confront one of the most sensitive issues of the war and to report the truth that matters most, a historical truth thereby disentangled from individual personalities. True or not in its particulars, then, the conclusion of Leo's story is true in its evocation of certain realities of the war. Whatever Wolff's role may have been in these events, his role in narrating them now is significant. In a way, he has taken on one final responsibility as battalion commander nearly six decades after the fact – the responsibility of testimony and witness. Whether Wolff's narrative here is fictional or confessional, however, readers are free to decide for themselves. Yet even then people will need to decide whether Wolff is relating – on behalf of himself and the battalion – a necessity, an injustice, or a complex mixture of history, fate, character, policy, and accident.

Throughout the book, then, Wolff has his own character take on a relationship with which he did not want to burden any other recognizable veteran. That decision delicately balances the fact that this is not merely a novel – that it is also the historical testimony of the battalion's last commander – with the license available to the novelist. In a gesture so distinctive that I cannot think of any comparable example in another book, Wolff also uses fiction to take responsibility as a commander for actions his troops may have had a role in carrying out. In the end, Wolff opts for a fictional method of putting forward a truth that could not be recounted in any other way.

There is one other incident – at the battle of Quinto – that requires some qualification. Wolff has based this chapter in part on what other veterans have told him, but after all this time their memories of the incident differ. They disagree, for example, about the number of people involved. Once again, the form of the novel allows him to pass on to us what matters most about this kind of event (the capture and treatment of prisoners under fire): a sense of its basic character and plausibility in the midst of battle. Here and elsewhere in the book Wolff's most important contribution is to put potentially unacceptable violence into context. Whatever morality we might want to impose on these events has to confront the exigencies of combat. The much-debated questions about the existence of punitive battalions, about the fate of prisoners and of volunteers who deserted more than once, are here given answers Wolff stands by.

Wolff has not written the kind of book he would or could have written immediately after the war in Spain. Of course World War II intervened rather soon, and Wolff's service in that war was not without its drama either.

He served with the British Special Services before Pearl Harbor, with Still-well in Burma, and with William Donovan in the OSS. But it is equally important to remember that for the next two decades, the Americans who went to the defense of Loyalist Spain were under fire in their own country. As last commander of the Lincolns and first commander of their veterans organization, Wolff was called to testify before the House Un-American Activities Committee in 1940 and again before the Subversive Activities Control Board in 1954. Other prominent veterans were harassed for years, and support for the Spanish Republic – even minimal support such as do-nating money or signing a petition – was often considered evidence of po-litical untrustworthiness. It was one reason why some people lost their jobs and saw their careers destroyed in the long postwar inquisition we call the McCarthy period. Whatever the motives of individual volunteers – and those motives varied – whatever the merits of the effort to aid the Spanish Republic, and despite overall military control of Republican forces by the Spanish army, it was enough for HUAC to know that the International Bri-gades were organized and politically controlled by the Comintern. About 65 percent of the American volunteers were members of either the Com-munist party or the Young Communist League; others were liberals, dem-ocrats, or socialists. Wolff himself had joined the YCL (but not the Party) in 1936. But even those who were Party members were not necessarily in Spain primarily *as* Party members. Under the conditions that prevailed through the 1950s, however, such distinctions could gain no hearing, and a book – like this one – that deals frankly with the contradictory human realities of the war would have been impossible (and perhaps counterpro-ductive) to write. There was no room in our national imagination for any-thing other than unqualified heroes and villains in Spain. It took thirty years before Wolff could feel that enough cultural space was available to give a fair hearing for the more complex life in the battalion that is report-ed here.

A novel seemed in many respects the best way to take advantage of the layers of memory and reflection that now stand between Wolff (and us) and the events of 1936–38. There are many passages here – a freak moment when enemy artillery shells come skipping horizontally across the field without exploding, the death of Bill Titus against barbed wire at Seguro de los Baños, the patrol from which Jim Lardner never returns – that take us back to the war so persuasively that we feel we are reading battlefield report-age. Indeed, in these passages and many others that describe events Wolff was part of, he has tried as much as possible to recount them exactly as they happened. But it is impossible for other events to escape refraction in the medium of their recounting. Wolff emphasizes this in the final elegiac chapters by adding another narrative layer between us and the story he tells. The last great campaign, therefore, the campaign across the Ebro River in the summer of 1938, is explicitly *retold* in *Another Hill*. Mitch Castle relates the story of the campaign to the sculptor Jo Davidson in the Hotel Majestic in Barcelona. Wolff, of course, did meet with Davidson in the Hotel Majestic, and Davidson did sculpt Wolff's head there and later cast it in bronze.

In writing *Another Hill* Wolff felt he needed at once to exploit and to resist the tricks of memory. He could make some events palpably real – give them more presence, make their historical testimony more persuasive – by risking elaboration. At the same time, he wanted to reject the tendency to glamorize his own role. He was more interested, moreover, in giving us a sense of what he felt in Spain than in relating how he was viewed by others. His self-portrait in the person of Mitch Castle is thus less admiring than what others have written about him. For the later view, we may consult Hemingway's brief sketch, or perhaps the dedication Edwin Rolfe, himself a Lincoln Veteran, wrote in the copy of *The Lincoln Battalion* he gave Wolff in November 1939: "With deepest admiration and friendship. – Certain qualities remain with a man all his life: things he did, said, thought, felt. What you were and what you did in Spain, Milt, can never be lost; it remains deep in the memory and in the consciousness of all of us who at one time or other were under your command, all of us whose acts were more perfect because you were there with us, leading us. The stature you achieved there – the respect, admiration, love that we had for you, and the confidence and trust you inspired in us, will always be part of us and a part of you in our eyes."

Note

This introduction is based in part on a series of conversations with Milton Wolff that took place in 1992. The quotations at the beginning and end of the introduction come from the Milton Wolff Archive in the Rare Books and Special Collections Division at the University of Illinois Library. That archive also holds earlier drafts of *Another Hill*.

ANOTHER HILL

1

The way was up.

In the dark of night, forty Americans dressed in business suits had been assembled at the foot of the Pyrenees. They had been cautioned to maintain contact, and instructed to tell any gendarme or border guard encountered, "We are mountain climbers on an expedition."

Mitch Castle was in a state of ecstasy, unconcerned with the incongruity of it all. He would have danced on his toes if he had known how.

"Stupid, stupid," Earl Glenn protested beside him. "Either they're stupid or they're in the pay of the imperialists. Criminal one way or the other." Mitch and Earl had been tablemates on the ship coming over. Earl was big, his big bones piled high and loose, asymmetrically supporting a large sand-colored head in which his small blue eyes operated mistrustfully of each other. On the *Ile de France* he had regaled Mitch with tales of hardship and struggle among the northwestern lumberjacks. As a kid he had been a Wobbly organizer, then a member of a commune that had seceded from the USA; and, in his years of wisdom, a seaman, a longshoreman, and a maverick member of the Communist party. Earl knew what went with the *vin blanc* or the *vin rouge*, knew who were the spies among their fellow passengers, and which waiters and busboys were union members and which were working for the Sûreté. All this knowledge he had shared with Mitch, who at twenty-one was ten years younger and knew none of these things.

Earl stared morosely at his feet. Too big for the rope-soled canvas *alpargatas* that had been issued for the climb, they remained encased in the thick-soled brown brogans he had worn over from the States. "We'll never make it," Earl groused.

While Mitch was impatient for the column to get moving, he rejected his mentor's prediction of failure. After all, he had successfully navigated some three thousand miles from Brooklyn. "What the hell are a couple of hills," he said in an attempt to overcome Earl's pessimism. "A lead pipe cinch."

"Mountains, not hills, comrade," Earl said.

Mitch did not want to think of mountains or any other obstacle in the way of his getting to Spain. As far as he was concerned, it was a miracle that he was here, and he had accomplished this by simply raising his hand when Cy Wolfert, Young Communist League section organizer, had tentatively asked the members gathered in the club's meeting hall: "Are there any comrades who want to join the International Brigades fighting fascism in Spain?"

Mitch smiled now. His hand had been the only one raised. Embarrassed as much for himself as for the others, he had quipped, "Well, if only for the boat ride."

The reaction to the call to arms had been a reflex. It had been, he realized now, an extension of what he had already been doing to fight fascism, and particularly to help the Spanish people. There had been ample time to withdraw. Instead, he had found additional reasons to go.

There were plenty of those.

For instance, the women complicating his life. There was his "steady," Blanche, the housepainter's daughter who had almost been the mother of his child. She had wanted that baby, and if not that one, the next. He had promised to marry Blanche someday, and when he'd raised his hand, "someday" had become his return from Spain. That was good enough for Blanche, and she had come to see him off. They had been well into a last passionate embrace when Earl had burst in on them announcing, "Hey, I'm your cabin mate, comrade."

Then there was Irene. Irene was the mistress of Mitch's married older brother. But Irene had seduced Mitch, and now his loyalty to his unfaithful brother was compromised. And what about his own fidelity to Blanche? All was confusion.

Besides the women, there was Ladies' Hat Body Forms, Inc.: factories jammed into lofts crowding the upper Thirties between Fifth and Sixth avenues. Mitch had been an errand boy there, a job his sister had gotten for him. Mitch's starting salary had been eighteen dollars a week in 1934, and by the time he left for Spain, he was making twenty-one dollars per fifty-four-hour week. Or that had been it until Artie, the keeper of stock, and David, the shipping clerk, had recruited him into a shady business they ran on the side.

Dave had packaged the stock and Mitch had carried the packages, along with all the other deliveries, to Artie's brand-new Ford, from which it was delivered to one or another storefront shop. His share in this enterprise had earned him eighty to a hundred dollars a week.

Now Mitch looked around at the men shuffling in the dark, talking in whispers, waiting for something or someone. They were all American volunteers, men who had come to this place for whatever reasons. He figured that at least one of the reasons he was here was that he had wanted to get away. Away from Artie's shady "business." Away from Irene, even from Blanche. He sighed. Maybe to get away from himself. He imagined them all now, YCL'ers, Artie, Blanche, Irene, all awestruck at the notion of Mitchell Castle, the kid from Brooklyn, boy antifascist, gone to fight the Nazis in Spain. The kid who got away. He liked that.

Two men, both small and broad, materialized out of the dark. They wore black berets, black jackets, and dark baggy trousers cinched at the ankles and held around the waist by black sashes. Gesturing, they formed the forty men into a column of two or three abreast.

The man who took the lead smiled reassuringly. His mate fell back to bring up the rear. Between them they worked the men like sheepdogs working a flock, heading the column toward the towering mass of black hills.

"They're Andorran smugglers," Earl whispered in Mitch's ear, "our mountain-climbing expedition guides. Been smuggling contraband for centuries." Earl flaunted his superior knowledge. "Now us," he snorted. "Live contraband."

At first the ascent was easy, the slope gradual and soft underfoot. After a while dogs began barking, and tiny yellow and orange lights blinked on and off to either side of them. The barking dogs and the lights formed an aisle through which the column passed, the guides picking up the pace as though to outstrip the hounds and their owners. The lights went on and off like candles in a windy place, the dogs barked and bayed, and Mitch could feel nervousness building up in the column.

"Keep it quiet, watch those clodhoppers," whispered Nate Nolan. Mitch, like Earl, had not been able to find a pair of *alpargatas* to fit his 11D feet. The $8.80 Regal wingtips he wore were not designed for silent climbing, or silent anything else.

Leo Rogin, ahead of Mitch, breathing heavily and slowing down, opened a gap between himself and Jack and Manny, who were hurrying to keep up with the rest of the column.

Nate Nolan, Leo Rogin, Manny Spear, Jack Altman, and Mitch Castle had been stashed away in a farmhouse in Capestan while waiting to be called to the mountain crossing. The owner was a member of the French Communist Party, a busy man who was always off on some urgent mission, his motorcycle wheels spinning clouds of dust that hung in the air long after he was gone. While waiting, they had played poker using cards that Leo had fashioned out of paper. Leo came from the Bronx. He was fair, his cheeks rosy, his eyes blue, his lips full and curved. He had been separated from his friends Aaron and Murray, who had been left in Paris when Leo and the others had entrained for Beziers – something to do with logistics, shortage of transport. Leo kept wondering when they'd rejoin the group. After all, they had been inseparable since their college days, when as a trio named the Voluntarios they had performed satirical songs at rallies, in trade union halls, and on campus. They had done everything together, including volunteering for Spain.

Mitch, light-footed with excitement, passed Leo, waving him on as he did so. He passed Jack and Manny and kept going, hardly aware of what he was doing until he came to the guide at the head of the column. The Andorran greeted his arrival with a smile and a gesture that dismissed the dogs and the lights as things of no importance. Mitch returned his smile; it was nice to know they hadn't mattered.

From his position up front, he could see the crest of a hill black against the bright night sky, and it seemed to him not very high nor very far, and that when they got to the top of it, Spain would be on the other side. But when they got to the top, another hill seemed to rear up before their eyes, cutting off a slice of star-speckled sky. This one was higher and steeper, the going more difficult than the first, and so it was the rest of the way, each hill seeming to be the last, the stars bright on the rim, and then the sky cut off by the dark mass of yet another rise.

They were well into the mountains now, dogs and lights gone, dropped away far below.

They came to a stream cut deep into the soil and rock. Spaced stones crossed the trench, and the guide slowed to point them out to Mitch. Then, using arm signals to instruct him, he posted Mitch there to guide the others across. The men came puffing and trudging by, and Mitch showed them the stones and how to cross, and they went across, one by one, too tired to acknowledge his presence.

When the last man had crossed the stream, followed by the rear guide, the lead guide came down along the column signaling the men to sit, to rest. Mitch went forward to see how Manny and the others were doing. He found Earl, who had fallen behind, sitting on a rock, cutting slits in one of his shoes with a pocket knife.

"Why are we sitting here like sitting ducks for the gendarmes to pick off," Earl asked, not expecting Mitch to know. "If I ever get out of here in one piece, someone's going to get a report. Heads will roll, don't you kid yourself." He inspected his work, put his knife away, and then, putting the shoe on, said, "What are you doing?"

Mitch's back molar had acted up, and he had taken a small tin of aspirins from his pocket; while trying to get it open he had spilled the white pills. Now he was on his hands and knees gathering them up. "Aspirins."

"Aspirins? What're you going to do with 'em? Eat 'em?"

"That's an idea. Six, seven . . . I guess that's all I had." Mitch straightened up. He replaced all but one of the tablets, snapped the lid shut, and put the tin in his pocket. He used his finger to position the aspirin between his cheek and the sore place on his gum. His tongue picked up the bitter taste. He coughed. He did not tell Earl about his toothache because he was ashamed of his damned teeth, beautiful but rotten.

They came off the slope onto a dirt road, white in the light of the stars and level, and after the hours of climbing, it was like flying. The stars were close and moved with them, and Mitch thought they looked bigger and softer than he had ever seen them. Bigger than they had seemed in the night skies of the Alleghenies, where they had bristled like spikes of blue ice. He silently thanked President Roosevelt for the CCC's where forestry in the Allegheny Mountains had conditioned him for the Pyrenees, though in 1933 he hadn't known it would. Neither had FDR, who along with France's Leon Blum and England's Neville Chamberlain had closed the border and embargoed Republican Spain. Mitch's passport, like those of all the others, was stamped NOT VALID FOR TRAVEL IN SPAIN.

His strides lengthened on the hard-packed road. He cast himself in the role of d'Artagnan, with plumed hat set jauntily on his head, cape billowing out behind him, seven-league boots devouring the distance. He led the queen's swashbuckling musketeers into the fray – the French Foreign Legion across African deserts to relieve a fort under siege, the tricolor torn and riddled by shot but still brave under the Saharan sun – a troop of cavalry on a western plain, pennants whipping, bugle blaring "Charge!" These dreams held off the weariness of ten hours of steady climbing, made the aching tooth more bearable.

They did not stay on the road long. The Andorran turned the column off to the left and up again into the mountains, finding trails where there seemed none, the twists and turns revealing themselves to him as though they were on a well-lit avenue marked by directional signs. Mitch marveled. How would they know when they got to the border? Would there be a dotted line, a marker, a fence?

What was a border? Mitch, pumping his long legs, which did not pump as well as the Andorran's short ones on the steep path, thought about borders. A ditch. A wall. Soldiers lined up facing each other, bayonetted rifles held at the ready. Barbed wire. How wide was a border? On this side you were a Frenchman, on the other a Spaniard. One inch difference, a foot, a yard, a mile, a river, an ocean. Here it was a mountain. That mountain? The next one? Or the one after that, which he couldn't possibly climb after having driven himself up the last one, just barely making it because he had convinced himself that it was the last one?

The guide went back down the slope to make sure that he was not leaving any stragglers behind. Mitch, raising his eyes, saw that the stars were less bright, the sky turning grey. He found Earl, his face white in the half-light, his pile of bones collapsed, his head sagging. Earl did not answer or raise his head when Mitch greeted him. Black-stockinged knobs and bumps swelled through the slits he had cut in his shoes.

"You still on your feet?" Manny, crouching nearby, was still cheerful. "Why come all the way down here and have to go back up again?"

"I think this is it," Mitch said, and seeing that they were all there, added, "I want to be with you guys when we go over."

"Oh, no." Jack's smile was strained. "There's another mountain after this one and another after that and another – "

"How do you know this is it? You have inside dope or something?" Leo said. His lips, white now, hung thick and loosely open. His eyes were red-rimmed and glassy and the pink flush of his cheeks had changed to pastel violet and tints of green.

"It's getting light, so we have to be almost there. These guides know what they're doing," Mitch said.

"I hope so." Nate spoke softly. "It's been a long night."

"If I was sure someone would carry me one way or the other I wouldn't take another step," Leo said.

The guide came back up the trail, motioning them to their feet. Beginning again after the brief rest made the going tougher for Mitch. The aspirins he had used during the night were making him drowsy. He had to concentrate to keep awake, to force himself to take each painful step. Putting one leg in front of the other was like lifting a lead pillar, lurching forward with it and putting it carefully down. It was a formidable task that absorbed his whole attention, so that when they reached a crest in full morning light he stood there with the others, looking down the grey-green slope at two figures waving at them, not knowing who they were or where they were.

The doll-like figures stood next to a white stucco hut. They wore blue coveralls and had rifles slung over their shoulders. In the east, where a yellow sun broke above the horizon, the Mediterranean lay flat and shimmering. In the west, a range of snow-clad peaks, pale gold in the early morning

light. Thank God, Mitch thought, we didn't have to climb those to ge
where we are. And now he knew where they were, because down there
where the two soldiers stood waving at them was the beginning of a plain,
its flatness broken by a scattering of hills – hills, not mountains.

Then everybody was running down the slope shouting and pounding
each other on the back. When they got to the hut they embraced the soldiers, lifting them off their feet. Loyalist soldiers of the Republic. They saluted the soldiers, examined their guns, their bandoleers, the blue monos
they wore. They saluted with clenched fists held shoulder high.

"¡Salud! ¡Salud!" *soldados* and volunteers shouted, and "¡Viva la Republica! ¡VIVA!"

The *soldados* dished out barley coffee in tin mugs along with slabs of
hard white bread; and they ate greedily. "Bueno, bueno," they said, hungry
and happy and safely in Spain.

Mitch moved back up the slope a little way, away from the others so he
could see where he was, so he could get a feeling about it. The sun was well
up now, and the sky was big and high and a thin blue. The land going south
showed a brighter green with long black shadows of trees. He did not look
back to where they had been.

The feeling he had was not in his head or stomach or heart. It was something that filled him from skin to skin. It washed into him and out again
across the plain, filling him and all the space in between.

"I'm in Spain," he said into the tin mug of barley coffee.

The fort at Figueras, a massive pile of stones and mortar,
crouched on a low-lying hill, a dried scab on a browning boil in the Catalan sun. Quarters for the new arrivals were below ground level, shadowed
cavernous halls that had once stabled the horses of Napoleon's cavalry.
Wooden bunks lined the bare stone walls. The belching and farting of hundreds of men added to the sour stench of unwashed bodies, rancid olive oil,
the rank fumes of crushed Gaulois – the strong French cigarettes issued to
the men – and the stink of snuffed candles, smoking kerosene lamps, and,
when the draft was right, open latrines on the verge of overflowing.

All this, along with the lingering aroma of long-gone horses, was as much a part of the permanent defense works as the meters-thick walls on which earlier International volunteers had inscribed in their many languages slogans expressing the motivation that had brought them to Spain.

Two and sometimes three times a day the men were led outside of the fort and spread out in thin lines encircling the fort, their leaders shouting commands in a babel of tongues culminating in some universally understood "Charge." They would storm up the slopes of the fort, assault the walls, and, sweating, cursing, and laughing, never fail to triumph over the defenders, who were nowhere to be seen.

One day after having once again conquered the fort, they assembled on the parade ground and formed up in squares, outlines blurred by swirls of dust, each national contingent standing apart: Czech, Pole, English, German, French, Italian, Hungarian, American. Like separate banners snapping in the wind, Mitch thought. The dust and tobacco smoke, snatches of strange words and songs, the bursts of sound rose compactly before fragmenting and spreading in an excitement of bubbles that broke all around him, as he stood, still sweating in the thin March sunshine.

A smartly uniformed officer stepped forward. He was, he said in French, the commandant of the fort, a statement reinforced by the gleam of his polished boots and Sam Brown belt. He rattled off a chunk of oratory, broken by an occasional pause for other men to translate his remarks into one of the Slavic tongues, into German, into Italian, and finally into English.

The speech began with Napoleon and the fort, and how the Spanish people had driven the invaders from the sacred soil of Iberia. The Internationals were foreigners, but now the Spanish people welcomed them, for this soil belonged to all antifascists; and now the Spaniards, Frenchmen, Germans, Czechs, Poles, and all the others were gathered here to drive the fascists from Spain. They were, he declaimed, the vanguard charged with the sacred duty of defeating Hitler's plan to enslave the world.

There was more, all translated into four or five tongues, interrupted by cheers and clenched fists raised in the sunlight. When he finished by announcing that they would soon leave for the Madrid front, the cheers changed to a concerted roar of approval. Madrid was where the fighting was.

On their last day at Figueras, the Americans were called to the parade grounds again. A man that Mitch remembered seeing at Beziers on their way to Capestan announced that there was a critical need for truck drivers. The Americans, he explained in accented English, were more familiar with vehicles than the comrades from the other countries were, and he called on them for volunteers. Mitch did not think that anyone would step forward; they had come to fight, and to fight meant with guns. But to his surprise, six men stepped forward. They took that one step and became truck drivers. He didn't know why, but it didn't seem right; it bothered him.

But it wasn't until they were on the train heading south, after they had passed Barcelona on the way to Valencia, that he spoke.

"I don't know about it not being the right thing to do," Manny said. "If I knew anything about cars, let alone trucks, I would've felt that I had to help out."

"Come all the way here to drive a truck?" Leo said. "Not me. And I can, you know. I drove army trucks on National Guard maneuvers. Big sons of guns, too."

"Okay. So maybe you should have volunteered, then," Nate said. "The way I figure, I can imagine a situation where a good truck driver could be worth more, contribute more than, say, twenty infantrymen."

He opened the window and tossed out a handful of orange peel. The coach reeked of oranges. There were oranges everywhere; everyone in the coach was eating oranges. At every place the train had stopped, there had been people pouring bushels of oranges in through the doors and windows. Men and women, kids with fists raised in the salute of the Spanish Republic, gave oranges to the Internationals on the way to the front.

Mitch was getting sick from having eaten so many oranges, and from the swaying of the slow-moving train.

"Oh, yeah," he said. "That's the ticket, all right: you go where you can do the most good. Like the story I cooked up for my mother, telling her I was coming here to work in a factory because more than anything else the Spanish people needed workers . . ." Feeling the oranges he had stuffed himself with coming up, he tailed off.

Leo was saying, "You came here to fight, so how can you wind up driving a truck? They can always find truck drivers somewhere."

"We can find men to fire rifles easier," Manny reasoned. "One of the comrades who volunteered was Al, Al Alexander, a kid from my club. A good guy – "

"I think I'm going to be sick." Mitch stuck his head out the window and heaved into the clouds of steam and coal smoke and cinders blowing by from the engine. Somehow, neither the sickness, smoke, nor cinders came to mind when he settled back onto the seat: what rattled around in his mind was that Leo had said "they." "They can find truck drivers." Manny had said

"we," "we can find." He wondered about that, and in the midst of wondering why he wondered, Mitch fell asleep.

The base at Albaceté was 250 kilometers from Madrid. There had been
fighting in the town, and there were bullet holes in the building that had
housed the Guardia Civil and now was the headquarters of the International Brigades, or IBs.

Once inside, they stacked what little baggage they had on top of a pile of
suitcases left by men who had come when the border was still open. They
were issued uniforms, khaki pantaloons and tunics, *alpargatas* and berets.
They were told that they would receive ten pesetas a day, the same amount
paid trade union workers; and they were now in the army. It was the first
time they had heard about being paid at all.

Then they lined up to sign in. The clerk asked each man to turn in his
passport.

"What's the idea," said Earl, who was in line ahead of Mitch. He held
onto his passport as though it was about to be taken from him by force.

"No idea, at all," the clerk said. "Just keeping it safe for you, along with
the rest of your belongings."

"I can take care of it. I don't need anyone taking care of it for me."

"Aw, come on," Leo said. "We're all turning them in." He threw his onto
the table before the clerk. "Don't make an issue of it."

"It's marked not valid for travel in Spain," Mitch said. "What the hell
good is it, anyway?"

"It's my identification, my proof of American citizenship." Earl patted his
hip pocket. "Hell, it's me!"

"Comrade, if you lose it," the clerk said patiently, "you will have a great
deal of difficulty when the time comes to go home. Every comrade is issued
a military *carnet* for payroll and identification purposes."

"Give him the damned thing," Nate said quietly, "and get on with the
business you came to Spain for. You're holding up the line."

"I'll identify you," Jack said, showing all his teeth in a steeplechase smile,
"dead or alive."

"Thanks a lot, comrade," Earl said. He picked up his *carnet*, a piece of
thin white stiff paper folded to make a two-by-four-inch booklet, and
walked away.

The clerk shrugged. "Next," he said. Leo pointed to his passport on the
table.

Mitch would not remember about the passports until later, when Earl no longer had a need for one. What he did remember was the suitcases, piled every which way, stacked almost to the ceiling. It struck him that each suitcase had belonged to someone who had been there before him, someone who was now somewhere else and might never come back.

≡ 3

The village of Madrigueras seemed to Mitch a collection of orderly rows of temporary shelters arrayed along narrow dirt streets that had been set down a thousand years ago and forgotten. The church, by contrast, seemed a skyscraper, its tower dominating a square and the fountain and a stone trough in the center of the square. The buildings facing the square had been taken over to house the troops. Mitch bunked with Jack and Manny, who were now members of a newly formed Machine Gun Company.

Leo's long-awaited comrades, Aaron and Murray, had finally caught up with him. They, along with eight others, had been arrested at the border and jailed in Perpignan. Demonstrations of protest, and the work of French lawyers sympathetic to the Loyalists – as the supporters of the Republic were called – had sprung them. As the Blum government had tightened the blockade, arrangements had been made to get the men to Spain by boat.

"A good thing, too," Earl said after Aaron and Murray had left for a rifle company, taking Leo with them. "Fat as they are, they'd never have made it over the mountains."

The Americans voted to name their new outfit the George Washington Battalion. The Abraham Lincoln Battalion, Americans who had arrived earlier, had been in action at Jarama on the Madrid front since mid-February, and had suffered heavy casualties. Word of the fighting filtered through to Madrigueras, including names of the fallen and the wounded.

Word also arrived of the first casualty in Mitch's group: Al Alexander. Al had left Albaceté with a convoy bringing supplies to Almería, and the convoy had been shelled by a German warship cruising off the southern coast.

"Well, I guess I was wrong, thinking he should have stuck with us," said Mitch.

"Or maybe right," Earl mumbled. He kicked at the dirt with his big feet. "Sand gets in through the slits," he said to no one in particular.

Mitch turned it over in his mind. "I think I'll go with the first-aid outfit. I mean, I was a first-aid man in the C's. Not that I got to aid anyone the whole time I was there," he said, trying to cover his sense of guilt at having questioned Al's motive for going with the truckers. "Maybe I'll get more action bandaging you guys up, ha?"

Old Doc Taylor was English, tired-looking, casual to the point of near-collapse, and a great teacher. He taught his *sanidads* bandages, knots, splints, and tourniquets, and he had them learn how to use a hypodermic syringe by administering injections to Catalan oranges. And when they had learned all that and had run up and down countless hills bearing each other on stretchers, he taught them the proper procedure for delivering babies on the theory that every captured village or town was bound to have at least one woman in labor.

Doc Taylor supplemented his lectures with stories of hawking the *Daily Worker* at night outside London's theaters. Few playgoers had bought, but many had stopped to argue, giving him the opportunity to speak on behalf of the Loyalist cause, free Soviet health care, and the miserable lot of Welsh coal miners. When, in the course of these debates, he was called upon to reveal his profession, there was invariably a great deal of surprise and disapproval. One did not expect a member of the medical profession to be a street hawker of the Red press. Were things so bad these days that it had become necessary to supplement one's income by selling papers? "And I say, old chap," some old boozer, splendidly got up in evening clothes, would inevitably demand, "you're not proposing socialized medicine are you? Be the death of us all. We won't have it, you know." "Bloody well right," another would add, "back to Russia with you, with the whole lot of you Bolsheviks. Practice your infernal socialized medicine on the ruddy Russkies. They deserve no better, the blighters."

Doc Taylor would go on, mimicking his pompous hecklers, the patients of high-priced Harley Street surgeons and the long-suffering victims of gout, diseased livers, and abused intestinal tracts.

"And they deserved the treatment they were getting," Doc Taylor would comment, adding, "I gave better care to eighty workers each month of the year, for what it cost just one of those dying Johnny Bulls to go on dying."

Classes were much more thorough than the single instruction Mitch had received as a first-aid man in the Civilian Conservation Corps, for which his father had volunteered him in the depths of the Depression. However, there was no set schedule for lectures or practical work, and more often than not, the men were in the dispensary until late at night. They were issued *salvoconductos*, permits exempting *Sanidad* personnel from curfew.

Pedro shooed all stragglers out of his cafe at curfew, *soldados* and civilians alike. But Mitch, armed with the *sanidad salvoconducto*, had an arrangement with Pedro. He'd rap out "shave and a hair cut, shampoo" on the wooden door.

"¿Quién eres?" Pedro would whisper through a crack in the door.

"Soy el Castillo solo poco loco," Mitch would whisper back.

The door would open just wide enough for Mitch to slip in. Pedro would warm the milk for *cognac con leche caliente*, Mitch's sleeping potion. It was understood.

Some nights Pedro was not alone. Mitch would find Manny sitting at a table behind a mug of *café con leche*. Pedro's sisters Immaculata and Constanzia kept Manny company, a small glass of wine untouched before each. Constanzia, a plain, solidly built peasant type, sat like a duenna between Manny and her pretty younger sister. Immaculata wore black. A large silver crucifix on a chain around her neck rose and fell gently on her breast with each breath. She gazed at Manny, her enormous eyes black pools of luminous shadow in the candlelight.

So Manny had his *novia* and Mitch his nightcap, and all was well until the night Mitch brought Roberto into the picture.

Robert Gardiner, called Roberto because he spoke Spanish like a native and with his dark good looks could pass for one, was the most serious and the most advanced *sanidad* in Doc Taylor's dispensary. He knew the Latin names for the bones and muscles, and was the only one who took notes at the lectures. Gardiner, Mitch had learned from Earl, was a university student who had interrupted his studies to volunteer. Earl was not impressed, did not approve. "These college kids'd be more useful to the cause with degrees on the wall," he'd said. Mitch, who had left high school a term early to join the C's, thought Earl had a point.

Mitch and Gardiner were the last ones to leave the dispensary. They left together, walking without a word. As they were about to pass by Pedro's door, Mitch, who was feeling stupid, not knowing what to say to an intellectual like Gardiner, seized the moment to break the silence.

"Wait a minute," he said, "watch this." He rapped out the familiar tune. "This'll kill you."

Pedro's muffled voice came through the closed door. "¿Quién eres?"

"Aquí es el Castillo solo poco loco," Mitch replied and then, turning to Robert, "Just like a speakeasy, huh?"

Gardiner frowned, and when Pedro opened the door for them, he did not follow Mitch in.

"Oh, you have a companion," Pedro observed. "Welcome to my place."

"This is Roberto," Mitch announced, pulling at Gardiner's arm, "a medico-*sanidad* like me. This is Pedro and this is his sister, Immaculata, and his other sister, Constanzia. Do you know Manny? He's Immaculata's Leslie Howard."

Manny did not look happy. Pedro asked Roberto if he would have the same as the others, *cognac con leche*, or *vino*, and did the *compañero comprend*?

"I understand very well," Gardiner said. "And many thanks, but it is better that I do not partake of your hospitality. I really did not mean to come here at this hour."

"Doesn't he speak Spanish like a real Castilian?" interrupted Mitch, whose vocabulary consisted of only the basics, put together by ear rather than the laws of grammar.

"It is true," Immaculata said, "but will you not do us the honor of having one glass of cognac or wine with us? We serve you as our guest."

"Yes," Manny said, "they're not open for business now. We're just friends, you understand."

Mitch took his hand out of his pocket, leaving the coins there undisturbed. "Yeah, that's right, Roberto," he said, "nothing illegal . . . just a friendly drink."

"You realize," Roberto said, "that this is a violation of the curfew, a breach of discipline. I did not want to come here and I am going to leave now. However, I think that you should know that I will take this matter up at our next meeting."

Manny looked at Mitch with great displeasure. Pedro and the girls sensed that all was not well; Roberto's speech sounded hard and threatening.

"Oh, shit," Mitch said, "you can't be serious. What the hell harm are we doing just having a drink after hours? You're liable to get Pedro's ass in a sling if you make a stink, and all he's doing is being hospitable. Hell, you don't want to do that."

"I have my responsibility as a Communist and as an antifascist. This action of yours may have all sorts of ramifications. It erodes discipline, it's an abuse of a privilege extended to you as a first-aid man, and furthermore," he paused and looked at the sisters and then at Pedro, "we have been given talks on security."

Manny blanched, and Pedro asked, "What does he say? What is the matter? What is going on here?"

Mitch laughed. "Pedro?"

Pedro looked at him questioningly. "¿Qué pasa?"

"He thinks you may be a . . ." – he did not know the Spanish for "spy" – "a friend of Franco."

Pedro and the sisters shook their heads in disbelief. Manny smacked his forehead with one hand and used the other to finish off his drink in one gulp.

Mitch laughed but no one was laughing with him.

"You're crazy." He turned to Robert, "plain loco. Pedro is as much an antifascist as I am. Maybe more. Immaculata's got the looks of a Mata Hari, but a Mata Hari she is not. What she is, is madly in love with her Manue-lo." He finished off his drink. "Come on, let's get the hell out of here and forget the whole thing."

Manny got up and said good night to the girls and to Pedro. Though everyone understood that Manny and Immaculata were destined for marriage after fascism was defeated, they did not kiss or touch each other. But there was a tenderness in Manny's "Hasta la vista," and Immaculata dropped her eyes and murmured lovingly, "Va con dios, Manuelo." More than enough under the circumstances.

"Hey, Roberto," Mitch said outside, "I don't think that you ought to involve these Spaniards. The spy business is crazy. Pedro voted Popular Front and when the uprising took place he was with the people when they ran the *alcalde*, the *Guardia Civil* and the *padre* out of town."

"I noticed," Roberto interrupted, "that they used the *adiós* form of farewell instead of *salud*. I noticed that Immaculata – is that her name – was wearing a crucifix . . ."

"One thing has nothing to do with the other," Manny cut in. "Sure, they're Catholics, but they're against the clergy that went with Franco, and they're against the fascists. They've been saying *adiós* all their lives and they're not about to change overnight."

"Who goes there?" the guard challenged as they approached the building where they were billeted.

"Sanidad," said Mitch, relieved to see that it was one of the guys from his billet who knew him and knew he had a pass and had passed him by with Manny before.

Once past the guard, Manny continued, "We will submit to any disciplinary action that is decided on." He looked at Mitch, who nodded in emphatic agreement. "No more Pedro's after hours. Just leave him out of it."

"I don't see how I can," Robert said.

By this time they were inside, and Robert turned off to mount the stairs. Manny and Mitch went on to their room. They undressed and got into their beds, straw ticks with rough sheets and blankets occupying assigned spaces on the tile floor. Mitch, who had slept on folding beds and army cots for most of his life, had no difficulty sleeping on the hard floor. He turned to Manny, who was in the space next to his, and whispered, "I'm sorry I brought that guy to Pedro's . . . Jesus, I knew he was a pretty serious guy but I didn't think he'd be a squealer."

"That isn't squealing," Manny said. "He's right and we're wrong. We're endangering the lives of our comrades by breaking the rules."

"Nuts," said Mitch, "we have a drink, play a little cards, get in a little late . . . nobody's hurt, nobody's complaining."

"Look, Mitch, you schmuck." Manny sat up. "You can't make an independent, individualistic decision like that. Certain rules and regulations have been established, and they are meant for everyone on the base, no exceptions. If individual comrades begin to decide which rules apply to them and which don't, we'll have anarchy here."

"Okay, already," Mitch said. "You sound like Gardiner. And he sounded like a Party organizer laying down the law."

Manny laughed, "I don't think you know what I'm talking about."

"You're wrong," Mitch said. "I know you think I'm a babe in the woods when it comes to these things. I understand the need for discipline. I think I understand why Gardiner will have to inform – I mean, will have to report this thing. It's just that there are some relations between men, it seems to me, that take precedence over the relations between men and organizations."

"That's a bourgeois *bubba-miessa*, Mitch, and you don't understand a damned thing." Manny was still laughing. "I wouldn't report you and you wouldn't report me and that doesn't mean that we're right and he's wrong. What it means is that I have a long way to go before I'm worthy of the name Communist. And you – you'll never make it. And with that, I leave you for to sleep and to wake up tomorrow to whatever tomorrow brings." And he lay back and covered himself.

"That was well done," said Jack, who was on the other side of him.

Manny sat up. "You up?"

"That was well done," Jack repeated, "and you couldn't have been more righter if you tried. So what's it all about? Are they going to shoot you in the morning?"

"Go to sleep," Manny said.

"Yeah," Mitch put in, "go to sleep. Tomorrow will unveil the next chapter – will Roberto tell all, will Manuelo confess his horrible crime? Will I scorn the blindfold at the very end? Come back next week for the next chapter in this thrilling spy adventure."

Then they all sat up as they saw the hulking outline of John McGivney, the oldest volunteer in their outfit, loom against the moonlit window. They listened to the rush of urine into the tin mess-kit taper off into the drip-drip of the last drops.

"You comrades have no consideration for the sleep of other comrades," McGivney complained. "I'm going to take this up at the next meeting."

"Oh no," Mitch whispered, "we're getting it from all sides."

"Does he eat out of that?" Manny asked.

"Of course," Jack said. "He claims it improves the flavor of the garbanzos, cuts the grease. Very healthy."

"Ugh," Manny said, "we've got all kinds. To sleep. To sleep."

And they went to sleep listening to McGivney grumble on as he settled back in his space, leaving the now-full mess tin on the window sill. The ammonia smell of urine carried on the gentle breeze across the room full of sleeping men.

"So what's up?" Mitch greeted Roberto at the dispensary the following morning.

"We're considering the matter." Roberto said this with such gravity that Mitch refrained from asking him who "we" was.

On Sunday, Mitch, Manny, and Jack got up before sunrise, skipped breakfast, and put in their share of volunteer Sunday farm work so they could cut out early to picnic in the countryside with Pedro and the sisters.

Pedro laid out bread, red wine, cognac, cheese, and smoked pork, and when they had eaten, they walked among the olive trees. Pedro sang Spanish love songs, accompanying himself on his guitar. Manny and Immaculata walked together, and Jack walked with Constanzia. Mitch tried to sing along with Pedro, who was very sympathetic and encouraging even though Mitch was off key most of the time. At Mitch's insistence they sang "Adiós, muchachos" three or four times because it had been popular back in the States. He was surprised when Pedro sang it through from beginning to end, because he had thought it was strictly a Tin Pan Alley production.

Afterward Pedro talked about life after the war. "These hills and olive groves now belong to the people," he said. "The owner was seldom here and now he will never come back. The *campesinos* who worked for him and his family, generations and generations who owned nothing, now have all this. Spain has always been the most beautiful land in the world and now it will be the most beautiful to live in."

Mitch leaned his head back against an olive tree and tried to squirt the wine out of the goatskin *bolsa* into his gaping mouth. First he missed and splashed his face with the wine. He flooded his mouth and could not swallow without choking, the wine spilling out in front of him. Then Pedro showed him how it was done, moving the spout to his lips and then up and as far away as his arms could hold the pouch, the thin blood-red stream arcing gracefully, only the movement of Pedro's Adam's apple signaling that the wine was on target. Then he brought the spout close to his lips, and in one swift movement twisted it up and away.

"Sonofabitch," said Mitch in admiration, "never spilt a drop."

"Why son of a bitch?" Pedro wanted to know. "What is it you say?"

"Nothing, nothing . . . nada, de nada," Mitch said, then tried to explain that he was complimenting Pedro on his skill, not cursing him . . . and cursing himself because his Spanish was so lousy. Half the time he did not know what he was saying for sure. Or no – he was sure of what he was saying and he said it with a great deal of confidence, but when he came up against something like this where he had to be understood precisely, he became painfully aware of the inadequacy of his mixture of Yiddish, pidgin English, high-school French, and rudimentary Spanish.

The little old lady who came around in the morning selling warm *churros* from a towel-covered basket and hot milk from a metal canister strapped to her back would stop for a minute or two and patiently teach him a few Spanish words. *Plaza* for the sun-washed square, *iglesia* for the church, *agua* pointing to the fountain, the only water supply for the entire town, and *niños* and *niñas* for the little boys and girls he bought milk and *churros* for. She explained the pesetas, duros, and centimos to him as she made change. The kids chipped in with *Madre*, *Padre*, *hermanos y hermanas*, *casa*, *comer*, and *borracho*, which was what they said he *habla*'d like.

"Como un borracho," they laughed. And after a while he understood what they said even though he did not understand all the words, and they seemed to *comprendo* him even though he did not have all the words.

So now he laughed and put his arm around Pedro and said, "Nada . . . nada . . ." With his other arm he took in the olive grove and the adobe wall with the red tiles of the *casa* showing above and pink in the hot sun, and said, "Sí, todos es nosotros . . . ," and hoped he was saying "all this is yours . . ."

"Ours, yes," Pedro said, "but will you stay after the war or will you go back to your home and to your families? That is what I think you will do and that is why I worry about Immaculata and Manuel."

"Do not worry about them," Mitch said, "for it is too early to worry. I think, too, that we will go home afterward because there is much to be done at home. It is a beautiful land also, and we must make it beautiful to live in too." He sang,

> We are the fighting antifascists
> We'll stay here till the fascist's tomb is laid
> And when we get back home once more
> We'll do; we'll do the same thing there.

He felt good singing and took another swallow from the goatskin, this time without spilling a drop, though he cheated by holding the spout close to his lips and tilting it only slightly so that he was not overwhelmed by a swift stream of *vino*.

There were burros on the road back to town. They were loaded with faggots, and a man sat on top of one of the burros. A woman walked behind, a black shawl over her face to keep her from breathing in the white chalkdust of the Castilian plain. The man, the burros, and the women looked like they were floating along on top of a white mist. The church tower shimmered in the sun ahead of them and the glare of light washed out the houses huddled beneath. The sky was pale blue and only under the trees where they stood and talked and drank wine was it green and cool. Mitch knew that what he had said had no real meaning for him. He was here, someday he would be in the midst of battle, and someday they would win. Winning would mean the defeat of Franco, and indirectly the defeat of Hitler and Mussolini, and that was good.

They would advance the cause of socialism all over the world. That was what they told each other at bull sessions, at political meetings, and in their songs. And Mitch thought that was fine. The only thing that bothered him about the coming victory was that it might happen too soon, before he had had a chance to do something about winning it. When the news of the big fascist defeat at Guadalajara was announced, he had had a sinking feeling in the pit of his stomach and had looked guiltily around at the cheering men to see if they noticed his disappointment.

"The war will go on for a long time," Pedro said. "You will be leaving Madrigueras soon and only God knows what will happen. It will be enough if he keeps you all from harm."

In the dark little houses, the Virgin and the bleeding heart of Christ still ruled over the bedstead, but there was no priest now, and the church had been converted to an army mess hall. Now the Spanish soldiers cursed on the milk of the Virgin Mother and defecated on the twenty-three testicles of the twelve apostles. Now there were more fiestas and meetings, more dancing and entertainment, plays and performances. Now all the children went to school, and most of the adults, too, learning to read and write. They read the government papers and the posters of the parties that made up the Popular Front which defended the Republic they had voted for, and they no longer inked an X where their proper names were to be affixed, but proudly spelled them all out with many flourishes.

"Pedro," Mitch said as they walked back to the village, stepping carefully so as not to raise the choking white dust underfoot, "why do you say *adiós?* Why do you not say *salud* like so many of the other people now do?"

"I say *salud*," Pedro responded, "I say *salud* to many people, but to my friends and to my family I cannot say *salud* . . . I must say *adiós*. It is perhaps a superstition . . . I do not know, but the others are like that too. To each other they say go with God, to you and others they say *salud*. It is natural, I think."

"Pedro." Mitch was wandering in his curiosity. "Does it bother you that the soldiers now eat in the church?"

"The church is a building," Pedro said. "The *padre* was not a good man. He did not concern himself with the people. We do not miss him and therefore we do not have a need for the church. We are satisfied that you have found a good use for it."

"Is this something you tell me also, while among yourselves, you do not like that we eat in the church?"

Mitch did not expect him to answer this truly, and so he did not listen closely to Pedro's "No. It is as I have said. We do not need the church."

Mitch thought for a moment that he would like to tell Pedro about Irene. How she needed the church, and about the letters she wrote telling him, "I pray for you every day, every morning and every night, that God will keep you safe." But it was too complicated, and so he did not.

"What are these? What do you do with them?" Mitch asked Manny. They were sitting at one of the long plank tables that filled the interior of the church. The tables were heaped high with steaming artichokes. Mitch had never seen an artichoke before, his knowledge of their existence barely recollected from something he had come across in his voluminous reading.

"These, you ignorant bastard," Earl Glenn said, "are artichokes. They're a delicacy only our filthy rich can afford."

"Wow," said Mitch. "There are tons of them here . . . how come?"

"How come? Because there's no way of exporting them now, and so rather than let them rot in the fields they're letting us eat them. Look," Earl said. "Pull off one leaf and dip it in the oil and vinegar and suck the meaty part off. Keep doing that and then you'll get down here where it's white. This is the heart of the artichoke. Delicious. The best part. But be careful, there are spikes, and if you try to swallow one it's like getting a fish bone stuck in your throat."

Their farewell feast, and on the morrow off to the front. The green smell of the artichokes filled the cavernous nave. Green leaves littered the tables and the tile floor; the smell of olive oil and vinegar clung to their fingers. Mitch thought, Things will never be the same in Madrigueras.

On the way back to the barracks, Mitch decided to stop and say goodbye to Pedro. He knocked at the closed doors and was relieved to hear the familiar "¿Quién eres?" Immaculata and Constanzia greeted him. They had set out four glasses, a bottle of wine, bread and cheese.

Constanzia went to get another glass and Pedro said, "Where is Manuel?"

"Oh, he can't come in here after curfew. No more of that since Roberto . . . or did he say he'd come?" Mitch asked.

"Yes. He was here earlier. He said he would return. To say goodbye," Pedro said. They all looked very sad.

"Give me a drink and I will go see why he has not come."

Back at the barracks, he asked, "Manny, are you asleep?"

"Not now that you woke me," Manny said, turning on his pallet. "Why the hell don't you get to sleep? We're leaving in the morning and you haven't packed your gear yet. When are you going to do it?"

"In the morning," Mitch said. "They're waiting for you over at the cafe. They said you said you'd be by."

"I said goodbye this afternoon," said Manny.

"But you said you'd be back tonight, they're waiting."

"Oh, they know I don't violate the curfew anymore. I just said 'see you later,' or something like that . . . it's hard to say goodbye, you know, so I just said something indefinite like that."

"So what'll I tell them? They're waiting for us to come back."

"Tell them I'm sick," Manny coughed. "As a matter of fact I think I am. My throat hurts so I can hardly talk."

"That's just from the dust. You got too much of it today."

"I don't think so," Manny croaked, "I think I have a cold. Anyway, tell them I have a cold. I'm sorry. I'll come back . . . maybe . . . someday . . . Tell them I'm sick, okay? Now beat it and let me go to sleep."

"He's sick," Mitch said. When he saw the look of alarm on their faces he added, "It's nothing. A bad throat. A painful throat. That's all. It's nothing." There must be some way of saying "a sore throat" in Spanish but he did not know it and in the end he had to do an imitation of a man trying to speak with a sore throat and then they understood. "He tells you all goodbye and wishes you well," Mitch said. Immaculata turned away.

Constanzia said, "Well, then, I shall go to my room. I wish you all well. Good night." Mitch thought she looked relieved. He wanted a drink but he did not feel that this would be a good time to ask for one. Instead he said loudly and cheerfully, "Well, *salud* and *adiós* and *hasta la vista* and I'll be seein' you . . ." and let himself out the door.

He was stopped twice on the way back to the barracks, and the second time he asked the guard, "How come all the vigilance?"

"The word's out that we're moving tomorrow, and they think the Fifth Column might try something in the way of a farewell send-off."

"No kidding?" Mitch said. He looked around the square. The *paseo* was over and the dust had settled for the night. The one-storey adobe houses with their black windows and black doors stood quietly in the night, close to one another, close to the ground, standing small beneath the soaring bell tower of the church. A glint of light caught his eye. It was the fountain. He could hear it splashing into the trough where the women would come in the morning to fetch water or to wash clothes and talk, and they would be small in the shadow of the church. The men would come to water their burros before they left for the fields, blowing small clouds of blue smoke from the crude cigarettes they rolled. And the church would stand over them, hands on its hips, menacingly. Then when the sun was up and the men were well on their way to the fields, the soldiers would come out of their barracks and march into the wide-open doors of the church and fill the insides with their talk and the sound of eating, and the smell of roasted barley-coffee and fresh bread and orange marmalade. But now the village of Madrigueras was asleep and it was the last time he would see it at night.

He told the guard, "Keep your eye on the church. If they're going to come, they'll come from there." He laughed and went into the barracks. Manny and Jack were asleep, as were all the rest of the men. He considered packing some of his stuff, and then thought that the noise would wake them and he'd better not. He undressed and got between the coarse sheets, but before he could pull the blankets up around him his ear caught a hissing sound from the window. He saw a shadowed form there, and sat up.

"Manuel," the voice whispered, "Miguel, it is me, Pedro. Come to the window."

Mitch got up, and the tiles were cold on his bare feet. "What goes?" he asked. "What are you doing here? You'll get killed, you *loco* you. It is very dangerous tonight."

"I bring this for Manuel, for his sick throat." Pedro passed a bottle to him. It was very warm. "Leche caliente con cognac," he said. "You will give it to him from Pedro, yes?"

"Wait, do not make a sound. I will tell Manuel you have come to say goodbye."

"Oh, yes." Pedro was happy.

Mitch bent over Manny and placed the warm bottle against his cheek. Manny came up and awake, grabbing the bottle out of Mitch's hand. "What? What? What?"

"Quiet," Mitch whispered. "It's leche caliente con cognac. Pedro brought it. He's there by the window. For your cold. To say goodbye to you."

"Oh, you son of a bitch." Manny struggled out of his bedding and headed for the window where Pedro waited to say goodbye.

"So much for security," Jack said.

5

Sometime toward the end of April, the American troops were moved to Tarazona.

The commissars told them that Tarazona, which was to be the American training base, was solidly pro-Republican and very happy to have the Americans. And it was true. The people took them into their homes and had them stay for the late dinners the Spaniards fancied. Steaming soup was ladled out of black kettles that had been sitting on the fire since early morning. And the troops had stewed rabbit and chicken and garbanzos, and even eggs, which were a great treat. After the meal they would join with the families for the nightly *paseo*, walking around the square two or three times before turning in. The people of this town were not as poor as the people of Madrigueras. The houses were a little larger, they were whiter, and the roofs seemed to be in better repair.

Mitch's first sight of the new doctor was like his first sight of Tarazona. Dr. Mark Stein was younger, more ambitious, and better organized than either Madrigueras or old Dr. Taylor had been. He shone in the April sun like a well-lit bathroom fixture, his tile-blue eyes moving brightly from face to face. His first lecture to the *Sanidad* unit – held outside the dispensary – was quite different than anything they had had from Doc Taylor.

"Venereal disease can inflict more casualties than the fascists." Dr. Stein coughed, cleared his throat; the *sanidads* seated on the ground turned to look at each other. "A casualty is a casualty no matter what the cause. A man laid up with VD is as much a liability to the army as one hospitalized by a fascist bullet."

Mitch Castle had been prepared to be impressed. This was the doctor who would lead them into battle. They were part of the Washington Battalion, which was all set up in companies, sections, and squads, and just starting intensive training for the fighting ahead. But so far they had not actually been in any fighting, nor had the doctor, and so the whole idea of casualties was still an abstraction. There had been fighting and other men had been wounded, and yet the young American doctor from New York was talking to them about VD.

Holding a condom at arm's length, Stein bravely carried on. "This," he said, "is a weapon in the war against fascism." With his other hand he picked up and placed on his head a steel helmet. The 1915 French helmet was quite stylish, with flared rims and a metal crest across its crown from front to rear. It gave the doctor the appearance of a Greek god, perhaps Hermes, imperiously dangling a rubber offering from Mount Olympus with outflung arm. "This is a condom," he went on. "It offers the same protection as this." He rapped his fist on the helmet.

Mitch decided that the time had come to leave *Sanidad*. Thinking about how he would do it, he stopped paying attention.

The Machine Gun Company was the logical choice for Mitch because Nate and Jack were there and Manny was already a section leader. Manny didn't question his reasons for wanting out of *Sanidad*. Dr. Stein honored his request for a transfer without any sign of regret, and Lieutenant Walter Garland, MG Company commander, assigned him to a squad as water carrier, the last man on the last crew in the company. This gun crew was distinguished for having the oldest water-cooled Maxim in the battalion, possibly in Spain, and the shortest ammo bearer in the International Brigades, Gus Heisler. Gus had a leonine head mounted on a mouselike body. He seemed poised for flight, his huge ears straining to take wing. The sight of little Gus followed by Mitch, the water-toting beanpole, was too much for the men. "Our own Mutt and Jeff," they called them. Garland had probably planned the mismatch; he had a great sense of humor.

Walter Garland, a tall, handsome Negro, had been wounded at Jarama in February. He was an expert with all types of weapons, and Mitch idolized him. There was an air of mystery about him that had to do with his having been acting battalion commander at Madrigueras.

There was much gossip among the men as to who would take official command of the Washington Battalion. Walter Garland, Vanderberg, Steve Nelson, Lenny Lyons, and Mirko Markovicz were mentioned. Everybody had their favorites, but since Mitch had been with *Sanidad* he knew little about any of them except for Garland. There seemed to be a great deal of animosity toward the one named Lyons, as the rank and file, ever class-conscious, was averse to uniforms, especially the spit-and-polish kind, and Lyons sported sharp riding breeches and gleaming leather boots. On the other hand, Nelson was much admired by those who had heard of his leadership at Jarama. Others questioned whether Garland, who had also distinguished himself at Jarama, was qualified or whether the policy of the Party to promote Negroes would be the deciding factor. Only a few insiders knew anything about Vanderberg or Markovicz. Mitch wondered how such decisions were made. He had no doubt that, however made, they would be the correct ones.

Markovicz was named commander of the battalion, Garland commander of the Machine Gun Company.

There was a Russian attached to the company as instructor. The guns were water-cooled Maxims from the last war, and Maxim was the name the Russian went by. Russians attached to the brigades were identified as Mexicans, a subterfuge that fooled no one; the men called them Mexicanskis. Maxim was above medium height, his hair straw-colored, his rubicund face as wide open as the Soviet steppes.

Maxim instructed them in theory; range-finding for the gun, fields and cones of fire, what the gun could and could not do. Each man was subjected to the same training routine because, as Garland put it, "You never know when you're going to find yourself number one on the gun." Garland taught them the mechanics: how to strip down not only the Maxim but also the Dicterov, the latest in air-cooled automatic infantry weaponry, and the 1903 Remington rifle, a long skinny affair that took a five-cartridge clip. Every man in the company learned to take the guns down blindfolded, simulating night battle conditions.

They went on long hikes. Sometimes three men carried the gun broken down into three parts: shield, wheeled carriage, and gun; other times one man carried the gun fully assembled, the U-shaped hinged steel harness folded over his head, resting on his shoulders and held against his chest, and, the carriage's heavy wheels hard on his back, the armor-plated shield affixed to the gun, the gun's muzzle pointed down. Or the fully assembled weapon was hauled on its wheeled carriage, bumping over the rough terrain.

At the firing range, Maxim oversaw the work of setting sight elevations and estimating trajectories and windage allowances. If a gun jammed in the course of firing, Garland showed how to unjam it, finding out why to prevent a recurrence. Mitch developed a great sense of security with these two men, and surprised himself by how quickly he grasped the fundamentals. With very little effort he was soon able to strip, assemble, clear, load, and fire the gun as fast as anyone in the company, even blindfolded. Out on the range, he was generally on target by the second or third burst. He was very good with the rifle.

Apparently it was a thing that came to him naturally, and he did not think about it one way or another.

But none of that moved him up in the company. He had been the last man to join, and so he remained the last man on the gun – water carrier – behind little big-eared Gus, Jack, Nolan, a Swede named Jacob Jorgensen, and David McKelvey White, who was a skinny semi-bald black-browed highbrow with steel-framed glasses, a one-time CCNY professor.

Every now and then there would be a battalion formation, and off in the distance he would see Earl Glenn in the Second Company, or Leo in the First with Aaron and Murray. The musical trio had become a quartet when Lehan Larner joined the group. With Harry on the piano, Aaron and Leo on guitar, and Lehan singing, the Voluntarios entertained the troops and the people in town whenever there was a fiesta or some sort of occasion, and, of course, a piano.

Now Mitch could enjoy their performance without feeling envious of Leo's talent, as he had been in Capestan. His mastery of the machine gun had given him a new sense of achievement, had given him an identity. Leo played the guitar and sang, and Mitch applauded. Mitch couldn't carry a tune, but he could strip the Maxim in record time and even play out a tune with his thumb on the trigger the way Garland did. That was talent enough for him.

There were political meetings as well as military ones, but Mitch did not pay much attention to them. The political line did not go through any basic changes, and he was already sold on it: the Popular Front, sometimes called the United Front, was an electoral bloc made up of parties ranging from the Communist on the left to the Republican somewhat to the right, and had run on a reform program promising universal education, land to the *campesinos*, a better deal for organized labor and women, and so forth. Mitch's devotion to the cause was unaffected by the complex problems created by the multiplicity of parties and the changing roles of generals and government officials.

When he wrote to his mother, he still pretended to be working in a factory. His letters to the YCL'ers, and to Blanche and Irene, urged more intensive work, more political work, more help for the Republic.

 **6**

Murray and Aaron, and me sandwiched between. It's a song. It's raining. The poncho's leaking. If I make a move I'll roll one of them out into the wet black night.

Leo made a problem of it to keep from thinking that now he was in the lines; well, not exactly . . . in reserve, at Morata, wherever that was. Between the Washington Battalion – between himself and the fascists – was the thin line of the Lincoln Battalion. It wasn't much, he thought, but if there was a breakthrough, he'd know about it by the change in the sound of gunfire, now only sporadic and scattered. But what if the Moors silently infiltrated the positions? He opened his eyes wide in the dark and imagined a scimitar-wielding Moor bursting into the shelter, intent on cutting his head off.

He shut his eyes tight. "Listen to the rain," he whispered.

If he turned onto his left side – the correct thing to do, politically speaking – he would flip Murray onto his right side and out of the tent. And if he turned the other way, it would be the old heave-ho for Aaron. It was all a matter of leverage because both Aaron and Murray were big and both were well padded, and he could not move either one of them unless he caught a shoulder just right to pivot him. What with the number of hard-boiled eggs and chocolate bars they had consumed, moving them any which way was out of the question.

Maybe there was a song in this somewhere. Something about "Hard-boiled eggs / Chocolate bars / Gifts from the very merry / dairy maids of Holland / They came in kegs / to fight the war" (not the maids, dammit, the eggs and chocolate) . . . No, no, comrade, is not political enough. Is funny, maybe, but a message it hasn't.

"Made in Holland" stamped in purple ink on each egg. How did they get them from there to here? And when it comes to chocolate I'll take a Hershey bar any time.

Does anyone know anything about Holland? I do, teacher. Holland is famous for its chocolate. It is a picturesque country with quaint windmills dotting the landscape and blonde, rosy-cheeked milkmaids daintily tripping over the dikes in cute little turned-up wooden shoes. The chocolate beans are brought in from Holland's colonial possessions. The Dutch people are noted for their cleanliness and industry. Also for their famous painters Vermeer and Hals. What about Van Gogh and his dirty, pale, rheumy-eyed potato eaters? All the commissars will now leave the room. But, teacher, what about those African slaves sweating brown sweat into the Dutch chocolate? Imperialists, brutal colonists. Yet all those eggs and all that chocolate we ate today (is it still today?) stamped "Made in Holland," a gift of the Dutch people to the International volunteers fighting for the Spanish Republic. Confusing? Anyhow I will take a Hershey bar any time. One of those big ones with thick squares of chocolate. With nuts. Without nuts.

Oh, no, you don't. He fended Aaron off with a sharp elbow so that Aaron, turning in his sleep, did not roll on top of him. Murray stirred on the other side, and he quickly cocked his other elbow against any possible encroachment from that flank. Their movements loosened the ponchos, and the smell of dampened bodies and soft, damp farts swept over him so that he caught and held his breath and then let it out with a loud Ph-s-e-e-w.

Goddamn it – the rain must be getting in. Listen to them snore, nothing bothers them. They eat like pigs and they sleep like logs and I love them dearly. Why else would I be here? Sleeping on the ground, yet. This is war? Sleeping on the ground in the rain? Some war! I should've joined the Ambulance Corps or something, like where they have beds and it's dry. The Medics.

Leo Rogin had not wanted to come to Spain in the first place. He had avoided the meetings where the recruiting was done, using as an excuse his membership in City College's Reserve Officer Training Corps, in which he had enrolled at the suggestion of the Party. Revolutionaries never knew when military training might come in handy. He had attended only three sessions of the ROTC before quitting.

Murray and Aaron, though fellow students, had no taste for the military. The ROTC was not for them. They were, after all, musicians and it was well known that musicians made lousy soldiers. On the other hand, it did not occur to either one that volunteering to fight fascism in Spain was a particularly military venture. When the recruiter had asked for volunteers, Aaron had looked at Murray, and Murray at Aaron, and then both had stood and signed up. When they had told Leo they were on their way to Spain, he had had no choice but to go with them. They had been friends ever since P.S. 44 days in the Bronx, all through Stuyvesant High School, at City, and as the Voluntarios.

Why can't I sleep? Something is going to happen tonight. I feel it. I know it. Something. Rain, rain go away / Come again another day / Little Leo wants to play . . . It's snowing, it's snowing / A little boy is growing . . .

Mama, mama, did you raise your boy to be a soldier? Or a YCL'er? Ha! Be a doctor, my son. My only child. Go . . . go to college. Yes, go to shule, go to school, go to college, go to music lessons. She was always sending him. Go. He went. Diplomas, bar mitzvah. But no violin. What can you do with a violin? There's no message for the masses in a violin. That's what Aaron said. She sent me to college to be a doctor and I went to City and became a guitarist and a Communist, and here I am in the rain.

How does the old man feel about that? Bragging about his son who is a hero? Nah. Probably dreaming up a grievance for the shop committee. "It's a no-good union by the bosses." Who knows how he feels about anything? "Do as your mother tells you." What did Mama tell me to do? Half the time he didn't even know what I was doing or what I was supposed to be doing. When

I joined the Party I thought he would be pleased . . . thought he would talk to me for once. "Papa, I joined the Communist party in college." "You know what you're doing?" . . . That was a surprise . . . What did it mean? I should have asked him. I should have said, "What do you mean? Isn't that what you want me to do? You're always talking about socialism, you're the one that's always fighting the bosses. When I took Hebrew lessons you gave me Freiheit to read, remember? Come on, Papa. Oh, I know I'm not as important as your fellow workers, or the union, or all those meetings you go to. I'm only your only son."

Night after night so that sometimes I hardly ever saw you much less spoke to you for days and days. Sometimes on Sundays . . . on Sunday, if it was raining like it's raining here and now. Is it raining in the Bronx? In the Bronx you have to look out the window to see if it's raining . . . "You know what you're doing?" I wanted to tell him about Murray and Aaron and the club at City. How Mama's music lessons and Mama's insistence that I go to college paid off . . . how you won, Papa . . . because from the violin to the guitar it was nothing, and now Murray and Aaron and me, we're a group. We sing union songs and revolutionary songs . . . but he was back behind the paper, not listening . . . funny voluntario songs. Why can't I sleep?

Something out there in the night had changed. Leo opened his eyes, strained to hear. The sound of machine guns opening up, the whomp of artillery and rifle fire no longer sporadic, now a fusillade. Aaron sat up, throwing off his poncho. "What's going on?"

The tempo of the firing increased. Someone was shouting orders. Leo could hear men cursing and slogging around in the rain. Murray and Aaron were wrestling themselves into their clothes, struggling to get out of the crude tent. They thrashed about clumsily and, half standing, half crouching, stumbled out through the narrow, low opening, dragging the makeshift tent wetly over Leo's head.

Leo drew his poncho up over his head to keep out the rain. But then, afraid of being left behind, he sprang up. Tripping, he ran off, turned, and ran back looking for someone to follow.

He found himself facing a ridge line that was intermittently revealed by flashes from the guns. The rain beat in his face. He was alone in the night. Visions of the Moors breaking through came back. He stood facing the gun flashes, not wanting to expose his back to an unseen attack.

"Sorry, sorry, comrade. I didn't see you." The tall skinny figure that had knocked him to his knees helped him to his feet, then stooped to pick up something that clanked metallically.

"Are you all right, comrade? Hey? Where can I get some water?"

Leo knew it was Mitch. He wanted to laugh. *Everybody is drowning in this goddamned rain and Mitch asks me where the water is.* He imagined telling Murray and Aaron about it.

"It's for the machine guns," Mitch persisted, thinking Leo hadn't heard or didn't understand. "Commander Garland is setting up the guns and we need water . . ." He trailed off in the darkness, the water canister clanking against the equipment dangling from his waist.

Murray's huge bulk loomed out of the wet and dark.

"Leo? For Christ's sake, whataya standing there for? Come on, we're forming up." Murray grabbed him roughly by the arm. "Come on. Where's your rifle?" He rummaged in the bedding, found the long skinny weapon, bayonet attached, and pushed it into Leo's hands. Leo let it slip through his fingers, but Murray grabbed it before it fell into the mud. He thrust it hard against Leo's chest.

"Don't ever leave your rifle behind. How many times have you heard that, huh? Your rifle is more precious than your life. The lives of your comrades may depend on it."

All the time the rain is coming down, the shooting is shooting, and he is talking to me like a commissar giving a lecture. What the hell . . . What the hell . . . they call this relic a rifle? He remembered his guitar, left behind in the slit trench and probably full of water. As he shifted the rifle it hit Murray.

"Jeeeeesus Christ!" Murray pushed him toward the dark mass of men lined up, milling around, trying to make sense out of the shouted orders. The water running down his face had the taste of salt. Angry with himself for crying, for acting the damn fool before Murray. "Come on," he said loudly, "Find the company."

It stopped raining as if a faucet had been turned off. Leo hunched his back against the scatter of gunfire and with great surprise found himself wondering if Mitch had found water – perhaps enough to drown in. "Now that's funny," he said, and Murray and Aaron laughed, too, when he told them of his encounter with Mitch. He did not tell them about the guitar, left behind.

Mitch was all geared up. Garland had rousted them out as soon as the shooting started. Manny had seen to it that their tent had been pitched correctly, with deep gutters all around the sides, and so they had slept well and dry; and when he had come out into the rain it had not been too bad.

The gun crews lined up and Garland looked them over. "All right. All squad leaders check equipment. Check for dry ammo, belts, water. Clear the chambers and report."

Manny came down the line. "How's the water, Mitch?"

Mitch held the canister at shoulder level and shook it. The rain drummed on the empty metal container.

"Jesus, get it filled," Manny laughed. "There must be water around here someplace." He held his hand out, palm up.

The ridge up front was flashing blues and yellows, the guns crackling and thumping away. Where did you get water in the middle of an olive grove? Even if it was raining? He saw Garland going by, looking very efficient.

"Castle, what're you doing away from the company?" Garland asked him, not stopping.

"Looking for water for the gun." Mitch held up the empty can.

"Oh, Christ, now I've heard everything," Garland said. "I'm on my way to HQ and you better have some of this water collected and be back by the time I get back. Hear, soldier?"

"Yes, sir." Mitch was thrilled that Garland had called him by his name and had bothered to tell him he was on his way to battalion HQ. For orders, no doubt. To report the company assembled and ready for action.

In the dark he knocked someone down and stopped to pick him up. It was Leo, his face white and shiny in the rain, his full lips looking black in the night. Just standing there. Well, he was no help. Mitch turned and went on. He stepped into a water-filled hole and with his free hand braced himself against the fall. There was a musical twang, and when he looked closely, he saw that he had fallen on a guitar.

He lifted it and sloshed around the water that had accumulated inside. Not enough. He took the top off the water carrier and submerged it in the foxhole. The water gurgled in, and the can filled quickly. He screwed the cover on and started back. He met Garland again.

"Good man, got your water. That's the stuff."

"Yes, sir," Mitch beamed.

Garland looked at him closely. "What's with this 'sir' stuff?" he asked. "We're all comrades here."

"Yes, sir. Yes, Commander." How could he explain the satisfaction it gave him to call his hero "sir"?

Garland shook his head.

They stopped to look up at the sky and around to the ridge.

"You hear that?" Garland said. "That's Slater's antitank battery."

Mitch hadn't noticed, but now he could pick out the flat sharp crack of the antitank guns.

"They broke it up," Garland went on. "Nothing more's going to happen tonight." And nothing more did.

They spent the rest of the night cleaning their equipment and talking about how the attack had been beaten back by the Lincolns and the English antitank battery, trying to decide among themselves if this had constituted being in action or not.

"No matter," Manny said. "It settled the hard-boiled eggs."

Mitch sat down on the water can and looked toward the ridge. Up there the Lincolns had been under fire. They had been under fire off and on for three months. That was as long as he had been in Spain, and this was the closest he had gotten to the action. "So far," he heard the words escape his lips.

The Washington Battalion left Tarazona around the end of June for an encampment outside of Valdemorillo, where they were joined by the Lincolns, who had been withdrawn from the Jarama front. The Lincolns were now seasoned veterans; they had been in attacks and counterattacks, had repulsed attacks by the fascists – and had suffered heavy casualties. Mitch, like the rest of the Washingtons, looked upon them with respect. Tales of exceptional bravery ran through the ranks, of how this or that comrade had been cut down, of how Bob Raven had been blinded by a grenade, of how Bob Campbell, the battalion commander, had been wounded leading the Lincolns in an over-the-top assault. There had been many killed and wounded, and the attack had been beaten back. Some of the survivors called it an asshole operation.

The names were those of comrades known to many of the Americans in the Washington Battalion. Leo had known the three Stone brothers from New York, one of whom was killed at Jarama. Earl Glenn had known the three Gordon brothers – now two; and Manny knew Nick Stamos and his brother Mike. Mike had also been killed at Jarama. It seemed to Mitch that a hell of a lot of brothers had volunteered and too many of them had been killed.

The American battalions were joined by the British to form one of the regiments of the Fifteenth Brigade. The other regiment was made up of a French, a Slav, and a Spanish battalion. The Lincolns were led by Oliver Law and the Washingtons by Mirko Markovicz.

The Lincoln and Washington battalions joined in arranging a July Fourth celebration. The Voluntarios entertained, speeches were made, cigarettes and chocolates were distributed. Then the orders of the day were read and posted: the brigade was to move out that evening to join the offensive at Bruneté that would break Franco's siege of Madrid and relieve the pressure the enemy was putting on in the north.

"Aw." Jackie Altman held up his pack of Luckies and a Hershey bar. "Ain't that nice. A last cigarette, a final treat, and off we go to do or die . . ."

The forced march to the jump-off position lasted all that evening and well into the next afternoon, the day getting hotter by the kilometer as the July sun arced high in a cloudless sky. Before they got to the last leg of the march, they were drawn up into a sort of hollow square formation to await the arrival of Dolores Ibarruri, the famed La Pasionaria, who was crossing the entire front of the advancing brigades delivering send-off orations. Mitch had heard of Pasionaria, the Asturian miner's daughter who had become a leader in the coal miners' strike of 1934; and who, according to Earl, had escaped to Moscow when the army, under this same bastard Generalissimo Franco, broke the strike.

The troops waited in the hot sun, and waited. After a while the British troops started to sing:

> Waiting, waiting, waiting
> always bloody well waiting
> Waiting in the morning, waiting in the night
> God send the day
> when we'll bloody well wait no more.

The Americans joined in once they caught the hang of the words. When Dolores finally arrived, she apologized for having kept them waiting, explaining that the roads were jammed, making it very difficult to move from brigade to brigade. She said, however, that such a hardship was as nothing – that in the coming days, in solidarity with the people of Spain, the International antifascist volunteers would go forward under the banner of the United Front to smash the rebellious Falange and the fascist generals.

The government now, she explained, was in the best shape since the start of the uprising. Juan Negrin, a socialist, "*Un hombre,*" she said, giving weight to the words, "who has taken the War Ministry in hand and who is direct and capable, who has the will to lead the Republic to victory over the fascist insurgents."

Her remarks were interrupted with shouts of "¡Viva La Republica!" For the finale, she called for the death and defeat of the fascisti, and the victory of the Spanish people, the Internationals, and all mankind. She raised a clenched fist, and the men responded with a roar.

"¡VIVA LA PASIONARIA! ¡NO PASARAN!"

And for another moment she stood there, her head bare in the July sun, her black hair reflecting its light, her sturdy figure erect in a black dress, dark shadows in the hollow of her eyes, her pale face lined with exhaustion, and yet a small smile on her lips. Seeing her there like that, the men repeated "Viva Pasionaria" three times over.

Mitch searched the sky where the rushing, whooshing, arching shells made a rainbow of sound; he thought he caught sight of a black and silvery flash, but only for a split second, so he wasn't sure.

The single file of men snaked its way over the gentle green hills. The sun beat on their backs. When they came to rest on a rise, Mitch looked behind just in time to see a puff of smoke snap the line in two, the broken ends recoiling, separating into fast-moving black dots.

"That was a lucky shot," he said to McKelvey.

"Not for the man who was hit. Or men." McKelvey removed his steel-rimmed glasses and polished them with a remarkably clean handkerchief. He replaced the glasses on his nose, adjusted them, wiped his brow with the handkerchief, and returned it to his pocket. He sat down on an ammo case and looked off to where the shell had landed.

"Who's back there?" Mitch asked, his eyes on the small puff of smoke now slowly rising against the blue sky, the delayed soft "poom" of the explosion sounding harmless in the distance.

"Another brigade," said McKelvey. "Men. The first casualties."

McKelvey picked up his two cases of ammo and Mitch fell in behind with the water canisters. The heavy ammo cases dragged McKelvey's shoulders downward in a simian slope, bowing his thin legs. As he plodded on, his head and neck were thrust forward, his beard a bluish black against the white of his cheeks, the French tin helmet slipping and sliding on his balding brow, dust powdering the bushy black eyebrows, glasses blank and glazed in the strong sun. Mitch marveled at this skinny one-time professor, now the ammo carrier for a Maxim. McKelvey had come to Spain to fly planes for the Republic, only to find that there were no planes for him to fly. Offered the choice of going back home or staying to serve in some rear-line capacity, McKelvey had opted for the infantry instead.

Ahead, Mitch could see men running up to the crest of a hill, falling down, firing, moving forward. Garland came down the line giving orders to the section leaders.

Manny gathered them together. "There's snipers up ahead. When we get to the foot of that hill, hit the dirt until I say go over, and then get up and run like hell. Don't stop on the way to read the *Daily Worker,* okay? Let's move!"

Garland knelt just below the crest, waving the men on one at a time.

"Listen, Dave," Mitch nudged McKelvey, "let me take one of those ammo cases till we get over to the other side of this hill. I can handle the extra load."

McKelvey turned on him. "Just who do you think you are? Giving orders!"

"I'm not giving orders. I mean, I can easily carry one more thing and you look . . ." Mitch stammered, taken aback.

"You just carry yourself over and don't you worry about me," McKelvey said.

"Okay, okay, comrade, hit the dirt!" Garland bawled, and McKelvey flopped to the ground, still holding onto the ammo carriers, which he flung out before him. There was a pause, and then, "Now!" McKelvey scrambled awkwardly to his feet and ran up the hill, but the ammo cases banging against his thighs slowed him so that he was barely moving when he reached the crest. There was the *spftt* of a bullet, and McKelvey pirouetted gracefully, the ammo boxes fanning out as he settled to the ground.

Garland raced to his side. Mitch waited his turn to go over. He could see Garland searching McKelvey's body for the wound, prying loose his grip on the ammo cases, and then starting to lift him in his arms. There was another swift *spftt;* Garland dropped McKelvey and looked at his hand. Mitch got up and started for Garland, but Garland waved him on past.

"Keep going! Keep going!"

Mitch veered off to where his gun crew waited. He looked back and saw Garland half drag, half carry McKelvey off the hill.

"Whadda we do now?" Gus said.

Before Manny could reply, they saw Garland come over the top, loping toward the head of the company, waving his hand wrapped in a white handkerchief.

"It's just a scratch," he called as he ran past.

"Yup," Manny said. "How hit is McKelvey?"

"He's okay." Garland slowed his pace. "The wound doesn't look like much, but that and the heat has him down. He'll be all right. Only man we lost. Pretty good. Get your section ready to move," he called over his shoulder as he picked up the pace, heading for the lead section.

"Mitch, you go up and retrieve those ammo cases. We're going to need them," Manny said.

Mitch turned and scrambled up the hill. Now there were men coming from another outfit and they looked at him questioningly as he moved toward the rear. He felt a need to point to the ammo cases, and he got there as fast as he could. As he bent to pick them up he looked for blood on the ground, but there was none.

Loaded with the two heavy cases, he turned and ran back. Mitch thought, *He wouldn't have been hurt if he'd've let me help.* But Mitch wasn't really thinking of McKelvey. His concern was for Garland. What a stupid fucking thing to do, he thought. *The guy we need most going out there to pull him in. He could've gotten killed, or hit so bad we would've lost him. He should have let me take care of it. Or somebody. Goddamn it.*

And when Mitch came panting back up to Manny with the ammo cases, he blurted out, "That wasn't brave, that was stupid. We need Garland. Who needs McKelvey. Whyn't you tell Garland it was stupid – "

"Whaddaya mean, 'Who needs McKelvey?'" Gus said.

Mitch looked at Gus, at his grey-blue eyes staring up at him from between his immense flap of ears, and flushed.

"Well, someone else could have gone and got him. Me or someone else, someone not so important – "

"Holy shit, what are you saying, Castle." Gus stood up, all five feet of him bristling. "We're all important, comrade, all, see?"

"Oh, hell." Mitch sensed that he was losing the point. "Of course," he waffled, "I didn't mean he wasn't, or that we should have left him there." But as he said it, he was not sure that that wasn't what he had meant. A guy was hit. Okay. A guy went out for him and he was hit. Also okay? The daisy chain could go on forever.

They set the gun up behind a stone wall and Mitch lugged up the ammo and the water. He looked out across a flat field of wheat to a row of stone houses. The fascists' machine guns were firing from somewhere in those houses, pinning down the infantry companies in the wheat field.

Nolan got the Maxim going, firing across the field at the line of houses. Mitch strained to see where the bullets were hitting, but nothing showed. There was the row of houses, and the chatter of guns, muzzles arcing above the wheat where the men lay close to the ground, baking in the sun. That was all.

He moved back to his water carrier's position and listened to the firing. After a while the stretcher bearers started to come by carrying the wounded, rolling from side to side in the sagging canvas slings, as the bearers, sweating, dirty, their faces grey, drained of blood, backs bent in a sort of half-walk, half-trot, bore them to the rear.

The empty water can was passed back to him and he followed the stretchers. They came to a place in a dry riverbed where the wounded were being assembled. There was a dead burro lying in the middle of the cut. The stretchers were in a line against the near bank and the medics were working over the men. There were bloody bandages all around.

Bob Gardiner came by carrying a wounded man over his shoulder. His black eyes shone as he gently laid his casualty on the ground.

Gardiner's eyes held Mitch's for seconds, and then he turned away, to hurry back to the lines, to where other comrades lay bleeding. Mitch watched him go. The guy had never forgiven him for the incident at Pedro's – or maybe for having quit *Sanidad*. Anyone could see – Mitch looked to where Dr. Stein, unshaven, his blond locks smeared with what looked like mud but was blood, his white tunic all smudges and blobs of the same, no longer squeaky clean, was feverishly working, while others waited, and still others who had been attended to wondered if they'd ever get to a hospital – anyone could see, all right, that there was a crying need for medics. Mitch felt silly, holding the empty can, with the wounded bleeding all around him. Water carrier.

He noticed craters in the riverbed, and that the bottoms were damp. Remembering how as a kid he had dug to water in the sand at Coney Island, he dug until water seeped into the hole. He scooped it up with his tin cup and poured it into the can. It was a slow process, digging ever deeper, less than a cup of water at a time. And in the background the groans and cries, the urgent voices of the medical personnel, and the coming and going of the stretcher bearers intensified his sense of futility. The can half full, he turned away and took off.

Manny was firing the gun and Gus was feeding. When Manny saw him, he turned the gun over to Gus and told Mitch, "Here, you feed. The rest of the guys have passed out from the heat."

They pulled the gun down and changed the barrel and filled the jacket with the water he had brought up. They repositioned the gun, and Gus sat behind it, his short legs braced on the wheels of the carriage, his fists hanging onto the handles, his ears flapping, his whole body vibrating as the Maxim snapped up ammo.

Mitch fed the belts carefully, making sure that the cartridges went in flat, that the canvas holder wasn't twisted. The gun hammered in his ear until Gus stopped and said, "I can't . . . too hot . . ."

His face was powder gray, his eyes bloodshot. He rolled over and Mitch got behind the gun. He thumbed the trigger and the gun jumped. He stopped. "Wait. What am I shooting at?" he hollered to Gus. "What are we shooting at?"

Gus just rolled his eyes. Mitch got to his knees and looked over the shield. Nothing had changed. The wheat field, the row of houses in the distance. He couldn't see anything to shoot at.

He looked for Manny. Or Garland. He knelt down and sighted along the setting on the gun. He saw nothing, just the tops of the wheat, the roofs of the houses in the distance.

"Wait for me!" he yelled at Gus, who was flat on his back. He ran into the wheat field looking for someone to tell him what to shoot at.

"Get down, you crazy bastard!"

Mitch fell down beside Aaron. Murray and Leo were there staring through a swathe cut in the wheat.

"Aaron, what's up there? What are we shooting at?"

"They're in pillboxes right along that fence row, below the line of buildings. We can't move, they've got us pinned."

Mitch looked to where Aaron was pointing. He could see narrow rectangles of black close to the ground. "Out of them slots?" he asked.

"Yeah."

Murray pointed his rifle and fired. Aaron pointed his rifle and fired. Mitch saw a puff of dust appear near one of the black slots. "Good," he said, "we'll get the gun on it." He got up and ran back to the gun.

When he got behind the sights, he could not find the pillboxes, but he could when he stood up. He looked around for a piece of high ground and there was none. Then he lifted the gun, carriage and all, the ammo belt trailing, and mounted it on top of the stone wall. He bent behind the sights; now he could see. He adjusted the rear sight and knelt behind the gun. He fired a short burst but couldn't see if he was on target. He pulled Gus into a sitting position.

"Listen, Gus, see those black slits over there? Along the fence? See 'em? Watch 'em. See if we're hitting them."

He fired another burst and looked at Gus expectantly. Gus shook his head. He fired again, and again Gus shook his head.

"Well, where are the hell am I hitting?" he screamed. "Correct me, give me a reading!" Gus just kept shaking his head. Mitch got up and loosened the clamps on the shield and removed it from the gun. He sighted the gun in and then, as he fired, he stretched to see where the burst impacted. At first he couldn't see anything. He freed one hand to shade his eyes, holding the trigger down with the thumb of his other hand, the safety off with his ring finger. Then he picked up grey puffs hitting low on a house behind the row of pillboxes.

"Now!" he whooped. "I see 'em! I see 'em!" He adjusted the rear sight and fired again. The bursts were landing on the pillboxes, on top of them, in front, kicking up dirt, obscuring the black slits. He had them! He kicked Gus back into life and made him feed the belts. It was something! He had no room in his head for thoughts about the men between the gun and target, about Gardiner and Stein and the wounded in the riverbed, or about the fascists who were in the pillboxes. His whole connection was with the gun and the puffs that appeared wherever he aimed it. The noise of the gun covered the sound of incoming fire, so that he barely heard the whisper of bullets flying past his head. He ran the belts through until Manny pulled him down and away from the gun.

"Get the gun together, you crazy bastard. We're moving forward. Hurry!"

He threw the bolt, lifted the flap, and pulled the belt out of the gun. He became aware of the stillness. Except for a distant sound of firing, the immediate area was quiet. He threw the bolt twice more and pressed the trigger to make sure the gun was cleared. He clamped the shield back on and helped Gus fold the empty belts into the ammo cases. Mitch asked Gus if he wanted to drag the gun or carry the ammo, the two of them being all that remained of the crew. Gus said he would carry the ammo. Mitch rolled the gun down off the stone wall and, dragging it behind him with one hand and the empty water can in the other, he and Gus started forward, following the line of men ahead of them.

When they reached the pillboxes, Mitch got hold of Manny, and together with Jack, they went over to look. There were three bodies in the first, and two in the second. The bodies were just there, sprawled on the dirt floor, dead, some face up and others face down. They had been stripped of their guns and papers by infantry that had passed through earlier. Inside the dark of the pillboxes, they all looked alike. There was nothing to mark them as fascists, and there was no way of telling who had killed them.

They were just there dead and they looked as if they had never been alive. Mitch wondered at his acceptance of their being dead, but there was no time to think deeply on it.

A bullet snapped viciously above Leo's spine. He hunched his shoulders and buried his face deep in the wheat stubble. There was another and another. He pressed down as hard as he could. Another, closer. He tensed himself to get up and run. He held himself together. He gathered all his bones and muscles and flesh into a small ball and held himself, all of him, braced against the snap of the bullets, his skin raw and stripped and aching in anticipation.

"Leo! Leo!" Aaron was calling to him. He forced himself to open his eyes. Murray was to his right, looking around at him squinting in the bright sun, then past him to where Aaron was calling.

"Come on," Murray shouted, "we're moving up. Let's go, the charge of the Light Brigade." Murray's fat face smiled wildly. His glasses glinted in the sun and he pumped his rifle, with the long skinny black bayonet fixed in place, up and down like a drum major leading a parade down Fifth Avenue.

"Yeah." Lehan Larner rose out of the wheat stubble, his Dicterov at the ready, singing, "Hold the fort for we are coming . . ."

They were waving him on, Aaron in the lead, Murray and Larner following, singing. Leo came to his knees, paused as though waiting for the bullet that would get him, and when nothing happened, came to his feet and ran after Aaron and Murray. He imagined the fat of their bulky bodies melting in the sun. Larner was dancing ahead, singing.

"Spread out, spread out," Leo shouted at them as he veered off to one side. "Please, please, put space between us."

Leo could see that they were going to bypass the town, which was a relief, better than a frontal attack against fixed machine gun positions. The wheat field sloped down and off into grass and brush and stunted trees; the downward slope became more steep, and pools of cooling shadow patterned the land.

They rested at the bottom. Nelson and some other officers formed a tight little group that included Max Frank, a slim dark kid Leo had talked with about crystal radio sets at Figueras. Frank was furiously working a telephone that seemed to be resisting his efforts.

"The heck with it, let's go, we've got to take this darn town today." Nelson's voice carried to where the troops rested. He stood up and shouted, "Come on fellows, let's get the job done."

Oh, my, Leo thought, *"job," "heck," "darn," "fellows," who is this guy?* But the men were coming to their feet, the Lincolns first, then Leo's company. They spread out and started the ascent to take the town on the flank of its defenders. The climb up was tough, but there was little incoming fire. The combined covering fire of the Lincoln and Washington guns poured over the advancing troops in a steady chatter and whine of bullets that only let up as they approached the crest of the hill. They came into Villa de la Cañada unchallenged. The town was theirs. The battle was over.

Aaron and Murray collapsed on the narrow sidewalk in the shade of a building. Larner, holding the Dicterov at the ready, remained on his feet, guarding against surprise from any quarter. Leo sat down, back against the building, and closed his eyes.

The day was over. They had fought all day under a scorching sun, and now they shivered in the cold Castilian night. They had thrown away their ponchos, not knowing or caring how the night would be. Their teeth chattered as they huddled together for warmth and tried to understand and define the long day by calling the roll of the dead, the wounded, and those who had passed out in the heat – too tired and too cold to sleep.

Scattered over the hill where the Machine Gun Company had set up for business, the scrub oak and sagebrush cooked in the heat of the rising sun, greening the air. The fascists were on the ridge across the valley. In between, down in the valley, the men of the Lincoln and Washington battalions struggled part way up the ridge or lay pinned down on the slopes. The Machine Gun Company waited for orders to give cover fire when the attack on the ridge, Mosquito Crest, kicked off.

Casualties had forced a reorganization of the gun crews, and now Nolan, Jorgensen, and Jack Altman manned the gun that Mitch and Gus had had at Cañada. They had set up shop under one of the scrub oaks, where they had a clear sweep of the crest some 150 meters away; Mitch and Gus were under another tree about ten meters away, water canisters and ammo boxes piled around them. Mitch watched Jack squeeze off a burst now and then. Jack would fire and then look around at Jorgensen and Nolan and laugh excitedly.

Far off to the right, a flat plain unfolded. Mitch saw tanks, like toys, slowly moving forward across the plain, and puffs of smoke and brilliant flashes exploding in the path of their advance. A tank stopped and a finger of flame spurted from its turret gun. Then it moved on, trailing a wisp of blue smoke. He saw a tank spin at a right angle to its path; it stopped and burned, a cloud of black smoke enveloping it.

The sound of the guns barely carried to the hill, and after a while the entire plain was covered with clouds of dust and smoke, only occasionally flashing a yellow or orange burst. It looked unreal to Mitch. Though he tried to visualize the men as sweating, bleeding human beings, stopping, moving their machines, firing, being fired at, under clouds of smoke and dust, it all seemed mechanical to him; machines not men, sound and fury but no sense of human feeling.

Nolan called to him, and he stood up and loped over.

"Don't you ever crawl, comrade?" Nolan said. "Listen to me. Manny is over there by that tree; you see it? Get over there and get us some firing instructions. Get some water on the way back."

Mitch trotted – it had not yet occurred to him that he might be hit – to the tree where Manny was with a gun squad belonging to Nick Stamos, the black-eyed, black-haired Greek whose brother had been killed at Jarama. The two were in solemn dialogue with Jerry Cook, who was fair, handsome, and Irish.

They were discussing the fate of someone who seemed to be asleep. His legs stretched out, his back against the tree, a hole in his helmet.

Jerry was saying, "That's a good way to go if you have to go. He never knew what hit him."

"I want to be awake when I get mine," Stamos said, shaking his head. "I want to have those last visions. The ones you're supposed to have before you die."

"Maybe his dreams were better," Jerry said.

"How do you know he was dreaming?"

"He was asleep."

"I don't dream when I sleep. Not everyone does," Stamos said.

"Right through the helmet?" Mitch asked Manny.

"Yeah, he was sleeping there and . . . What are you doing here? Why aren't you with your gun?" Manny said.

"Nolan wants to know the score," said Mitch, his eyes still on the sleeping figure. He wanted to contribute something about the relative advantages of getting killed sleeping or awake, but all he could think was that he would like for there to be something between being and not being.

"Earl?" he ventured, though he knew from the size of the shoe, the shoe with a slit cut in it where a bunion might find relief, the shoe attached to the foot thrust out before the sleeping figure. Earl Glenn, no longer asleep but dead, the kind of sleep that ended all griping, all suffering from bunions and the foolishness of his fellow men. So Glenn was gone. Though many had gone before him, he was the first comrade that Mitch had known as more than just a name.

Then the shelling began. Shells exploded in the trees, two or three bursts in quick succession, a pause and then a burst or two. Behind them, enemy planes flew overhead strafing and bombing the Loyalists' lines. For the first three or four days all the planes had been their own, old French fighters and Mexicanski fighters and bombers, and almost all the artillery as well. But when the French had closed the border, the Republic had run out of steam as far as air and artillery support went.

"Tell Nolan he'll be the first to know," Manny said.

The exploding bombs and shells had turned the sweet, green-smelling, sunlit air into a sulphurous brown stinking haze. On the way down to the dry riverbed, he threw his helmet away.

The river now had many more bomb craters scattered along its sandy bottom. In one spot where the bank was high, there were three *soldados* plastered against the embankment, profiled in bas-relief like a Greek frieze. They had been blasted flat, the life blown out of their intact bodies by concussion.

Mitch went on down to the place where he had gotten water before. The dead mule had inflated, its hide glistening against the corruption expanding in its guts, an aura of shimmering green and violet hovering over it. It smelled bad.

The collecting station for the wounded had moved on, leaving broken stretchers and bloodied bandages, thick with opalescent flies.

Chow had come up while Mitch was away. Manny, who had come to tell them to move the gun and to dig slit-trenches, had stayed to eat with the crew. He had saved Mitch a good portion of garbanzos and grey, tough meat, and a cup of *vino del campo*. Mitch went to work on the meat, putting all thought of the stinking mule out of his mind.

They all heard the shell coming at the same time. They dropped their food and sprawled flat around the tree; Manny and Mitch, who had been sitting together, flung themselves into an unfinished foxhole just as the shell exploded in the tree, sending a torrent of leaves, branches, and shell fragments raining down on them.

When the smoke cleared they came up for air. Nolan and Jorgy were on their feet looking at the muscle torn and dangling from their upper arms. Mitch saw that the exposed bone of Jorgensen's arm looked yellow, while the bone showing through the torn red flesh of Nolan's was white. The thought crossed his mind that Jorgensen was old and Nolan was young and that that was why the bone was different in color. There did not seem to be much bleeding, and both men stood there looking at their wounds, Jorgensen with a worried expression and Nolan with the same quiet, intense look with which he addressed himself to all problems.

Nolan said he could walk to the first-aid station. He looked at Jorgensen, who nodded and set off after him.

Jack, still prone, twisted his head to gaze up at Manny, an apologetic smile splitting his face in two. His protruding blue eyes seemed enormous.

"I can't move," he giggled, all white teeth and pink gums.

Mitch knelt beside him; there was a hole in each side of the seat of his pants. He laughed, "You lucky bastard, the shrapnel went in one cheek of your ass and out the other. Come on, get up. You ought to be able to walk to the station, too."

"I know," Jack said, "but I can't get up. I can't move."

"What'll we do with him?" Mitch asked Manny.

Manny called for *Sanidad*. When the stretcher bearers came, they turned Jack on his back before lifting him onto the canvas. Still grinning, his face now chalk white and tears rolling down the sides of his face, he strained mightily to muffle the cries escaping through his clenched jaws. Blood stained the front of his pants, making black splotches around two gaping holes there.

"Oh . . ." Mitch said softly. "All the way through . . . in two places."

"I guess it's bad," Jack groaned. Then, forcing a smile, he said, "I'll see you guys later. I hope. Mitch, you take care of my cousin for me. Take care of Manny."

Mitch sighted in on the ridge. He elevated the sights two notches so that he would be shooting over the ridge, and got off a short burst, then a long one and a short one. Then he tried various combinations, working out some kind of rhythm. Straining his eyes at the ridge across the valley, he kept seeing the yellow bone in Jorgensen's arm, the bas-relief of the three *soldados* plastered against the embankment, the black hole in Glenn's helmet, the inflated mule swelling and stinking in the hot sun on the dried-up riverbank. He fired and fired, trying to blow the sights out of his mind. He fired, wanting the fascists to know they weren't all dead or wounded. And when he fell back from the gun, it was getting dark and the lines were growing quiet.

Now Mitch was number one man on the gun. Gus was happy being number two. There was nobody else.

Mitch slept, and in his sleep he wondered what had become of Earl's passport.

"Aw shit!" Leo cried when he saw Aaron up ahead fling his rifle away before falling out of sight behind the sagebrush. Leo and everyone else hit the dirt.

Murray raised himself on his elbows, sighted down the long barrel of the Russian Remington rifle, and fired. He worked the bolt, and Leo saw the ejected cartridge flash in the sun.

"Get up there and see how bad he's hit," Murray yelled at him. "I'll cover you."

I'm not moving from here, he thought. *I'm safe here. I'm not moving. I can't move.*

But Murray kept yelling at him between rounds. He forced himself to crawl forward, the undergrowth tearing at his uniform, until he reached the brush behind which Aaron had disappeared. Using his rifle as a lever, he pried the short branches to one side and moved his helmeted head forward. Aaron's head was turned to him as though he had been waiting for him; his eyes were wide open and flat, his mouth gaping, his face dead white, except for the stubble of black beard.

There came a whoosh and whine of bullets overhead. Pieces of the brush whispered against Leo's helmet, dirt kicked up into his face, and a new sound that he instinctively identified as bullets thudded into and tore at the thing that had once been Aaron, his Aaron, now his shield.

Leo was conscious of the wetness between his legs and the warm lumps there. He had shitted himself and this gave him comfort. It took him back to his childhood, to his mama, to a warm bed in a warm room full of warm smells and the comforting warmth of shit between his legs.

He began to relax, the sun on his back easing the tension of his muscles. He heard the bullets whip overhead, but now he listened easily to the sounds around him. He heard a machine gun firing from behind, and every so often Murray would fire a round and then he heard the pull and slam of the bolt. He thought he heard the spent cartridges fall into the stubble. He was so close to the ground, almost part of it; his muscles, nerves, brain all gone limp and washed into the bittersweet smell of earth.

"Get up! Get out of there! Get out of there!" Murray's shrill screaming penetrated the blanket of calm that had engulfed him. When Murray reached down to pull at his blanket roll, Leo saw that his cheeks were streaked, his brown eyes swimming in tears.

It wasn't until they came to where the men were assembled waiting for orders, and he collapsed beside Murray, who was choking back sobs, that Leo realized that he had not shed a tear for Aaron, that a sense of loss had not yet set in.

"Come on," Larner was on his feet, "let's move it." Leo found the rifle heavier and more difficult to carry than it had been. He shifted it from one hand to the other, trying to find an easy way to carry it.

The company came to a stone wall and Larner deployed the section behind it. He heard Larner say, "When I give the word, move up. Let's get them bastards off the ridge." They clambered over the wall and into another wheat field. Leo was hot and thirsty. He laid his rifle down and reached for his canteen. The water was warm and smelled of sewers, but he drained it dry. There was a lot of firing, and when he looked around he saw men falling, disappearing into the high wheat. There were shouts of "I'm hit, I'm hit!" and "*Sanidad!*"

Leo got up and stumbled four or five steps, the sun blinding him. The rifle, too heavy to hold, he cast aside as he fell to the ground. He heard Murray fall beside him, and then the whipping of the bullets passing over him.

His mind was in a turmoil as he fought against the heat, the exhaustion, the crack of the gunfire. He had to do something . . . there was something he had to do . . . something about home . . . about going home . . . about not being here . . . about stopping. Stopping!

He made a decision: he would go no farther. It was easy. All he had to do was stay put. They could all go on without him. He was not with them anymore.

He felt good about it, and he dozed off, dreaming lightly and pleasantly about how nice it would be to be coming home. He half woke to hear the arrival of Mitch – to hear him asking for targets. He thought kindly of Mitch now, of how he was always asking something silly like where to get water in the middle of a downpour, and where to fire when all hell was breaking everywhere around them.

Murray was beside him and shaking him. "Leo, are you all right? Are you hit? What's the matter?"

Murray pulled at him, but he stayed limp, letting Murray roll him over.

"What's with him?" Larner said.

"Christ, he stinks," Murray said. "I don't see any blood or anything. Leo, Leo, can you hear me?"

Just don't move. Don't say anything.

He let his mouth go slack, he felt the spittle roll down the corner of his mouth.

"Maybe it's the heat. Heat exhaustion," Larner said. "Leave him. Come on, the section is moving up."

"Let's get *Sanidad* over here first!" Murray said and hollered, "*Sanidad!* First Aid!"

Someone poured water over Leo's face and into his open mouth. It was warm and brackish.

"Come on, let's get him out of here. We can't fuck with him all day."

Leo recognized the stretcher bearer's voice: Butch.

Just don't move, he thought . . . it's their problem now . . . just don't move.

They rolled him onto the stretcher. He felt himself soar into the air and then they were running.

Please don't let anything happen now.

He could hear the gasping breath of the men carrying him. They came to a stone fence and rested him and the stretcher on top of it. He felt the hard stones through the canvas. He opened his eyes.

Mitch was off to one side, standing behind his chattering gun. He'd found a target, Leo thought. Then the bearers scrambled over the fence pulling the stretcher after them.

Leo heard the thwack of a bullet, and at the same time Butch let go of the stretcher, banging Leo's head against the ground.

"Sonofabitch!" Butch said, then picked up his end of the stretcher again.

There were stretchers and men lying all over the place. People running around. "Sorry, comrade," Butch said, wiping blood from his hand.

Leo realized that he had been holding his breath for a long time. He let it out with a heavy sigh that sounded like water rushing past his ears, washing over his eyes, and passed out.

Each day, and sometimes at night, they moved forward some and backward some. Mostly they moved laterally and down the dry riverbed from one flank to the other. It was impossible to drag the gun through the sand on its wheeled carriage, so Mitch carried it, carriage and all, on his back. His back was a mass of boils and carbuncles, and the gun mashed them into bleeding, pus-filled sores. The muscles of his back and legs ached. He trudged along half sleeping until he bumped into something or someone in the dark path ahead of him.

They were ordered to move the gun over a field the infantry had passed. Looking for a place to set up shop, Mitch came across Aaron's body. Aaron had been big in life, but now he seemed grotesquely large. He lay in a clearing against a chewed-up bush; stripped naked, his black hair, black brows, and the black hair on his chest and between his legs, like ink washes against the whiteness of his stretched skin, reminded Mitch of a Japanese painting called *Women Taking Bath* that he had seen in a book.

Though Mitch could not have said so in so many words, the deaths of Glenn and Aaron had added a new dimension to the venture. While he accepted their vulnerability, his own sense of being invulnerable was reinforced.

Casualties had reduced the ranks of both American battalions, and now the Lincoln and Washington battalions were combined to form the Lincoln-Washington Battalion. They swapped tales of heroes, victories, and disasters. Battalion commanders had come and gone – between the two battalions, they had gone through eight. The greatest loss had been that of Oliver Law, who had been killed leading the troops up Mosquito Crest. But though there was speculation, no one knew what had happened to Markovicz or the others.

The newly hyphenated battalion held a position behind the front line, near a bridge that spanned a *barranca*. In the rainy season the *barranca* became a river, but in July, in the heat of summer, it seemed to Mitch that all the rivers in Spain, or at least all the rivers on the Bruneté front, had dried up. During a pause in the fighting, they lolled about in the sand reading mail that had caught up with them. Mitch was reading his letter from Irene to Manny and Nick when Doug Roach, who was digging himself a foxhole, said, "You oughtta knock off the reading and dig yourselves some holes, comrades, that bridge's gonna be attracting company. And not the kind you want to be standing around entertaining." Doug's muscles bulged and his smooth black skin glistened in the sun.

"You dig the hole big enough," Mitch laughed, "and we'll crawl in."

"Not into my hole," Doug said. "You be crawlin' up your own 'fore long."

As though on cue, the thick, thrumming sound of approaching bombers interrupted his reading. Mitch watched them come in, trimotors, Fokkers moving slowly, so low Mitch could see the helmeted heads of the crews. The bombs came tumbling out, wobbling from side to side before arrowing down, their whistle rising in pitch up into the sky. Then he felt the ground heave beneath him; his head filled with the roar of the explosions.

Clouds of black smoke closed out the sun, and the smell of burnt powder choked him. He fell face down onto the warm sand, his back turned to the falling bombs. For an instant he had an exact vision of the structure of his spine and a sure knowledge of which vertebra would feel the impact of the next bomb; it felt like all his nerve endings were bunched at the spot waiting for the blow. The *barranca* contained the roar of the planes, the booming bomb-burstings, the shuddering thuds of the big bombs that buried themselves in the sand, many not detonating.

Then it was over. The sounds echoed in memory, the smoke cleared, the sky above was unoccupied, no longer menacing. Mitch hauled himself out of the deep impression he had made in the sand. Men were getting up all along the riverbed and on the banks alongside, taking stock of themselves and of each other. No one had been hit.

Mitch looked at the crumpled letter he still held. Irene's closing line, the line before "I love you," was there: "I pray for your safety and the safety of all the boys. This Sunday I lit a candle for you."

Now, laughing, he read it out loud to Manny and the others and said, "See, God's on our side," and everyone laughed except Doug, who was trying to figure out whether his labors had been necessary after all.

Mitch and Gus set up their gun on a mound and commenced firing toward the fascist lines even though they did not see anyone to fire at. It was the only gun in the company in working condition after the bombing. The only gun on the firing line.

After twenty or twenty-one days of going up and down the hills, back and forth along dried-up riverbeds, what was left of the Lincoln-Washington Battalion was taken out of action. Manny and Mitch bunked together on a ledge on the side of a hill where the battalion had come to rest. They had been in battle, they had seen men die, they had suffered thirst and hunger and unbelievable heat during the day, and had been chilled to the bone at night. But they were alive, unscratched – discounting the mass of raw flesh on Mitch's back – and they were happy about that.

There was a meeting going on down below them. All the men were assembled, but Manny and Mitch remained on the ledge looking down on the proceedings. The commissars from the English battalions spoke, and then Nelson; and when Mitch, deafened by the prolonged sessions behind the hammering Maxim, asked what they were talking about, Manny shouted, "We gotta go back because the lines are breaking again."

There was a sinking feeling in Mitch's stomach because the big thing had been that they were alive, that they had come through this and it was a victory – a personal victory. Later he would write home that it had been a victory for the Republic, for the cause, and all that. But now it was his victory, all his.

He hadn't been the one to decide when to stop fighting at Bruneté. It had come as a surprise, since he had assumed that once they had started, they would go on until they won the war or were all dead or something.

So if it was back into action, that was that, and, while he did not stop to think about it then, later on he wondered why the commissars had made a meeting of it when all that was needed was the simple order. Later he knew that commissars were concerned with "morale," and were always seeing "crises of morale" or "crises of discipline" where there were none – where there was only weariness and hunger and sometimes fear.

That was how Mitch saw it. It was quite possible that the men who had been in battle before, the British and American veterans of Jarama, might have been ready to debate the issue and take a vote.

But as it turned out, there was no need to go back into the lines that same day, and so they rested. That meant getting cleaned up, deloused, eating a hot meal. There was also the reading and rereading of the mail that had piled up while they were in action. Mitch had five more letters from Irene, all of them flowery and full of religion and love, their very oddness in this place having a terrific appeal, so that he read them to his comrades – atheists all, he assumed – and passed them around. Their reaction was one of disbelief and laughter. And in a peculiar way it set him apart from the others; they looked upon him with curiosity and even a certain amount of respect. There was also mail from his family and one letter from the YCL club, asking him what he needed.

He replied to that letter first: boots, size 11D, since nothing so monstrous was even conceivable, let alone obtainable, in Spain.

Then he was handed huge sums of pesetas representing back pay, and a *salvoconducto* for ten days' leave in Madrid. Mitch had expected neither, the promise of ten pesetas a day from the base at Albaceté already forgotten. No pay, the contacts in the States had said. No one would be responsible in any way for anyone or anything in this business of going to Spain to fight fascism.

"I know exactly what you are thinking, Comrade Rogin." Bill Lawrence spoke with the precision common to someone who has adapted to a language not his own. "You are wondering what right has this rearguard bureaucrat to tell me that it is my Communist duty to be at the front, is it not so?"

Leo looked at the handsome Slavic features across the desk. He had not been thinking that at all. After all, there had to be men in the rear. As a matter of fact, in the rear was where he should be, perhaps would have been if not for his loyalty to Murray and Aaron. The second he thought of Aaron, he relived the shock of Aaron's glazed eyes staring at him. He leaned against the desk.

"What's the matter, comrade? Are you ill? Sit. Sit down."

"No. I'm okay." Leo forced himself to stand erect.

He had been carried out of Bruneté alive, and that was better than being carried out dead. He wondered if Aaron still lay where he had fallen. Did anyone bother to carry out the dead? Still, there was Murray, and Murray was wherever the Washingtons were. Murray was alive, he told himself; he had to be, and Lehan Larner, too.

He brought the conversation back to Lawrence's challenge. "Being in charge of the Americans at this base is a very important job," he said earnestly, "as important as being at the front." He noted with satisfaction that some of the belligerence went out of the dark blue eyes. The heavy lashes closed lazily and then opened again, and Comrade Lawrence leaned back in his chair sweeping long waves of brown hair back from his forehead.

The base at Albaceté was under the command of French IB'ers, and there had been some grumbling about packages, which came in relative abundance for the Yanks, being diverted to IB'ers who, because of the restrictions imposed by their governments, were receiving little or nothing from home. Leo had picked up the rumor that Lawrence – obviously not the name he had been born with – had been sent to regain control over the Lincoln Battalion's packages.

"I just thought," Leo went on, the idea surprising him, "that with my experience I could make a more valuable contribution at the base training the men."

Lawrence glanced at the papers in his hands. "And what experience is that, comrade?"

"Isn't it there?" Leo pointed to the sheets in Lawrence's hands. "It should be. I was in ROTC in college, I was slated to join the National Guard. It was a Party assignment . . . to become proficient in military matters, to familiarize myself with tactics and weapons, if we should ever need . . . Well, you understand these things."

"Not so, Rogin. Only to win the future soldiers over to the side of the working class, is the understanding. But never mind. Did you become proficient?"

"Yes, of course. For two w – " He caught himself, he was thinking on his feet now. It was a matter of staying alive. That instinct had gotten him carried safely away from the bullets that had cut Aaron down. "I trained for two years – "

"Was this information available when you were in training with the Washingtons?"

"Yes."

"So?"

"So. You know how it is."

"No," said Lawrence. "How is it?"

Leo squirmed. He knew how it was, but he doubted that he should say so. Lawrence had been preselected; he had been made co-jefe of a base in Spain before he had even set foot on the gangplank. Should he tell Lawrence now that that was the way it was at Madrigueras and Tarazona? That all the officers were predesignated by powers on high? Then why not him if he had Party experience in the ROTC?

The truth was that he did not know why. Someone who did not know one end of a rifle from the other did the picking.

"Well, all the positions were filled," he said, and saw the bushy eyebrows go up in disbelief. "Anyhow," he went on, "I've been in action. It seems to me that you would want me to work with the new men at Tarazona."

Lawrence riffled through the papers.

"You were at Bruneté for exactly four days."

"Yes, but I was under fire. You must take that into consideration. It is very important to have men who have been under fire training the troops."

"Four days?"

Four days? Leo had thought it a lifetime. "Once you've been under fire it doesn't make any difference whether it's four days or four years." The eyebrows were climbing again. "You may not be able to understand how . . ." He trailed off, afraid of going too far.

"It is also important to have seasoned men at the front." Lawrence leaned across the desk. "And let's get this straight, Comrade Rogin. There is no place I would rather be than at the front. No matter how tough, it cannot be as unpleasant as having to sit here and deal . . ." He paused. ". . . with people." He leaned back. "The circumstances under which you were removed from action at Bruneté are questionable. The report reads . . ." He referred to the papers again, and Leo eyed them with suspicion. ". . . Possibility heat exhaustion feigned; symptoms at variance, comrade uncooperative. Probability of malingering . . ." Keeping his eyes on the papers, he said, "Well, what have you to say for yourself?"

"Oh, you can't think that. They can't say that!" Tears came to his eyes. He leaned forward and put every ounce of sincerity that he could muster into his words. "I would never leave my comrades on the field of battle like that. What are they saying? My best friend, Aaron Adler, was killed at Bruneté." He swept his sleeve across his eyes. He recalled the skeptical faces of doctors and nurses at the hospital. "Believe me, Comrade Lawrence." He reached for Lawrence's hands. "There is nothing I want to do more than get even, to kill fascists. For Aaron, do you understand? Nothing more than that . . ."

Lawrence's expression revealed an opening.

"But . . ."

"But what?" Lawrence waited.

"But we can't let our actions be determined by our emotions. I'm a Communist. I want to make the best contribution I can to the struggle. That's what's important. That's why you're here and not at the front where you want to be, isn't it? And my experience, used properly, for training men . . . can be a much bigger contribution than just my one rifle at the front. Isn't that right? Isn't that the way to look at it?"

Lawrence looked away. Leo held himself. Would it be wise to go on? Everything he had said he believed in a way. It was true, he thought, he had more experience than most of the men who had come to Spain. Of them all, of all those he knew, he was the only one who had fired a rifle, who had had target practice, who had known how to sight a gun. He had come to Spain to kill fascists. He hadn't killed any, but there was Aaron. Something must be done to avenge Aaron. Yet when he had been at the front, it had been too much. The heat, or the stink, or all the marching, taking the strength out of him, weakening his defenses so that he was helpless before the fear that engulfed and crippled him as he lay behind the bush staring into Aaron's dead eyes, hearing the thud of bullets tearing at Aaron's body, shrinking into the ground as bits and pieces of the bush were clipped by bullets to rain down on his head. The only clear recollection he wanted to hold in his mind was the feeling of security that had come over him when he had decided to go no farther. He wished now that Murray had let him lie there. Maybe he would have gathered the courage to go on.

Then the hospital. The wounded, the sounds and smells of pain all around but not in him. The dying and the wounded; himself alive and in one piece. That single fact, so vividly underlined, had made a deep impression on him. What else was there but to be and stay alive?

He watched Lawrence weighing his words. He knew he had put forth the correct argument. It would appeal to a man like Lawrence, the business about doing the most good. He had made it sound convincing because he believed it. Anything was true – if you wanted it to be true.

"Look," he said. "I'll do whatever you say. I want to do the right thing, the best for the cause."

"All right." Lawrence put the papers aside. "I will send you to Tarazona with a recommendation that you be used to train cadre. But it will be up to the *comandante* of the base, Captain Johnson, to make the final decision."

Leo tried to conceal the relief that swept over him. He leaned forward and set his face, waiting for Lawrence to go on.

"You'll like Captain Johnson. He has had considerable experience in the U.S. Army. And he was in action at Morata and Bruneté, so you can be sure that he will use you in the best way possible."

"You won't be sorry, Comrade Lawrence."

Lawrence looked up at him. "I hope not, comrade."

11

Manny Spear, MG section leader, and Mitchell Castle, MG numero uno gunner – no fancy rankings or titles and damned few men left to command after Bruneté – checked into the elegant Gran Via Hotel, Madrid, on the first bright and sunny day of August. Their room was large, the centerpiece a huge bed, its blankets turned down to reveal dazzling white sheets. The bathroom was all tile and marble, and, wonder of wonders, had hot water at the twist of a tap. They took turns soaking in hot baths. Afterward they searched out a tailor and were measured for uniforms, each to his own fancy. Finished and delivered in thirty-six hours as promised, Mitch's selection was done up in a chocolate brown corduroy from England; trousers made pantaloon-style, topped off by a double-breasted, many-pocketed, epauletted jacket. Fit for a captain, at least, and far outranking Manny's more modest khaki broadcloth. The tailor had been unhappy about the many yards of cloth needed for one so tall. Mitch offered to pay extra, but the man had been insulted.

Manny was for seeing the sights. This was Madrid, he said, the symbol of resistance to the fascist hordes; Moors, Nazis, Falangists, Guardia Civil. Ten months earlier, the four enemy generals, leading four columns of heavily armed troops, had boasted that they would take the city in the first few days of November – with the aid of a fifth column operating within the city. Mitch and Manny took to walking the streets, Manny in search of inspiration and Mitch looking for signs of battle and a fifth column. One side of the Telefonica, which seemed to be the one unadorned, modern-looking building in all of Madrid, was pockmarked by artillery fire.

At the Plaza del Sol, statuary from the now-dry fountain was protected by stacked sandbags, a reminder of the early days of the uprising, when Fokker, Junker, and Maserati bombers had held the sky above Madrid unchallenged. But then the Mexicanskis had arrived with speedy single-wing Chatos and bi-wing Moscas, and swept them away.

When they came to the Café Chicote, Mitch suggested that they pop in for a cold *cerveza*. But Manny was determined to see more of the city, for, as he put it, "Hey, I'm an orphan kid from Brooklyn, when'll I get another chance, huh?"

So Mitch waved him off and went in alone. Since he had a pocketful of back-pay pesetas, he sat at a table instead of at the bar. The menu offered only beans and fish, which he did not want but ordered anyway because he was too shy to ask only for beer. The beans and fish turned out to be the standard staples: garbanzos and *bacalao*. Though elegantly served on white china, the all-too-familiar aroma of salted cod and hot olive oil killed what little appetite he had. He poured the *cerveza* into a crystal glass and drank slowly.

At a table nearby, Mitch spotted a fellow brigader, whose name he did not know. Nor did he recognize any of the others at his table. They were focused on a man who looked too military to be a civilian and too civilian to be military, a tall, heavy-set character with dark hair and a black mustache, a handsome broad-faced man whose wide shoulders were in constant motion.

But Mitch's eyes were mainly for the girl beside him. She was definitely Spanish – altogether too brunette to be anything else – beautiful and definitely out of Mitch's class. So thoroughly did she command his attention that he did not notice when the mustachioed gent got up and approached him.

"¿Americano?" the big guy asked.

"Yeah," Mitch said.

"Just in from Bruneté?"

"Yeah." Then he remembered security. They had been warned not to reveal anything that might be of use to the enemy. "Er . . . who are you?" he stuttered.

"Hemingway, Ernest. Why don't you join us? Buy you a drink?"

"Oh. yes," Mitch said. The name sounded familiar. He stood to shake Hemingway's hand. "Mitch Castle."

"You know Captain Phil Detro? And this guy here is Evan Shipman, a great poet and pony handicapper and not a bad ambulance driver. And Eddie Rolfe with the Radio Madrid outfit . . ." He went down the line until he came to "Eulalia, who speaks for herself in Spanish. ¿Tu sabe?"

"*Un poco,* but maybe *bastante,*" Mitch said, taking the chair Hemingway brought from a nearby table, nicely placed between Shipman and Eulalia.

The conversation at the table was over his head, having to do with strategy and tactics both political and military, the art of weaponry, the merits of one gun over another or one whiskey over another. Hemingway tried to get him to talk about Bruneté, but Mitch was vague. He had not yet digested those twenty-one days and nights. He was, in fact, not even thinking about it; he was in Madrid, on leave, drinking cognac and soaking in the perfumed presence of Eulalia, whose closeness made him feel good all over. He left the telling to Detro. Detro seemed not to have any problems with security.

Detro was a Texan, a company commander he had seen in action. Tall and rangy, grey-eyed and tanned, his sandy hair was burnt almost white by the sun. Mitch pictured him as a character out of a Zane Grey western. Sipping the cognac, Mitch looked around the table. He had not seen Shipman before. Shipman was built more or less along the same lines as Detro, though not so tall. His sandy hair, blue eyes, and the fine-boned planes of his face and a certain remoteness and kindness about him appealed to Mitch. Eddie Rolfe looked more like Mitch's idea of a poet, lean and hungry-looking, but not with a hard hunger, more a searching hunger, Mitch thought. They all looked so damned clean, so damned intelligent, sounded so knowing. They weren't from Brooklyn, that was for sure, not from Mitch's Brooklyn.

But he had come through Bruneté at least as well as any of them, and now the beer and the cognac imbued him with a certain amount of confidence, not enough to participate in the sophisticated talk, but enough to get a conversation going with Eulalia. It was clear that she was in the same position as Mitch, but for a different reason: she didn't understand a word of English. So Mitch made small talk in bastard Spanish, not understanding what she said, but happily convinced that she understood him.

Fortified by a second drink, he announced that he was hungry, and, without waiting for a reaction from the others, invited Eulalia to join him for dinner at the hotel. To his delight she agreed, and they got up and left without saying goodbye or it was nice to meet you, or waiting for anyone to offer to join them. Only Shipman stood up to see them off.

After they had eaten their *bacalao* and garbanzos, they repaired without discussion to Mitch's room. Eulalia was perfect in every way. She tossed and turned in a frenzy of passion that was new and wonderful to Mitch, and he fell in love with her. It was a long and beautiful night, and for the first time he fell asleep with a girl in his arms. The war was far away. Blanche, Irene, and Brooklyn no longer existed.

He awoke with Eulalia sleeping in his arms, naked against his nakedness. The room was full of sunlight, and Evan Shipman was sitting on the edge of the bed looking at her.

"What the hell are you doing here?" Mitch demanded.

"She's beautiful," Shipman whispered, not taking his eyes off her. Mitch looked at the uncovered girl in his arms and agreed that she was beautiful. He was glad that she was beautiful.

"Yes," he said.

"Beautiful," Evan repeated, shaking his head slowly back and forth. "Beautiful."

"Yeah, but how did you get in?"

"Through the door. Unlocked door."

"What're you going to do, sit there all day telling me how beautiful she is? Come on, get the hell out of here." Eulalia stirred and came awake, her nearly black eyes opening to the sun, warm and glowing, stretching against him, softly saying something in Spanish too low for Mitch to catch. She saw Evan but did not seem to mind his being there.

"Would you let me have her?" Evan said.

It was so natural and easy, and Mitch felt good about a guy like Shipman wanting something he had. "Why don't you ask her?" he said.

Shipman spoke to her then, his Spanish fluent and persuasive.

"No, no," Eulalia said and pulled the sheet over her bosom, snuggling closer to Mitch. "No . . ." and then a lot of other talk of which Mitch only understood that she was all his.

Evan got up off the bed saying, "Oh, you're lucky . . ." and two or three more "beautifuls," as he left the room, shaking his head.

Eulalia was beautiful, and it turned out to be a beautiful morning and a beautiful week in Madrid. Manny was beautiful, too; he had left a note for Mitch saying he had gone to other pursuits, and not to wait up. Wherever he had gotten to, and for whatever reason, he did not return to the room. The week was theirs, Eulalia and Mitch. It was, as Shipman had never tired of saying, beautiful.

The week ended when Eddie Rolfe came to tell him that the Americans were being rounded up to return to the battalion.

"Something's afoot," Rolfe announced. He nodded toward the open door of the bathroom. "Who's in there?"

"Eulalia, the gal who was with you and those other guys at Chicote the other night. It's all right. She can't hear and she doesn't understand a word – well, not quite – of English."

"Hemingway's girl. He let you walk away with her."

"He did? Well, if he did, thank him for me; tell him it's the best thing he's done for *La Causa* as far as I'm concerned."

"I'll tell him," Eddie laughed. "But there's nothing else I can tell you except to get down to the Plaza de los Torres and grab a truck."

"How much time?"

"You're late now. Kiss her goodbye for me." As he was leaving, he called over his shoulder, "The rent's been taken care of."

As he dressed Mitch broke the news to Eulalia.

She shrugged. "Nothing is forever."

"If all goes well," Mitch said, "I will return to Madrid and to Eulalia." Then he laid all the pesetas he had left on the pillow.

Later, when he wrote home about Madrid, he did not mention Eulalia. He wrote about the beauty, courage, and devotion of the people of Madrid; of the magnificence of the shell-scarred city, the heroism of the people under bombardment – though this was hearsay – and of the people's great love for the International Brigades.

He felt it necessary to write forcibly in defense of the Republic, adding violent denunciations of the fascists and phony liberals, democrats, socialists, and others who in their passivity or uncertainty gave aid and comfort to the enemy. It seemed to him that the IBs, who were mostly Communists, and the Spanish regiments under the command of such Communists as Lister, Campesino, Modesto, and Galan, were doing all the fighting. He urged his comrades and even his mother to join the struggle. He even demanded that Irene rouse her fellow Catholics to denounce the Church's defense of Franco.

Writing these letters, by candlelight or by the light of a low-grade incandescent lamp, was his way of seeing one side of the truth of Spain. He was not drawn into the political or social phenomenon of the war; he did not go looking for evidence to support the case for the Republic, for the Communist party, or against the fascists. These things he took for granted, and he went about the business of fighting without being distracted by political niceties. But when he sat down to write – to his mother, for instance – he wrote long letters about his support work in factories or agriculture, depending on the point he wanted to make. He described in great detail the Spaniards and the men and women who had come from all over the world to work at their side: their problems, the oppression and the terror that had been their lot for centuries. He wrote of the zeal and the glorious feeling they brought to their work, and how through labor they would defeat the Nazis in Spain – and how they would pave the way for a better world for all workers and peasants.

None of this was said with tongue in cheek. He was a true believer.

 **12**

Manny had left Madrid before Mitch. Mitch found him now wearing a visored officer's cap and carrying a sheaf of papers. The brigades were shaping up near Hijar on the Aragon Front.

"Well, so you tore yourself away at last," he greeted Mitch.

"It wasn't easy. What's going on?"

"We're going into action."

"¡*Bueno!* What do we do now?"

"The battalion's been reorganized. I got back early so they made me commander of the MG Company." Manny chuckled as though it was of no importance.

"Wow! Great! You gotta give me a section."

"Well, you're late . . ." Manny let it hang.

But Bruneté and Madrid revealed something about Mitch that he had not known was there. The accumulated experience, the move from speechifying about fascism back home to fighting it in Spain, and then Eulalia, a love affair where he had given as much as he had received, and which had been easy and natural, without complications. It was so unlike the secretive sessions with first Blanche and then with Irene. He had made the passage from boyhood to manhood under fire and in that great big room in the Hotel Gran Via.

"What do you mean, I'm late?" he demanded. "I got here when Rolfe told me to get here. As fast as the fucking camion could make it."

"Christ, you're pushy. Well let's see if I have anything for an ex–water boy," Manny said. "Nick is my adjutant, Dave Reiss has the first section . . ."

"Nick your adjutant? How come he didn't get the company?" From what Mitch knew, Nick Stamos was senior in experience, having seen action at Jarama; he had outranked Manny at Bruneté. Moreover, he had organized furriers under Ben Gold who, in addition to being the president of the Fur Workers Union, was also a member of the Central Committee of the CPUSA. Nick had also been one of the few Americans to be special guests of the USSR, in Nick's case to get away from difficulties arising from his particular method of "organizing." Furthermore, he had been the number-three man after Garland and Maxim at the training base; Garland had been sent home to do political work.

But Manny chose not to answer. "I'll tell you what," he said. "We just got replacements from Tarazona, mostly seamen and longshore. Do you think you can handle them as a section?"

"Why not? What's so special about them?"

"They're tough and they're all a hell of a lot older than you . . ."

"Oh. Well, that might be a problem."

"I think you can handle them."

"Okay, where are they camped? How many guns do we have? When do we move out?" Mitch banished any doubts about his ability to lead a section. In combat he was unimpressed by a man's stateside credentials. They had all volunteered to fight, and under fire it had not made much difference if a guy had been a student or a steelworker. He took it for granted that some men would take more care protecting themselves – deeper foxholes, more sandbags – but that was their business, just so long as they were doing what they were supposed to be doing when the shit began to fly.

As they approached the section's *chabolas,* Mitch spotted Carl Nielsen, the battalion commissar, talking to one of the new men. Mitch had seen Nielsen, a tall, blond Scandinavian, in action at Bruneté.

Nielsen had seen to it that the machine gun company got its share of food, water, clothing, mail, and other morale-building things when they were available. At Bruneté, he had served under a succession of officers without confusion, constantly but unobtrusively in evidence. He was sparing in his speech and exact in CP political orientation. An ideal commissar.

"Here I am a good Catholic," the new man was saying. He shook his head, as though finding it hard to believe what he was saying. "And like any true American, hating you no-good priest-killing, nun-raping Reds . . . who is this guy?" He pointed to Mitch.

"Mitchell Castle, commander, third section," Manny said. "Comrade Castle, Comrade Fred Rupert, your section commissar."

Rupert was medium sized, stocky and strong-looking, with a broad face and a knowing smile. The sparkle in his blue-grey eyes gave Mitch the impression that he was on the verge of saying something either witty or cutting.

"Please to meetcha, comrade," Rupert said, leaning heavily on the "comrade." "Pull up a chair, comrade, I was just telling this other commissar the story of my life."

There was no chair to pull up. Freddie sat on his helmet, Carl likewise. Mitch's helmet lay rusting on some hill back on the Bruneté front, so he squatted on his heels instead.

"With the Depression and all, I took the first job I could get, which was running a freight elevator in the garment district. Thirty bucks a week, no time-and-a-half for overtime, of which there was mucho. I only been working a couple of months when this guy comes around quitting time and invites me to join him for a brew . . . turns out he's an organizer for the Building Workers Union. To make a short story long, his pitch was long, the beers short, and five or six beers later, I'm signed up, I'm a union member. All I know about unions is they're a bunch of Reds out to ruin the country."

Mitch laughed. "I don't know about ruining the country but when they pulled that strike it damned near ruined me; climbing stairs ten, twelve stories delivering hat bodies."

"Oh, yeah? Crossed the picket line, did you?"

Mitch felt blood rising to his face. "Well," he argued, "it was the Depression, and everything. If I hadn't done it, the boss would have found someone else to, and there I'd've been without a job and you know how tough it was, still is, to find a job; and, shit, I was supporting my mother . . . groceries, rent . . ." He trailed off, seeing that he wasn't moving Rupert, or himself, for that matter.

Manny looked away; Nielsen looked serious.

"If you'da respected the picket line of your fellow workers you'da stayed healthy," Rupert snarled.

Rupert then ran on about the exploitation of the building workers: their low pay, long hours, and how they had suffered during the strike, had had to keep warm huddled around wood fires, while their families lived on bread and water. By the time it was over and the union had won, Freddie had been "converted to the cause," he said. "The Reds in the union worked harder than anyone else. They weren't ruining nothing, only making things better for the workers." He paused, turned to Manny and said, "He's gonna head the Third? Hah."

It was a poor introduction to the new section. Mitch felt like a shit, a scab, a strikebreaker. And so many of the replacements had been, like Rupert, part of hard-fought union organizing battles. Their leaders were already legendary in the pages of the *Daily Worker*: Joe Curran, Blackie Meyers, Fernando Smith, Harry Bridges.

"So Mitch became a convert, too," Manny came to the rescue. "He's here, you're here – I bet you were recruited by the Party as Mitch was by the YCL?" Without waiting for Rupert to answer, he pulled Mitch to his feet. "Come on, I'll introduce you to your section while Fred, here, cools off."

They were a hard-looking gang – his section – older than he had expected, strong men with names like Connors, Bianca, Dion. Mitch Castle was to lead these men into action. He would be responsible for them. It was not going to be easy. He knew that. But then, he braced himself with the thought that he'd been baptized under fire, and they had not.

As he got to know his section better, he was impressed. They had traveled, had seen and done things that Mitch had never dreamed of. The seamen had read every book on the shelves during their long voyages; they knew about philosophy and physics, and had seen places he had never heard of. Nor were they new to the fight against fascism. Bill Bailey, longshoreman and something of a poet, had torn the Nazi flag from the *Bremen*'s bowmast when it had docked in New York.

For them, everything was generally "fucked up." The "pie carders" back at the training base "didn't know their asses from a hole in the ground," were a bunch of "white-collar appointees." They considered themselves castoffs, troublemakers that the base at Tarazona had selected to beef up the decimated ranks of the Lincolns in order to get rid of them. There was a kind of daring about their rank-and-filism that appealed to Mitch.

He quickly discovered that they knew the Maxim's workings intimately. They kept the three guns in the section oiled, primed, ready to go. Their uniforms were clean, they were clean-shaven, and their gear was neatly folded and compartmentalized. They obviously knew how to live out of a bedroll. He had no doubt that they would acquit themselves well under fire.

The battalion went into the lines in the middle of August, taking up positions outside the town of Azaila. The armies that had fought on the Madrid front were now preparing for the Aragon offensive. This was a maneuver designed to take the pressure off the Euzkadi and Asturian fronts, which were under siege by Franco's legions. The Luftwaffe's April bombing of Guernica, the Basque holy city, was already part of the bloody history of fascist atrocities.

The Lincolns came into the trenches of a departing Spanish unit of Anarchist militia. The trenches were narrow and shallow, deep enough for the Spaniards but not for the larger Americans. The single line of trenches was strung along a high plateau; there were no secondary positions prepared. The fascist lines were nearly half a kilometer off. There was no gunfire, and when Mitch had his crews fire for range settings, the rattle of the guns sounded intrusive in the silence.

Stamos came up to see what all the noise was. Mitch said he was checking to make sure the guns worked, and that the men got some feeling for distances in relation to landmarks. Stamos informed him that this had not occurred to anyone up above as necessary. The firing, Stamos said, alerted the enemy to their arrival. There was to be no firing until an order was given.

Mid-morning of the next day, Al Kaufman, a short, stocky, bug-eyed seaman, barged into the command post Mitch had set up for the section.

"Comrade Castle, come on over to our gun. There's something fishy going on out there."

"Out where?" Mitch said.

"Out in front of our positions." Al was impatient. "Between the lines," he said, and then, as though he doubted Mitch's ability to grasp the message, "in no-man's-land."

"No-man's-land?" Mitch laughed and repeated the phrase, posturing as though delivering a line in a film.

"Okay, Castle, cut the bullshit. You coming or ain't you?" Al was in no mood for horseplay.

Joe Bianca acknowledged their arrival by inviting Castle to look through the sighting slot in his gun's shield. Mitch crouched down behind the gun to have a look.

"Goddamn!" he exclaimed, unwinding to gawk over the top of the shield. "What are they doing down there?"

"They're Spaniards from our side meeting with the fascists to exchange papers and tobacco."

"How long has this been going on?"

"We watched them for a little while, maybe five minutes, before we got you."

The MG position was in a section of trench that had a clear sweep of a dip in the plateau, green and gold beneath the August sun. Mitch did not have binoculars, so he could not determine whether there were any signs of life out there, but less than two hundred meters in front of their lines was a group of men, black ciphers against the green field.

"How do you know what the hell they're doing out there?"

"We been told that that's what they do," Al said. "Exchange things, newspapers and the like, and work on the fascists. The *soldados*, anarchists, I guess, figure they can win the fascist soldiers over to our side. They say they're peasants and workers just like themselves." There was doubt in his voice.

"Where'dja hear that bullshit?" This was news to Mitch.

"Freddie," Al reported. "He came by last night and told us to watch for it, to hold fire, and – "

"Oh, yeah." Mitch cut him off. He stared at the figures out in the field and thought about Rupert going over his head with information to his cronies from training camp. Rupert must have gotten the information from Nielsen and then passed it on to the men.

As he watched the men below, a thought occurred to him. Somewhere over there on the other side of the valley a fascist officer, or more than one, was probably checking on the palaver between the lines. There could be only one thing they were interested in, only one reason for allowing these sessions to take place. Information.

"You know what those bastards are doing down there?" he said.

"Yeah, I told you," Al replied.

"Bullshit. That crap about swapping newspapers and cigarettes is for the birds. What they're doing is giving the fascists information. They're telling them right under our noses and in full view of everyone just what is going on up here on our side."

Al looked at him curiously. It was a look Mitch had noticed when he took over, a silent, questioning stare, as though Al was weighing him. "Like what?" Al said.

"Like the Lincolns have come into the line, for instance."

"Yeah? If that's the case, why aren't we doing something about it?"

"We ought to blast them out of there." Bianca, who had listened without commenting, now spoke decisively. These two were always together, the one short and chunky and bug-eyed, and Bianca a head taller, lean, hawk-faced, black of eye and hair and fierce mustaches.

"Give the word." Bianca positioned himself behind the gun.

"It's gotta be close. Just break it up – well – wait." Mitch remembered Stamos chewing him out the day before. "No, I'd better check with Manny. Hold it, don't do anything, just keep an eye on 'em."

Manny took Mitch's report more calmly than he had expected.

"Whaddaya say we blast them out of there with some warning bursts from Bianca's gun?"

Nielsen, who had listened to the report, said quietly that the fraternizing men were to be left alone. The Anarchists were being difficult, and anything done to offend them might have horrendous effects.

Manny added, "The word is no firing, no exposure of our positions or strength. You already got me in a jam yesterday, so lay off."

"As if they don't know that already. What the hell do you think they're talking about out there, the Dodgers' chances to win the pennant?"

"Orders are orders."

"Well," said Mitch, "then why the hell didn't I get the order before we went into the lines?"

"I thought everybody had been briefed," said Manny.

"I told Rupert and he was supposed to tell the men – " Nielsen protested.

"He did tell the men, but he didn't tell me."

"I should have told you," said Manny. "I meant to tell you but something came up. We're new at this, we'll work it out."

"I hope it doesn't take forever."

"I'll tell you what," Manny said, looking at his wrist watch, "I'm due at battalion right now for a meeting. Why don't you come along and raise the question with Commander Amlie?" Hans Amlie, who had been a company commander at Bruneté, was now commander of the battalion.

"No," said Mitch, "I have to get back to my section. You take it up with them. But for Christ's sake let me know what the decision is." Mitch was shy of battalion headquarters, peopled as it was by members of the upper hierarchy who were quartered in buildings and held meetings and made decisions and brought the word down from Mount Sinai chiseled in stone.

When he got back to his section, he explained as best he could the "ramifications of the situation," to use a phrase he had recently acquired at one of the lower-echelon meetings he now attended as a section leader. They discussed these "ramifications" for some time. Al and Joe Bianca spoke in a different idiom when discussing politics, dropping the rough seamen's lingo. They had the line down pat, and it did not include the Anarchists other than to debase them. Given the evidence – the inactive front the Anarchists manned, the conniving, as Bianca called it, with the enemy – left no choice for Mitch but to agree with them. Still, the idea of the meetings appealed to him the more they discussed it. After all, they were a political army, and no one was more politically conscious than the Anarchists.

"Al, do you think it's possible that in their own way these Anarchists may have inflicted as many casualties on the fascists by conversion to the Republican side, as the fighting troops have by kills on the other fronts?"

"That's not likely, because as you said, those fascisti are meeting out there with the blessings of their officers, and if they were suffering the kind of defections you're talking about, you can bet your sweet ass there'd be no more of these little tête-à-têtes between the lines."

"Yeah, but on the other hand, the Anarchists haven't suffered any casualties and they haven't lost any territory here, which is something you can't say for the other fronts."

"Oh, sure, that's just great," Bianca snorted. "They also ain't inflicted any casualties or liberated any territory. They've made it nice and cozy for the fascists, who can concentrate their punching power at Madrid, or up north, Asturias, wherever – you sure do raise some funny questions, Comrade Castle." He looked quizzically at Mitch and then at Al for confirmation.

"It's not just the Aragon; between the Trotskyites, POUMists, and the Anarchists, they've got the whole of Catalonia sewed up. If the government doesn't get off its ass pretty soon and take over this here part of Spain and make it fight like the rest of the country, they're going to lose this war . . . Comrade Castle, don't you read the press? Don't you know – "

"Sure I read the paper," Mitch said hastily, "I know what's going on – I just like to pose a question, frame a problem from another angle, try to see it the way they're seeing it, so I can understand it better, so that even if I don't agree with their approach, I'll know better what I'm not agreeing with." He hurried on. "Not just looking at it the way I see it, the way I see it working out, but at the real effect it's having, and assuming from that that it's the way they actually want it to happen, that they are carrying on, doing the things they believe in, with the knowledge that it will have the effect we observe."

"In plain English, which you don't seem to speak," said Al, "you want to give them the benefit of the doubt?"

"Yeah, that's it."

"Have you ever tried?" Bianca asked.

"No," Mitch admitted.

"Don't," Bianca said. "There's always some of them on board wanting to do something stupid like blow up the ship they're sailing on, to make some dumb point."

Al Kaufman and Joe Bianca went at it, the one beginning where the other left off, each reminding the other of forgotten points, reinforcing the other's arguments, citing the Bolsheviks' experiences and a book Mitch had had to buy as a YCL'er but hadn't read save for one chapter – on dialectical materialism – which had satisfied his need to know how the world functioned. They cited these as empirical proof of the correctness of the Party position. Everything had been tested and revised by the Russians. The two looked at Mitch questioningly.

"Don't look at me that way," Mitch said. He mimicked them: "'All I'm doing is putting the question in a dialectical way, opposing conflicting ideas in order to arrive at the truth.'"

"You should've arrived there before now, or what the hell are you doing here?"

"Well, there are all sorts here. The Anarchists have their own truths and I think we've got to find a way to work with them."

"It's too late," Joe said. "Talking with them is like those guys talking out there this morning with the fascists. It can only help the enemy."

"Besides," Al said, "we're in a shooting war and there ain't no time for talking. Let's win the war and talk afterward."

"That's my intention," Mitch said.

"What's your intention?" Manny asked. They had not noticed his approach.

"To win the war," Mitch said, relieved.

"I'm glad to hear it," Manny said. "Meanwhile, you'll be happy to hear that the Anarchists have been told to cut out meeting with the enemy. Anyone appearing in no-man's-land will be shot at starting as of twelve midnight tonight. Those are the orders."

But the next day the Lincolns moved out for the beginning of the Aragon offensive; there had been no shooting of Anarchists.

≡ 13

The thing Mitch liked most about being a section leader was that he no longer had to lug the heavy gun, or its supporting equipage. The boils, carbuncles, and general rot on his back could now fester and burst without being rubbed raw by the guns. He wore his blanket roll across his chest one way and his bandoleer the other, in an X. He carried his Remington carelessly over one shoulder, and he felt as light footed and swift as Mercury. He gloried in the sweat and grunting of the Finns, the Greeks, and the seamen as they lugged the heavy armor into battle, the sweat rolling down their faces in the hot sun. He strode up and down the section line, exhorting the men to keep closed up and get their asses moving, while they cursed him and struggled along on their way from Codo, their first and uneventful objective, on to Quinto.

At Quinto, the fascists withstood the initial shock of the attack, perhaps forewarned by the fraternizing Anarchists. The Machine Gun Company, following the rifle section, approached Quinto across a wide plain dominated by a hill called Purburell, just outside of town, and by the belfry tower of a church at the edge of town. The fascists opened fire with what must have been old artillery pieces, and the shell trajectory was so flat that the shells came whistling by, struck the ground and bounced, and disappeared without exploding. It was like skipping flat rocks over a pond. The section hit the ground or froze standing every time one came by.

"Hey, did you see that? Did you see that one? Look at them skip! Come on, get up, get moving! They can't hurt you unless you catch one directly . . . hell, they ain't none of them going off, they're all duds . . . look at that . . . look at that one . . ." Mitch was fascinated by the bouncing shells, and he wanted them all to share in the excitement, but he could see that they were preoccupied with something else, and that something else was fear. They were tight lipped and silent, their faces grey and tense, their eyes staring.

He had not expected fear; he had not been aware of anyone at Bruneté either talking about it or showing fear. Mitch mused that maybe at Bruneté they hadn't known – what they didn't know couldn't hurt them – while these new guys, veterans of stateside strikes, many of them violent, were much more aware of the possibilities involved when someone started shooting.

Now, to help the men deal with this, he acted the clown, racing up and down the section line, pointing to the skipping shells as he would to rockets bursting at a Coney Island fireworks display.

"Looks like the working classes spiked the fucking ammo!" he roared. Laughing and chattering, he kept the men moving forward.

Up front, as they neared the town, a battalion runner contacted Manny. Stamos came back along the file of machine gunners with orders to set up positions. The gen coming in was that the enemy was dug in at the cemetery, by twin green-black cypress trees snaking skyward behind pale grey walls – the Sisters of Sorrow, the Spanish called them. Stamos laid out the order of battle: first the artillery would open up, then there would be a pass by Republican planes, and then the infantry would go in. The machine guns would provide cover fire. Stamos tried to put conviction in his voice, but Mitch could sense that he did not believe that the attack would go as planned.

Mitch got his crews into position on the only rise he could find; the plain seemed as flat as a football field. They sighted the guns in on the area before the cemetery wall, where the enemy trenches might be; Mitch had no way of knowing if they were there or not, as he was still without binoculars.

Division artillery commenced firing on schedule. The exploding shells seemed to bounce off the church, digging shallow craters in the thick walls. Then the bursts moved along the near side of the cemetery wall. Mitch had the guns open up, using the shell bursts as target markers. As he did so, a flight of bombers and fighters roared overhead, unloading their bombs on the approaches to the town. The artillery stopped, and for a moment, a second, the drawing of a breath, it seemed to Mitch that all was quiet.

"Look sharp," Stamos said. "Keep firing – make sure it's over our guys' heads – until I give the order to stop."

The gunners could see the Rifle Company rise up and advance, the sound of cheering streaming back, sounding through the clatter of the still-firing MGs.

"Okay, okay!" Stamos shouted through cupped hands. "That's enough. Hold your fire, hold your fire."

Mitch picked up the command, and up and down along the line MGs fell silent. The men came up from behind the guns to see their comrades leaping in the air, disappearing into the enemy trenches, whooping it up.

"Son of a bitch." There was a note of wonder in Stamos's voice. "A picture-perfect operation . . ." He turned to Mitch. "Can you believe it? I mean," he said, "it's hard to believe."

"There's a first time for everything," Mitch said, sensing in Stamos's tone the "fucked-up" operations he had been in at Jarama. "Could make a believer out of anyone, even Earl Glenn if he wasn't beyond – " Mitch broke off.

"Yeah," Stamos agreed absently, "sounds quiet now, right? You hear any firing? Castle, keep this section where it is until further orders, you hear? I'm going forward to see what the fuck is up. Spear's somewhere around there with the other sections."

"Okay," said Mitch, "but I want to go with you, as far as the cemetery, anyhow. I want to see how we did." He waved at his gunners. "They'll be okay."

The trench, when they came to it, was much better constructed than the Anarchists' trench they had occupied when the brigade had first come into the Aragon front. These zigged and zagged as they were supposed to, with sandbagged gun positions and well-dug-in command posts. There were a few bodies bent in awkward angles between the narrow walls of the trench, and the usual litter of papers, helmets, mess kits, and debris.

Five men of the First Company moved along collecting weapons, now and then stopping to collect papers from the dead. They said that the infantry had moved into town to clean it up, and Stamos, after telling Mitch to stay put, headed for the town.

"Keep close to the wall, and the buildings. They're still in the church."

"Hey," Mitch called to the man who had shouted the warning to Stamos. "Murray! Murray Amov. Last time I saw you was early on at Bruneté."

Amov held an armful of rifles, his face glistening with sweat, his shirt soaked black. One of the lenses of his glasses was cracked, a fine line running diagonally across from his eyebrow to his right nostril.

"I'm Mitch, Mitch Castle," he reminded Amov, "Leo's friend from Madrigueras."

"Oh, yeah," Murray said, more in accommodation than in confirmation. "Aaron was killed at Bruneté."

"Yeah, I saw him – "

Murray looked closely at him. "Leo – you know where Leo is now?"

"Well, no," said Mitch. "Do you know? Larner's around, I saw him on the way here – "

"I looked for Leo in Madrid," said Murray. "At the hospital they told me he had been sent to Albaceté – "

"Albaceté?"

"Yes, that's what I wondered. Why Albaceté? The commissar at the hospital told me he was okay, nothing wrong with the comrade so far. I've been puzzled by that 'so far,' so far." Murray's instinct for comedy surfaced briefly. "How far is so far, all the way back to the Bronx?"

Mitch laughed.

Murray, his arms full of weapons, used his foot to point to a nearby corpse. "I killed one . . . of these," he said. "You know," he said absently, staring at the broken figure, "I didn't think I'd ever kill anyone, ever. Then we were on the top of this trench, and they were below us down there, and I was just as scared, and even surprised, as this fascist . . . Well, I guess I thought . . . no, I don't think so, I must be thinking of him as a fascist now, but then, at the moment we came face to face . . ." He turned to Mitch. "I saw myself in his eyes, and then it was too late, we were moving too fast, it was as though our momentum just carried me down into the trench, and the bayonet on the end of the rifle into the neck . . ."

Murray paused, looking again at the dead soldier.

"Hey, don't feel bad about it, for Christ's sake," said Mitch. "That's one dead sonofabitch for Aaron. Come on, hand me the rifles and get out of there before it begins to stink."

Murray looked at him now as though he were seeing him for the first time, seeing him as a man untouched, or unmoved, by the dead. He handed up the rifles he had collected and came out of the trench.

"I hope these are better than ours," Murray said, "but how could they not be." Looking at Mitch as though seeking understanding, he said, "I pulled the trigger first, but the bolt jammed . . ."

"C'est la guerre." Mitch wasn't giving an inch.

Murray retrieved the rifles from Mitch, saying "Thanks" as he did so, and moved off to join his detail.

"Take it easy, take care, comrade," Mitch called after him.

Manny and Nick returned to the MG positions just before nightfall, Manny carrying his poncho like a loaded sack. He said he had been checking out the houses down one side street.

"Everyone came into the streets when the artillery let up, and it was all clear with the *aviónes*," he said, the words gushing out, "and they came smiling, crying '¡Viva La Republica! ¡Viva Russia!' – Viva Russia, can you beat it. *Americanos*, I told them, no *Russos*, *Americanos*. But I don't think they could grasp that, what the hell would *Americanos* be doing in Spain fighting Franco's *insurgentes?* Anyhow," he went on, "I took off down a side street and came to this shop – at first I didn't even know it was a store, just a narrow door, no windows, and dark as hell inside. But it was a store, all right." He put down the poncho, unfolding it to show eggs, bread, strips of ham, links of sausage, and a few cans of fish. "No one answered my calls, there was no one in the back room, no one anywhere. So I just loaded up, left all the pesetas I had in my pockets on the counter, and here it is. Let's share it out to the men."

Mitch, who had been rummaging in the poncho, looked up. "Shit, Manny," he said, "there isn't any tobacco, no cigarettes – "

"That's the first thing I looked for," Manny said. "I couldn't find any."

"Cigarettes," said Stamos, who knew everything, "anything tobacco is like gold. The store owner took off, must've took off if he wasn't there guarding his stuff, probably a fascist afraid of what the townfolk would do to him, probably because the bastard has them over a barrel with credit. Beat it, like I said, taking all the tobacco, cash, and I bet the books he kept on the dough the peasants owed him."

"Ha, he'll never come back for the dough you left," Mitch said. "Let's go get it."

But when they went back into Quinto the next day, enemy snipers, still holed up in the church tower, commanded the square and forced them into detours and dead-ends that confused Manny. The only sounds of firing came from the church, and more distantly, from the hill outside the town. They stopped in the shelter of a building across the plaza from the church.

"Christ," Manny said. "The whole brigade staff is here."

Mitch recognized a few of the officers standing in a group, some just inside the main entrance to the church, others along the wall: there were Copic and Dave Doran, brigade commanders, Campbell and Nelson and Amlie, the battalion command, and several others he did not recognize. Doran was shouting into the church, pleading and promising at the same time, his voice carrying across the empty plaza.

"Look over there, the side of the church," Manny said. "They're coming out of that side door."

One by one, the men who had been holed up in the church came through a small opening and lined up against the building with their hands behind their heads.

Manny, apparently assuming that all the fascists in the church were surrendering, moved away from the building from which they had been watching the operation. Then shots rang out from somewhere in the church, kicking up a cloud of dust into which Manny disappeared. Mitch threw himself down, arms outstretched to grab Manny and pull him back to safety. He got kicked in the face for his effort as Manny scrambled backward on his belly, his heels flailing.

There was another burst of firing, but this time it was not intended for them. Two or maybe three of the prisoners – it was hard to tell with all the milling around – slumped against the church wall, sliding into sitting positions, heads falling forward. The guards' rifles were still pointed at the slumped figures.

Now there was a threat rather than a promise in Doran's exhortations. And sure enough, the remaining fascists filed out of the main entrance. There seemed to be hundreds, though probably one hundred at most, waving white rags.

"Let's get out of here," Manny said.

"What happened?" Mitch asked.

Manny lit out on the street that led out of town, moving so fast that Mitch had to trot to keep up with him.

"Dammit," Manny said when they got back to the MG HQ, now set up at the far end of the trenches in the cemetery, "where the hell is the *vino?*" He pawed at the blanket rolls on the floor of the *chabola.*

Mitch unhitched his canteen and shoved it against Manny's rear end.

"*Vino,* not *agua,*" Manny said.

Mitch nodded.

"Ah," Manny said, "of course." He unscrewed the top of the canteen, sniffed at the opening, then placed it to his lips and drank deep and long. When he was through, he passed the canteen back to Mitch. Mitch screwed the cap back on and hooked the canteen onto his belt. His motions were slow and his eyes seemed not to be focusing.

"Whatsa matter, Mitch, you're not drinking? You okay? Something the matter?" But Manny was not really interested. He turned away to search the blanket rolls yet another time, and then, satisfied that there was nothing in them, sat down on top of them.

Stamos and Rupert joined them. "It's all over," Stamos said. "We took the church."

"I'll never forget this," Rupert said.

"You saw what happened?" Manny said. "You'd better forget it."

"How can I?" said Rupert. "I mean, a church, a church still means something to me. I never thought we'd be fighting and killing inside of a church."

"Oh, that," Manny said. "I forgot, you were an altar boy."

Stamos said, "I can imagine how it must feel. Superstition clings like dog shit once you step into it."

Rupert had stopped listening.

14

Manny had to come back to Mitch's section to get it moving; the battalion had already left Quinto and was headed for Belchite. There were signs of bombing and strafing on the road: craters, scorched vegetation, abandoned rifles, helmets, and other gear; the stink of cordite charred the air.

As they came into the brigade camp, the first thing Mitch saw was Dr. Stein working over a man lying in a stretcher on the ground. Stein was on his knees and there was blood on the sleeves of his jacket. There were several other occupied stretchers nearby, and some walking wounded standing or sitting on whatever was around to sit on.

"Caught on the road," said Manny. "I don't know how you do it, but dragging your ass kept us from catching it like they did."

"Someone's praying for me," Mitch said.

They bivouacked for three days. The usual bull sessions went on about Quinto: how one strong point after another had been taken, sometimes after Carl Bradley's dynamiting squad had blasted the way; the taking of prisoners; and the warm welcome given by the townspeople.

Mitch was immersed in the same feeling of unreality that had overtaken him once at Bruneté when he had wandered alone beside a tank, sent to patch a break in the lines that never happened. He had briefly encountered Lehan Larner on the same mission, Dicterov on the ready; Lehan had said later that he remembered nothing of it, and no one had missed Mitch or known why he should have been where he said he had been. Now he had the same sense of unreality: did it happen or did it not? As he listened to the stories, he began to wonder if he had been there, though now they all insisted that he had. He recalled the artillery duds skipping alongside the column, but no one else did. And no one spoke of the prisoners who had been executed. It was as though it had never happened.

On the fourth day, rested and refurbished, the brigade moved on to lay siege to Belchite, another heavily fortified town on the way to Zaragoza, the main object of the Aragon offensive. As at Quinto, the churches were the strong points they had to contend with.

There was a stone retaining wall that held a terrace sloping up to where a church sat, its tower commanding the surrounding terrain. On the side facing Mitch, there was a large ragged opening that had been punched in the thick wall by artillery fire. The fascists were in the church, according to Manny. The guns inside had to be silenced for the rifle companies to move into town.

Mitch placed one gun just off a dirt road leading into town, a second in line with it about fifteen meters to the left, and the third another fifteen meters on, all along the wall.

Al and Joe were on the first gun, near the road, and they set to work to cover the belfry. The second gun, manned by the Finns, was targeted on the hole in the church wall; the third gun was assigned to cover both the belfry and the belfry tower. Mitch stayed with the Finns.

He felt strange among them, and for that reason he wanted to be with them. They were a quiet lot, blonds with frosty blue eyes. They sang the familiar tunes of revolution in Finnish, and had names like Marti, Makki, Makkilo, and Holomen. They were mostly farmers from Minnesota who had come to Spain after Bruneté.

Mitch watched one of them sighting through the oblong aperture in the gun shield. The Finn fiddled with the sights, with the elevating and lateral screws, his face white and pink. The white skin stretched tightly over his nose, his cheekbones reflecting the blue of his eyes. Before the Finn could fire a burst, there was a sharp snapping sound and the Finn's face disappeared. He fell away from the gun, as though someone had jerked him from behind and sent him sprawling.

Before Mitch could say anything, one of the men pulled the dead man gently aside and himself got behind the gun. The same thing happened to him. A loud snap and he was gone.

Mitch stared at the black hole just above this second gunner's blue eyes, then looked at the opening in the gun shield. Clearly he had been picked off by a sniper who, with terrible accuracy, was firing at the sighting aperture in the shield.

Somewhere inside the church, Mitch reasoned, a sniper patiently waited for that small oblong of light to be blacked out by the gunner behind it, then, squeezing off his round, seeing daylight again as he counted another victim with businesslike satisfaction. The sniper was positioned somewhere well into the body of the church – somewhere above the floor, sighting down on the gun through the opening the artillery had blasted.

Meanwhile, another Finn had manned the gun. Mitch directed his fire at the opening, and the Finn got in a single burst before he was hit. Mitch did not see him fall; he was peering at the opening, looking for the muzzle flash of the sniper's rifle. But he felt as much as heard the sound, the bullet smacking into the Finn's face – just as he spotted a spark, like a struck *machero*, flash deep in the blackness of the church's interior.

Holding the image in his mind's eye, he straddled the dead Finn. The gun grips were warm and sweaty. The son-of-a-bitching MG was sighted in too low. He unlocked the elevating screw and the traverse clamp and swung the muzzle upward, not bothering to sight in, for he knew that there was no time. A bullet clanged off the shield; moving the gun had saved his ass. He opened fire – a sustained burst and then a short one, and another and another. Makki crawled over to handle the belt. Mitch set the clamps and triggered a fast "shave and a haircut." He stood up behind the gun and turned to the remaining Finns, now leaderless after losing their number one, two, and three men. One of them was smiling, and Mitch made him number one. He told him to reorganize the crew and to keep the church under fire, especially up around the middle where there must be a balcony of some sort. Then he went to see what was doing with the gun that had originally been assigned to fire into the church. He found the men crouched behind the gun and the embankment.

"Why aren't you firing?" he asked the squad leader, a tall broad-shouldered seaman with a craggy face.

"They're hitting the gun," he replied. "They hit the water cooler on the gun. Don't stand there like that, you'll draw fire."

"Get up on that gun, get up there and lay it on." Mitch was furious. He could see that the water jacket was dented, but it was not pierced. He thought about the dead Finns on the other gun. "What's your name?"

"McCall, what's yours?"

"Oh, yeah. McCall. You know my fucking name. Now get your crew up there." He could hear the other guns firing. "The church is covered now. I'll give you new targets."

He turned away to search the line of buildings facing them. He felt embarrassed to be standing while McCall crouched below him. It did not seem to him that there was any more firing coming from the town, though he could hear a rattle of rifle fire in the distance. He had had no further orders from Manny and no idea of what the infantry companies were up to.

McCall came up alongside of him and peered cautiously toward the town. "I don't see nothing to fire at," he said.

"I want you to fire at each of those windows, there to the left of the church, the upstairs windows – to your left – a burst into each one of them, and then back and over again, and at anything you see move, at any flash of fire. And don't let me hear this gun dead again." And when the man turned doubting grey eyes on his, he added, "That's an order."

The expression on McCall's face informed Mitch that he was not accustomed to being ordered around, not by the likes of a green New York kike. The look enraged Mitch.

"Get this gun going – okay?" he said sharply. "Now!"

He glared at McCall, forcing him to turn away and busy himself with the gun. Puffs of white powder appeared around the first window and then the second. "Good work," Mitch said. He patted the big shoulders and moved off to Kaufman and Bianca's gun.

They were firing short bursts at the church tower, Bianca behind the gun, Connors feeding the belt, and Kaufman kneeling beside them observing their fire. The church tower did not look like a profitable target. Mitch looked down the road. There was a body in the middle of it, a big body, swollen and shimmering in the August heat. Black hair spilled out of the helmet, which was pushed to one side, exposing the face to the sun, and one earpiece of a pair of spectacles stuck crookedly upward, the cracked lenses glinting.

"Amov," he said. "What's he – How'd he get – "

"They got the road covered," Al said. "He ain't the only one."

Staring at the body brought back the sight of Aaron lying dead behind the sagebrush at Cañada. He wondered what had happened to Leo, and where Larner was, and who would sing those funny songs now.

"Listen, Joe," he said. "The Finns are covering the church. Why don't you get your gun on those shell holes in that factory to the right of the road?"

"Okay, but I don't see anything to fire at . . . anywhere."

"That's how it is. You got to fire at likely places, no matter. Amov got it crossing the road and so there must be – "

"There is. Two or three other guys got it, maybe more, trying to pull him off the road. Some snipers got it covered."

"So okay, you cover them, right?"

"Right." Joe changed the alignment on the gun and started to work on the factory wall. While they were doing this, Mitch caught sight of Manny waving to him from the other side of the road. He waved back before he understood that Manny wanted him to come over.

"Why did you cross that way?" Spear asked.

"Because you called me, or did you?"

"I mean standing up, strolling across like that, you schmuck. You know how many guys got hit crossing this road?"

"Maybe they aren't covering it anymore."

"I give up," Manny said. He pointed toward the factory. "That's a mill and there are no fascists in it."

"What do you mean? I got one of my crews firing into it."

"What? We have a section in there. Stop them!"

But Mitch was already on his way. He ran across the road to where Al was with the gun, and as he did so he could hear two separate shots whistle by.

"They still have the road under fire," Al said excitedly. "Did you hear them shooting at you?"

"Yeah, I must have caught them by surprise the first time. Anyhow, I'm not much of a target. No more firing at the factory. It's in our hands. And get one of your men to tell the other guns to lay off the factory. See if you can find something up the road for a target, or just hold it . . ."

Now he had to go back across the road because he had not heard Manny out and he could see him waiting for him. He looked up the road to where Amov lay. He waited for Al's gun to open up and then he very deliberately walked across the road. Remembering the sound of the two shots fired before, he walked across the white road in the sunlight, his skinny figure throwing a pencil of black shadow before him. Just as he got to the other side, there was a ping and another miss, and then he was behind the terrace with Manny.

"Oh, you dumb bastard," Manny said.

"I'm too skinny for them to hit me," he said, thinking, *I do not want Al and Joe to see me run across like a scared rabbit.*

"If you just waited until I finished – "

"But they were firing into the building, they might've hit one of our guys."

"They're not hitting anyone. The men are down on the floor. We knocked a hole in the far corner; it commands one entrance to the church and the street going up into town. I want you to put one of your guns in there for cover fire. We're going to have to go into the church and take it. Get a crew, I'll wait for you here and show you where I want the gun."

Mitch trotted back across the road. There was no firing this time.

"Al, wrap up the gun and take your crew across to Manny. He'll show you where he wants the gun. I'm going to tell the other crews where we're going."

When he came back, Al hadn't moved. He noticed how blue Al's beard had become against the pallor of his drawn cheeks. "What's the matter? Why're you still here?"

"How're we going to get across the road?" Al asked.

"What do you mean? Just get across. Go ahead, you first, and I'll send your crew after you one at a time."

"But the road is covered. We'll get picked off."

"Hell, you won't. You saw me go back and forth."

"Yeah, but that's different. With all this heavy gear."

Mitch could see that that was the way it was going to be with Al. Al was constantly aware of death. He knew fear and he knew he had to live with it and do whatever had to be done in the class struggle and the fight against fascism – but not recklessly. Mitch could see that Joe Bianca would not take the first step either.

Al studied the road, glanced at Mitch, and looked to Bianca, who looked at the ground between his feet and shifted his gaze back to the road. Mitch knew then that the first move was up to him. He picked up the shield, tucked it under his arm, picked up an ammo carrier for each hand; thus burdened, he crossed the road to where Manny watched and waited. When he looked back, he saw Bianca tearing across the road, lugging the wheeled

MG behind him. Al sent the men over one at a time and then came over himself. A few rounds whistled by, but the quality of the fascist marksmanship was deteriorating rapidly as they took casualties from the other crews.

They used the sacks of grain in the mill as sandbags around the hole where they mounted the Maxim. It was set up to cover the street, the houses along the street, and the approaches to the church from the plaza. By the time Joe was satisfied that the gun was well positioned, protected, and ready to go, night had fallen and the chow detail had come up with hot food. Mitch left to check on his other gun crews. Murray Amov's body had been carried off and the road was no longer under fire; the gun crews had been fed, guards were posted, and all seemed in order. The church tower thrust straight up and silent against a sky coming alive with a scatter of stars.

When Mitch got back to the mill, Al's squad and some of the riflemen were deep in a bull session. The riflemen were always better informed than the machine gunners. It had become increasingly apparent to Mitch that battalion HQ tended to ignore the MG Company, seeming not to know what to do with it or how to use it, especially in offensive actions. Manny seemed free to do whatever he could think of with his guns, and was constantly looking for ways to use them effectively.

The scoop from the riflemen was that the battalion commander, Hans Amlie, had been relieved because he had refused to order the infantry into a frontal attack; or that he had done that and then been wounded and sent to the hospital; or that there had been a political uproar between battalion staff and brigade staff. Commissar Nelson had taken over, and then he had been wounded and evacuated. Many of the men, who had served under Nelson at Jarama and Bruneté, had chosen him as their lodestar. Now they shuffled their feet and wondered what would happen.

Mitch could only listen, for his heroes were no longer on the scene. He had lost track of Maxim the Mexicanski, and Garland had been sent home after being wounded at Bruneté.

He remembered the time when J. B. S. Haldane, the famous British physicist, had arrived to lecture on gas warfare. Everyone had been pleased to have him on the side of the Loyalists; and they had listened carefully to what he had to say about hanging blankets over the entrance to dugouts, about gas masks, washing off mustard gas, and all that.

Mitch had listened to him unbelievingly, barely able to keep from laughing at the funny way Haldane spoke and the way he bustled about, his face florid and sweating. Mitch did not think anyone would be using poison gas, not after the horrible experiences suffered in the World War. But then, who could know what the fascists would pull – they had bombed the open city of Guernica. He supposed he should have paid more attention to Haldane, and perhaps he might have if everyone had not made such a fuss over him. Mitch always reacted badly to what he thought of as kowtowing to big shots.

He laughed at the riflemen now. He made fun of Nelson's wound, which was easy to do since it had nearly deprived the commissar of his manhood. He scorned the battalion commander who had questioned the order to advance, even in the face of heavy enemy fire, even without the promised artillery and air support that had shot their load in the first few days of the Aragon offensive.

It had been a long day. The gabfest became tiring, and one by one the men dropped off to sleep, making pallets of flour sacks to keep them from the cold cement of the mill floor. There was only the distant sound of an occasional single rifle firing at shadows, followed by a short burst of machine gun fire, a lonely shell winging somewhere in the night followed by the hollow cough of the gun that had sent it, sounds that did not disturb the stillness, which seemed all the more quiet for their intrusion. The soft breathing of the sleeping men was reassuring.

Thinking about what they had been talking about kept him from falling asleep. He recalled his YCL days, the days and nights he had devoted to speaking against war – when he had approached war from the human and not the political side. He thought about the insanity of the war business, and how he had known then that if he was ever forced into a war, the one thing he would never do was go over the top. The bastards who started the wars, who profited from them, *they* never went over the top, never put themselves in danger. It was inconceivable to him that any intelligent person would get up out of a trench where he was relatively safe, climb out onto the top of the ground, and run toward other men who were dug in and protected and who were firing rifles and machine guns at the advancing figures. No, he had read too much about that 1917 insanity. Besides, the "war to end all wars" hadn't. If Hitler and Franco weren't defeated in Spain, if Madrid did not become the tomb of fascism, a second war to end all wars was in the offing and all those guys who died going over the top should have . . . There Mitch drew a blank.

But, as his father would say, there are two sides to every proposition: this was a different kind of war. It was a people's war, a just war. And since everybody dies in due time, what better time or place than this?

Thinking about death, he remembered something he had read, about how certain characters experienced a premonition of death, of falling the next day or in the next battle or in the next hour. Not likely. He was, after all, a half-assed Marxist, and Marxists were scientific about these things. People did not get advance notice from some mystical source about coming events. Of course, if you were being constantly exposed to death, it was only logical that you might get to thinking your time was up. The longer you were exposed, the shorter the odds would become, so someday you might call it right on the button.

He got up and lit the candle stub he carried in his pocket. He filled his pipe with sour, dry cigarette-issue tobacco, and used the candle flame to get it going. He coughed, and sparks showered out of the bowl of the pipe as he smoothed out the writing pad he kept in his bedroll. He would write a letter to Irene.

She was practically the only one who had written to him so far. There had been no letters from Blanche, which did not surprise him. Irene's faithful letter-writing made her his number one, the one he thought of when he thought about home at all.

"Tomorrow," he wrote, "we shall have to storm a church. I imagine the fascists crouched behind the altar, barricaded behind pews and statues of the crucified Christ and the Virgin Mother, waiting for us – for me carrying in my pocket your letters, the prayers on my behalf. This particular church, like the one before it . . ." No mention of Quinto or Belchite, for the censor would delete that. ". . . is an armed fortress now. I bet you never dreamed that a church, perhaps even a cathedral, could become a strong point. Somebody must have, though, for every goddamned – excuse me! – church around here commands all approaches to the heart of a town. What do you think of that? In any case, we shall see which – the guns or your prayers – prove most effective. Many of my comrades have already been killed by gunfire pouring forth like holy water from this holy fortress. Meanwhile, your Christ looks down on all, and like the heads of state, professes neutrality while the fascist war machine rolls on. Oh, well, you may not need to do further praying for this member of the masses. There is something about the coming day, the chosen arena of battle, that seems to me very familiar. Like a place I have been to before to do a thing I have done before. If my being here serves in some way to make you rethink what this is all about and where the world is going and where it must go, then it will be worthwhile, for I am sure that, once convinced, you will make a bigger contribution to the final victory than I have. Excuse the past tense, and, as we say here, *Salud y Amor.*"

Irene was the only one in the world to whom he could write the way he had; spiritual . . . Mitch searched his mind for the right words to describe her aura of saintliness, so in conflict with her expressed sensuality. Saint and sinner, something like that . . . it was a combination that appealed to him.

In the morning he downed the fake coffee and white bread that Fritz, the cook, had brought up; he tore the letter up and stuffed it in the garbage sack hanging from the side of the chow truck. It was another day and there was the church, a rosy blush laid on its forbidding stone by the rising sun. It was too fine a day to be prophesying his demise.

 **15**

The sun came up fast, as though hurrying to see the day's killing get underway. Bared to the hard August light, the church looked like a square of ocher papier-mâché that some giant had kicked holes into. Seen close up, it loomed scarred and threatening. There was a walled-in courtyard facing the mill, and several attempts had been made to secure it, but without success.

Manny pointed to the courtyard. "That is now no-man's-land. We can get in but we can't stay. The fascists get the hell out of the church when it's under fire and then run back before we can get in. I want Al's gun to cover the openings facing the courtyard so that we can go in there and from there into the church. Then turn the gun up the street. Keep anyone from coming back, or get them as they go out."

"You going into the church?" Mitch asked.

"Yes," Manny said, "I'm taking the other sections in with a rifle company."

"Why not the rest of my section too?"

"The other sections haven't taken any casualties. Yours has. Just give cover, okay?"

"Okay, but if you're going in, I'm going in with you. I'll give Al the dope, he can handle the section and the firing assignments."

"If you want to," said Manny. "I'll feel better having you with me, you seem to lead some kind of charmed life – maybe it'll extend to me."

"Irene is burning candles for me in some church just like this, somewhere in Brooklyn. I should've told her to include you."

"There aren't any churches like this – "

"In Brooklyn, I know."

"Why not the whole company, the battalion? Can't she get wholesale protection?"

"She can't afford candles for everyone. You don't get these blessings for free."

"Everything has a price." Manny looked toward the church. "We're paying a big price for the fucking church." He paused and then looked at Mitch curiously. "Why the hell are you messing around with a Catholic broad?"

"She's working to convert me and I'm working to recruit her. Who're you betting on?"

"If she's no better a Catholic than you are a Communist, it's going to end in a standoff. Go ahead and get your men."

Al was not happy about being given the section, but Mitch argued that he needed to go into the church to see the setup for himself. He tried to make it sound official and very tactical, but he did not think that he had succeeded in convincing Al that this was not just a stupid, undisciplined foray dreamed up to titillate himself – which he knew it was.

Slater's antitank guns, the only artillery available, put five rounds into the church. The machine guns hammered away until the order was given to hold fire as the infantry charged out of the mill and made for the courtyard.

"Follow me." Manny led the way, Mitch at his heels. They made their way through a shell hole in the wall, then raced to reach the back entrance, its one door open and held in place by a bent iron hinge. Each man knew it was a matter of life or death to get into the church before the fascists could get back.

The interior of the church surprised Mitch, because there was no smoke or stink of exploded shells. Many holes, big and small, breached the thick walls. "Aired out," he thought. His eyes took in the ruined interior, resting for a moment on the balcony from which sand poured in the steely light, catching a slant of sun on its way down to the debris below.

"Here they come," Manny whispered.

Mitch saw them clearly, crowding through the huge wooden doors that now hung lopsidedly inside the front entryway. Some were in uniform, with and without helmets, others in white shirts and blue trousers. Later he would remember it as a tableau, like a reproduction of a Goya etching that had been pinned to the wall in the classroom of the WPA art school he had briefly attended. They seemed to group themselves in a prearranged order and then freeze as though waiting for a photographer to take a class photo, each face set, waiting for the flash, each one a recognizable personality.

"Don't let them back in!" Manny sounded like one of the street kids in Brooklyn, protecting a snow hill, protecting the den in a game of Ring-O-Leary, his cry tense and bubbling with anticipation. Mitch and the others rushed forward, shouting "¡Viva la Republica, Viva!" Forgetting to use their weapons, they charged the fascists, who panicked, pushing and shoving in retreat.

There was a rush of machine-gun fire from the mill, rattling rifle fire from the windows of the houses around the plaza, and the explosion of grenades tossed by the retreating enemy. Mitch heard bullets striking all around, the impact on flesh and bone as men started to fall. Manny was kneeling just outside the door, firing his rifle as fast as he could work the bolt. Mitch stood behind Manny, the Remington at his shoulder, and fired at the backs that scurried down the street, that ducked into doorways, that scrambled and separated. The fleeing men were no longer Goya-esque, they were targets, and he kept firing until there were no more targets, until the plaza was empty except for scattered bodies and the echoing of screams and gunfire.

Manny came to his feet and deployed the men along the front of the church; Mitch fired at doorways and windows, stopping only to reload after the five rounds were gone, when the firing pin fell on an empty chamber.

"Okay, that's enough already," said Manny. "Now we've got to hold the church. Get one of the guns in here. Mitch, do you hear me?"

"Yeah, I heard you," Mitch said, but he did not see him. The image of the men standing in the doorway was fixed in his head; he saw them in greater detail now, their different heights and builds, the young and the older men. He was trying to figure out why they were standing there, why they kept standing there . . .

"Sanidad!" Manny was checking the casualties. "No, this comrade is dead, so is this one. Two dead, two wounded. Sanidad!" he yelled.

"Now you know why I wanted you with me, you lucky son of a bitch," Manny said, his blue eyes ablaze with excitement and laughter. "You're a charm."

"Am I?" Mitch replied. "How about the rest of these guys?"

"As long as it worked for me . . . Never mind. Get the guns in here. Go ahead, get going."

The church itself was nothing to look at. Everything had been reduced to rubble. Here and there a bit of gilt caught the light, a tatter of red velour poked through a pile of splintered painted wood and masonry; a torn prayer book lay open, its illuminated Latin tongue mute under the sky that was visible through the shattered walls and ceiling. From the balcony, Mitch looked out to where the Finns had manned the gun positions. The sandbags along the edge of the balcony were torn and shredded, and sand still trickled from them, falling silently to the floor below. There were no dead fascists there, or anywhere else in the church. There were only dark patches, stains made by blood – or sacramental wine – everywhere.

Mitch came down from the balcony and investigated the doors that led from the main body of the church. One door opened on a dark narrow stairwell. Holding his rifle at his hip, safety off, Mitch climbed the stone steps, which ended in another door. It opened to his touch to reveal a large room with a table covered with white linen. There was half-eaten meat, potatoes, and bread on the plates. There was wine that had turned brown and cloudy in pewter goblets. The bread was hard and the meat smelled bad. There was no silverware at all.

"Rupert would love this," Mitch muttered, "the priest taking off with the silverware."

There were other rooms, but the one that caught his fancy was the bedroom.

It was large, with one big window facing out on the square, a huge chest of drawers against one of the walls, a couple of massive upholstered chairs, and other odds and ends. There were no crucifixes, nor were there any icons. He examined the objects on top of the chest of drawers. An ivory elephant, a shoehorn, a comb with several teeth missing that was stuck into a less than clean bristle hairbrush. But here, too, there were no religious objects. He went through the drawers, finding them partly full of linens, clothing, and some remnants of sewing kits.

Now he confronted a massive bed piled high with down mattresses, pillows, and comforters. Though it was unmade and had been slept in, the white sheets seemed clean. Mitch flung himself onto the high pile of down. With the exception of the ten days in Madrid on leave, Mitch had done all his sack-time on the hard tiled floors of Spanish *casas* or out in the fields, and the Spanish earth, blood-soaked, wine-soaked, nut-flavored by rotting olives, was quite hard.

The bullhorn got going below. Dave Doran, as at Quinto, harangued the fascists, trying to talk them into surrendering. Mitch went to the window to listen to the mechanical voice bounce off the walls of the old buildings. There was no sound of rifle fire now; the windows of the low houses were black and empty. He envisioned that same group of men, those he had seen in the doorway of the church, behind those windows and walls. Standing, sitting, crouching, listening to the words of the Rojos.

". . . Surrender, surrender . . . you are surrounded . . . the traitor-generals and the clerics have abandoned you . . . nothing can save you now . . . join your brothers, peasants and workers like you . . . you will be welcomed into our hearts . . . into our homes . . . stop this killing . . . you do not want to die for the landowners . . . the enslavers . . . join the people . . . come out and join your brothers . . . no harm will come to you . . ."

On and on, across the plaza and up and down the streets, ricocheting from wall to wall, brushing by the darkened windows, invading the places where men crouched, weapons at the ready. Mitch imagined himself there, looking at the others, consulting with unmoving lips, hearts and stomachs clutched with fear. What would he do? Where did safety lie?

At least we're giving the bastards a chance, Mitch thought. *If it was the other way around there would be no choice. If they were trying to sell us that bill of goods . . . What would I do? Shoot it out, try to get through the ring in the dark of the night? Anything . . . but not surrender or get captured.* The fascists killed Reds out of hand so there was no choice. And that's what they must be thinking: the terrible Reds kill the Falangistas out of hand – so what to do? Believe their promises?

He went out into the street and saw to it that his men were set for the night and that guards were posted. He showed Al where he would spend the night, pointing to the window and telling him which door to use to get there. Al was too tired to ask questions.

When he woke up, he knew he was sick. He had thrown off all the comforters during the night. His eyelids stuck together, there was a bad taste in his mouth, and his bones felt exposed, aquiver with pain and apprehension. Doran's tone on the speaker had changed, now almost conversational. Mitch dragged himself out of the priest's bed to the window in time to see the fascists coming out of buildings, holding their hands high in the air. The Lincolns who flanked Doran kept their rifles trained on the emerging figures.

Doran held the microphone to his mouth, urging them on. He stood erect, trim in boots and breeches and peaked military cap. As Mitch watched from the window, Doran handed off the speaker and turned to interrogate some of the prisoners, who were being lined up against the side of the church. Doran was joined by other members of brigade staff, one of whom was translating. Doran wanted to know who the officers were, and if there were still *soldados* hiding out in the town.

Just then the chow truck hove into sight. Fritz was standing on the running board, hollering, "¡Comida, camaradas, comida!" His arrival put an end to the questioning. Mitch had no appetite. He watched as Fritz and the driver dished out the food. There was enough left over to feed the prisoners as well; there were always more rations than men to feed after a firefight. Mitch searched the faces of the prisoners as they ate, to see if any of them had been at the church door, but none had.

A sudden itch, a demanding itch, struck at his crotch. When he scratched, he discovered the area crawling with lice. He eyed the mussed-up bed, and called down the most anticlerical Spanish curses he could think of on its former owner's head.

The war seemed over for Belchite, at least for the time being. Men were sprawled on the narrow walks, backs up against the walls of the *casas* eating *pan muy duro con* "fake" *café con leche*. The prisoners were standing around finishing up the goat – or burro – stew and talking animatedly with Doran, sometimes through interpreters, more often – with much gesturing – directly. They were pouring out information and complaints, and also expressions of solidarity with their captors, whom they were relieved to find were not wild-eyed Bolsheviks sworn to cut off their *cojónes* and eat them alive.

Mitch joined the men moving up and down the street, poking into the deserted houses and shops. He turned a corner into a street leading to a small square. The brigade ambulance, one Hemingway had brought over from the States, was parked on the square. He went over to see what Dr. Stein had to get rid of the crabs. He hoped they would not have to shave off all his body hair, since he had heard how uncomfortable it was when the stubble grew back. The thought made him shiver – like scratching a thumbnail over a slate.

He leaned against the warm side of the ambulance and watched Stein at work. Eyes red and face unshaven, the doctor seemed to be using his patients to hold himself together. Mitch didn't know what to say to him because, aside from the crabs, he just felt bad generally. He had no specific symptoms that he could describe.

"I feel lousy, I am lousy, and I'm crabbed-up, too. You see, last night I slept in the priest's bed and . . ." He trailed off as he saw the doctor focus in on him. "Can you give me something?"

"Get in the ambulance," Stein said and turned away to write something on a sheet of paper mounted on a clipboard.

"I mean something for the crabs. Some salve or ointment," Mitch explained.

"Get in," the doctor said. "You're sick." He hung a tag around Mitch's neck.

"Oh," said Mitch. He walked to the back of the ambulance and looked inside. There were men sitting on the benches on both sides. They looked at him and he looked at them. He turned back to the doctor.

"I don't think you understand," he started.

"Get in, get in!"

"But I can't. I have a section to take care of."

"It's all over now, don't worry. You won't miss anything."

"Yes, but . . ." But what? He was feeling lightheaded, and the discussion was tiring. He thought he would sit down on the step leading to the back of the ambulance. Later he remembered starting to sit down.

16

Johnson, Leo thought, looked like a typical U.S. Army captain. Maybe he was. Maybe he was working for army intelligence. They must have had a couple of men with the American volunteers. But from what Leo had heard about Johnson, it was not likely. Johnson had gone to the front at Jarama like the rest of the men. He had gone over the top, been badly wounded, had risen in the ranks without a political assist, had fought again at Bruneté, and had refused an opportunity to return to the States. He had accepted the job as *comandante* of the training base at Tarazona under protest, as he had wanted to be with the front-line troops instead.

Leo studied the smooth, sharp face, the neatly brushed sand-colored hair, the tight lips: so unlike Lawrence. He wondered how he would move him.

Johnson, finished with the file, looked up, studying Leo's face, making him feel uneasy.

"No, I think not." Johnson's diction was precise; the words clear, clean, and unbending. Leo's heart jumped. But he waited for something more, something that would give him an opening, a hint of how to proceed.

"Our training cadre is complete. We will include you in a contingent we are sending to the Lincoln-Washington as replacements."

"But Comrade Lawrence said – "

"He only recommended. We make the decision here."

"We? Who's we? There's only you and me here. This isn't the U.S. Army, you know. I'm entitled to more consideration than that." Panic caused Leo to lose control.

"Do you want a meeting on the question?" asked Johnson.

Leo searched the whitewashed walls, looking for a clue as to which way he should go. There was a map of Spain on the wall to his right, divided by a red line that snaked its way up from Estremadura to the outskirts of Madrid, darting east to Teruel and then more or less north to the Pyrenees. The fascists were on the Portuguese side of the map, while the Loyalists had the Mediterranean to their back. On the opposite wall there was a poster of an undivided Spain, with figures of a worker, a peasant, an intellectual, and a *soldado*. Underneath, emblazoned in red, was the slogan "¡En Unidad es Victoria!"

"No," Leo said. A meeting might include people even less sympathetic than this goyish army type. Losing control had been a mistake. "But I do think, Captain Johnson," he said respectfully, "you ought to let me state my case, perhaps give some consideration to Albaceté's recommendations?"

"And just what is your case, Comrade Rogin?"

"Well, I think you have it there." Leo indicated the file. "I have some stateside military training. I mean, more than most of the comrades." He had to be careful not to make too much of his ROTC time, lest doing so would lead Johnson to probe further than Lawrence had. "I think I can handle a command. Or at least train the new men."

"I'm afraid you're going to have to prove that."

"How can I prove it if no one will give me a chance?"

"You had your chance," Johnson said. "In combat."

"I got sick before anything happened. I wound up in the hospital before I had a chance."

"I am giving you another opportunity. You shouldn't have any trouble rising to a position of leadership. Do you know that almost every officer in the Lincoln-Washington, from squad leader to battalion commander, is now a comrade who has risen from the ranks after demonstrating his leadership qualities in battle?"

Yes, Leo thought, I know that, and I know what happened to the officers whose places they took. Dead. Dead. Dead. The words "combat" and "battle" irked him. Johnson could talk, the lucky bastard. Johnson had lived through it and he was out of it now. Sure. Combat. Battle. Johnson was going to stay in Tarazona.

Leo reached for one more straw. "I would like to request a meeting, after all."

Outside in the sunlight, Leo wondered why he had asked for the meeting. Out of desperation? Perhaps he would find someone more his kind, a type he could reach. Johnson was hopeless but at least he hadn't questioned the Bruneté thing.

He stood in the square before the *estado mayor* and listened to the rattle from the firing range. He saw men executing close-order drill on the parade grounds, partly obscured by a cloud of white dust, and heard the commands shouted by the training cadre. He considered canceling his request. Johnson was right, the place to prove himself was in combat. After all, Bruneté wasn't the definitive test. There had been the heat, Aaron getting killed, and the realization that they, with their lousy 1903 Remingtons, ten airplanes, handful of Russian tanks, and who knows what vintage artillery (Leo got increasingly bitter as he listed the odds against them), hadn't had a chance against the better-equipped, better-trained fascists.

But that was Bruneté, he tried assuring himself. Now they had better arms, the men were receiving better training. General Miaja was the new commander of the Central Sector – civilian as well as military; the Republic was getting its act together. Who knows, he shrugged, maybe Johnson knows what he's talking about.

Leo saw two familiar figures turn into the door of a cafe down the street, and quickly walked to join them.

It was cool and dark in the cafe and it took a minute or so before his eyes made the adjustment from the bright sun beating down on the white turf of Tarazona.

"Say, I know you comrades." He sat down at their table. "We were at Bruneté together. I know you from Madrigueras, Tarazona. What are you doing here?"

"Who are you? Oye, una botella de vino . . . rojo, por favor."

"I'm Leo Rogin from the First Company. You're with the Machine Gun Company, right?"

"That's right. I know you now. You're one of the Voluntarios. My name's Manny Spear. Nick Stamos."

"Gracias," Stamos said to the man who brought the wine and two glasses. "Another glass if it is not too much trouble."

"De nada." The proprietor picked up the pesetas Nick had put on the table, and whipped a cloth over the white oilcloth table covering.

"De nada, de nada. Everything is nothing, no problemas." Stamos poured the wine, raised his glass, ruby red in the shadowed room. "Here's wishing that it were only so. No problems, everything according to Hoyle, or maybe Clausewitz." He emptied his glass. "Mierda," he said through wine-stained teeth, and refilled the glass.

"So you're one of them, eh?" Stamos raised his glass again. "So here's to the last of the songbirds – "

"What do you mean 'last?'" When Stamos did not answer, Leo turned to Spear.

"Aaron got it at Bruneté – "

"I know, I was there."

"And Murray at Belchite. You weren't there? You didn't know? I'm sorry."

See? Leo screamed silently. *See! Murray, Aaron . . . me? Leo next?*

"Big and fat and blue in the middle of the road in the hot sun. Cooking all day," Stamos said into his glass.

"What?"

"Don't pay any attention to him," Manny said kindly. "Snipers. It was a while before we could get to him. I thought you would know."

"I was in the hospital, I wasn't there. What happened, how did it happen?" But he wasn't hearing himself or them. *See! See!* the voice kept screeching inside, demanding his full attention.

". . . really a shame," Spear was saying. "All the best guys. Block, Aaron . . . guys with real talent with so much to contribute."

"¡Mierda!" Nick repeated. "What talent? What difference does it make? What about the others – Janus, the dumb seaman, or Schwartz the candy-butcher, or Gordon or Krauss or Joe Blow. How do you know what they had in the bag? They were just as important. My brother Mike, the first day at Jarama, never fired a shot, a sweet kid, a good union man, for Christ's sake . . ." Stamos's eyes watered, his voice caught. "Shit!" he said, turning away.

"The Party ought to keep our most talented people in reserve," Manny said, "doing more important work, not wasting them on the battlefield unless it's absolutely necessary. If it could've been me instead of Aaron . . ." Manny drank to cover his embarrassment. "Well, are they sending you home too?"

Leo sat up. "What do you mean, sending me home?" The words drove all thoughts of Aaron and Murray out of his mind.

"We've been selected for preservation," Stamos said grandly. "Snatched from the battlefield to be sent forth to bring the message to the masses back home."

"It's a problem," Manny said.

"What problem? I'm staying here. Who wants to go home?" Stamos stared into his glass. "What's to do at home? Let someone else be a hero."

"But it's a Party decision."

"It won't be the first Party decision I've ignored. They'll let us stay, don't you worry your little ass about that. Whoever the hell dreamed up the idea that you serve your time here and then go home to fight the battle there is going to get his ass in a sling. Is for the birds, comrade. Is going to demoralize the *tovarisches!*"

"Time? How much time?" Leo's hopes rose. He had as much time as Manny. "How long – ?"

"Yeah, how long?" Manny asked Stamos. "You've been here since Jarama but I've been only since Bruneté."

"Time plus battles plus political necessity minus desire multiplied by shit. I don't know. Makes no difference. We're staying, right?"

"We'll see." Manny filled his glass. Stamos waved for another bottle. Leo sipped from the first glass poured for him. "I quite agree with you," he said to Manny. "But the Party knows what it's doing. You'll make a great contribution."

"¡Mierda!" Stamos said.

"Say, Manny, who's in charge . . . who's taking care of the details?" Leo made it a casual question.

"What details?"

"Oh, arranging for passage home and all that . . ."

Stamos looked at him closely.

"Who? I don't know. Do you?" Manny asked Stamos.

"Where d'you say you been?" Stamos changed the subject. "Hospital? Where'd you get hit?"

"They sent me to Albaceté from the hospital and Comrade Lawrence assigned me to train the new men," Leo dodged.

"Oh, Lawrence. Ha!" Stamos snorted. "Lawrence, eh? That's it."

After a moment's silence, Leo asked "What do you mean? I don't understand."

"No comprende, eh?" Stamos said. "I'll tell you. Lawrence's the man the

Party sent from the States to run the base at Albaceté." He paused. "To bring the word that after X amount of combat you get to go home." He stopped, his black eyes hard and questioning. "So Lawrence sent you here to train new men? You know what I think? I think you're a lot of shit. I do not propose to sit here and drink with you. C'mon, Manny. I've been telling you, stay away from the rear if you want to keep the faith."

"I'm sorry about Murray, and Aaron too." Manny got up with Stamos, stopped, and added, thoughtfully, "If someone explained about the Voluntarios . . . You're the last, right? I know Lehan Larner joined in with you, but you and Murray and Aaron are – were – the originals from New York. Maybe it would be a good idea if you were sent home to keep alive the songs and music. It would mean a great deal to the people back home."

Leo looked at him, tears coming to his eyes. He was glad now that he had asked Johnson for the meeting. He had approached the whole problem from the wrong end. Manny had shown him the way to go.

17

Mitch awakened to find himself in a room filled with sunlight. The room was long and narrow, and beds lined the walls in orderly rows. There was a lot of white linen, white bandages bright in the sunlight. A few men were sitting up, or on the edge of their beds, but most were sleeping or quietly lying back staring at the high whitewashed ceiling. Beside his cot there was a chair and his personal belongings, his military *carnet* and other documents neatly stacked, his clothes washed and folded.

As he sat taking stock of himself and the room, trying to figure out what to do next, a nurse or a nurse's aide – she was young and pretty – came into the room and, seeing him sitting up, came up to the bed saying something that sounded like "Buenas dias," but wasn't. She smiled. "Catalan" she said, and rapidly spieled off a great deal in that language, which he did not understand, before switching to Spanish at the same pace.

He gestured to slow her down, and found out that he was in a place called Bals, that he was now *limpia*, which he took to mean clean of lice and crabs (he felt surreptitiously for his hair and was relieved to find it intact though sticky with salve), and also *muy afortunado* to be here where he could stay until the medico ordered him back to his unit. Furthermore, she looked forward to his staying as he was the only *Americano* in the hospital. He wondered how that had come to be, but he did not ask.

When she left, he got out of the bed and dressed, collected his papers, and looked for a way out. He had not been wounded, and though at first he felt a bit weak in the knees, once he had retraced the nurse's steps, the weakness disappeared. He came into a large entryway, bare of furnishings save for a simple desk and a couple of chairs. There were no people around, so he walked out onto the steps, down a gentle grassed-over grade to a road. He did not look back to see what the hospital looked like, and he had no idea how long he had been there. He was feeling fine and the priestly crabs from Belchite were gone. He did not know what else had been the matter with him, or why Stein had sent him to the rear, or why he had been the only American in a place called Bals, which he had never heard of.

He walked away from the rising sun, hoping Belchite and the Brigade lay in that direction. He wanted to get away from the hospital, and when a camion came along going his way he waved it down and got in.

The driver was an American headed for brigade, which was no longer at Belchite but in a rest area to which he was carrying a load of new uniforms. The truck driver looked at him and asked, "What are you doing here?"

Mitch didn't answer because he did not know. When they got back to brigade, he found out where the battalion was and went to look for Manny, but Rupert told him that Manny, along with Stamos, was no longer with the battalion.

"So, Commander Castle, congratulations. You are now commander of the Machine Gun Company," Rupert said, with something of a flourish.

"Where is everybody, where's the company?" Mitch asked.

Rupert took him by the arm and pointed him in the direction of the Machine Gun Company. He started to go to it when a thought occurred to him.

"Where's Dr. Stein?" he asked.

"With Division *Sanidad*. We have a new doctor. Why, are you still hurting?"

"No, I just wanted – I just wanted to ask him – it doesn't matter." It really didn't, Mitch thought. Whatever had hit him in Belchite, or more specifically in that goddamned priest's bed, had not been lasting. He had hardly been gone long enough for Rupert to have missed him. Besides, he'd have more to think about now, now that he had a whole company, nine guns and maybe a hundred men if they were ever at full strength – which was unlikely. Maybe only eighty or seventy-five men – to . . . to what? He was at a loss for what he was supposed to do as company commander, but not for long. He would do whatever had to be done when they got into action. And that, Rupert had said, would be soon. Zaragoza or Huesca, one or the other, was the next objective.

18

The meeting wasn't going well. Johnson had read Leo's file aloud and then announced his decision to ignore Lawrence's recommendation.

"Comrade Rogin wishes to appeal my decision," Johnson had said, and had turned the floor over to Leo.

He had been nervous at first. The faces in the room crowded in on him. Besides Johnson, there was Joe Bullard, tall and very military-looking, commissar of the new Mackenzie-Papineau Battalion. Both Mac and Pap, as he thought of them, had been Canadian heroes. He had heard the men speak of Bullard as a martinet, a stickler for discipline. And then there was Bob Carter, the commander of the new outfit. Carter, like Bullard, sat erect. As far away from the overhead light as he could get, someone to whom Leo had not been introduced lounged against the wall, only his Sam Brown belt picking up a bit of the light. Manny and Nick, who sat apart from the others, had been included to represent the combat veterans.

Leo presented his case, haltingly at first, and then, as he convinced himself of the justice of his position, with earnestness, and tearfully when he spoke of Aaron and Murray.

"If only one of them had been spared," he concluded, "not me, but Murray or Aaron, to return home with our songs and music to tell the story of Spain! What a tremendous contribution to the cause!" He paused. "Someone must – " He broke off, unable to say "if only me."

Johnson turned to Stamos and Manny. "How about it, comrades? You were in his outfit."

"I think your decision is correct," Stamos said. "And while we're at it, I don't agree with this policy of sending guys home. We came over to do a job. We're supposed to stay here until it's finished."

"Let's not get into that again," Bullard said.

"It's bad policy, a demoralizer," Stamos persisted.

"I don't want to go into that anymore, either," Manny broke in. "I don't agree with Stamos. What I want to say is that since it has been agreed that Stamos and I will not go home, why not let this comrade go in our place? You comrades did not know the Voluntarios, but they were a very big part of the Washington Battalion. Their songs and skits were terrific. We loved them. They even managed enough Spanish to delight the village people, they had 'em rolling in the aisles, like they say. I bet they're still remembered here in Tarazona. Comrade Rogin was part of that, he has the story and all. They can use him back in the States to rally support for the Loyalist cause. . . . Well, I guess I spoke too long. Anyway, what I'm saying is he can take my place, or Nick's . . ." Spear trailed off.

"There's a great deal of merit in what Comrade Spear says," Carter said. "I wonder if Comrade Lawrence was aware of the facts. Do you know?" he asked Leo.

This was the high point of the meeting for Leo. He could have kissed Manny. His heart sang with joy, not only because it seemed that they might see it his way, but also because he believed it. It sounded great, even inspirational. He would go home and write the songs down. He'd write their story and travel all over the States telling the story of the group, the story of their heroic deaths, the fascists they had killed, the contribution they had made to save the Republic, to stem the tide of fascism, to forestall the coming of another war. They had given their music and their lives so that others could sing and dance in peace and freedom. The words rang in his head; his heart overflowed.

"No, Comrade Carter," he said. "I only wanted to do what was right, what was best for what we're fighting for. I trust Comrade Lawrence's judgment. As I trust yours. I am prepared to do anything for the cause." His eyes shone.

But now the man he did not know, whose name no one had mentioned, spoke from the corner of the room. "Why, comrade," he asked, "did you allow yourself to be carried from the field at Cañada when there was no reason for it? When stretcher bearers were needed for the wounded?" The tone was menacing.

"I didn't allow myself to be carried," said Leo. He was not afraid now, not even of this mysterious character. He was enthralled by the image of giving his all for the cause. "I was unconscious. I didn't have anything to do with it. I woke up in a hospital."

"The medical record says," the voice was flat, "that you feigned unconsciousness."

"It's not true! How could I?"

Bullard took his pipe from his mouth. "You must realize, Comrade Rogin, that it would be unwise to send you home under the circumstances. I
propose we accept Comrade Johnson's decision with a qualifying recommendation: that Comrade Rogin be returned to his battalion for assignment, and immediately after the next action – if Comrade Rogin carries
out his assignment in a manner befitting an antifascist fighter – he be withdrawn and sent to Albaceté for assignment home to do political work."

Leo thought to protest, but a glance at the man in the corner checked
him. There was something about the way he positioned himself in the
shadows, about the gleam of his Sam Brown belt, about the way he eyed
each speaker as though taking mental notes to be filed for future use.

Johnson, nodding, turned to look at the others. Manny and Stamos had
had their say. Carter went along with his commissar.

"Fine," Leo said. "Of course, like I said, anything you decide. I object to
the so-called 'feigned unconsciousness' in my records. It shouldn't be there."
He looked at the man in the shadows, at his folded hands, white like a clerk's,
soft like his face. "I am ready to go the front again if that's the way, but – "

"Good," Johnson interrupted. "You'll get your orders when we've assembled a group of replacements and arranged for transport. That's all."

Dismissed, Leo wandered off to his quarters, turning down Manny's offer to buy him a drink. He was tired; the emotional strain had drained him.
He had trouble getting to sleep, playing the scene in Johnson's office over
and over again in his mind. That was it. It was a letdown. But on the other
hand, now there was a definite end in sight. One action and then home.
Terrific. All he had to do was take care, not stick his head out, and then
home. Home! The sole survivor of the group, a hero. But this thought
brought Murray and Aaron back. His eyes moistened and some of the de-
termination went out of him. He'd be alone in the battalion. Who was left
that he knew? Nolan and Jorgensen were out of it, he'd seen them at the
hospital with their arms in plaster. Jack flat on his stomach with shrapnel
deep inside his ass. Glenn killed at Bruneté, Spear stuck here in Tarazona,
waiting with Nick to be sent home as ordered, or to stay . . .

Replacement . . . awful word . . . replace the dead, the wounded.

Castle. If he wasn't dead or wounded. Leo remembered Castle looking
for water in the pouring rain at Morata, and at Bruneté – "Where do I
shoot? Where are the fascists?" Dumb.

But never mind; all he had to do was what was asked of him, giving a good account of himself but making sure he wasn't put in some stupid position where he might get himself killed. He turned on the pallet trying to find a soft spot on the hard floor. *Back away*, he hummed, *and live to fight another day.*

Leo recognized the battalion commander from the early days at Tarazona. Leonard Lyons had been one of the few better-dressed, military-looking types in the outfit. He was one of those comrades who seemed always to be part of, or at least constantly in the company of, the upper echelons. In the hospital and out on the streets, Leo had heard that as many as seven battalion commanders had come and gone during the twenty-one days of Bruneté. The big news reported in the *boletins* posted on the rec room wall was that Hans Amlie, the brother of a congressman, had led the Lincolns at Quinto and Belchite. What with all the turnovers, Leo did not bother to ask the whereabouts of Amlie. And he was relieved that Commander Lyons spent little time querying the replacements.

Leo and the others were directed to report to the Third Company, which he found in an olive grove, the rows of trees sheltering the *chabolas* the men had dug. Each century-old tree had its cluster of *chabolas* arranged haphazardly around its base, the odd shapes, the newly turned soil, and the makeshift roofing covering the dugouts like flower petals on a twisted giant stem turned upside down. The men sat "reading" the seams of their shirts in search of lice, cleaning rifles, reading papers and pamphlets, writing letters and poetry, or just talking. Looking up to see the new men coming in, one of them called out, "Hey, Rogin, the Voluntario. Hey, Leo, what'cha doin' so close to the front?"

"He's come back for another ride," someone yelled. "Stretcher bearers! Here's a passenger!"

"Hey, wait a minute," said a tall, lean man, whose steel-rimmed glasses glinted in the sun as he came to his feet. "Let's cut this crap out, comrades."

He approached the group of new men with an outstretched hand. "My name's Harold, Harold Smith. Commissar of the Third Company. Good to have you join us." He shook each one by the hand, saving Leo for last.

"Hello, Comrade Rogin," he said warmly. "You don't know me, but I remember you from Madrigueras and Tarazona. You and Aaron and Murray. Don't mind these guys. Shithouse rumors fly thick and fast around here. We all spend a lot of time in the latrine, lots of time to bullshit between, during, and after the runs. Ah. Here's Comrade Williams. The new men, Commander."

The company commander had emerged from a *chabola* no different from the others and approached the group. Leo recognized him as one of the original Washingtons; he had been a squad leader in another company. Williams was short and slight, with soft brown eyes and straight brown hair on a small head. His voice was thin and midwestern as he welcomed the replacements.

"We all start out even here. All alike whether you've seen action or not. If you're worried about being green, forget it . . . we'll help you one way or another. If you're out of a hospital, you're healthy now. Uh," Williams paused, looking over the heads of the men before him, "if you've, uh, had some kind of problem, uh, it doesn't mean a thing here. If you have any question, the office door's always open – mine or Harold's." He smiled, pointing to the crude shelter.

"When are we going into action?" one of the "green" men asked, excitement pitching his voice into higher ranges.

"Soon enough," Williams replied dryly, a tight smile on his lips.

Harold walked Leo to his assigned section.

"You know," he said, "it would be really great if you could put together another group. I know no one will replace the original . . . but you could get a couple of guys together . . ." He laughed. "I'd love to sing along. Do you think you can do that?"

Leo's first impulse when the men had greeted him with "Get a stretcher" had been to bolt. But before Smith had finished talking he knew that he had a friend, someone to attach himself to, as he had been attached to Aaron and Murray. Here was someone he could deal with, who would listen and perhaps help him get through in one piece.

"I don't know," Leo said, "I'm in a kind of funny position here."

"You mean about what the guys said? Forget it. I'll put a stop to that."

"Not only that. It's been decided I'm to be sent home . . . as soon as possible . . . to do work there. For the Loyalists."

"What?" said Harold. "Who decided? What do you mean as soon as possible? We'll all be going back as soon as possible."

"Don't you know? There's a policy to send some of the comrades home as soon as they've served their time – "

"Served their time? I never heard of such a thing."

Leo sensed that he was in danger of antagonizing Smith. Apparently the men at the front had not received word of this policy.

"Anyhow, the thinking at Albaceté is that since I am the last of the Voluntarios I should be sent home to do propaganda work, fund raising, memorials for Murray and Aaron."

He could see that Harold was mulling it over, and he moved to strengthen his case. Smith could be helpful in expediting whatever was necessary to satisfy Albaceté.

"Comrade Lawrence has discussed this with me, as well as with some of the other leading comrades." He thought of the stranger in the shadowed corner of Johnson's office. "Spear and Stamos, you know them? They're in Tarazona waiting to be sent home." He did not add that they had asked to be sent back to the outfit.

"Hmm," Harold grumbled. "Look, I don't want you talking about that here. We've had no such word. After Belchite some men were taken out of their companies and sent to the rear to be trained as officers." He paused. "That's my understanding, anyway. We're not through on this front. Quinto was a bitch and Belchite worse. But none of the main objectives have been taken . . . Zaragoza, Huesca . . . I don't know them all. All I know is we have a lot of fighting to do here, and . . . well, it won't make it easier thinking it's time to go home."

"Of course, of course. I'm not thinking about it either . . . just when you mentioned starting another group. I don't think I can go through that again. It would be too painful. Still, if you thought it important enough . . . if I had enough time – "

"We'll find time. Okay? It's settled then." Harold slapped him on the back. "Here's your section and here's Gabby, the section politico. Gabby, I have fresh blood for you. Leo Rogin . . . remember him? From the Voluntarios."

Harold was as good as his word and no one hassled Leo about Bruneté. There was a wait-and-see attitude toward him, and most of the men seemed to think he would be okay. And he felt he would be – except that it rained a great deal in the days that followed, and the battalion was constantly on the move. It was unsettling. No sooner did they arrive at one location, with the understanding that they were supposed to go into action at that point, then new orders came and they marched back or trucked farther north. The uncertainty, the marching, the cold food, the soaking rain – all began to wear down his resolve.

He tried to form a group to do the old songs and skits, but the men were too tired and the seemingly aimless maneuvering of the outfit depressed him.

He couldn't understand how the men kept sloshing along from one place to another, tired, wet, dirty, gagging on rancid olive oil and cramped by diarrhea. They packed their gear each and every time and fell into formation for the next march, and the next, and the next. They complained, but they harbored no resentment or doubts. Gabby, a skeleton-like collection of bones, his face like a hawk, talked incessantly about food, the food they had had at home and the meals they were going to eat when they got home, when he wasn't lecturing about politics: the POUMists, the United Front, the meaning of President Roosevelt's "Quarantine the Aggressors" speech, what their unions were up to.

Leo tried to keep up with them, join in, but he'd lose some of his composure. His remarks became more bitter, more pointed, his attitude more questioning. Men laughed at him, jeering, "Hey comrade, you're in the fucking army, not picnicking in Bronx Park." Nothing went on forever, he assured himself. The rain would stop, they'd finally get to do something, whatever that might be. Everything would turn out according to plan – his plan, of course.

19

They had bedded down in the wet, cold earth of the northern sector of the Aragon front near Huesca. It was still raining, a hard rain, and Leo was trying to find a way to stay dry under the poncho he had rigged as a tent when he was startled by the close explosion of a gun. They were supposed to be behind the lines, but in the wash of blackness there was no telling where the lines, if any, were. It was reminiscent of the night at Morata, when firing had broken out all along the ridge and he had felt the same tight clutch in his gut that was part anticipation and part fear.

As he listened, holding his breath, he heard voices raised in alarm, the slosh of hurrying steps on the wet ground. He debated whether to stay put, crouched in the shallow foxhole under the woolen poncho, or to get out and see what was going on.

The sound of an approaching motor decided for him. Cautiously, he stuck his head out. The *chabolas* left a clear avenue closed off by a real honest-to-goodness canvas tent, the kind you'd find in an army and navy surplus store back home. The flaps of the tent were thrown open and a triangle of yellow light skidded down strings of slanting rain. An ambulance, slewing from side to side, slid to a stop before the opening. There were only the sounds of the rain tin-panning on the roof of the ambulance, the irregular laboring of its engine, and a voice calling out, but not the flurry of fire that was often set off when some half-asleep sentry dreamed an attack and opened fire at imagined figures in the dark.

Two men came out of the tent supporting a third between them. When the third man turned his head back to the light, Leo recognized him as the battalion commander. Arms around the shoulders of the men supporting him, Lyons one-legged it to the rear of the ambulance. One man got in with him and the other slogged around to the cab and waved the driver off.

The wheels of the ambulance spun, spraying mud on the man who had stepped away from the cab.

"Sonofabitch," he hollered after the departing vehicle. He followed this with a string of Spanish curses before turning away abruptly, a cape flying out from around his tall skinny body, a fantastic apparition Leo barely recognized as Mitch Castle. As Castle drew nearer, Leo saw that he was hatless, his black hair a swirl of wet curls dripping across his brow, snared in the black moustaches that cut across his cadaverous face and flew out from under a huge nose like the wings of a crow.

As he came by with long, loping strides, Leo caught at his cape and tugged.

"Hey, Mitch! Hey, what happened?"

"Fuckin' mud!" Mitch bent to scan his face. "Leo! What the hell are you doing here? Let me in out of this fuckin' rain. When'd you get back? How the hell are you? This your hole?"

Mitch squirmed, fishing under his cape, and came out with a pipe which he stuffed from a Bull Durham sack and lit with a *machero*, sparks spraying in every direction.

"Goddamned dehydrated horseshit!" he cursed, pulling in sunken cheeks, the white of his teeth flashing as he drew his lips back with each puff.

Good Christ, the kid from Bensonhurst, Leo thought, looks like a cadaver, a pirate, a roaring, fire-spouting dragon. But Leo was glad to see one of the men he had known from the bucolic days in Capestan here on this muddy plain somewhere near Huesca, wherever that was. He avoided Mitch's questions and repeated his own instead: "What happened to Lyons? I saw you put him in the ambulance – "

"He had an accident, but – Oh, hell, everyone will know by morning if they don't know already. The stupid bastard was cleaning his pistol . . . a little bit of a thing . . . it went off . . . and powie! a neat little hole in his foot."

In the dark Leo thought he saw a smile on Mitch's face. "Powie!" Mitch repeated. "That sonofabitch has more bad luck than anyone I know."

"Bad luck, what bad luck?"

"Aaagh!" Mitch said. "He's been bucking for battalion commander ever since Tarazona. He finally gets it when Amlie chickens out at Belchite, and before he can take us into action, powie! Tough shit."

Crowded and huddled as they were, they warmed the space under the poncho. The stink of mud that Castle had brought in combined with the smell of wet wool and the sharp reek of burning tobacco. They were silent for a moment and then Mitch asked again, "When'd you get back?"

"As soon as I got out of the hospital." Leo wanted to bring the talk back to Lyons, away from himself. "How could he shoot himself in the foot cleaning a pistol?"

"When was that?" Mitch persisted. "Were you at Quinto? I didn't see you there, did I?"

"Didn't he know it was loaded?"

"Belchite, hah? Did I see you there . . . I don't think so."

"There was a guy in the hospital where I was, in Madrid. They say he shot himself in the hand. Shot his finger off."

"What guy? Who says?" Mitch was leaning toward Leo now, blowing acrid smoke into his face. Close up, he smelled of damp mold, and there was a gleam in the blackness where his eyes, sunken hollows, fixed on Leo. Leo regretted having stopped Mitch.

"Are you still with the Machine Gun Company?"

"Just back, huh?" Mitch leaned back. Leo could feel the wetness coming through the poncho where his humped shoulders pushed against it. "You got a ride out of Bruneté, didn't you? That was in July. This is September or October, shit, I don't know which. So where've you been all this time? What in hell'd you come back for?"

"What d'you mean? I was in the hospital. I was sick. You're not spreading that rumor too?"

"No, I ain't spreading nothing. I just listen." Mitch twisted to a crouch in order to crawl out of the pup tent. "They sent me to a hospital, too, only I didn't go until the shooting was over. I came back the next day. Where the fuck you been all this time, in some kind of limbo?"

"In a way, yes. Wait, listen to me, will you? We were in Capestan together. Listen. I don't care what you heard. Aaron and Murray are dead – "

"So what's new?"

"They're sending me back to the States after this action, to carry on the Voluntarios, to work for the Loyalist cause, and – "

"What?"

"Yes, some of the guys. Manny – I met him in Tarazona – he's going to get sent back – "

"No! I thought they pulled him and Nick out for officer training. That's why I got the Machine Gun Company. You telling me they're going home?"

"You're the commander?" Leo was taken aback. Mitch in command of the machine gunners? The battalion commander out with a self-inflicted wound? What would happen to them in action? More to the point, what would happen to him?

"Listen, wait, I didn't know you were the commander. Listen, why don't I get transferred to your company? Why don't you get me transferred?" He did not know Williams, Smith had been nice to him, but both were unknown quantities. He knew, or thought he knew, Mitch. Mitch was younger, less educated, and at Capestan had been, it seemed to him, willing to be led. Castle had come alone, without friends or comrades, with damned little political savvy and no Party clout. It was entirely possible that he could use Castle to make a safe place for himself.

"What for? According to you, you're going home."

"Sure, I'm going home but first I have to – I want to – get this action in . . . I want to do my share . . . don't you see?"

Leo had moved closer to Mitch, seeking some sort of expression of sympathy. Mitch pulled back, but Leo could still make out his features. As Mitch moved, the pistol he was wearing under his cape slipped out of its holster. He picked it up and wiped it with the end of his cape.

"Sonofabitch!"

"Me?" Leo was startled.

"Not you, the damned pistol fell out of the holster. Quit pushing up to me like that, will you?"

"Look, I know you, you know me. I'd feel better being in your company. Maybe attached to your staff. Huh? You know I had military training back in the States. I could help set the firing fields for the guns, you know?" Leo watched nervously as Mitch wiped the pistol with a corner of his cape. He drew back as Mitch held the gun out to him.

"Look at this beauty. It's a German Luger. Look at the handle, carved bone. Picked it up at the church at Belchite. The cape, too."

"Don't point it, please! What do you say, will you?"

"Will I what? Yeah, I might, I might." Mitch withdrew the Luger and held it on his lap. "Don't worry about this one going off. It's loaded. Lyons's wasn't." He roared.

Leo laughed weakly. "Listen, you won't be sorry. And don't worry, I won't tell anyone about Bullard's decision to send me home."

"Bullard? What the hell does he have to do with it? He's the commissar of the Mac-Paps."

"He's more. At a meeting in Tarazona where they . . . where they took up this question, it was his decision – "

"Joe Bullard!" Mitch shook the pistol under his nose. "Bullard? Let me tell you about Bullard." He fished the pouch of Bull Durham from his pocket. Leo kept his eye on the pistol. "See this?" Now Mitch was waving the tobacco before Leo's eyes. "Cigarette butts, dried leaves, dehydrated horseshit. That's what I've been smoking since Quinto. And here comes Bullard, fresh and clean, pressed and ironed, the commissar of the Mac-Paps. No action yet, see? But he looks down at us scurvy, filthy, demoralized bastards. Demoralized! That's what they say. Why? Because we ain't singing the Internationale every hour on the hour. Because we ain't having political meetings three times a day. Bullshit!" He caught his breath. "I don't know why I'm telling you this, anyway."

"Telling me what?" This was the first Leo had heard of the Lincolns being demoralized. "What about Bullard?"

"I'm wandering around the Mac-Paps who have just joined the brigade after Belchite, and I'm looking to see if any of the comrades from my Bensonhurst branch have gotten up enough moxie to come over, which they haven't, and suddenly I smell real tobacco. You know what real tobacco smoke smells like when you haven't had any, when you've been smoking this crud for months? I sticks my nose into the air, picks up the scent, and follows the nose to where it leads. And it leads to Joe Bullard. It leads right to this big fancy tent in which is Joe Bullard and a guy called Carter who is the battalion commander of the Mac-Paps. But Mr. Fancy Bullard is the one smoking the pipe."

Leo shivered. He was getting cold, and he would have liked for Mitch to have settled his transfer and gotten the hell out. He didn't know what this was all about: tobacco, pipes, Bullard.

"I go up to Mr. Bullard. I'm gently tapping the empty bowl of my pipe against the heel of my hand. 'Comrade,' I say, not knowing then who he was but seeing that he was a somebody, 'could you spare a pipeful of tobacco? I haven't had any in a month of Sundays.' I had no doubt that I could cadge a pipeful because we pipe smokers are clannish. We'd never turn down a fellow pipe smoker in distress. Well! He looks me up and down. 'No,' he says, 'I can't.'

"Meanwhile I have seen past him, into the tent, and there on a table stands a red can I recognize as being a one-pound tin of Prince Albert, which is not my favorite brand and those that smoke it are basically a conservative bunch who have had no adventures in tobacco sampling, or maybe anything else. But then maybe he didn't have a choice. I certainly didn't, and Prince Albert is a hell of a lot better than this shit." He waved the pouch in the air and pushed the Luger under Leo's nose. "'See this Luger?' I said to him, 'I took it from a fascist officer at Belchite.' Stretching it a bit to make it more appealing to him. 'I tell you what I'll do. I'll swap it for whatever tobacco you have in the can, sight unseen. Here,' I said, 'you can look at it.' He pushes it away and says, 'What do you think I am?' Well, I wasn't about to tell him. Instead, out of desperation, I said, 'For half of what you have. I know how you must feel about having a supply on hand.' But I was not moving him and so finally I said, 'Here, you can have it. Just give me a pipeful.' 'What company are you in, soldier?' he shoots back, quick as a flash, nasty-like. 'What company?'

"'The Machine Gun Company. Why?' I ask, still holding the pistol out to him and feeling foolish.

"'I think your company commander should know about this. We don't trade in arms in the Mac-Paps.'

"Hah! I could hardly keep myself from laughing. 'Well, you must tell him that,' I said. 'His name is Castle, Mitchell Castle.' Now Carter pipes up with 'We don't talk that way to officers in this outfit!' 'You men have a great deal to learn,' Bullard throws in.

"'Not from you,' I say. They look properly pissed off."

"I bet," Leo said. "But how about me, how about my transfer?"

Mitch shoved the gun into its holster and scrambled for the exit. "Ask Bullard for it; he's laid it all out for you. Go ahead and ask the . . ." Mitch's last words were lost in the rain.

Leo lay awake the rest of the night thinking it all out. He tossed and turned, always coming back to the same point. The only peace and security he had had since they had first gone into action was when he had made his decision out there in the heat, in the wheat field, with the bullets whistling over his head, Aaron's dead hulk his only protection: when he had decided to go no farther. But everything had gotten fouled up. Aaron and Murray were dead, and no matter how many times he said this or had it said to him, the effect was always the same. His guts collapsed, his heart fell like a cold stone into the ruins. Now he was a marked man. He had had a meeting with Lawrence and Johnson and Bullard, and most of the guys in this outfit had never even heard of these people. And no matter what he said, it seemed to be the wrong thing. His hand fell on the rifle he kept by his side. He sat up.

What if . . . how . . . could he? He wondered if it had been an accident with Lyons. Lyons might have wanted the battalion, but when it came to leading it into action, it might have weighed on him. And on a rainy night, after trekking all over the countryside day and night in the cold and the rain, not knowing when they were going into action, suppose he broke. Took the easy way out. Happened in all wars.

Let's see, he mused. He would have to get the cleaning kit spread out to make it look good – guys were always having accidental firings when cleaning their weapons. Hand or foot? The foot. He'd best keep his hands intact for the guitar.

The rain let up and grey light filtered through the loose opening in the poncho. He sat up and rubbed the soft down on his chin, wrapped himself in his blanket, and crawled out of the *chabola*. He made his way to the latrine and urinated. As he stood over the trench, the chow camion came up with the morning's food. He watched Fritz get out of the truck to unload the steaming canisters of coffee, the sacks of bread, and the tins of marmalade. He wandered over to the truck and saw that some of the cookhouse detail were to be left with the food while the rest were about to mount the truck for the return trip. None of the men of the battalion had turned out as yet.

"Where're you going?" he asked the driver.

"Back to brigade," the man replied.

"That's where I'm going," he said without thinking. "Give me a lift."

"Jump in."

At brigade he found an ammo truck that had been unloaded, and he hitched a ride. Getting in and out of trucks all morning, he finally found himself in an empty lorry that was on its way to Barcelona. No one had asked for papers, or questioned where he was going, or who he was. He simply asked where they were going, and if they were going toward the rear, he asked for and received a lift.

He hadn't fully realized any plan to account for his actions, but there was no way he was going to shoot himself in the foot.

 **20**

The late afternoon sun gilding the ornate cupolas on the roof-tops of the tall buildings, and the civilians going about their business on the tree-lined streets, lifted Leo's spirits. He stretched to relieve the stiffness that had set in after more than a day's riding in the camions.

The last camion had let him off on the waterfront, and now he walked up the main street leading from it. White enamel street signs plastered on corner buildings read Via Ramblas. Seen close up, the buildings bore the scars of warfare: broken and boarded windows, and fronts pockmarked with rifle or machine-gun fire. There were posters everywhere proclaiming the virtues of the UGT, the CNT, FAI, the POUM, Catalonia, the Republic, and so on. Some were defaced or partially stripped from the walls.

He passed a group of uniformed men coming out of a shop. He nodded when they smiled, but kept walking; he had no papers. Hunger got the best of caution, however, and he approached a civilian. His Spanish was good enough now that he had no trouble asking directions to the nearest *comida*. The Catalan seemed in no hurry to reply, though he impatiently barked *sí, sí* when Leo kept repeating his words. The Catalan wore the usual black jacket and trousers, an open-necked shirt that was clean though no longer white, and a small black beret to cover a balding head. Leo felt uneasy under his searching black eyes; the man seemed to be checking him out, and he wondered why. What sort of test had he to pass before he got a simple answer to a simple question?

Finally the man nodded and, gesturing for Leo to follow, led him back the way he had come, to a narrow alley. Buildings three and four storeys high lined the alley, and a canopy of drying laundry strung from balcony to balcony stirred in the slight breeze, catching shafts of sunlight slanting between the buildings.

They turned into the alley and stopped before a building that looked residential. The Catalan looked up and down the street, and then, taking Leo by the arm, urged him into the doorway.

By now Leo was apprehensive, and resisted the tug on his arm.

"What is this? What passes? Where do we go?"

But the man smiled reassuringly, putting one hand to his mouth in the universal gesture of food, and, gripping Leo's arm with his other hand, guided him through the doorway.

Leading Leo up a flight of stairs and still holding his arm, the Catalan knocked on a door: one-two, one-two; one. The door opened, and a woman who instantly reminded Leo of his mother slid her glance past the Catalan and looked him over. She nodded questioningly at his guide, who whispered in a language Leo later learned was Catalan. She beckoned them in.

Her first words to Leo were in Yiddish, and a wave of relief swept over him. The woman, the apartment, smelled like home, a smell he could not identify right away but which turned out to be chicken soup simmering on a burner in the kitchen.

A short dumpy man appeared through another door, and the woman said to him, "A *yiddisher kindelah*. He's starving." She beamed at Leo. "From America."

"So what are you standing in the hall for?" The man took his arm and led him into another room, leaving the woman and his guide talking.

The room might once have been two separate dining and living rooms. Combined now into one large room with a number of tables and chairs, it looked like a restaurant dining room.

"You're early," the man said, "but we'll feed you anyhow. You have money? Good. You shouldn't starve. What was your name? Leo? Leo Rogin? Call me Sebastian, Leo, call me Sammy, whichever you prefer. You're on leave? Don't answer. It's none of my business. Wonderful boys, the Americans. Crazy, you don't mind my saying, but wonderful."

Not letting Leo get in a word, seeming to sense answers and reactions by watching him closely out of the corner of his small brown eyes, the man set a table. The woman, whom he called Feigelah, brought a steaming bowl of chicken soup and a plate of boiled chicken and greens to the table. "Eat, eat, poor boy," she urged as she set the food down.

It was the best meal he had had in Spain, better than any he had been able to buy in restaurants, better than the food at the hospital, and not to be mentioned in the same breath with the food they got at the battalion.

When he was through, he stared at the empty plates in disbelief. He had had no idea that this kind of food was available in Spain – not with the war, the blockade *and* food rationing.

"So where are you going now? What are you going to do?" Sammy asked, his tone almost conspiratorial.

"I don't know. Contact the Americans."

"That's a good idea. You know where the consul's office is?"

"No. That is, I didn't mean the American consul. I meant – What would I want to contact the consul for?"

"That's a good question. They watch the foreign consuls' offices like hawks. There are ways. Tell me, you have a family in America? Yes? They have money . . . a little money? They would send you money if you asked?"

There was a knock at the door, the one-two, one-two, one. "Oh-oh, here comes the customers. We'll finish another time." He started to his feet.

"Wait." Leo held him. "What customers? Who?"

"Of course, what a dummy!" Sammy hit his forehead. "Come with me."

He led him through glass-paned doors into a bedroom adjoining the dining room.

"Wait in here. Here is something to read. The toilet's through that door." He started to leave. "Don't open the curtains . . . I'll be back." He went out, closing the doors behind him.

The French doors, like the one window in the room, and the windows he had noticed in the dining room, were all curtained. The newspaper that had been thrust into his hands was Spanish. The bed looked inviting, and he fell into it with a contented sigh, letting the paper fall out of his hands. Before he fell asleep he promised himself that he would part the curtains to see who the customers were.

Sammy – Sebastian – had taken to him; and Feigelah had embraced him as a long-lost son. Surrounded by their love, the warmth of the combination home and black-market restaurant – for that was what it turned out to be – he succumbed in part to their philosophy, which was a queer mixture of humanitarianism and materialism. The humanitarian part stemmed from a religious need to help anyone in distress, whether that had to do with getting a good meal not otherwise available or illegally leaving the country if the war had become too much. The materialism was also based on need; to be a practicing humanitarian took money. And besides, what were they to live on? Charity?

Leo did not accept this philosophy at first. They were violating the law. Rationing was supposed to be for everyone. The Republic was fighting for its life, for freedom, for democracy, a better life for all Spaniards. The stakes involved people the world over, especially the Jewish people. He argued this with Sammy on mornings when there was time to waste. Food was scarce, he insisted, and should be shared among the people who were involved in Spain's life and death struggle. It was politically and morally wrong to be doing what Sammy was doing.

Sammy was patient and gentle, for, as he said, he had had to deal with this dilemma many times, within himself as well as with others. "In the first place," he would count off on his fingers, "what we are able to get to feed a few well would amount to less than a drop in a bucket in a city the size of Barcelona. In the second place," he raised a second finger, "I'm proud of giving a little pleasure where there's damned little of it around. It takes plenty of moxie and brains to keep this operation going. And number three –

"Tell me, so what are you doing here?" he interrupted himself, his tone implying that Leo too was into a shady piece of business.

But that was different, Leo insisted. His personal problem stemmed from the failure of the powers that be to utilize his talents to the full, his inability to function under fire (which he only intimated), the death of his friends, and the need for him in the States. "Even if you were to go so far as to call me a coward," he said, "still cowardice is not" – he thought "treason," rejected the word as too pejorative to apply to Sammy's operation – "is not illegal."

"And what about the others that come to eat at my table?" Sammy would point out. The "others" were members of the International Brigades who were in Barcelona on leave or recuperating from wounds, men who would be returning to the front and offering their lives for a cause that in Leo's opinion – not Sebastian's – they helped undermine by being patrons of Sammy's black-market chicken soup.

Leo had no answer. If anything, he found some justification for his own behavior in the brass's patronizing of this illegal operation. He had seen them come and go: officers, commissars, and Party organizers. They came to eat, and they ate heartily; they laughed and joked like schoolboys doing something slightly wicked. It seemed to him that they were privileged to do this openly, while he had to hide behind the thin curtains of the bedroom doors. It separated him from them, and consequently from the brigades. And so he went along with Sammy. For the time being, he thought.

But with Sammy it wasn't only a matter of chicken soup. Sammy introduced him to the mysteries of black-market currency exchange. Swiss francs, English pounds, American dollars, and even, to his horror, German marks and Italian lire. It became clear to him that all other currencies, no matter where they came from, were more valuable than that of the Republic. Unless coins were involved; Sammy collected silver duros with a passion equaled only by his fondness for the American dollar.

"So what?" Sammy had said. "Everything is illegal in wartime – except murdering each other – and if everyone obeyed the law, then there would be no one to make money during a war, and then there would be no wars.

But you must be realistic. While you are shouting your slogans, Señor March, the tobacco king and the richest man in Spain before the war, is still making millions. Señor Marches on both sides, and sometimes on both sides at the same time, believe me. Making money has nothing to do with who will win the war in the end. They'll break each other's heads until they get tired and then they will stop and rest until the next time. It has nothing to do with if Sebastian Maressa makes a peseta here and there. I'm surprised a *yiddisher kopf* like you doesn't know the simple facts of life."

Sammy had an answer for everything. Leo had questioned his dealings in forged or stolen passports, which were much in demand, even by a few IB'ers. "Listen, you want a man here when he doesn't want to stay?" was Sammy's ready answer. "What good will he be? More trouble than he's worth. If a man wants to go he should be sent on his way with blessings. A horse you can lead to water but can you make him drink?" Passports cost fifty dollars, or twelve pounds, or one hundred Swiss francs, either that or a bushel of Republican pesetas.

Sammy had suggested that he ask his father to send him money. "Just get the money and I will take care of the rest." But Leo had rejected the idea. He had no intention of going home, of fucking off, of deserting; he still saw his situation as one in flux, or undecided. It was a matter of time, of figuring out how to make the best deal and still go home in one piece, if not as a hero then at least not dishonorably. All his friends were in the Party or involved in some way. Spain was the big struggle, the Cause. You did not come home to the Party a deserter from Spain.

As for enlisting the aid of his father, it was unthinkable. His father had not wanted him to go to Spain. His father had wanted him to be a reformist operating out of their comfortable Grand Concourse apartment, always just this side, the right side, of respectability. Though when Leo had told him he was going, he had seen in his father's eyes a glimmer of pride mixed with fear and disapproval. It had expressed itself in a firm handclasp and the emptying of his pockets as he had handed over all the bills and loose change, saying, "Here, give it to the cause. I'll do everything I can to help. From now on, I'm on your side."

The gesture had signified a momentary exchange of roles, his father accepting his lead, not insisting on Leo's following his.

But Sammy made it clear that charity was charity and the best place for it was at home. If Leo did not want to get money from the States, then he would have to earn his keep. Unable to draw pay as a *soldado*, and unwilling to send home for money, Leo had no choice. He went to work. Sebastian sent him on errands to mysterious addresses, carrying money away and bringing back sealed envelopes. The days passed and became a month. Leo grew more careless about being seen in Barcelona, more resigned to his tasks. He progressed from running errands to making contact with the men who were looking for a good place to eat or who wanted out, or who were looking for black-market currency.

Under the tutelage of the Catalan who had brought him to Sammy's, and whose name was never spoken, Leo learned how to spot likely marks. He frequented bars, cafes, whorehouses, and the lobbies of hotels; he learned to distinguish a soldier on leave from a soldier on the lam. There was something in the way the latter dressed, in the way he examined people around him. It was a slipped phrase in an otherwise idle conversation, an air of being cut off, adrift, of looking and waiting for a break.

Leo became good at what he was doing. He was earning his keep.

 **21**

When Mitch came into the room at the Hotel Florida in Madrid, Hemingway was standing at a dresser, a bunch of paper in one hand, a glass in the other. There was a typewriter on the dresser. Mitch thought that that was probably a good way to type if you needed to keep off'n the piles.

"I'd like for you to read it," Hemingway handed the manuscript to Mitch.

"Another book?"

"No, a play . . . How about a drink?"

"*Gracias.* What's it about?" Mitch ran his eyes over the top sheet, studying the layout of the page.

"Take it over by the window. I want to know what you think. It's a rough draft now. The theme's the Fifth Column in Madrid."

"Oh, the Fifth Column, fascist spies in Madrid. Boy, that oughtta be great stuff."

"Something like that. Their Fifth Column, our Counter–Fifth Column."

"Counterfeit?"

"Counter-Fifth . . . fifth, five . . . counterintelligence."

They both laughed.

"I don't hear so good anymore," Mitch said. "The goddamned Maxims are making me deaf."

"Keep your mouth open when you're firing . . . it equalizes the pressure."

"Really? I never heard that one before. Why don't they tell you things like that?"

"We learn as we go along, *hombre*."

Mitch accepted the "we." A generous shot of scotch in hand, he sat himself down and read. He did not tell Hemingway that it was the first thing of his he had ever read. While he read, Hemingway stood at what he called an armoire, not a dresser. The scratching sound Hemingway's pencil made as he worked over a typed sheet, which Mitch recognized as the kind used to cable press stories, kept time with his reading.

When he had finished, he said, "Was the shelling that bad?"

"Worse." Hemingway went over to the window and looked out. "They couldn't get at us here. The angle isn't right."

"I didn't know," said Mitch. "When I've been here it's been kind of quiet. I saw shell scars on the Telefonica, that's about all."

"You've been busy with other things. Some nights it's bad. They're just playing with the Telefonica. After all, it belongs to them."

"Belongs to them?"

"Not now. But that's how they're thinking. They're laying them in where the property damage won't be too great. In the streets, when the people are likely to be there. When the cinema lets out. Or in the workers' districts."

"Yeah." Mitch was bemused by the idea that the fascists were careful about private property in the belief that it would be restored to them. The idea that the fascists might win the war was something he had not considered at all.

"Well, what do you think?" Hemingway asked.

"They'll never get it back. The Spanish people will never let them have it."

"Of course. I wasn't asking about that. What do you think of the play as she now stands?"

"Oh, I like it. I think it's great. Of course I don't know anything about the Fifth Column except what I read in *Mundo Obrero* and what we get at meetings. And I sure don't know anything about this counterespionage stuff, but it sounds real. Except," he hesitated and referred to the manuscript again, "we don't shoot our people for messing up. We don't torture prisoners for information. I think that's what you're saying here?"

Hemingway took the manuscript out of his hand. "We're not playing games, *mi capitán.* They play dirty, we play dirty. You guys at the front don't know what it's like back here. It's tough up at the front but at least you know where everyone is and what everyone is doing and who's who. We have something else, something nasty going on here in the rear."

"Yeah. Well. Like I said, I like it, and what I don't know about these things . . . What I'd like to do is see it, see it on Broadway." Then he added, "I wish the hell we did."

"Did what?"

"Know where everyone is and what everyone is doing." He held the empty glass to Hemingway. "¿Reenganchos?"

Hemingway took the glass and filled it with half scotch, half water. He handed it to Mitch. "Don't wait for me, I don't drink a lot when I'm working."

"Salud y Republica." Mitch raised his glass.

"Fuentes was our big foul-up, wasn't it?" said Hemingway. "Especially with the tanks?"

"The tanks? Oh, that. I don't know. After all, it was the first time it was tried. Infantrymen riding tanks into the enemy lines. I thought sure as hell they were going to go all the way to Zaragoza." He caught himself, not at all sure that this was the kind of stuff you were supposed to talk about to civilians. Even to Hemingway, who kept saying "we" and "our," who seemed to be in on everything, including the action – according to the play, even being a prime target for the Fifth Column.

"Don't worry, *capitán.* We'll get the sons of bitches who sabotaged the operation."

"Sabotaged? Was it sabotage? I didn't say anything like that."

"It was sabotage," said Hemingway positively. "There is going to be one very dead ex-general before long."

"So that was – I thought it was – I mean it just didn't work out is all. It happens. But even so . . . well, I hate to tell you this. But they knew where we were. Whenever we moved, they fired right where we were. Even if you didn't get hit it was close enough so that you knew it was personal, like . . ."

The second drink had loosened his tongue. "Why, once we went back for showers. The delousing truck had come up and we went back in groups of four or five to take showers. All the way we were under cover until we came out into an open stretch just before some trees. As we walked across this stretch, maybe fifteen, twenty meters, we could see a line of puffs walking parallel to us, but about thirty feet short. We heard the machine gun very slow and far away. We just kept on walking and the gunners kept firing – short, maybe at the limit of their range. But you knew the bastards could see us and were reaching for us. Yet all the time we were up there in Fuentes I never saw one of 'em and I don't think anyone else ever did, or if they did, they never told me. You know, I could never find a target to shoot at . . . to get my Maxims zeroed in on . . . just places, things out there that looked like they might be . . ." He finished his drink. "It was downright frustrating."

"They're pros, comrade *capitán*," said Hemingway. "But you'll catch up to them."

"I sure hope so," said Mitch. "Some decent binoculars to start with would be a great help."

Hemingway was standing at the window looking down at the street.

"No glasses up there? Mother of God . . . what a simple thing, a small thing like glasses. Listen, comrade *capitán* . . . we'll get you some binoculars, we'll get you some if we have to cut the *cojónes* off Blum to do it."

"Well, that'd be great." Mitch stood up. "When and if you get any, I'm staying at the Majestic – eight days."

"Will do. Where are you off to?"

"Eulalia. She's probably chewing up the rug right now. She is one hungry señorita."

"Give her my kindest." Hemingway held the door open for him.

Madrid had softened Mitch. Hot baths, meals served on real china in the hotel restaurants. Even the food seemed more palatable than when he had been in Madrid in August. Though skimpy, and mostly the same kind they had at the front, it was better prepared, the *bacalao* not as salty and rotten-tasting, the burro meat chewable and seasoned, the garbanzos not nearly as oily. And of course there was the soft bed.

He had started to think soft Eulalia. But she was hard. Hard and quick. In bed her movements were hard and quick. In the streets her laughter was hard and quick. She laughed at the "ugly people" on the street; the sight of a cripple amused her. This second tour with her was not as good as the first. It never was, he thought, but that was not true. With Irene each time had seemed the first. With Irene, he had been forever discovering something new about her, forever doing a new thing when they made love. Even when they walked the same streets they had walked before, or when he watched her at the piano playing the Moonlight Sonata, it was as though he was hearing it for the first time. Each time with Irene was both more stimulating and more unfinished, like a great book you must put down – he smiled at the thought – knowing that the story promised more surprise and delight and would be there for you when you got back to it.

Still, he would keep in touch with Eulalia, even though she was hard and quick and always the same. If he ever came back to Madrid it would also mean coming back to her. Irene and Brooklyn were three thousand miles away, and this was war and Madrid.

Madrid. What was Madrid to him? Well, of course, it was the banner of the antifascist fight. Madrid would never be defeated. The four generals, the sons of whores who were trying to take Madrid, would never take it . . . that was the song.

The Internationals had helped save Madrid. And at Bruneté they had been part of the offensive that had relieved the pressure on Madrid, and again at the Aragon. All for Madrid . . . except that at the Aragon there had been something about relieving the pressure on the Basque country in the north as well.

But the north had fallen to the fascists, and now Franco was moving all the tanks, artillery, and *aviónes* south to the Madrid front.

Mitch felt uneasy about all that stuff coming their way, but he did not feel uneasy for Madrid because this was the city of heroes. They would defend the city to the last citizen. That was how the song went. The city in the center of the plain.

When he had read Hemingway's play, which was about how it was in Madrid, over and beyond – or rather underlying all the heroics and every-thing – he had come out of the reading feeling the tiredness and weariness of the Madrileños. Even in the heroic action and in the way Hemingway had described the shelling of the city and how the people lived with it . . . through all that there was a weariness. It had started in July of '36 and now it was November '37. A long time, even for heroes . . .

There had been a great weariness in the hero's sidekick in the play; and Mitch thought that that weariness was so great, so overwhelming, that it bred a kind of cynicism that spread out to envelop all the characters in the play . . . it was the reason the guard fell asleep at his post . . . the reason Antonio resorted to Gestapo methods in his interrogation because he was too tired to work out other means. Too tired, or didn't have enough time – or what?

But Mitch preferred to think of the play as a dramatic concoction, the brainchild of Hemingway, without much truth. He was disturbed by the overall impression of veracity that Hemingway had given to the story, and

by the impression Hemingway had given that he was involved and partici-
pating. Even if it was only a literary device, that he could write it better by
play-acting the part, still it would have to be based on actual events.

"We," Hemingway had insisted.

The Plaza del Sol was practically deserted, it being the late hour when
Spaniards were at dinner. While he was thinking about the problems the
play raised in his mind, he circled the fountain in the center of the plaza a
couple of times before heading for the Gran Via. The fountain was still dry,
the statuary still sandbagged. There were no lights in any of the windows.

The hell with it in every way, Mitch thought. He didn't want to know
about interrogations and torture . . . and what's more, he wouldn't take that
job if they offered it to him on a silver platter. Of course, if "they" ordered
it he would have to do it. But when it came to beating someone, arm twisting or even – Suppose you had to shoot a guy . . . for falling asleep on guard
duty? Christ! Maybe you wouldn't have to shoot him yourself. You'd be part
of a firing squad. What did they do? Put a blank in one of the rifles so that
each man could think that it was not he that fired the killing round? But
he was an officer now, and none of that had anything to do with him. The
dirty work was for the *soldados*, the rank and file.

Except in Hemingway's flight of fancy where big shots went around
shooting people.

Maybe an officer would make up a firing squad and take some man out
to be shot. Give the order: "Ready! Aim! Fire!" BANG . . . step over to the
body and administer the coup de grace. As a child in Coney Island, Mitch
had seen a policeman shoot a dog that had been hurt and lay broken and
howling. In the open street the pistol had sounded like a small firecracker
going off, and he remembered that the hole in the head of the dog was
small and neat.

And one summer . . . one hot summer . . . when this old brown horse
had slowly collapsed between the wagon tongues, had sunk into the melting tar of the street with an immense sigh, he had seen a policeman use his
service revolver. He winced, remembering the fine line of blood left on the
ramp as they hauled the carcass up into the body of a truck.

The thing was, nobody was going to ask him – or order him – to do anything like that so why think about it? And the answer was, as he knew it was
all the time, that what he was thinking about was the guys who were doing
it, like Antonio or Philip – Hemingway? – in the play. And the only way to
think about something like that was to put it in its place. This was war and
someone had to do these things. There had to be discipline, and discipline

was not always voluntarily given. So if you wanted to make sure that your guards stayed awake, then you did not rely on a political understanding of the mission . . . not that alone . . . you put the fear of God into them.

As for when you were dealing with one of "them," as Hemingway put it, they played dirty, you played dirty. Though it shouldn't be that way because if "we" did everything the way "they" did, then what would be the difference? The difference, of course, would be in the end . . . what you were doing it for was what counted and not how you were getting there. But that did not make much sense either, since it did not seem likely that one would ever arrive at a noble goal if one did not get there as a result of noble ethics and modest, moral, and righteous conduct.

All of which sounded very nice, and would make good reading, something you could debate for a couple of lively nights at the corner cafeteria over steaming cups of coffee. But what you really had to do was weigh the facts. Where and how would the greater loss of life and the most suffering occur? Suppose you did not shoot the guy who fell asleep on guard duty. What the hell, it could happen to anyone. And what's more, so what? No one came in the dark of night and slit ten or twenty throats. But they could. They could, and the only way to prevent it was to make sure your guards were alert. And that was a damned good way to make sure, huh? Damned good way.

Only he would never do it. And as for "them" . . . if you could get one bastard to give you the intelligence, twisting his balls might save a couple hundred lives . . . hah? Wasn't it justifiable?

He let it rest right there. He was at the portals of the Majestic and Eulalia was waiting.

≡ 22

Leo spotted McCall in the bar of the waterfront saloon. He recalled seeing him lugging a Maxim on the long marches along the Huesca front, his balding head bare in the ever-falling rain. McCall's reputation was well known in the battalion. He had been a seaman whose toughness and daring during the organizing of the National Maritime Union had earned him a reputation that had followed him to Spain. He was a big man with immense sloping shoulders, a bull neck, and huge head. They had

had a tough time finding a uniform to fit him; and he was dressed now, as he had been then, in a mix of army khaki and civilian whites. Now the white shirt was soiled and the baggy khaki trousers stained and wrinkled. His wide-set water-blue eyes were bloodshot, and wisps of thin reddish hair stirred untidily on his domelike skull. He sat at a table in the corner with two men who appeared to be seamen, probably from one of the Dutch freighters that had made it through the blockade to the harbor. He was drunk and he was drinking, trying to communicate with his companions in a tongue that was obviously not theirs, signing with his massive hands.

Leo waited for an opportunity to approach him. Though he recognized McCall, he was sure that McCall would not know him. He was also fairly certain that McCall was where he should not be, even though there were many Lincolns in town on leave now that the fighting at Fuentes was over; Leo had been ducking them for days. There was a certain aura of detachment, of not belonging, of having cut loose – it was difficult to put into words, but easy to recognize. The men on leave were intent on making the most of the moment, before returning to the front. But there was a great deal of indecisiveness in McCall's unattended look.

This one looks like a live one, Leo imagined the Catalan saying. He waited at the bar until the two foreign seamen, seemingly despairing of making themselves understood, or of understanding the drunken American, paid the tab and left.

"Can I buy you a drink, comrade?" Leo brought his glass and placed it on the table before one of the vacated chairs.

McCall eyed him suspiciously.

"Why?" he growled.

"I don't like to drink alone."

"That is a sad and queery line. I ain't sure I like you. You look too familiar." McCall peered at him through narrowed eyes.

"Well, that's that." Leo stood up, but McCall's big hand grabbed and held him. "I mean, I wouldn't want to force myself on anyone."

"Sit down. You already have." McCall shouted "Cognac!" to the man behind the bar, and then to Leo, "You're one of our noble comic-stars, right? No? Somewhere I seen you doing something . . . yah, yah . . . singing, singing wit' dem other guys . . . wit' dem fat guys, yeah." He drank the raw cognac down in a single gulp. "Yeah. 'Fly higher and higher / Our emblem is the Soviet star.' Haw, haw. Hey, *garçon*, commodore, waiter, what the hell ever they call you . . . Bring the bottle over . . . bring the bottle. Right, comrade singer?"

"We never sang that."

"Well, who the hell did? They were singing it all the time. All the monkeys marching up and down the hills singing 'Fly higher and higher and higher.' Fly! What a joke! Fly what?"

"Yeah, well, I think I'd better be going." He did not like that McCall had recognized him, nor that he seemed to be without funds. Besides, it was not safe if he was known, if he had made a mistake and the guy did not want out. He couldn't tell what McCall's problem was and he did not think that he could pump him since McCall seemed to be suspicious of him.

"Not without paying for the bottle, you asked for it . . . Aaah, sit down, I ain't going to hurt you. Whatta ya doin', looking for a little action, hah? Maybe I can fix you up with one of the seamen. They're loaded and nuttin' to spend it on but booze and whores. And dey don't all go for the broads. How about it? Ya gonna cut me in?"

"Cut it out," Leo protested, feeling the blood rush to his cheeks. "What do you think I am?"

"What are you?"

"Not a fairy, that's for sure."

"Then whattaya want wit' me?" McCall was watching him closely.

Leo had an investment in him now, the bottle of cognac. He couldn't think of any way to recoup that short of wringing something out of McCall.

"I just thought you might need help. You look like you need some, and maybe I can help you."

"Help me what? What kinda fink are you?"

"Forget it."

"I ain't about to."

"Listen, you want to get out? A lot of guys are cutting out. You want to?"

McCall sat up, bloodshot eyes squinting. Leo came right to the point. If he was wrong about the man's intentions or predicament, well, the *conjo* was *borracho* and would become even drunker when the bottle ran dry. He'd remember damned little of this, and Leo had not given him a name.

"You want to, I can help, that's all. If I'm wrong, forget it. The bottle is yours."

"I can break you in little pieces, pretty boy. Remember that. You try to fuck wit' me, it'll be the last time you fuck wit' anyone."

"I said forget it."

"And I said I ain't about to." McCall held his eyes. "Supposing I said I wanted to. Then what?"

"I can get someone to fix you up with a passport and papers to get you across the border. The American consul will take it from there. It'll cost you sixty bucks, or the equivalent. Not for me, for the people who take care of these things." Leo spelled it out in a hurry. If he had made a mistake he could deny the whole thing. McCall didn't look or sound like someone who would turn him in; or if he did, like someone whose word would hold up.

"Sixty bucks?" McCall said quietly, reflectively. "I can get that easy from the sailors. Sixty bucks? What about you?"

"What do you mean?"

"You know what I mean. How come you don't go over the hill, you can fix it so easy?"

"I have to work it out some other way. I can't explain it. But if you want to make it, I can help."

"Yeah." McCall was drinking again. He did not bother to offer Leo any since Leo had not finished his drink. He spoke now, more to himself than to Leo. "Yeah. Gotta work it out. You do a lot of this, huh? Sixty bucks a t'row, that ain't bad. You gonna leave here a rich sonofabitchin' antifascist, ain't you? Not bad. Ah, me," he sighed prodigiously. "They got me in a bind. Listen, no one likes a fight better'n me, you understand. There ain't nuttin' better I like to do than bust in the face of a lousy scab, you understand, or a goddamned cop, nuttin' better." He paused. A puzzled look came over his face, his eyes wandered, one huge hand caressing the hand that held the glass. "But you know? It's different, it's a different thing."

Leo sipped his drink. He could sense that McCall had to explain something, perhaps something that would explain why he himself was having this conversation. It was gratifying to Leo that McCall might be a deserter; there was no longer any doubt about it. This brute, different in every way from himself. A myth on the waterfront, a seaman fighting for the rights of sailors all over the world, fighting fascism, fighting the bosses, fearless in the face of goons, thugs, cops. After all, if such a one was on his way out, how much better it made Leo look. Or if not look, then feel. He drank more deeply and gave his complete attention to McCall, who, though he paused from time to time, needed no urging to go on.

"Different, different, different, goddamn it. You might think I'm just an ignorant, illiterate sailor, hah? Let me tell you, pretty boy, there ain't none such. We got too much time to think, to read, to know where the cargo is and where the ballast is and where the bullshit is. But I never knew . . . Hah? Why don't you ask me what?"

"What?"

"I never knew it would be so different." He spread the words. He was obviously trying to think of a way to say what he had to say.

"You see, it's so goddamned fucking impersonal, you know what I mean? Listen, you're on da picket line and a scab, ten scabs, wanna go t'rough, right? You see dem, you see dere faces. You know dem, you seen dem a t'ousand times. Dey're bigger'n you, smaller, fatter, shorter, taller . . . hell, it don't mean a t'ing. Scabs. You bust into 'em. Busting into scabs . . . that feels good . . . you kin put your meat hooks into somtin' you know, somtin' you kin feel. Sure, dey're busting you wid brass knuckles, sure da cops are busting their clubs on your bean. But you can see 'em, you can smell da stink on 'em, you can taste da blood. And best of all, you can feel your knuckles in da meat, da bone, and already, y'know, you can see yourself afterward, down at da saloon, talkin' it over wit' da boys, feelin' da hurt and da bumps and da bruises, feelin' 'em good . . . feelin' your knuckles still pounding from da poundin' on some scab's thick skull . . . aah . . ."

McCall had a sweet smile going for him, a smile that softened the craggy face. But it faded as his eyes clouded over and he drew his brow together in a pained, querulous frown. He turned a pleading look on Leo. He surprised Leo by dropping the rough speech it seemed he had taken on up to that point.

"But it's different, you know. You don't see the bastards out there. No, you get stuck out on some fucking hill, on top of some fucking ground, in the fucking hot sun, and you sit there while the shit falls all around you. There isn't anyone to see to hit back at. You have this skinny ancient rifle in your hands and they're dropping tons of bombs on your head, they're laying down artillery fire, covering the trenches with MG fire, from guns two, three times faster than ours, and you're sitting there with a popgun in your hands watching this comrade and that brother get his head blown off, wondering when you're going to get yours and nothing you can do about it, just sit there and – goddamn it – pray . . . pray. How you like that, comrade? Pray!"

He was waiting for some reaction, so Leo said, "What good is prayer?" knowing it did not matter what he said. McCall wasn't talking to him; McCall was having it out with himself.

"Yeah, what good. What good is anything? But . . . but there isn't anyone to hold onto, don't you understand? It's all so goddamned impersonal. You like that? You don't know who is out there, and out there, they . . . whoever . . . don't even know who they're trying to take apart."

McCall lifted the glass and downed its contents. He slammed it back onto the table. "Yellow!" he exploded, lapsing back into his thoughts. "It don't make any sense. But I tell you this, and listen to me good. It don't make no sense to fight all dem bombers and cannons wid pea shooters. You hear me? The odder side has got all the stuff. They're gettin' more and we ain't gettin' any. You know what that ship dem two Dutchmen sitting here is unloading? You know? Chocolate and eggs and marmalade, and a bunch of other shit like that. Not even a lousy pistol. It don't make no sense." He shook his big head. "Yellow! Hah! You know that jerk Castle?"

The question took Leo by surprise. He was dismayed by the panic it stirred in him. Mitch was the last person he had talked to. And Mitch remembered Bruneté.

"Crazy sonofabitch, running around in a goddamned cape like a movie actor. Called me yellow to my face. I could break the skinny bastard in half. 'Fire!' he yells. 'Fire!' Up and down he runs, the goddamned cape flying all around him. 'Fire!' Pointing into the smoke and dirt, not giving a shit about all the guys that's been killed and buried by bombs . . . 'Fire!' . . . 'Fire!' . . . 'Fire!' At what, I ask you? The bombs went right across the trench, busted them wide open, busted my head open with the noise. Fire! Sonofabitch!"

"You mean Mitch Castle?" Leo said. "When did this happen?"

"Mitchell Castle, yeah. Where did what happen?" McCall held the bottle up to the light and swirled the cognac in it about. "Almos' all gone. Yellow! That kid calling me – me! – Red McCall – yellow." He slammed the bottle down and reached for Leo. Bunching the front of his jacket, he held him and shook him as he had the bottle. "Dere was guys buried alive . . . alive . . ." His eyes slewed wildly about and then opened wide as if he saw something over Leo's shoulder. He released him and fell back into his chair. "I better go now. When'll you have the stuff?"

"Tomorrow. Noon. Here. Get the money. And get cleaned up. You'll have to have your picture taken."

"Yeah, cleaned up – "

There was a sharp crack. Leo sat up straight, his head cocked, listening. Out of the corner of his eye he could see McCall, his big hands moving flatly over the table, his eyes darting from one corner of the room to another, his mouth open, hunching his shoulders as though expecting a blow. Leo bunched his muscles, ready to take off. He reviewed in his mind the possible *refugios*, estimating the distance and the time. One thing he knew for sure, and that was that the waterfront was not a good place to be.

There were three more sharp reports as antiaircraft batteries zeroed in and then opened up in earnest. Somewhere a siren wailed belatedly.

"Let's get out of here," Leo yelled to McCall and rushed for the door. He noted that the Spanish bartender, looking up to see him dash past, stood polishing a glass, a slight smile on his lips. Just as he reached the door, he was met by several men pushing in from the street. The colliding bodies rebounded, and Leo found himself sitting on the tile floor, dazedly staring up into the white face, now even whiter, of the man he had seen in Johnson's office in Tarazona. The same Sam Brown belt, the tiny polished leather holster. Two *Carabiniers, bandoleras* crossed, rifles at the ready, came in behind him. And then there was the whine of the first bombs falling.

He scrambled to his knees and scurried under one of the tables. As he crouched there, holding his insides tight against the din, the crack of the antiaircraft guns, the exploding bombs, he saw McCall under one of the other tables, the empty cognac bottle clutched in his hands, his eyes tightly shut, his lips moving furiously. The *Carabiniers* leaned against the bar. "White-Face" had his little pistol out of its shiny holster. The tiny black hole of the muzzle pointed his way looked exactly like the tiny black holes that were his eyes. It held Leo fixed as the snapping ack-ack fire and crashing bombs held the room suspended in a balloon of noise.

23

The seat in the cab of the camion was not soft, but it was a lot better than being in back on the hard benches or on the iron floor inhaling exhaust and Castilian dust. Being commander of a company had its compensations – not that Mitch sought them out, but that was how things were arranged. The Madrid auto-park dispatcher had said, "Captain Castle rides in the cab," and the men who had been on leave with him had filed into the body of the camion.

He had rank – captain – *el capitán*, lowercase "c" not sounding so damned U.S. Army, sounding more comradely than "captain." Still, captain, with five times the pay of a *soldado*. *Mucho* pesetas even after deducting substantial contributions to the Socorro Rojo and the Partido Comunista de España.

The men saluted him and Mitch saluted his superiors, though neither the men nor Mitch always remembered to do so. The important thing was not to take it too seriously. It had to be done for the United Front, but that didn't mean that all that military crap was going to change him – not at all.

The first thing he had done in Madrid was to buy the patches with the three gold bars and one red star embroidered in silk, look up Eulalia, and have her sew them on his uniform. Badly, for she did not sew well, or perhaps because she was indifferent to rank – had she not loved him equally well when he was a mere *soldado?* Or perhaps because she was embarrassed by his insistence that she read the flowery citation that had come with the promotion – when she could not read at all, as he should have known.

At Fuentes de Ebro they had organized "trench classrooms" for the Spanish replacements – *hermanos de sangre* – who could not read or write. *Analfabetos.* Back home "you goddamn illiterate" meant you didn't read the *Herald Tribune* and the *Daily Worker.* What was the world like if you could not read at all? *Analfabetos.* Spaniards living out their lives without the alphabet. "How you gonna reach them down on the farm . . ." if they can't read *El Mundo Obrero*, the world of workers? How they going to reach you . . .

Time. Time had been replaced by action. Had stopped at Quinto. Quinto had been in August. Time had not started again until the action had stopped, when October was almost gone and a lot of comrades were also gone. A whole year had slipped away, because he had become twenty-two somewhere in there and hadn't stopped to think about it until just now. So no matter how relative time was, it passed at its assigned pace. He had lived more in a year – in not quite a year – than most people lived in a lifetime, and he did not think he would live to be thirty. How could you make it against the world beyond thirty? Without compromising, without saying, okay, I'll take it easy, give me another thirty years, old pal, just like the last thirty? But how could he know that he had lived a lifetime in one year? In Bensonhurst, as in Fuentes de Ebro, a year was a year and you only lived a lifetime in one year if you were dead at the end of it. Which he wasn't.

He would put that in the letter he had had no time to write. He would write about the *analfabetos*; and maybe he would casually mention in his letter to Irene or the gang in the Bensonhurst YCL, "By the way, I'm a captain now."

He closed his eyes, but the green, greyed-over landscape remained, moving past under his eyelids, keeping pace with the noise of motor, wheels, springs, and rattling men in the body of the camion.

How much could he put in a letter and still get by the censor? Why worry? He'd put it all in and make the censor earn his pay. Who was the censor, anyhow? Did he merely censor, or did he note and report? Very necessary *hombre*. Kept vital information from falling into the hands of the enemy; also into the ears of friends. The censor as screen through which history was sieved . . . all the censors screening out all the stuff that wasn't allowed. Is not permitted, comrade. Vital information. Did Mitch have vital information? You never knew.

The best thing to do would be to start at the beginning, as he had read over and over again. If he really began at the beginning and was truthful, the impression would undoubtedly be that he was – and not just had been – extraordinarily naive, even stupid; and though later on it would become clear that he had grown with the passage of time, that first impression would be the lasting one. On the other hand, he'd only be writing a letter, not a book.

At long last, after countless maneuvers, north short of Huesca and south short of Teruel, by truck and by tramp – during which the only casualty had been Leonard Lyons, the new battalion commander, who had shot himself in the foot while cleaning his pistol – Captain Phil Detro, Lyons's successor, had gathered together the officers and commissars of the battalion and announced that the battalion would strike at Fuentes, aiming for Zaragoza, neither north nor south of their wanderings, but sort of in between.

Detro, whom Mitch had first seen at Hemingway's table in the Café Chicote in Madrid, carried his holster low and tied to his thigh with a leather thong. Unlike the heroes of dime novels, however, Detro had read a book.

"The capture of Zaragoza," Mitch remembered him saying, "will break the back of the Aragon front. It will break the damned backs of the fascists and relieve the pressure on the northern front where our Asturian comrades are making a heroic stand." He had stopped as though embarrassed by what for him was a lengthy and flowery speech; the word "comrade" did not come easily. Then he went on, brusquely detailing the timetable for aviation, tanks, and artillery. He discussed the role the other battalions would play, advising the company commanders to impart all this information to the troops under their command – "The way we do in this here army" – and brought himself to a halt.

None of the company commanders had doubted Detro. Fuentes would be taken, as had Quinto and Belchite. Zaragoza would follow. There was no need for discussion. Mitch had filled the silence that followed Detro's remarks by asking if Rogin had asked to be transferred from the Third to the MGs, adding that if he had, it was okay with him. He was surprised when Detro looked at him sharply and demanded to know why he asked.

"Why the why?" Mitch had asked.

"Private Rogin is missing without leave." Detro's lips barely moved.

"Never said a word to me about a transfer. If he isn't with you, he's fucked off," Williams said.

"Well." Mitch had tried to register surprise, but surprised he was not. He had been uneasily thinking that his mention of Rogin's intentions some-how connected him to the fuck-off's defection. This was the first time he had heard anyone called Private. He had made a note of that. "Who carried him out this time?" he'd said, attempting to lighten up the situation.

They had all laughed except Detro, who never laughed. Detro's amuse-ment ranged from a slight dimpling at the corners of his mouth, as now, all the way to barely revealing the tips of small white teeth, indicative of un-controlled mirth.

Mitch had wanted to say "Wait until Bullard hears about his going-home-boy," but thought better of it. Detro seemed anxious to cut the talk and get on with the fighting.

The Mac-Paps were going over the top. They looked huge as they came out of the trenches against the skyline – until they fell. Mitch had had all his guns firing, giving cover, firing into the trees, the stone terraces, the vineyards, firing at things and places, scars and marks on the ground, but never seeing fascists to fire at. That's how it had been, the guns banging away in his head as he watched the Mac-Paps go over, Bob Carter leading the charge, Bullard a step behind. Going over the top to some place be-tween the trenches and where a church steeple spiked distantly in the sun. The fascists were in between, the fascists whom they could not see, who "cut them down like wheat." Bob Carter came back on a stretcher, badly wounded but alive, and then his commissar, Bullard, with two men carry-ing him, not knowing he was dead. Afterward, when Fuentes was over, Mitch had asked the new commissar, Saully Glaser, a short, blue-eyed po-litico, for Bullard's can of tobacco. Glaser had looked at him out of round eyes, his face ashen, his head swaying back and forth in disbelief. He hadn't gotten the tobacco then, either, goddamn it.

Between the wind rushing through the window that would not close and the rough ride of the lorry, Mitch filled his pipe with spraying crumbs from discarded cigarette butts as best he could. The driver laughed as he watched Mitch trying to get the pipe going, puffing furiously as he held the smoldering end of a rope lighter to the bowl.

There had been damned little artillery support for the attack. The air support had come in late, and then, marvel of all marvels, a bunch of tanks had come roaring up, men riding them topside hellbent for Fuentes.

Over the top! Detro had sent line companies over the top. Mitch had watched them go, down the hill into a tangle of brush, following the tanks. When they'd come straggling back through the battalion's open right flank, where he had made his HQ and where he had placed two guns to protect the battalion, Mitch was there to greet them.

Harold Smith had come up holding his bleeding arm, saying, "It's murder down there."

They came one by one, drawn and grey. "It's murder down there." Their eyes accused him.

"Goddamn it," he stormed along the guns, "what the hell are you shooting at? We're supposed to give cover fire. What the hell . . . ?" Bianca, Kaufman, Makkelo, Sharp, Sandos, Connors, McCall. He had cursed them. And then he had looked over the parapet to check out the targets, such as they were, once again.

Now he sat up straight in the cab, reestablishing all the details.

His bare head over the sandbags, his hands on either side, he had tried to spot the fascists' gun positions. A single shot had cracked, and out of the corner of his eye he saw where the bullet had smashed into the small space between his right hand and his head. He fixed on the dark patch of ground where he thought the shot had come from, sighted Bianca's gun, and fired. When he looked again, there was a snap, the bullet close overhead. Someone over there held him in his eye and fired – not indifferently, but intimately, intent on killing him.

It was not a thing he had thought of before. It made a difference. He hadn't felt that way about the bombing that had come later. He had watched the Italian planes coming in slow, silvery formation, and he had followed the flicker of bombs as they fell toward the trench, and he would swear now that he had felt the trench lift and then settle before he heard the whine of falling bombs and everything getting buried in a huge ball of fire, dirt, and deafening sound. His only thought then had been for the wall of smoke that had engulfed them, the sudden fear that the fascists would come storming up the hill under cover of the smoke and into the trenches before his gunners recovered from the shock. Even while the dirt was still raining down, he had gotten the gunners up to the machine guns, firing blindly at shapes that materialized in the whirling smoke and dust. Perhaps the fascists were surprised by the guns alive in the heart of the bombs' towering wake, where there should be no one left to fire. The gunners had held onto the grips and fired, holding onto their fear and firing not only to hold off the enemy storming the hill, but also to still the echo of the bombs that howled in their guts, to shut out the sound of men shouting and clawing at the earth digging for comrades buried in the collapsed sections of the trench.

McCall had collapsed with the trenches and had not come back to his gun. Mitch had called him yellow, not a thing he had ever called anyone before. But he saw McCall huddled against the loose dirt, not getting to the guns, not helping with the digging, withdrawn from them and defiant in his withdrawal – yellow.

Mitch tapped the bowl of the pipe, now gone cold, on the open window ledge, upsetting the driver, who mistook the tap-tapping for a sudden engine knock. Mitch was about to apologize, when he remembered he was a captain. He smiled at the driver and leaned out the window to clear his lungs. The air was grey and chill and damp. The hills were no longer scenery to be admired, he thought, they were possible enemy positions, or good commanding hills where he could place guns to sweep the flatlands. He thought about how he had been as commander under fire.

He had placed the guns and tried to find targets. The riflemen had gone over the top and down into the plain and had come back crying it was murder, but they had been unable to indicate a target, not a single target for the guns. He had gone down the ditch along the sunken path, an awful long way, without seeing or hearing anything until he came upon a burnt-out tank, and then farther on another, blasted off its tracks, a dead *soldado* nearby. He had despaired and returned. "Maybe not far enough," he mumbled aloud now.

He could not find anything to shoot at. Battalion had never found targets during the eleven days of Fuentes de Ebro. And only a few of the tanks had made it back to the lines. It occurred to Mitch that he hadn't known what happened, why they hadn't broken through the fascist lines. The whole frustrating blindness would jolt his thinking from time to time, enraging him and causing him to lash out at the men.

Discipline. Rupert had warned him that Sullivan had to be sobered up, dried out, and brought into line. The problem was, however, that Marty Sullivan denied was Sullivan astray in search of the wherewithal. Sullivan supplied, on the other hand, was where Mitch wanted him, stringing lines of telephone wire, running errands and messages, happy, reliable and, while not fearless, uninhibited by the enemy.

Mitch had obeyed the battalion commissar by taking the problem directly to Sullivan, man to man; and Sullivan had agreed to forswear. Mitch and Sullivan having satisfied Rupert's wishes, they continued as before.

Mitch was still smiling, thinking about the letter he was composing in his head. He would not include the bit about Sullivan's love of the sauce. Back home they would not understand. A hard-drinking antifascist *soldado* would be hard to take.

Thinking about Sullivan drinking brought to mind an incident when O'Mara and Reilly had gotten drunk at Tarazona. He no longer smiled. Sullivan, O'Mara, Reilly. The driver of the lorry demanded, "¿Qué pasa?"

"Nada, de nada," he murmured, and in English, half to himself, "you wouldn't understand. Shit. It's not supposed to be that way . . . if we're going to have drunks in the outfit they shouldn't all be Irish, for Christ's sake." But Mitch could not think of anyone else in the battalion with the same passion for booze. Oh, there were drinkers, for sure, but in moderation. He himself had become partial to the rough red wine that came up with the chow.

Reilly had been wounded in the fighting at Bruneté. And O'Mara had caught one from a die-hard sniper on the last day at Quinto. Well, he thought, if I mention them at all in the letter, it will be to tell how well they served.

That had been Captain Mitchell Castle in his first command. Eleven days in the trenches, and on the twelfth day the Spanish Brigade had come up to relieve them. For some reason, they had chosen to come right through the machine gun positions; and it had fallen to him to point out the enemy's positions – what little he knew of them – to the little Spanish commander who, looking unbelievably young and passionate, had announced that he was going down there right away and in one terrible *culpo de mano* take the fascista's positions.

The little commander had stood on top of the parapet haranguing his troops, the whole front quiet except for his voice. Even the enemy was surprised into hushed attention. He had finished with a rousing cheer:

"¡Viva la Republica!" and his men had amen-ed:

"¡Viva!"

"¡Viva el Ejército!"

"¡Viva!"

"¡Viva la brigada!"

"¡Viva!"

"¡Viva yo!"

"¡Viva!" they had shouted and over they went, down the slope.

Mitch had had the guns open up in support, watching the men disappear into the now-familiar gullies and ravines and ditches, appearing, disappearing, reappearing; becoming toy figures, running, shouting.

He had seen them stop and mill around when the fascists opened up. They had come back up the hill into the trenches carrying their dead and wounded, their fiery little commander all crumpled and crushed like a cold cigarette butt.

"Madrid," the driver pointed. A pillar of smoke rose gracefully.

"Artillery," the driver said, "every fucking day."

24

Leo looked around the room, at the desk, the file cabinets, the seating arrangement, the faces in the room. All the faces seemed aimed at him, the eyes multiple versions of the pistol's muzzle.

How familiar it all was. He was becoming a veteran of meetings, inquisitions, sessions that revolved around himself. He was once more looking for the face that he could reach. "White-Face," whom he now knew as Comrade Service Serrota, SIM, which he understood to be the arm of secret military intelligence, was a face he passed over quickly. Serrota had known him instantly, had had the pistol on him all through the air raid, had placed him under arrest when it was over; and, almost as an afterthought, had asked the quivering hulk that was McCall for papers – he hadn't bothered to ask Leo for his – and arrested him as well.

He did not relish the prospect of being returned to the cell, where McCall's drunken snoring and mumblings had kept him awake all night.

He searched the anonymous faces of the others in the room, but they revealed neither hostility nor compassion. He listened intently to the list of charges: desertion under fire at Bruneté; desertion before Fuentes de Ebro (he hadn't known about Fuentes, but it became clear that this was the action McCall had referred to, where Castle had called McCall yellow). Of course, McCall had said nothing about his own willingness to buy forged papers, just that Leo had offered to secure and sell them to him.

When the charges had been read, he was asked what he had to say for himself. He felt a warm and satisfying glow of self-pity sweep over him. Tears – the ever-ready tears – came to his eyes, and, sobbing, he confessed to everything, flaying himself, castigating himself, confessing his betrayal of the cause, his confusion, the innocence that had led him astray, his burning desire to go back to his comrades if they would have him, to go back and face them, face the fire, face the fascists, fulfilling his mission as a Communist, dying in the struggle.

Even though he was supposed to go home, though he had only thought that and it had confused him. He did not even want to go home. He had had ample opportunity to go home; but he had not.

On and on he went, gulping, sobbing, pleading, protesting, desperately afraid to stop talking, afraid to allow Serrota to pronounce judgment on him. He felt that if he could just keep talking, he would win his way into their hearts, out of this room with bars on the windows, roll all the camions in reverse, back to where he had been, determined to get in his action, the action that would resolve everything, wipe away the "cloud" which had by now become tangible, weighing on him, hanging over him, a black cloud like a presence. He cursed Sammy, cursed himself for having passed up the opportunity offered by Johnson and Bullard . . .

Exhausted, he paused to catch his breath. His chest heaved, his throat felt raw. He wiped his eyes and nose on the end of his sleeve, looking apologetically at the faces surrounding him, then casting his eyes down to gather his thoughts so that he could keep talking, though he knew that he had already repeated himself many times. But before he could think of a new approach, the man who had read the charges spoke.

"Comrade Rogin." He began slowly and calmly, but his tone sharpened and became more penetrating as he ticked off his points. "The penalty for desertion under fire is death. The penalty for dealing in the black market is death. The penalty for aiding and abetting in desertion is death. The penalty for buying and selling forged passports is death." He had reached the extreme range of intensity in his voice before he paused. He let it sink in.

Leo stared at him, at the handsome face with planes that went slightly flat under the cheekbones, flat lips under a strong nose that also tended to flatten out, the elongated brown eyes staring intently at him.

Leo was incredulous. "Death?"

"Firing squad," Serrota snapped.

Leo winced. "Oh, no. No, I'm a volunteer . . . a . . . a Communist. That's ridiculous. No, you can't. You don't have to stare at me like that. I said I'm willing – What do you mean? What do you want?"

"We want you to realize the seriousness of your actions," the man in the middle said.

"I do. I said I did. What more – "

He stopped as one of the men got up and went to the door. The man opened it and beckoned, and in came Sebastian, smiling, between two guards. A well-dressed civilian followed behind.

"Hello, Sebastian," Leo forced a smile. "I'm in a little trouble – "

"I can see," Sebastian used the English he had picked up from his customers. "I can see. And you want me in it for company, no?"

The man in the middle broke in. "Is this the man from whom you've been getting forged passports and other papers?"

"Sort of," Leo said.

"You have no jurisdiction over my client." The civilian with Sebastian spoke in Spanish. "He is not in the army. He is certainly not in *your* army."

"It's all lies, anyway," Sebastian broke in. "A meal, yes. A little chicken, a little meat, some vegetables. The *campesinos* bring to me. I should chase them away? They need to live, too. You all know my place. Why," he looked at them, "some of you were in just the other night. It does harm?"

"You don't have to explain to them," the civilian hissed.

"Why not? They're all my friends, even customers. They're good boys." Sebastian smiled around the room.

"What do you mean, 'sort of'?" Serrota asked Leo.

"I don't know. It's all mixed up. He told me where to go, who to see . . . I gave him the money. I don't know how much he had to do with it. I could have done it for myself, I could have gone over the border if I had wanted to. I didn't know what was right . . . what was wrong . . . But I didn't go. I was going to go back to the outfit before you arrested me . . ." He filled the room with words again.

"He's right, he's all mixed up. Crazy in the head, maybe, what do you call it, shell-knocked?" Sebastian said smilingly. "I don't know what he's talking about."

"It's of no importance," the civilian said. "These are the problems of foreigners. You are a Spanish citizen, they have no right. I shall complain to the Chief of Justice. Come." He took Sebastian's arm.

"Any time I can help you, just ask me," Sebastian said, allowing himself to be led out of the room. Serrota got to his feet, but the man in the middle stopped him with a gesture.

"He's right, we have no jurisdiction over Spanish citizens. We'll get all the facts from Comrade Rogin." Middle-Face looked at him. "And turn it over to the Catalans to handle. When we have decided what to do with you, comrade, you will dictate all your information to a secretary in Comrade Serrota's outfit." He paused and stood up. He walked over to one of the shadowed windows and smoothed his parted brown hair, tugged at the skirt of his tunic, flared his breeches out; turning to catch his reflection in the glass, he centered the buckle of his Sam Brown.

"Well, comrades," he said, "the gravity of the crime of desertion arises from the fact that, first, it imperils the lives of the deserter's comrades-in-arms; second, it undermines the morale of the deserter's unit; and third, it gives comfort and aid to the enemy." He paused behind his chair. "If this kind of behavior is tolerated, it will have a bad effect on the rest of the men."

The room was silent as he went on. "I am not familiar with the procedures," he said to Serrota, and when Serrota started to talk he interrupted him. "But as you know, I have just come from Quinto, Belchite, and Fuentes de Ebro. The men have been in action all of August and September and most of October. Good men have fought against great odds and have died. I am afraid that this may affect my judgment."

"Comrade Doran," Serrota said. "You know the procedures. You just spelled them out."

So Middle-Face was Doran. Dave Doran. Another man Leo had heard of, a leading political figure from the States like Bill Lawrence but, unlike Lawrence, a commissar who had been at the front. In one of the issues of the brigade paper, Leo had read how Doran had persuaded the fascists to surrender at Belchite and, before that, at Purburell Hill outside of Quinto. As he watched Doran march back and forth, pausing every now and then to admire himself in the glass, he assumed that Doran had read the same glowing accounts.

"Comrade Doran," Leo said. "You know that you can't have me shot. I mean, after all, we're not members of any army. We're volunteers, civilians actually – "

Serrota started to interrupt, but Doran waved him into silence.

"Go on," he said to Leo.

"I have civilian rights, rights as a citizen of the United States – not to mention my rights as a Communist – to a trial, a regular procedure. Not that it is necessary. I've confessed my guilt – no, not guilt – stupidity. I've told you everything, but the most important thing is that I want to go to the front, to make up for it – "

"You were given that opportunity and you ran out on it."

"I don't know what happened." He was thinking fast now, sensing an uncertainty in the room. To claim shell shock as Sebastian suggested could be a possibility. God knew he'd been bombed and strafed enough even in the short time he had been at Bruneté. He had developed a kind of internal weather vane that responded to the least shift in direction, and now he knew that he had a chance to talk his way out once more.

"I came back and the battalion commander shot himself in the foot. We were always being moved in the rain. I was waiting to get into action, but it seemed it would never come. I was cold, sick. Maybe not fully recovered from what happened to me at Bruneté, under the bombs there, the heat – Ask Castle, ask him. You know, the commander of the Machine Gun Company. I wanted to get into his company. I really wanted to fight. Ask him."

"Castle?" Doran was interested. He turned to one of the other men. "Isn't Castle on leave in Barcelona?"

"No, he went to Madrid. He's got a *puta* there."

They all laughed and Doran said, "With all the girls here he goes there?" He looked at his watch. "I tell you what we'll do. Comrade Serrota, you take this man's statement and then keep him locked up with McCall. What neither of them knows is that we are now operating under the same regulations as the regular Spanish Army. However, since the desertions predate this change, we will have to proceed on that basis. We'll have to find a punishment that suits the crime," he recited, "perhaps several months of hard labor with the *zapadores* . . . Something like that. I'll leave that to you. But don't send either one of them back to the outfit. We won't have them, is that clear?"

They nodded.

"Good! I've got a meeting. I'm late now. Salud, comrades!"

"Salud," they chorused.

Serrota brought the guards back in and they led Leo away. He was relieved and tired, and even when Serrota said, "You don't know how lucky you are," he did not react. He was safe for now, he was alive, and that was all that mattered. The idea of being a *zapadore*, an engineer, or sapper, did not appeal to him. Digging trenches, stringing barbed wire and the like was hard work and sometimes dangerous. There was no future in it. He would be lost, out of sight, forgotten with no chance to prove himself.

When they arrived at the room where he and McCall were kept, Serrota stopped him. "How did you know that Doran was high on Mitchell Castle?" he asked with a curious look. "Of course you know that mentioning his name saved your ass."

"How could I know?" asked Leo wearily. He was not interested in talking with Serrota. Serrota represented something he could not deal with.

"You bet your sweet life that I'm going to check out your story as soon as possible."

Leo did not answer. He walked into the room. McCall was sitting on a bunk, looking quite cheerful.

"Welcome home, pretty boy. You look like you've been through the wringer. Hey, cop! Wha'dya do to my boy here? Goddamn you, put away that peashooter or I'll moider ya!"

"Shut up!" Leo said.

McCall razzed Serrota as he slammed the door behind himself. "Yaaaaah."

25

Albarez was like most other Spanish towns Mitch had been in: the buildings marking off the square were two stories high, while the church towered above, commanding the square and the narrow shadowed streets. Mitch was beginning to have difficulty telling one town from another, a difficulty he solved by lumping them all together in his mind. He was not a tourist, after all. He had known about La Mancha and Don Quixote, and that Albaceté had voted solidly for the Popular Front. How Albarez had voted, he did not know, did not ask, and did not find out.

He took his truckload of charges from Madrid to the *plano mayor* of the battalion, which was quartered in the *alcalde*'s offices. The *alcalde* had either fled or surrendered his quarters in hospitality; it was always one or the other.

And now, as at Fuentes when he had returned from the hospital at Bals, Rupert greeted him. "Welcome back, Commander. You're just in time to take over the battalion."

He searched Rupert's broad face for some sign that he was kidding. He had accepted without question the promotion to Machine Gun Company commander. That had seemed natural – he'd been at it as long as anyone else in the company, was as good or better than the rest, and he had stayed in one piece.

But this was different. This was moving onto a level where he'd be over other company commanders, where he'd have to deal directly with brigade, for Christ's sake. Besides, what would he do with a battalion? He was a machine gunner and had no fears about running a machine-gun company, though he was beginning to have doubts. Doubts that haunted him asleep and awake: what to shoot at? "Targets! Targets! Targets!" hammered in his head every time he relaxed.

He shook it off, thinking now of another problem: he had not had a single day of officer training. Rupert's blue eyes revealed nothing, so Mitch said, "Where's Detro?"

"On leave," said Rupert. "I should've said Acting Commander."

"You mean until he comes back?" Mitch didn't know whether he was relieved or disappointed. The feelings got mixed up inside of him.

"Yes, supposing he comes back."

"What does that mean?"

"Well, you never know . . . you never can tell what'll happen." Rupert was sounding mysterious. He was sounding like people in the Party, the comrades who were in the in, who had meetings where others – like himself? – were evaluated and assigned. There was more to this than just a temporary command.

"And Spear, and Stamos?" he said.

"Pulled out for officer training."

"Jeezus, doesn't anyone hang around? Guys move on, or out – "

"Or die. Anyhow," Rupert went on, "your stuff has been moved in here. When you're ready, we'll talk about what has to be done. We'll go over to brigade and get filled in."

"How long're we going to be here?"

The answer was predictable. "Who knows?"

Everything was efficient at brigade headquarters. There was the brigade commander, Vladimir Copic, a bald, ugly little man with beautiful brown eyes. Given the right time and place, he was known to belt out Russian love songs in an adequate baritone. The commissar was Dave Doran, whom Castle remembered from Belchite, handsomely arrayed as always in full officer's regalia. And there was Bonner, the Party Activist, a thin, good-looking young fellow. All three were got up in uniforms that included Sam Brown belts, map cases, holsters, and binoculars.

Everything will be worthwhile, Mitch thought, if only I come out of this meeting with at least the promise of binoculars. Battalion commanders, acting or otherwise, should rate glasses.

Before he could check out the equipment of the other battalion commanders and commissars, Copic opened up the meeting with a brief outline of the brigade's last action. Aside from saying that the debacle of the tank attack was being investigated – he didn't say who was doing the investigating, or where – he did not add anything new. Then he turned the floor over to Doran.

Doran moved continually across the room as he spoke, his hand now hooked in the Sam Brown belt, now smoothing the polished leather of his holster or tugging at the flaps of his tunic.

"Discipline," he said, "is the key. We are now part of the Spanish Republican Army. The role of the International Brigades has been to win time for the Republic to recruit, conscript, equip, and train an army. That army now exists. What is important for us now is that we are part of that army and must organize ourselves along the same lines. This means not only equivalent ranks, tables of organization, and so on; it means uniform discipline."

Mitch caught himself checking out the uniforms of the assembled officers before he realized that he had misunderstood Doran.

"We have already made a beginning. But not enough has been done." He paused in his pacing to point in turn to each of the battalion commanders facing him. "It will be your task to instill discipline in the ranks. You will have to demand it of your subordinates, and you will have to see to it that they demand it of the men under them. The salute, the correct form of address, the rules and regulations for guard duty, work details and so on; the enforcement of disciplinary action for infractions of the rules and regulations of the Republican Army – I repeat, the Army of the Republic – will have to be carried out." Doran paused again as though to make sure everyone understood what was being said.

Mitch wished Doran would stay in one place. He was having enough trouble following what he was saying without having to keep track of his perambulations.

"Americans, Canadians, French, Italians . . . in short, the volunteers cannot and will not be considered exceptions within the army. The fact that they are volunteers and Internationals will not set them apart, except as an example of what disciplined military units should be. Is that clear?

"So." He turned to the assembled commissars. "It will be your responsibility to explain this to the men. The commanders will lay it on the line, and you will explain. And," he turned to Bonner, "the Party Activists will set an example."

"That's very fine," Rupert said, "but it's the Party people who will give us the most trouble. Not that they're opposed to discipline, they like it *mucho*. That's Party discipline, they're all for that. But salutin' and stuff? These comrades have been fighting the bosses, the higher-ups, all their lives."

"This is a problem peculiar to the Lincolns, especially among the seamen," Bonner said. "We are aware of it and we will have to correct it."

"We don't have any such problem," said Cecil Adams, the new commander of the Mac-Paps, rather smugly. Adams was a plump, puffed-up, military-looking guy. Steel-rimmed spectacles flashed on his ruddy face, his reddish hair was cropped, and his speech was clipped and precise. He had taken over the Mac-Paps when Carter was wounded at Fuentes, and Mitch noted that he too sported a Sam Brown belt. He wondered where they all came from.

"It has been made clear to the men of the MacKenzie-Papineau Battalion from the outset that our success as an antifascist fighting unit depends as much on discipline as it does on morale," said Adams.

Good for you, Mitch thought. *I know our seamen and I'll be damned if I can see them saluting and kowtowing to me!*

But when he spoke into the silence after Adams had finished, he said, "Uh, will I be issued binoculars? That is, I see Comrade Adams has a pair and I . . . well . . ." He trailed off, embarrassed. But he did need binoculars if ever he was going to find live targets for his guns. He was still thinking like a machine gunner.

Adams smiled and patted the binocular case that hung across his shoulder, the strap marking an X on his chest.

Doran removed his case and held it out to Mitch. "Take mine. We're especially counting on you, Comrade Castle, to overcome the difficulties in the Lincolns. You'll get all the help you need, but essentially it will be your responsibility."

Once out on the street and out of earshot of the command, Sam Wild, commander of the British Battalion, slapped his commissar's back. "Fletcher, you old sot, you've got your work cut out for you," he said. Wild's lank black hair fell across his brow, and his blue eyes smiled distantly.

"You mean, *we've* got the bloody job," Fletcher said.

"Right," Castle said, turning to Rupert, "that bloody well goes for you too, old . . . old, what did he call Fletch?"

"Forget it," Rupert said. "Just remember that Doran singled you out as the only one who could get away with it in our outfit."

"Hold it," Castle was alarmed, "As I recall, he pointed out the commissar's role in all this – "

"Bloody nonsense," Wild said. "Doesn't mean fuck-all. Pay it no heed."

"I wouldn't say that," Rupert said. "We're not fighting this war by ourselves. We're just a small part, and we've got to fit in, or there's going to be a lot of friction between the Spanish regulars and the IBs. Doran knows what he's doing. Castle is about the only officer some of our men will take this new approach from. Mitch is a machine gunner and it's in the Machine Gun Company we're likely to find the most resistance. Doran is one smart cookie."

Mitch, clutching the binoculars to his breast, went along with that assessment.

26

Leo leaned against the warmth of the wall, his face turned to catch the sun. He would rather have sat on the ground, but he had found early on that the dust kicked up by the shuffling feet of the exercising men made such a position impossible. Even standing, he caught an occasional whiff of the acrid stuff. He hacked and spat to clear his throat. The sun would not stay long, and when it went beyond the walls, a cold chill would fall on the enclosed yard.

He had no desire to exercise. He was not ordinarily a sun worshiper, but the cold damp of the cell had gotten to him, and now he looked forward to the warming half hour under the winter sun. The narrow yard gathered shadows quickly.

There had been French, English, and some Slav IBs in the time he had been here. What happened to them when they left, or why they had been jailed, was information that only McCall claimed to know. According to him, if one of the prisoners left and did not reappear, he had been "stood up against the wall and shot." And newcomers were invariably men like himself, he said, who had seen no point in fighting a war with one hand – more like both hands – tied behind their backs while the politicos and plenipotentiaries – a word McCall was fond of – lived off the fat of the land.

"Da finks are sending the men into slaughter like the Czar did with the Russkies against the Japs in 1903. With rusty peashooters and a crust of bread. Like they did against the Huns, with no ammo," McCall would hiss in the privacy of the cell they shared. "Dese guys just came from Teruel and dey've taken a pasting. Dey've been shelled and bombed for a month and they ain't got a goddamned t'ing to fight back wid'. The Great White Father in Moscow ain't learned a damned t'ing, but dese comrades have. 'Where's the planes? Where's the artillery? Where's the tanks?' they ask. 'On parade in Red Square,' I says."

Leo would interrupt to point out that the embargo and the League of Nations were strangling the Republic. But McCall would have none of it.

"Listen, if dey can't deliver the goods, den why bring us over here? Hah? How come da cannon-fodder gets t'rough and the cannons don't? Answer me dat."

"Dribbling men through is one thing and getting shiploads through the blockade is another." Leo was arguing as much to convince himself as to convince McCall. He knew that McCall could not be convinced, that McCall had built a solid argument to justify his own desertion.

"Okay . . . so supposin' you're right, and I ain't saying you are, because if dey mean business, dey could push the stuff right through. Dey could run over any scabs that tried to stop 'em, run it right into Spain in columns of four. But supposin' dey can't, or dey don't want to, or dey're scared about kicking off anudder war. What den? Why send the men over here to be butchered?"

"They're not sending anyone. The men are coming of their own free will."

"You betcha dey ain't sending anyone . . . not dere own. Not dem, dey ain't dat dumb. No. Dey send the word down to the other parties, you send so-and-so many jerks. It's good politics. It stirs the conscience of the world. All us dead dumb bleeding jerks stirring the conscience of the world. So what?"

Leo could feel the cold shadow of the opposite wall creeping up his legs, the slow shadows of the men slipping across the haze of light behind his closed eyelids in a ghostly file. The siren sounded and he opened his eyes. The guard stood at the open door, his rifle slung across his shoulder, waving them in.

"¡Adelante! Vite! 'Urry!"

The air raids were coming more frequently now, and more often than not the exercise periods were cut short by the sound of the siren. Beyond the wall Leo could hear the scurrying of feet, the acceleration of car and truck motors, the urgent voices of the people on the street, beyond the wall.

"Aviónes. ¡A los refugios!" Down below Mont Tibidabo and the castle that was now a prison as well as HQ of SIM, people were heading for bomb shelters, basements, cellars, ditches, whatever would give them some measure of safety.

Without haste, the men in the courtyard strolled past the guard, who urged them on with hard shoves. When they were all inside, he slammed the door shut. They filed down the corridors and into their cells, the anti-aircraft guns opening up as the door shut behind them. They sat silently on their bunks, staring up at the ceiling, listening to the thud of bombs exploding down by the waterfront. There was a certain amount of security in being behind the thick walls of Tibidabo.

"Listen, I been thinking," McCall said when the all-clear sounded. He looked around, went over to the door and looked out through the aperture, craning his head from side to side. He came back and sat close to Leo.

"When we're out in the yard and the siren sounds off, did you notice the guard? He is in one big rush to get inside. He has to get us all in and then he's in, see?" McCall's dropping of the "dese" and "dose" alerted Leo to the probability of something really important in the offing. "He doesn't take a count. He hardly looks at us. He's too busy looking up to where the ack-ack is breaking. You notice that? Well, I have. Matter of fact, he's standing more in than out of the doorway, and with his peashooter slung! Now, the next time we're out there – you listening to me? – the next time the siren goes off, you and I get into that corner where the wall and the building come together. Out of his line of sight. Get it?"

"Oh no, not me." Leo turned his head away.

"Yes, you! You and me." McCall jerked him around and held him close. "You and me. The wall's about twelve feet high. I have my shoes off, slung around my neck, see, and you . . . you're standing there like you always do. Now, while he's hustling the crew in, I'll talk to some of the comrades, get them to go real slow. You boost me up. I go first, see, because you're too goddamned weak to pull your own socks up. I go first, to the top of the wall, and then I reach down and pull you up. Over we go into the street where everybody is busting their asses to make the *refugios*. We join them, we run along with them, nobody is going to pay attention to anyone running. Everyone's running, see? We find a place to stay put until it gets dark. And then, comrade, we make your connections. That's why it's got to be you. You've got the connections."

"Oh, no." Leo pulled back as McCall released his hold. "I'll give you all the connections you want. Not that I think they're any good now."

"Why not?"

"They've probably been picked up, or moved, put out of business."

"Hah, they'll be around somewhere. Somebody'll know where to send us. You guys don't ever go out of business. Tell you what, you give me those names, all of them you remember, the addresses and where they fit in. It's a good idea for both of us to have them." He got up and rummaged around his bunk and came back with a scrap of paper and a pencil stub. "Write them down clearly so I can read them. Don't worry, nobody's going to find it. Maybe we'll be gone tomorrow . . . the first chance, see. The next raid." He put his huge calloused hand on Leo's thigh and squeezed, "And you're with me, see."

Leo jerked his leg away. "Ouch, goddamn it. Cut that out."

"Wotsa matter, did I hurtcha?" He reached to pat the injured thigh. "We don't want anyt'ing happening to you now. We're going to need our legs, ain't we? We don't want any accidents." He jabbed a stiff finger into Leo's crotch. "Do we?"

Leo got to his feet, doubled over, holding himself. "Oh, you bastard." There were tears in his eyes. "You bastard, you," he gasped.

"Aaaagh, dat ain't nuttin'. A little poke." McCall reached up and slammed him down on the bunk beside him. "Listen, Comrade Rogin, I ain't foolin'. I'm fed up with this." He had dropped the dialect again, his voice low and urgent, as he waved his free hand to take in the cell. "I'm fed up with Spain. And I'm scared of these politicos. There's no telling what they might decide to do with us. Anything can happen. They may get orders to shoot a couple of deserters for the political good and welfare of all. Nothing's been decided. I'm not waiting around to find out." He got up and stood over Leo. "We do this together, you understand? Or there's going to be an accident. A bad accident." He paused to let it sink in. "Now put down those names and addresses and let's get some sleep. We're going to need all our strength."

Leo lay awake staring at the ceiling in the dark. McCall's snores filled the tiny cell. He was thinking of the nights he had spent with Aaron and Murray, in Murray's apartment back in Manhattan. Kicking lyrics back and forth, composing music, playing snatches on the piano, on the guitar. The discussions they had had about the three B's, with Aaron, who looked like Beethoven but preferred the romance of Brahms, and Murray, soft and moon-faced, arguing vehemently for the intensity of Beethoven. The days and nights they had traveled together bringing their act to the "progressive" camps in New Jersey and upstate New York. The long talkfests about their dreams, and the weapon that their music must be for the making of a better world. A world without racism and wars, a world without exploitation, one in which the talents of millions of oppressed people would be released, would flower . . . a world full of great paintings and great music . . . a universe painted in gay colors singing hosannas to the stars.

McCall snorted, turned noisily on his side, mumbling, and farted. The ceiling pressed down. Leo turned over and buried his face in the pillow.

The planes came over the next day, at the same time. The Germans were like that. Once they got started on a schedule, you could count on them to stick to it. When the siren went off, Leo stiffened against the wall. He had made up his mind that if McCall was going as planned, then he, Leo, wasn't going to be jerk enough to allow himself to be hauled over the wall. McCall could fucking well fend for himself. He wasn't about to present his back to the guard with the rifle. A slung rifle didn't take very long to get itself unslung.

McCall was looking toward the door where the guard stood looking up at the sky. He had his shoes off and the laces tied together around his neck, his big bare feet, dirty and obscene looking, actually seeming to wriggle in anticipation. The sirens wailed.

The guard opened the door with one extended arm and followed it in. He stood holding the door with one hand, the other hooked in the sling of his rifle, and gestured with his head, shouting at the men. "'Urry! Vite, vite! ¡Adelante! ¡Vamanos!" The men moved slowly toward the door. One of them stole a glance back to where McCall was beginning to angle off in Leo's direction.

"Good Christ!" Leo muttered and almost said aloud, *He's going to do it.* He looked toward the door. Two of the men had tried to go in together. They pulled an "after-you-Gaston" act and Leo could hear the guard impatiently trying to disentangle them and get them in. Then he felt a heavy fist against his chest. He turned and McCall was on top of him.

"Cup your hands. Hurry!" McCall blew in his face.

Leo cupped his hands and McCall placed his bare foot into the stirrup and lifted up. Leo's fingers came apart and McCall came down, jamming him up against the wall.

"Son of a bitch!" yelled McCall. "Hold me, hold me!" He grabbed Leo's hands and brought them together again. "Don't do that again." His eyes were wild. Leo held his hands together and McCall, with a quick look over his shoulder to see that some of the men were still outside the door, hefted himself up.

For an instant Leo held McCall's full weight, his knees buckling. He held his breath and pressed his feet down against the earth, struggling to straighten his sagging knees. Then the weight was transferred to his shoulders and was gone. The breath came out of him in a rush. The bombs began to whistle down and he heard the door to the prison slam shut; he was alone in the yard, exposed to the sky.

Instinctively he turned to the wall and reached his arms up to McCall as though safety lay only in flight from the empty yard. McCall was still perched on top of the wall looking into the street. He turned back when Leo called his name in a loud whisper. His face broke into a grin, the parted lips showing yellow teeth, the blue eyes slitted. Then his features twisted up and he spat on Leo, laughed, and was gone, leaving Leo alone in the courtyard, his arms reaching, the siren's wail tailing off, and the crack of the antiaircraft guns ringing in his head.

Leo stood frozen, his eyes stupidly on the place where McCall had been, his arms upstretched. And then the starch went out of him. He slumped against the wall and shut his eyes to hold tight in his mind the face of McCall spitting at him.

He heard the chu-chu chu-chu of antiaircraft shell fragments tumbling into the courtyard and the street. There was no cover in the yard. He was alone in the walled rectangle, half in the shade and half in sunlight. He forced himself into as small a ball as he could make of his body, and pushed into the angle formed by the wall and the building, clasping his hands over his head. Down by the waterfront the explosions began, like heavy footsteps falling on a hollow floor in an empty loft.

He heard shouting. He looked up, and there were three guards in the doorway, all pointing rifles at him, shouting, "Rogeen, Rogeen! Migall, Migall!" The gun barrels circled the court searching for them.

He forced himself to his feet and sprinted for the door, still holding his hands clasped above his head as though trying to get in from a sudden downpour. The guards made way for him, shoving him as he went past. He fell into the corridor where he sprawled on the floor, hearing the guards keep calling, "Migall, Migall."

"Fuck Migall," he said to no one.

27

Castle stood at the window fiddling with the focusing wheel on the binoculars, sighting in on the buildings across the square, on the church tower where the bell was missing, and on the women drawing water from the fountain below.

"How do you propose to proceed?" Rupert asked.

"We'll line them up in the morning and put it to 'em. Lay it on the line," Doran said. "No questions asked, no questions answered." Castle turned to confront Rupert. "It doesn't take a genius to figure out what's what."

"Whatever that means."

"What it means is that they got Detro the hell out of here because the men wouldn't take this discipline garbanzos from him. He's a Texan and that's no good. He's not in the Party and that's no good. He looks too much like a Hollywood soldier and that's no good. So, 'aha,' they think – the powers on high, I mean – 'we put him aside and we stick Castle up there. Coming from him, a guy more or less like themselves . . .'"

Rupert held up his hand.

"Don't stop me. If it doesn't work, Castle's the fall guy. Detro comes back and one way or the other, he's got it made."

"That's a pretty good estimate, comrade. It sounds reasonable."

"Reasonable, my eye. You know that's the way it is."

"Hold it, hold it. Look at it this way. Doran didn't pick you to do the job because he needed a fall guy." Rupert's grey eyes studied Mitch. "Yours was the only gun in action the last days of Bruneté. Your section, which includes the toughest nuts, like Bianca and Kaufman, did a job at Quinto, and a damned better one at Belchite. You and Spear in the taking of the church in Belchite. Rallying your men, getting the guns into action the way you did after the bombing at Fuentes. Dave considers you a hero. Leadership material."

"What?" Mitch's tone was disbelieving.

"Yes. Him, not me, necessarily." Rupert waited for his words to sink in. "If guys like Bianca and Al are going to go along with this discipline stuff, someone like you has to convince them."

"How do you know all this?"

"What do you think we talk about at staff meetings, the price of garbanzos? We fight the actions over again. We evaluate each unit, the commanders . . ."

"So," Mitch said, "I'm the battalion commander now."

"Acting," Rupert reminded him.

"Acting," Mitch sighed. "Detro comes back . . ."

"You got it."

"Okay, Comrade Commissar. You go down there and get those two guys, Bianca and Al Kaufman, tell them what it's all about. And after you do that, send them up here and I'll read them the rules and regulations according to Hoyle, or whoever. And then we'll rehearse the whole thing. Saluting, the issuing of orders, the responses, and all that crap. And in the morning, either before or after you've laid it on the line for the battalion, we'll put on a goddamn show. Now where's that folder where it's all spelled out?" He went over to the table and shuffled through the papers there. "Here . . . in Spanish yet. ¡A sus ordenes, mi comandante! ¡Izquierda, ah! ¡Derecho, ah! ¡Mediavolt, ha!"

Rupert chuckled.

"And if you laugh out there tomorrow morning I'll go get myself a new commissar."

"Hey, watch that," Rupert shot back, "we're equal in command here. Read those regulations, *comandante*. Commissars and *comandantes* are on the same level in the table of organization. If anything, the commissar is more equal."

"Be that as it may, the *comandante* commands and the commissar explains, to quote my favorite comic-star." Castle waved the binoculars under Rupert's nose. "So if I can you, you can go and explain it to the boss."

They both laughed. "¡A sus ordenes, mi comandante!" Rupert saluted smartly and grinned as he wheeled and left the room.

Son of a bitch! Castle thought. He's going to love this.

Rupert had been gone almost half an hour before Bianca and Kaufman came shuffling in, slouching and surly, Al's square jowls blue-black, his dark eyes staring from under lowered brows, and Bianca's black eyes defiant.

"Rupert told us to report up here. What do you want?" Bianca said. "What the hell's going on?"

"Rupert told you?"

"Yeah, some bull about discipline. So?" Kaufman said.

"Well, Al, aren't you glad to see me back?"

"Not up here, I ain't. Whyn't you come back to the company? That monkey we got as a commander now won't make it."

"Who's he?"

"Reiss. For Christ's sake, he fizzled out at Fuentes."

Hell, he didn't even know who the company commanders were yet. Reiss. Dave Reiss had been in charge of one of his sections. He had always had the feeling that Reiss didn't quite trust him. Dave was ten years older than Castle, with a fringe of black hair framing a bare scalp . . . slow in speech, quick to anger. He had come from the States with a record won in struggle back home. But he had elected to join the ranks, or maybe by the time he'd arrived all the leadership cadre had been battle tested and men weren't being put into leadership positions on the basis of their at-home records anymore. Reiss had fizzled out at Fuentes, as Kaufman said. He had withdrawn into himself out of sheer weariness, an exhausted, hollow-cheeked shell with bloodshot eyes, who executed his tasks mechanically and without imagination. He could handle fear, but the grind from Quinto to Fuentes had worn him down.

Castle had not known what to do with him until the order had come for each company to select one man for officer training, and he had seized the opportunity to elect Reiss. Reiss had not been overjoyed. So Reiss was back? Mitch wondered what kind of training he had received, how much better equipped he was now to command a company. He thought to ask Rupert, and also to ask why he, Mitch, hadn't been sent to the rear for officer training as Spear and Stamos, and then Reiss, had been. But then he decided he didn't want to know.

"Not fizzled out, Al. I sent Reiss back for training."

"Yeah, well, he's trained and back."

"He's a good man, I would've picked him for the job myself."

"There's all kind of pickers picking around here," Joe said.

Castle looked at Joe. "Well, I might have picked you – "

"No, thanks, not me," Joe shuffled his feet.

" – except that I know you wouldn't want to lose your exalted status as Supreme Rank-and-Filer." He hurried on before Joe could react. "So. Let's get on with it. The three of us are going to put on a demonstration tomorrow morning of what an army should look and act like. Let's sit down and work this thing out."

Mitch knew that Joe would want to debate the pros and cons. He was instinctively suspicious of leadership no matter from whence it came; yet no matter how certain he was of having the correct solution to any problem, he would never accept a leadership position.

"Chicken shit," Joe muttered.

"And that is the last time we hear that. Now," he picked up the mimeographed sheets of paper and, translating as best he could, read from them.

"'The training of the International Brigades will be adjusted to the same regulations and instructions as those which are in force in the other units of the army.'" He looked up to make sure they were listening, then read the rest of it, all of it, to them. When he had finished, he said, "We will begin by your going outside the door and coming in, saluting, and reporting accordingly: 'A sus ordenes, mi comandante.'"

Neither man moved.

"Remember, Al," he appealed to Kaufman, knowing him to be the more "politically developed" one; besides, Al owed him for helping him over the rough spots at Belchite. "If you guys don't do it, no one will. And if no one will, then we don't deserve to be part of this army, part of the struggle of all people for the things we believe in." He looked at Joe. "This is what it's all about. We're not setting the rules for how this war is going to be run . . . or fought. That belongs to the Spaniards. It's their country, their war and their army. You want in . . . or out?"

He knew the answer. Neither Bianca nor Kaufman were about to quit. They had been around, knew the score, and had volunteered to fight fascism in Spain because they saw this battle as part of the working class's war against the bosses. It was a war they were determined to win.

It wasn't easy for them, they said, to accept the proposition that a People's Army, which was how they thought of the brigades, should be run like a goddamned imperialist army, whipping the lowly ranks to kiss the asses of the brass, to do their bidding unquestioningly, and all that bilge water.

Mitch listened, wondering where the hell Rupert was and what the hell he had done to prepare these comrades. But there was no Rupert in sight, and so wearily he went over the whole thing again. They had to keep faith with the Spanish Republic, with the Loyalists, with the United Front, the Spanish peasantry, the working class. On and on he went, ending with the same schmear Rupert had used on him. "If you two, the best and most respected *soldados* in the battalion, fall in line, the rest will follow and we can get on with the war. So whatta you say?"

"Ah," Joe snarled, "what the hell, it can't hurt. Whatta ya want us to do?"

At dawn, Castle had the company commanders form their units in an open square. The men lounged and stood at ease. Castle read the new decree to them, and when he had finished reading, he drew himself up and bellowed "¡Atención! First," he shouted, "all commands will be given in Spanish. We are going to receive more Spanish soldiers and officers into our ranks, and the language for all military procedures will henceforth be

Spanish." He liked the "henceforth." He consulted the mimeographed sheet.

The men had come to a sort of attention. He could see that there were some who were careful to be unenthusiastic.

"Sargento Kaufman and Soldado Bianca, por el frente!" he bellowed. The men tittered. He knew his pronunciation was less exact than uninhibited . . . still, it wasn't English, and that was what mattered.

His heart sank as he watched Joe and Al detach themselves from their unit, rifles carelessly held over their shoulders, their feet dragging across the main square. If they decided to act up now he was through.

He looked at Rupert, who was watching the pair as they approached, a smile on his face. No help there. Last night he had thought he had them convinced. He had not been very profound in his attempt to motivate them politically, but they were supposed to know more about those things than he. At any rate, they had gone over the routines of military courtesy, close-order drill, and commands several times; and while they had groused and Castle had joked in an attempt to make it easier, they had cooperated and said nothing about being opposed to performing for the battalion the next day – though they hadn't expressed any enthusiasm either.

"Listen, you two," he hissed at them through clenched teeth, "let's do this and do it right the first time, this one time, or I'll throw the whole fucking book at you – military, Marxist, maximum – everything. The works!" He smiled to take the edge off his words, and to cover his fear that they would somehow make him look silly. "Now, straighten up." He turned back to the battalion.

"Comrade Rupert and I have selected the best two *soldados* in the Lincoln Battalion to show you how it's done." He was conscious of Rupert shifting. Uncomfortable about being implicated in this little exercise, he thought. "These men know what it's all about. They are demonstrating their confidence, their respect, and their antifascist consciousness . . . not in respect to or for any individual or rankings or insignia, but in understanding and love for the Spanish people, their government and their army, which is ours as well."

Castle drew himself up and turned to face Bianca and Kaufman. "¡Atención!" he essayed with as much authority as he could muster, and to his surprise and relief the two men responded, after a fashion.

He proceeded to put them through a few commands, which they executed shamefacedly and not without an occasional error, but well enough to project the idea. Castle, too, stumbled over the Spanish commands.

They smiled, the men laughed good-naturedly, and the thing went off as well as could be expected.

Castle was immensely relieved, and when it was over he thanked Joe and Al on behalf of himself and Rupert, and of the assembled men, who applauded as they marched off to rejoin the ranks. Then he said:

"It will be the duty and the responsibility of the company commanders and their section leaders to carry this through. Company commanders, take over!" He gave the clenched-fist-to-the-brow salute and, without waiting to see the salute returned, turned and marched off the square.

Once back in the safety of HQ, he stood back from the window to watch the companies shuffle and mill about as the company commanders and section leaders tried to figure out how to put the new orders into practice.

He saw Rupert go from company to company, the men talking and laughing, going through the gestures, and he thought that was pretty good. This training thing was tough, but suppose he had to take the battalion into action? Oh, Mother!

Mother? To his mother he would report that he had been made a foreman in the factory.

And so Castle trained the battalion, working through the company commanders, the commissars, the Party *responsables*, any and everyone he could get his hands on.

At first he was uneasy with men he regarded as his seniors, some of whom had been his commanding officers, especially at battalion meetings when he summoned them to pass on information from brigade or to give them orders for the day and get their reports. But since they seemed to accept the arrangement, he soon got over his feeling of being somehow misplaced. At twenty-two he was commander of a battalion, if only for the moment. He had no trouble living with that.

But at brigade meetings it was a different matter. There was Colonel Vladimir Copic, his very name resonant of Balkan struggle and intrigue, fortified by rumors of a background that was said to include revolutions, underground work, and years of torture and imprisonment in Bulgaria or Montenegro, Mitch wasn't sure which. Arrayed in the full parade-ground dress, Copic intimidated Castle.

Yet it was Commissar Doran who dominated the proceedings. He prowled the room even when he was not speaking, and those who had the floor addressed him when answering someone else's question. Both Cecil Adams and Saully Glaser, the commander and commissar of the Mac-Paps, spoke frequently, as did the commander of the Spanish Battalion and his commissar, an American by the name of Reed. Sam Wild and George Fletcher of the English Battalion had little to say, and what little Sam did say he got off in asides to Castle, who had taken to him from the beginning. Rupert spoke from time to time, but Castle had nothing to say. For one thing, he did not want to take advantage of his temporary position as battalion commander, and for another, he feared to expose himself by airing any opinions. Any question he might think to ask would surely display his ignorance, since if no one else had asked it, obviously they already had the answer.

Still, he was now part of the meetings, of the cadre that got together and thrashed out problems. He took what he learned back to the company commanders, discussed it with them, and instructed them in turn to take these things up in open meetings with the members of their companies.

As a battalion commander, acting notwithstanding, he savored the power to delegate unpleasant tasks to the officers a grade below. For Mitch, the only thing that mattered was that the men would do what had to be done when the shooting started. So it did not upset him when the trappings of discipline did not last more than a week.

When, around the middle of December, the news came through that the Republican Army had captured Teruel and inflicted heavy losses on the fascists, and that this had been done by the Spaniards without the help of the IB'ers, it was confirmation of Prieto's wise leadership as commander of the Army of the Republic. Most of the American volunteers hailed it as the greatest victory since Sherman took Atlanta.

It was explained to the men that this great victory was a maneuver to delay Franco's plans – or his German advisors' plans – to use all the war materiel released with the Republic's loss of the Basque country, in an all-out attack on Madrid. Once again a major action had been undertaken; the objective: to save Madrid, buy time, and show the world that the Spanish government was capable of defending itself. The Western world was supposed to react by resuming normal intercourse with this most legitimate of all democratic governments.

The feeling of the American volunteers was that now there would be a change of heart. They believed that help would come, especially from the United States, from their great liberal, democratic, progressive president, Franklin Delano Roosevelt.

So Teruel was a big thing, and many an American happily made plans on the basis of the war's ending soon. With the end in sight, all things were possible. Parties were held, Christmas plans were made, and the raw cognac that Sam Wild called ferkin flowed like wine while wine flowed like water. And when the last party was over, Phil Detro came back to the battalion.

Castle hung suspended for one hour after Detro's return. There was a period of great activity involving all the commissars, the Party *responsables*, and the high command, but in which Castle himself had no part. For him, it was sixty minutes of silence. He assumed that he would be going back to the Machine Gun Company, either to resume command there or to take over a section under Reiss. The Spanish victory at Teruel cast everything in a golden glow, and where he was assigned mattered not to him.

When the news came, he was chewing the fat with Bianca and Kaufman over at the billets of the Machine Gun Company. Reiss was in the background, also looking uncertain.

The man who brought the news was not Rupert but Doran himself. It was a funny thing about Doran. Castle could sense that Doran took a personal interest in him. And yet up until that time, and even afterward when they met in Barcelona for a top-level discussion of the deserters who were crossing the border during the dark days of defeat, long after Teruel had been lost again and Spain had been cut in two, they never were alone together for Doran to tell Castle what he had in mind for him. He had only Rupert's report of Doran's "evaluation."

Now Doran came to Castle with the news that he was to be attached to brigade staff as a liaison officer. Reiss looked relieved.

Castle recognized this as a kick upstairs, one of those promotions of convenience that settled several problems at once. As a symbol of the new discipline in the army, it would not do to have him reduced in rank or status. At the same time, they wanted Reiss for the MG Company and Detro for the battalion.

"Why not Detro a brigade staff officer, instead?" Mitch said after Doran had left.

"They already got all-American-non-party-member Campbell in brigade," Al Kaufman said. "No room for another one. He'd be lost there. Commander of the Lincoln Battalion, Captain Phil Detro. Texan and so on. That's another story. You get the picture."

Mitchell Castle, Young Communist Leaguer, Jewish kid from Bensonhurst, got the picture.

28

The brigade staff captain rank was unreal. Mitch was on his own, free to wander about as he pleased, virtually without contact with the rest of the brigade staff.

The *estado mayor* was set up in a long concrete railroad tunnel through which trains no longer ran. It was dark, dank, and cold, and Castle wondered why Copic had chosen it. It was close to Teruel, and deep enough into the hill to be bombproof, but it was damned uncomfortable. Colder than a witch's left teat, Wild had commented after a meeting, colder inside than out, though January on the Teruel front was no summer picnic.

Men moved purposefully back and forth in the tunnel, the yellow light of oil lamps throwing their long shadows onto the curved walls, reminding him of the tunnel he'd dreamed – nightmared – when he'd had his tonsils out. Then he had stretched, extended himself to scratch and claw at the walls, seeking a way out. But the sides of the nightmare tunnel were warm and resilient, giving but unbreachable. The ether-inspired tunnel had been without beginning or end. But the railroad tunnel was cold and hard, and in his dreams now he kept falling in and out of either end.

"Hello, Captain. How does it feel to be on the brigade staff?" Fritz was a cheerful man and a fair cook.

"I'll let you know when I find out," Mitch said. "What's the *comida – bacalao*, again?"

"Don't make a face. I do the best – "

"I know, I know," Mitch said. "I can't stomach that dried-out slab of cod. I don't know how the hell anyone else can."

"So. Anyhow they do."

Mitch had more or less given up on the battalion kitchen. Most days he subsisted on the *pan duro* and *vino del campo* – bread and wine, the hard white bread dunked in the *vino*.

"You going to the battalion from here?"

"*Ja.* To the North Pole," Fritz laughed. He laughed seriously. He was cheerful in a serious way. Fritz was a political escapee from Hitlerland. Somehow he had made it to America, probably illegally, after Hitler had come to power. Now he was fighting Hitler in Spain by cooking *bacalao*, garbanzos, and goat stew, and by brewing barley coffee. It was a damned good thing, too. Cooks were hard to come by, and any kind of cook was worth a section of men.

There were Negro volunteers who were good cooks, but they had come to fight fascism. They wanted machine guns and rifles, not pots and pans. There were Negro gunners, and officers, and commissars, and just plain damned good *soldados*, but no Negroes in the cookhouse. The quality of the food did not mean all that much, but the caliber of the comrades meant everything.

"The North Pole?" he asked. "Where's the North Pole?"

"Where the battalion is. It's covered with snow and cold, very cold."

"I mean, where is it, what's its name?"

"Something in Spanish. I can't pronounce . . . Sel, Chel-something – "

"Okay. When are you going up there?"

"Now."

Though it was chow time, the men in the tunnel and their shadows, somehow inseparable in Mitch's mind, were still in motion. He stopped one who looked very brigade-official-like, with Sam Brown belt, boots, an official-looking hat.

"Captain." Mitch could see the man was a captain by the three gold bars on his sleeve. "I'm going up to the Lincoln positions. If anyone wants to know where I am."

The shadow paused. "Right, Captain Castle," he said, and continued on his way.

Well, someone in the *estado mayor* knew his name, knew he was there. He looked after the retreating figure, wondering what his name was.

Castle squeezed into the cab of the camion, sitting next to the door because of his long legs. Fritz sat in the middle next to the driver. On the way to the North Pole, which was all up hill, a battery of Italian guns laid in fire, and he watched the shells explode to the side, front, and rear. The truck moved slowly because the road was full of shell holes. Even so, Fritz kept saying, "Don't go so fast; you'll spill the soup."

The truck driver said, "If one of those shells lands in the soup it'll be an improvement," and Fritz, though he had evidently heard it before, laughed for Castle's benefit. Fritz was frightened by the shell fire, but he insisted that they move slowly for the soup's sake. Mitch wondered if they'd beat the enemy artillery gunners' bracketing before the soup got cold.

They climbed a long way, the last part without artillery fire because now they were on the good side of the hill. The company food bearers were waiting before the *plano mayor*, stamping their feet and swinging their arms. It had been warm in the cabin of the truck, but outside it was cold.

Rupert came out of the HQ *chabola*, his broad face red, his blue eyes sparkling in the cold, clear air.

"How about getting the chow up on time?" he said. But there was no anger in his demand. "Hey, Castle, they make you chief cook and bottle-washer? What's the word from brigade?"

"Hiya, Freddie. No word. I just want to see the positions and find out what gives."

"Let's eat and then I'll show you the sights." Rupert supervised the distribution of the food. The men laughed and quarreled good-naturedly, hurrying to beat the cold, to get the food to the men before it froze.

It was close quarters inside the battalion *chabola*.

"Just coffee and a chunk of bread." Castle could see that there wasn't going to be enough to go around.

"They must be feeding pretty good at brigade," Freddie said.

"Roast duck."

Detro glanced his way. He had nodded when Castle came in and waited expectantly for him to say why he was there. Castle, having no reason, said nothing and so Detro gave his attention to the food that Rosenblatt, the battalion secretary, laid out for him.

Detro ate quietly, taking small mouthfuls and chewing without showing his teeth. As he chewed, his large grey eyes looked around at each of them. A level stare. Castle had read that description somewhere. Zane Grey? Everything about Detro reminded him of a western hero. Clean-cut. Tall. Lean. Laconic. Fast on the draw? Castle watched him detach a small bit of bread with his long fingers and pop it in his mouth. His jaws moved smoothly and slowly, his lips not at all.

Rupert – shorter, stouter, talking through and around the food. A good pair. Quixote and Sancho. All-American team leading the Lincoln Battalion. White Christians. Should make the folks back home feel good. Made Castle feel good. No bewhiskered, long-haired, red-eyed Jewish Bolsheviks leading the operation. Campbell, from brigade, looked like a college professor – from an Ivy League college at that, Mitch thought. All good clean-cut stock. That was what Castle measured by and did not measure up to. There were times he felt, inside himself at least, that he did. But not here, not with these two in the same *chabola*.

Rosenblatt. Sydney. The clerk. The happy, happy clerk. With blue eyes, nothing but blue eyes. And a plump face, red and smooth under the thick wave of reddish hair. His curved lips, wet and bubbling with excitement and good cheer. Everyone was cheerful at battalion headquarters, sir, *mi comandante*, comrade commander.

Everyone was cheerful at the North Pole. "North Pole?" Mitch broke the silence. "What is this place anyway, doesn't anyone know?"

"Celades," Detro said. "That's the name of the village on the reverse side. You can hardly see it for the snow. This range of hills is Alto Celades."

"Time for the grand tour." Rupert got up. "Let's go."

The men they met in the lines were wrapped in blankets and ponchos, wore whatever headgear they had pulled over their ears, and had slung scarves around their necks up to and over their mouths. The Spaniards cheered when Rupert appeared, and laughed uproariously when he scolded them in bastard Spanish for imagined infractions.

At one of the outposts overlooking the village, Castle asked Freddie where the fascists were. Freddie wasn't sure if there were any. Castle turned to the *soldado* who seemed to be in charge.

"I think we ought to go out and find them," the *soldado* responded.

"Where would you suggest going?" Castle asked.

"Down there." He pointed to a group of buildings that were relatively free of snow and looked to be some sort of farmhouse and outbuildings. "At night you can see the trucks moving in down there."

"Well, why don't we go down and see for sure?" Castle said. "They may move in and out, maybe the joint could be ours without a fight."

"Don't include yourself," said Rupert. "We can't have brigade staff on patrols."

"Just between you and me, Freddie, brigade will never miss me."

The man who had pointed out the position introduced himself. "Bill Titus, commander of the Third." He held out his hand. "I've heard good things about you."

Castle looked more closely at him. His mouth was crooked, but that did not detract from his good looks. Made him look more interesting. His eyes were the color of violets, violets shaded with umber glaze beneath thick, curling lashes. The poncho he wore loosely added little bulk to his slight figure.

"I don't know what that means," Castle said.

Titus's hand was warm despite the cold. He swiveled his head to indicate the path down. "If we're going down there we ought to get started."

The buildings were maybe a kilometer down a dirt road that twisted and disappeared between outcroppings and showed a small stretch of brown here and there in the snow. They looked deserted. The sky was darkening.

Titus instructed his sentry details to look sharp and not be shooting them when they came back up. When they got to where the road began, floating blue shadows were settling into the valley along the road, and in the sky one big fat evening star appeared. Titus recited under his breath, "The road was a ribbon of starlight . . ."

The road leveled off as they neared the buildings. The night had come on fast, stars sprouting in clusters in the darkened sky. The sounds of people moving around, the sounds soldiers make, came clearly to them. They approached the first house, a low adobe building standing away from the others. There were men going in and out, and each time the door opened a splash of yellow light spilled out. The men carried their rifles carelessly or leaned them against the walls of the building, getting ready to eat.

Well, so here they were, crouching in the dark, and it was colder in the valley than it was on top. Damper. Castle shivered. They looked at each other. They should be doing something, he thought.

"Let's go in and blast them," Titus whispered.

Rupert looked at him. There was uncertainty in his expression. Castle took hold of Titus's upper arm; the hard, tight muscle in his grip was vibrating. He felt the resistance in Titus. Mitch pulled him back and onto his feet. He did not let go of Titus's arm until they were well on their way back to the battalion.

When they passed through the sentries, Titus peeled off without a word. Castle left it to Rupert to brief Detro, while he went off to visit his old company. When Fritz came up with the last meal of the day, he went back with him to brigade. He found the captain he had spoken to earlier and reported on what he had seen. The captain took him to a part of the tunnel where there were lights and a table and the brigade staff sitting around, the remains of their meal still on the table, and only Commander Copic standing. Castle repeated what he had told the captain. The captain, whom they called Dunbar and who spoke with a British accent, helped find the place on the map. There was some talk about what it all meant, but no one seemed to have any idea about what to do except to pass it on to division.

Later, trying to get to sleep on the cold, damp floor of the tunnel, Castle kept seeing Titus in the dark straining to do . . . what? Blast them with pistols and one rifle? They'd never have made it back up the hill alive. Still . . .

Castle took to patrolling the Celades, sometimes alone, sometimes with Rupert. Aside from an occasional cluster of artillery fire directed at the road, sniper rounds wide of their targets, and air activity, dogfights and bombings off in the direction of Teruel, there wasn't much doing.

"Except," Rupert said, "as Titus keeps saying, they are gathering up a storm. The comrade's a poet, and poets, as you know, can smell and spell out trouble before any of us mere – Whoa," he broke off, "Holy Mother, it's Dion!"

"What, is this guy dead? What's he doing out here? Where the hell is everybody?"

"Naw," Dion lifted himself on his elbow, the rest of him a brown mass sprawled against the whiteness of the snow. "I ain't dead, but you comrades will be if you keep standing around like that."

"Sniper?" Rupert knelt by his side.

Castle came down on one knee and scanned the hills facing them. Almost five hundred meters, he figured. Clear field of fire. But there was nothing to be seen on the blank white slopes. "Maybe a stray," he said.

"Yeah, that's it," Dion said, "It was like someone shoved a hot potato into my pocket. Right in the hip. Right here." He rolled over on his side and there was a circle of blood the size of a baseball on the snow, which had partially melted under the heat of his body and showed some green poking through. "I think it hit the bone. Feels like it. All numb now. Got me so I can't get up . . . not even to piss." Dion laughed, his close-set blue eyes sparkling. He looked, Mitch Castle thought, like a youthful Santa Claus: all pink and white and rotund, but without the beard. Cheerfully wounded. Celades was cheerful. Maybe it was because Rupert was always so cheerful.

Kaufman and Jorgensen came up carrying a stretcher between them. Mitch was surprised to see Jorgensen; the memory of yellow bone revealed when Jorgensen's biceps had been torn away at Bruneté remained vivid in his mind.

"Jesus," he said, "you healed fast. What's it been five, six months?"

"The bone she did not break, Mitch," Jorgensen smiled. "Them doctors put everything back in place. Sewed him up. Here I am."

"Let's cut the social and get this load on the stretcher." Rupert took one end away from Kaufman.

When they had Dion rolled onto the stretcher, Rupert told Kaufman and Jorgensen that he and Mitch would carry Dion down to *Sanidad* so that they could report back to company and get someone to fill in for Dion.

Dion was a load. As Rupert and Castle carried him, he asked them to stop whenever they came by an outpost, sentry, or section or company *chabola*, so that he could cadge loans from the men. "Lend me a coupla pesetas," he'd demand, smiling. "You can't spend them here, and I'm broke and where I'm going it ain't good to be broke, come on . . ."

As they carried him, Castle heard a bullet plunk softly into his hulk. Dion shifted on the stretcher. He rolled his eyes and chuckled, "I been hit again."

"I think you have. Freddie, Dion's been hit again. Put him down."

"No, no," Dion pleaded. "It ain't bad. Just a sting. Get me out of here." He waved his hand forward. His fist held a bunch of peseta notes, crisp in the cold air.

Drumfire. Mitch had read that in tales of the World War: "drumfire barrage." The day after Dion had departed, Castle had come back to the spot where they had found him. Reiss had a machine gun positioned there now, the water tank filled with *vino* so as not to freeze in the cold. Being there was like being in the bleachers at Ebbets Field, out in the open, up front, watching the flashes of orange, yellow, and red flickering in black-and-grey clouds of smoke. His head filled with the steady boom boom boomboomboom of the explosions. Bidaboomboomboom – on and on for what seemed an hour, or more. Now the enemy troops were coming up behind the barrage, red-and-gold banners leading black crawling things up the slope below. The storm Bill Titus had predicted.

The Spanish division on the brigade's left flank was catching hell. When the barrage lifted and the advancing enemy troops began their advance, Mitch was sure that the barrage had flattened the troops holding the line. He would have to hustle his ass down to brigade to let them know the flank of the battalion had been turned. But as he turned away, he heard rifle and machine-gun fire break out from the entrenched Spaniards, pitiful little whips of sound after the thunder of the barrage. The fascists broke off the charge and scrambled down the hill, leaving their dead, black lumps against the white of the slope. The barrage began again, the troops following as it lifted ahead of them. Again, they were met with bursts of fire from the trenches, throwing them back. Over and over again, Mitch lost count of how many times, the slope sprouting more dark splotches in the snow, markers for the dead and wounded – There was movement down there, Mitch noted, crawling wounded. The fire from the trenches got feebler after each artillery barrage, but the Spanish division was holding.

As he watched, he became aware of a shift in the line of shelling, the barrage shifting closer to the American flank, the explosions moving between the Lincolns and the Spaniards.

He felt a thrill run through him as he saw the Lincoln machine guns swing and follow the fascists and their banners, following the pounding, exploding shells. There had been no command given, at least none that he had heard. The gunners knew their job. They were veterans now, Kaufman, Bianca, Jorgensen, and the rest. Mitch clenched his hands as if grasping the grips of a Maxim; his stomach muscles tightened in anticipation.

"There they are, here they come," he shouted . . . no need for binoculars . . . He could see bodies, arms . . . legs . . . two legs, each one separately, clear in the grey late-afternoon light, no confusing shadows under the leaden sky, officers and banners in the van, moving forward, up the slope, which was not so steep there between the hill where the Spaniards held and the left flank of the battalion, which the machine guns anchored. They came on spread in a raggedy line, and now he could see that the officers and noncoms wore the tasseled caps of the Requettes, the black armbands of the Falange; they were Spaniards, the other side, the enemy – Mitch began to deal with the fact that they were Spaniards: the dead on the slope from earlier attacks, the dead in the trenches of the defenders, who were also Spanish . . .

And then the guns opened up, enfilading the line, catching the advancing troops by surprise. They milled around, came around to face the gun positions, split up, ran off in all directions as the guns fired and fired along the line of the advancing men . . . chopping into the ranks, kicking up clumps of dirty, blood-stained snow . . . breaking the line into segments . . . rolling them up into balls and clusters, careening them down the hill.

"Mother of God," Rupert came up to stand next to Castle, "did you see that?"

They stood together in the gathering dark, the guns silent, as the first star blinked in the western sky.

"A prettier sight I never did see," Castle said.

# 29

"Captain Castle," Malcolm Dunbar's shapely fingers darted over the map. "The British Battalion is presently positioned here. They should be on this hill and not" he stabbed at the red marker on the contour map, "here. Do you understand? They have been told to take the hill and they are having trouble. Will you go out there and see what's holding Captain Wild up? It is absolutely essential to the brigade position now that the fascists are trying to wedge in between the Second Division and our brigade."

Sam's eyeballs were blood-red. He was cursing, British cursing. Fuck this and fuck that and fuck all things. "Fuck-all" was what the Sahara Desert was filled with – "fuck-all." And bloody this and that and buggered be this and that.

"Sam, why haven't we taken the hill?"

"Why? Because the bloody buggers over there are shooting the bloody bejesus out of us."

"Well, you have to take it. That's what Dunbar says."

"What the fuck d'you think we're trying to do?" Sam yelled.

"Well, come on, I'll go up with you." How would this help them take the hill? He didn't know. But he did want to report back to Dunbar: "The hill has been taken and secured, Captain."

Sam yelled, "Up'n at 'em. Up'n at the bloody bastards." The Brits scrambled and struggled up the slope, firing as they went. Wild and Fletcher urging them on, Castle bringing up the rear, getting dirt kicked in his eyes. The hill jerked, spewing dirt and steel in a deafening red roar as the lead men hurled grenades into the trenches. Sam yelled for Fletcher: "The boys are up there, on the fucking hill! Get the MGs up, quick! Where's my ferkin? Who got it? How many?"

"Gimme a slug." Sam passed the bottle. Castle drank deeply, noticing that the bottle was pitted. "This stuff," he sputtered, "is eating holes in the glass."

"Tads from Brooklyn should be drinkin' bloody milk. Leave the ferkin to the Brits." Sam took the bottle. "How many?" he repeated to Fletcher.

"Miller's bought it. Only one. Four, five blighties. All taken care of." Fletcher tipped the bottle to his lips, drank deep and long.

"Good work, Sam. Any message for brigade?" Mitch was in a hurry to leave to report the taking of the hill.

"Think of something," Wild said.

Castle scrambled down the hill. Once, an angry burst of artillery fire turned him around; the hill had disappeared under a shroud of erupting earth and pillars of smoke.

In the tunnel, Dunbar and Copic were at the maps.

"Wild has the hill. They're shelling the shit out of it. Sam's being shelled to pieces." Castle was out of breath.

"Take them off the hill," said Copic. "We don't need it now." He made no explanation; Dunbar turned back to the map.

Castle was looking past Dunbar and Copic, seeing the men falling as they went up the hill. His mouth was open, but nothing came out.

The tunnel was closing in on him.

Mitch was up early the next day. He had spent the better part of the night trying to understand what went on in the tunnel, how decisions were made. There was no way he could face Sam Wild, whose battalion was now off the "bloody hill" and in reserve. Instead he went to the Mac-Paps, a battalion he disliked for no good reason at all. Maybe it was a holdover from the time they'd sent rejected seamen to the Lincolns, or Joe Bullard holding out on pipe tobacco. Or maybe it was Cecil Adams. There was no reason for not liking him except that Adams seemed to know what he was doing with his battalion and Castle had this feeling that he had not known what to do with his – when it had been his.

The Mac-Paps were on the outskirts of Teruel, on a plateau, and they were being heavily shelled. Behind them the plateau dropped sharply into town.

Teruel was warmer than Celades. The buildings were a watery-blue-and-sand color except where black holes and raw edges advertised war in the streets. *Campanillas* and steeples bearing crosses sprouted like tall weeds everywhere. A path zigzagged up the steep bluff to Adams's *plano mayor*. Glaser was listening to Adams talking on the phone.

Adams put the phone down and looked at Castle questioningly.

"Just checking the positions." The phrase had become Castle's password as he roamed the front lines.

"The mortars are bad," Adams said. "Even here . . . they drop in over the edge." He tested Castle.

"Have you taken casualties here?"

"Some," said Adams.

"Can't you find a better place?"

"Why?" Adams was still looking at him closely. Mortar shells woofed over the edge and landed down below, out from where the scarp started its rise. Smoke came drifting up.

"Well, we don't want our battalions decapitated." Castle met him head on.

"Decapitated!" Glaser said. "That's pretty good, Cecil."

"Not my head," Adams said. "I'm going up to the observation post. You can stay here and count as they fall . . . while you can."

"I'll go up with you," Castle called after him.

"Come later. We go up one at a time."

"He's a very military man," Glaser said, his big round blue eyes on Castle. "Too many go to the lines at one time and the fascisti will zero in on this spot. Nothing to see, anyway. Tell me, what's going on?"

"Everybody holding very *mucho bueno*. You comrades are doing a real good job here."

"Not that. What's doing at brigade. What's the dope?"

"What I know, you know," Castle smiled. "And I don't know nuttin'."

"Tell me, Comrade Castle," said Glaser, "do you like prune pie?"

"Prune pie? Never heard of it."

There was another set of woofs, this time off to the side a bit. They watched the shells explode harmlessly below.

"You never get down on it? You know. Muff dive. Eat it. Nothing wrong with that." Glaser's eyes were like blue china saucers.

"Oh, sure," Mitch howled. "All the time. You're a real nut, ain't you? Say, listen, tell me how to get up to that observation post. I better get out of here."

"What's wrong with prune pie?" Glaser's blue voice and blue eyes insisted.

"Nothing, nothing at all." Mitch climbed over the edge and took the first path that looked like it was going somewhere. He heard the mortars come over. The sound they made exploding was far away and hollow.

They took the Lincolns off Celades and brought them into Teruel. Castle spent most of his time with them, and some with the Mac-Paps. Glaser always greeted him with "How's the prune pie?" or "Had any lately?" and so while he was able to laugh it off, he did not expose himself to it, or Glaser, overmuch. Besides, he had found Bill Titus again, and Titus was a delight. He recited poetry and discussed plays as though Mitch, too, had read or seen them. Mitch sought to find meaning – working-class, revolutionary meaning – in Donne or O'Neill or whoever they happened to be on, and criticized their works if the meaning was absent or obscured, or so embedded in symbols as to be beyond him. He didn't know what he was talking about half the time, but the more heated and involved the discussions became, the more convinced he became of the correctness of his position . . . until Titus would bring in some other part, a further stanza or scene that seemed to reinforce his position. Castle would feel foolish, crossed up by the author like that, but not for long. His agile, if unlettered, mind would soon find something that he could bend to his point of view.

Titus's company held the convent on the outer rim of Teruel. Blackie, who with the discovery of the convent's larder had become the Third Company's private chef, specialized in pies, and being an ex–marine cook – a detail he'd withheld from the brass so he could carry a rifle rather than a spatula – he baked them well. The men of the Third Company would line up in rotating shifts for the hot pies. Those left to guard the company's positions shouted to have some saved.

The convent had been an institution for insane women. There had been nuns there in mortal terror when the company took over. Rupert had used his credentials as an RC, and his gift of Irish gab, to calm their fear of *Los Rojos*. That was before they and their charges had had to be shipped out to the rear when the artillery and air attacks became bad.

"Blackie, you're the best cook since my mother. Whyn't you take over the kitchen for the battalion?" Castle and Titus sat in his kitchen eating hot apple pie.

"Not on your life," Blackie snorted. "One of the reasons I came here was to get away from cooking."

"So here you are, in the kitchen and a good thing too."

"This is different. We ain't doin' anything out there." He waved to where the men were positioned in trenches and buildings facing the fascist lines. "Besides, I couldn't work with that garbage they call food at battalion." He turned to look around the room. "Look at all this equipment. Ovens and stoves. This is the kind of thing you need to do it right."

"How's the larder holding out?"

"Plenty. Last as long as we will." He looked at Titus sharply and then at Castle. "Providing word doesn't get to brigade and they take it all."

"They won't get the word from me. The sisters took pretty good care of their charges, huh?" Castle sipped real coffee from a real china cup.

"Hell, no," Blackie exploded. "They kept them down in the basement and fed 'em soup made from leftovers, two times a day. All this was for their own mess."

"You don't know that," Titus put in mildly. "We found the inmates down in the cellar, but I think that's where they stashed them to protect them from rape and other atrocities."

"Who the hell would want to rape them?" Blackie laughed. "Now the Sisters, that's something else again. They were eatin' good, they had some meat on their bones."

"You should've accommodated them," Titus said. "They seemed quite disappointed."

"Listen, I was horny enough to try it. But that's the trouble with being a class-conscious politico. It inhibits you and frustrates you. Instead of throwing them a piece, which, for most, wouldn't have been the first or the last, Rupert gives them a political lecture."

"That's no way for a Catholic to talk," Titus said.

"Ex-, comrade, ex-!"

"They're the worst kind," Titus said to Castle.

"Sure, we're the worst kind. We been through the meat grinder. You guys don't know what it's like to believe all that horseshit. You guys don't know what it's like to have a priest make a pass at you."

"Oh, nonsense," Titus said. "Every ex-RC I meet has had some priest try to seduce him, one time or another."

"Could be . . . could be . . . they're a horny lot."

"Which of course doesn't have anything to do with Catholicism, or Christianity as a church."

"Well, if them bastards don't practice what they preach, how the hell can any of the rest of it be any good?"

"How come you're defending the church?" Castle asked Titus.

"There are millions of Catholics in this world, most of them members of the working class and the peasantry. We're not going to win them over by attacking the church or the priesthood."

"Don't let them numbers fool you," said Blackie. "Most of the Catholics happen to be born that way. It don't mean a thing to them. There're fighting Catholics fighting the church, right here and now. I don't mean religious Catholics . . ." Blackie mumbled this last as he turned to his hot stove to lift the cover off a pot and spoon a sample into his mouth. "Aaah, just like the way mother never made it. Come to think of it, they won't be Catholics long. The *padres* are working overtime excommunicating 'em."

"You can't turn it on and off like a water faucet. You can't be an RC all your life and then some nut in black comes around and waves his hand over a candle and in sixty seconds flat you're a heathen." Mitch wondered how he was always getting involved in discussions on religion. "I mean, I'm not a religious person. I don't even believe in God. At least, I keep telling myself I don't believe in God – though I'll be goddamned if I can grasp either side of the argument. I can't get it straight in my head that there was no beginning, that there will be no end . . . Maybe man began . . . evolved . . . and most surely he'll end . . . destroy himself or be overwhelmed by some natural catastrophe or phenomenon that he is unable to cope with. That's MAN . . . what we know and don't know as MAN. But all this space loaded with cosmic gook which may be expanding or contracting . . . or whatever it's doing . . . If space is an entity, it has to be a thing in something, damn it, and if it is, what is that something? Infinity? What the hell is infinity – God?" Castle was alarmed hearing himself sound off. "Just you keep making coffee like this, Blackie, comrade ex-RC, and you'll go to heaven in spite of all the popes in this world."

"I'll go to hell before that," Blackie hoisted a canister off the stove, "if you comrades don't get your asses out of here. The men will be lining up any minute now for chow."

"They are already," Titus said, standing by the window. Castle joined him. Down in the courtyard nine men gathered near the door.

Afterward he couldn't tell if he heard the mortars coming first and then thought – this is no good, the fascists will zero in on this spot, if this is where they come all the time for chow they've got a fix on it – or if he thought about that before the rounds came in, or simultaneously with the sound. They came in slush, slush, slush – five or six rounds.

The explosions drove Titus back against Castle, who grabbed him to keep him from falling. Blackie carefully set the canister down on the floor. Mitch saw him wipe his hands on his trouser legs. They all started for the door together.

Smoke and dust hung heavy in the sunlit yard, settling on the men sprawled on the ground. They dragged some bodies into the doorway before the next salvo landed. Some of the men got to their feet and helped. They laid the men out on the stone flooring. Three dead, three wounded, three untouched. The dead were ripped, the wounded were cut, and all of them were like grey specters, covered with the fine dust of the masonry walls, the blood bleached out of their faces by the shock of the explosions.

The next salvo hit, and they flattened against the thick walls of the room inside the doorway. Except Titus. He stood in the middle of the room looking down at the wounded and the dead. His hands were covered with blood, his eyes opened wide, tears blackening his lashes, the violet irises drowning. Blackie leaned against the wall, wiping his hands on his pants leg as before, now leaving black streaks of bloody mud. "Not a good idea for the men to gather in the same place at the same time all the time," Mitch said senselessly.

Titus turned a twisted face to him, then away. Three, three, and three – a neat division. One of the three men who had not been hit came away from the wall.

"I better get *Sanidad*," he said, and waited for Mitch to agree.

"Yes. And pass the word: no chow line-up – we'll let them know. But no one is to come into the courtyard now – except *Sanidad*. Get them in here. You know where they are?"

"I'll find them," he said.

Castle looked at him. His face was streaked with dirt but it was calm, round and fair under the thin coating of dust. He had his rifle in his hands and he looked very familiar. He went out, hurrying but not running.

I've seen him around, Mitch thought . . . I always see him around. He's always around and he's always carrying his rifle . . . always calm like now . . . going from one place to another . . . a presence. There are a lot of guys in this outfit like that. They are always around, they are always composed. They are the comrades we move from one place to another. They never seem to say anything. They are never wounded or killed. Or never until they are, and then suddenly they become a personality, they crystallize into a figure, a person, because they have become a casualty and casualties are something you count, you give importance to.

He ought to find out who the *soldado* was.

Titus was busy with the wounded now, and when the *soldado* left, he turned to Castle. ". . . like locking the barn door. I should've known better . . ."

"It was the apple pie, Bill," Mitch said. "It gave us all a false sense of security."

≡30

The machine gunners had dug a trench between the buildings so that they could safely cross from their gun position to company headquarters. Detro ignored the trench. He moved so gracefully that he did not seem to be hurrying as he crossed the mouth of the alley. A blue beret tilted rakishly over one eye; his face was fair in the sun, the grey eyes catching the light like morning light on the surface of a pond before the sun is up. His arms arced gently, one hand brushing the pearl-handled six-shooter he wore slung low on his narrow hips. The holster laced around his thigh accented the length and leanness of his legs; the laced boots, every eyelet and hook caught up tight, shaped his slender ankles. Mitch watched him coming as he sat chatting with a gun crew on the left flank of the Lincolns.

They all looked up to see him coming, swinging along, tall and thin, alone on the street that led out of Teruel. It seemed to Mitch that Al and Joe and Jerry Cook and all the machine gunners had stopped whatever they were doing to watch as Detro came into the sunlight shafting between the buildings.

They saw him fold and sink into the light that lay on the stone paving before they heard the shot. He was like a thing becoming unhinged, a vital part giving way, causing the whole perfect unity to collapse, break up into separate parts, and fall in on itself, a ruin. Jerry and Al rushed out and got him.

The bullet had pinholed into his thigh, smashed the bone and come out the other side, leaving a gaping red crater, blood floating bits of pink flesh and pinkish-white bits of bone to the surface. Jerry applied a tourniquet and compress. Detro's face remained smooth and grave, his eyes serious but unclouded.

"So, Mr. Detro," Bianca snarled, and the "Mr." made Mitch jump, "you're too damned proud to use the trench and we lose another battalion commander."

The grey eyes turned to meet Bianca's anger. The pale, delicate face considered his scowling, swarthy face, the curved nose hanging over him like a scimitar.

"I'm sorry, sir," Captain Detro said.

"How long has this damned pig been dead?" Mitch said.

"Blackie just killed him. I've been saving him for an occasion." Rupert was sweating in the heat of the flames. The pig lay on top of the fire Rupert had had the men build in the middle of the street, its skin crackling and popping, the juice running out and sizzling, spitting, bursting into tiny blue flicks of flame. Teruel salivated in the smell and men gathered around in twos and threes.

"I hope you know what you're doing," Mitch said. "You can kill us all with trichinosis."

"We'll leave him on until he's done good," Lyons said.

"What's the occasion?"

"We got a new battalion commander. Roast pig in honor of Commander Lyons. An old Chinese custom." Rupert made it sound like a *pronunciamiento*.

Lyons limped up to the fire, the wounded foot still bothering him.

Rupert cut a piece out of the pig's rump, stuck the point of his knife into it and offered it to Lyons. "You first, *Comandante*."

Lyons steadied Rupert's hand and gingerly took the meat from the blade with his teeth. Fat ran down his chin. He chewed as they watched and waited for the verdict.

"Delicious," he said, wiping his lips with his fingertips.

They were standing singly, more or less evenly spaced, ten or fifteen men, on the paved road leading from Teruel to the coast, like beads on a string. Bead space bead space bead . . . All faced the same way, toward El Muleton, a kilometer or so northeast. At the end of the string a medium Russian tank, its gun silently facing the hill, hung like a locket. Copic, his sheepskin collar drawn up around his neck, his face a clenched fist, was to Mitch's left, and Dunbar, bundled up in a greatcoat, his profile sharp and white, was on his right. Then came the others, the members of the brigade staff – Doran, Campbell, aides, clerks. A crowd.

It was a clear winter day and visibility was good. Castle had no difficulty picking out the markings on the planes that bombed and strafed the hill, or the standards of the cavalry and infantry that periodically tried to take El Muleton.

The fascist planes would come in and circle overhead. One would peel off and dive almost straight down toward the crest of the hill. He could see the bomb, or sometimes more than one, separate from the fuselage. Then the plane would flatten out and scream upward, bank, and join the circling planes above, one of which would already be on its way down. When the planes had gotten rid of their bombs and the top of the hill was a ball of black smoke, they dived again, one after the other, the rattle of their machine guns clacking through the whine of the wings. Stukas, Copic had said, the hard word sounding like doom.

The cloud of smoke rose to meet the diving planes. They went into it, screaming out as they made their passes. Mitch could see fascist cavalry and foot soldiers forming for the attack, officers moving up and down along the ranks, standard-bearers waving red-and-gold banners to and fro at the foot of the hill. When the planes buzzed off, the artillery began and the formations started up the hill. When they got close to the top, the artillery lifted. Then the men picked up the pace.

There was a furious rattle of gunfire and the explosion of grenades. The enemy ranks broke and the men fell back in disorder. The planes came in again, then the artillery, and then the men, over and over. He had seen all this before. Too many times.

Meanwhile, in the rear, convoys of trucks brought more men and ammo for the artillery that was pounding the hill.

The Thaelmann Battalion was on that hill. They were Germans, Austrians, and other central Europeans, all exiles from their own countries. Mitch knew one who had been in the hands of the Gestapo for months, tortured and beaten, but not broken. Now they were in Spain on a hill called El Muleton on the outskirts of Teruel, and they were being pounded by Stuka dive-bombers and German artillery.

Mitch and the others stood in the road watching. Countless German and Italian camions, in broad daylight, fueled by Shell Oil Company, brought supplies so that the attack could be pressed. Pressed until there was no one left alive on the hill?

"My God, isn't there anything we can do?" Castle asked. Copic shook his head.

"Dunbar?"

"Nothing. We do not have the means." His diction was precise, very British. "All our units are committed."

"Why don't they take them off the hill? Why are they – "

"They won't come off. They are sworn to hold the hill to the last man."

"To the last man? That's bullshit."

"They're Germans." Dunbar looked like an Egyptian pharaoh, or at least like the photos and drawings Mitch had seen, except he was very white. His face was smooth, no sign of concern wrinkling the surface. Stiff upper lip. "I suppose they've decided that this is where the battle ends. They've been at it for an awfully long time, you know. One might say since 1930, perhaps before."

"How about that tank? What's the tank sitting there for? Why can't it – "

"It wouldn't last five minutes." Dunbar turned back to the hill. "I wonder how long they will . . ."

Castle sat on the fender of the tank; the metal was still warm from the bit of sunlight that had filtered through the overcast. It had not moved. He felt alone in the night, the stars his only companions. Dinner was being served in the tunnel and the tank crew had joined staff for the meal. He sipped from a tin mug filled with *vino del campo* and munched on white bread, watching the fascist camions snaking down the road into the saddle before El Muleton, coming to a slow stop, changing gears, starting up El Muleton, the hill that was now the graveyard of the Thaelmann Battalion.

The camions drove with their bright lights on, in a long twisting column. He could hear the motors race. They drove up the hill and down again, their lights on, all through the night, each truck with its two bold, blazing eyes defying him on the way up, the red tail lights mocking on the way down. Christ, it was galling, souring the wine in his gullet, his stomach watery with a helpless sort of rage.

He imagined the *soldados* who sat as he did, along the lines in trenches and *chabolas*, seeing what he was seeing, feeling the same helpless rage he was feeling. He wondered if that *soldado* who'd gone for *Sanidad* when they'd been mortared in the courtyard of the convent was seeing what he was seeing, feeling what he was feeling. Once again he saw the calm round face, the steady blue eyes; he was everywhere, come from everywhere to the outskirts of Teruel, a city taken and lost. Now, this night, this very cold, soft, starlit, fragrant night – watching, seeing, and feeling inside of them, in their guts – the fascist camions rolling up with tons of crap to hurl against them the next day, running freely in daylight, running without fear of interdiction at night, their lights blazing.

The men watched and weighed the odds. He knew that. Knew that they held unlit cigarettes between their lips, as he now clenched the stem of a cold pipe, unable to light up, even with a flint and rope *machero*, for fear that the tiniest spark of light would give their positions away. Aware as he was of how little chance there was of getting any air or artillery support. The embargo choked off all vital supplies, supplies piling up on the French side of the Pyrenees. No big guns, no spare parts, no fuel. Artillery silent for lack of ammunition. And no mortars.

Thinking of mortars and how they were always on the receiving end and why the hell they didn't have so simple a thing as a mortar themselves, a simple fucking tube on a plate – he remembered the round-faced blue-eyed kid at the convent in Teruel the day Titus's outfit was mortared . . .

"What the hell is his name?" Mitch addressed the steel hulk of the useless tank.

The tank grew cold in the chill of the night, the wine soured in his gut, the bread was hard and dry. He felt the presence of the tunnel behind him, felt it wanting him back inside, where the staff would be at the maps, charts of contour lines that told of elevations but divulged nothing about rocks or trees or shrubs or sudden crevices or booby traps, or craters or entrenched snipers. The hills on paper, Mitchell Castle had learned, were nothing like the hills they had to take and hold. Back there in the tunnel, staff was planning another move, on to some other hill, another Muleton.

31

The earth around Aguavivas was frozen and for that reason the digging was difficult. Even if it had not been so granitelike, Leo would have found the going tough. Ditchdigger. It was a fate worse than death, something for the "Talainos," Italian immigrants, to do; no trade for a Jewish boy. But for him, now, it was a fate better than death.

After McCall's escape he was summoned to yet another meeting. This one had been easier in one way and tougher in another. All the people he had to deal with on this one were SIM, and this time Serrota conducted the interrogation.

It had been easier because he could tell them exactly how it had been – how McCall had planned it, how he had been terrorized into cooperation. He even volunteered the list of names and addresses he had given McCall and had urged them to go looking for McCall in those places, but not to put them together again because McCall would kill him. If they executed McCall, that would be better, not only because the bastard deserved it – he recalled the spitting face on the wall – but because then he, Leo, would feel a hell of a lot safer. He hadn't told them that when escape had seemed briefly possible he had reached to be pulled over the wall. After he had repeated the story at different sessions, he forgot about that moment of weakness.

Still, Serrota had insisted on some punishment, and it was then that they had recalled Doran's suggestion that he be detailed to the *zapadores*. Here he was, had been for ten days now, quartered in a miserable little town called Aguavivas, sleeping on a cold tile floor, eating lukewarm, oily food; the work had nothing in common with engineering as he understood it, every morning going out to dig graves in the frozen ground. At least the holes did not have to be big enough for coffins. It was a good thing, because there were a lot of holes to dig.

Each morning when they got to the burial site, a truck loaded with corpses would be waiting for them. The detail would put a couple of men up into the truck to hand the bodies down to the men below, who would lay them out in a row as far away from the road as they could get in a hurry.

Leo was grateful for the cold because it deprived the stiffs of personality. If it had been warmer and the bodies soft and yielding, probably beginning to smell, it would have been impossible. Handling them now was like handling logs. The *zapadores* dug holes for the bodies and sometimes extras for the next shipment; they liked to be ahead of the game. But mostly there were as many bodies as they could dig holes for.

They did not talk because they had no language in common. They were from different nations, assigned to this work because for some reason they could not, would not, fit themselves into the purpose for which they had come. They were silent, listening to the distant rumble of gunfire, the crunch of artillery and bombs, estimating by the volume how many stiffs there would be the following morning. The stiffs were, like themselves, from all the countries. They came unmarked, unnamed, to be juggled into the graves and covered with Spanish earth.

At night, exhausted, Leo fell into terror-filled dreams. Awake and working, he was really asleep, indifferent to all around him. But at night, the pictures came. The men digging with picks and shovels in the earth, which was always soft in his dreams. Animated small black shapes, grotesque against a grey and lowering sky. The stiffs became soft and pliable, staring up from the graves, their faces fixed but alive. Aaron's, Murray's, and finally his own. He could feel the dirt clumping in his face as he shouted, *No no no no! I'm not dead, I'm alive!* But no matter how hard he struggled to get out of the grave, no matter how loud he screamed, no one heard him, and he realized that he could not move and that no sound came from his wide-open mouth, into which the dirt fell, choking him. He would see the iron shovel coming toward him, getting bigger and bigger, and he would scream louder and louder as the dirt came raining down on him. There would be a slice of sky hanging over him, and the shovel would reappear, small at first, getting larger, shutting out the sky; he would shrink into the hole, into his pallet on the hard floor, in terror of being buried alive. When the breath had all but left him, he would come awake, covered with sweat, blankets wrapped around his neck, shivering in the cold.

Castle was chucked out of brigade HQ and made commander of the base at Aguavivas. He had an iron stove in the center of the room, an ornate, potbellied, wood-burning gadget. It was much more complicated than the simple iron cone that had warmed his tent in the C's up there in the Allegheny Mountains. Here, a Spaniard came in with armfuls of wood for the stove. He left with a sackful of ashes. Aside from nodding and smiling slightly, he did not utter a word.

Castle was cold and miserable and unhappy. He had just finished writing a letter to his friend Herbie.

"It all comes," he wrote, "from being stuck somewhere in the rear with a base. This is not for me. I cannot be happy back here, and even though I know it is my duty, I do not think that I can even function well here. As a matter of fact, I do not know what a base is, what we are supposed to do here, and therefore I do not know what I am supposed to do. I don't expect this situation to last, however. I am sure that I will be back with the men shortly."

He put the letter in its envelope, not sealing it as per regulations, knowing that the brigade censor would read it, hoping the censor would report his discontent and effect his release. Who in his right mind would want a base commander who did not know what a base was?

Base headquarters was up one flight of tiled steps in a house off the square. It had belonged to the keeper of the general store. Out in back there was a little plot of ground, divided into rectangles by odd slabs of wood. In each rectangle, there was a pig. A big pig – bigger than Rupert's Teruel pig. There was not enough room for the pigs to turn around or even lie down. The owner, his wife, or one of his children was forever feeding the pigs some sort of slop that went in one end and had to be shoveled away when it came out the other end. It was something like feeding the stove, only the stove did not get any fatter. The pigs, enormous to begin with, got bigger and bigger. Castle spent a considerable amount of his time as base commander studying the pigs.

Officers and *soldados* arrived and left. They reported that they were about to do this, that, or the other thing. Castle never asked them why and they never told him. He neither approved nor disapproved of the actions planned since all these things had to do with tinned marmalade, picks and shovels, shoes, underwear, things of no interest to him.

His most frequent visitor was a certain Major Humberto Gennaro. He had not seen Gennaro in the tunnel at Teruel, or at the front. Castle accepted him as a member of brigade staff, though no one had ever bothered to introduce him in that capacity. The major was tall and handsome and sported a neatly trimmed black moustache and beard. He wore the most complete uniform in Spain, and it was always spotless and pressed. His boots were polished and his gloves black. Various leather straps criss-crossed his chest, and from them hung map case, binoculars, compass, and pistol. The breast pocket of his tunic bristled with the heads and clips of fountain pens and four-colored pencils. It was Castle's understanding that the major was responsible for him and the base, and that he was in constant touch with brigade. That is, he was constantly being driven to and from brigade in the pursuit of duties that seemed to Mitch rather esoteric, having as their main purpose the improvement of the officers' mess.

Mitch saw in Major Gennaro the perfect man for the job he himself was stuck with. Though he was not clear what the job was, he did know that he couldn't simply walk away from it. If, however, he took advantage of one of Gennaro's frequent visits to the base and left then, leaving the major no choice but to assume command, Mitch could not be accused of dereliction of duty . . . or he didn't think he could. But at the moment there was no need to leave. The battalions were resting. Once they got back into the lines, he would resume his self-appointed task of visiting with this battalion or that for a piece of the action.

The pigs got fatter while he waited.

A horrible scream, a penetrating yowl of pain, fear, and rage, followed by more screaming and still more, rising and falling, inexpressibly full of agony and terror, jerked Mitch out of bed.

The screams filled the room. He wrapped his cape over his BVD's and dashed out into the street. He followed the sounds down a sidestreet that opened into a small square. The square was lit by a fire in its center. Black forms hurried about, steam rising from their mouths, smoke coming from the fire . . . and the smell of hair burning, of flesh being charred.

He realized that the shock of the screaming had propelled him into the street unarmed and unescorted, with no idea of where he was, shivering in the blackest part of the night, the time just before dawn. He stopped to take stock of what was happening before determining on a course of action.

Next to the fire there was a long wooden table. On the table a pig was stretched out, its feet held by four Spanish peasants, its head hanging over the table. The pig was screaming, and blood, bright red and shining in the fire's light, streamed from its neck into a bucket on the ground. At its head stood a muscular man, stripped to his undershirt, sweating, in a cloud of white smoke, holding a gleaming knife. The screams diminished, as did the flow of blackening blood. The pig kicked weakly and grunted. The man with the knife inserted the point into a hole in the pig's throat and then drew it down the full length of the pig, pushing aside those who had been holding the struggling animal. He cut through the skin and peeled it back, cutting through the fat and then through the meat. Others now joined in the operation, and the hooves were severed, as was the head. The rest was cut into chunks and slabs and joints, and carried away. The insides were cleaned out, the intestines dipped in a kettle of water boiling on the fire, and then the women poured the blood, which they had been stirring in the pail, hot and steaming, into the pinkish-white guts, distending them into a long tube that shone obscenely in the night.

They were very efficient, and the huge bulk of the pig disappeared like magic, to be replaced by another squealing, screaming animal. Two women poured boiling water over the swelling hide of the pig, making the bristles stand up and pop as other women scraped the hide down, gathering the bristles. The butcher tilted the pig's head back and inserted the knife; the blood spurted and streamed into the bucket, the pig kept screaming, and the whites around its pink eyes turned red. It rolled its eyes, which mirrored the flash of the knife. It looked at Mitch. Mitch looked at the pig, at the people busy around him, at the dancing shadows cast on the adobe walls of the buildings around the square, up at the black morning sky where the stars still shone brightly.

He turned to go back to his room, and saw that some of the men from base had come down to the square.

"Es nada," he said as he pushed by them. "It's an old Spanish custom – "

"Mitch!" One caught his cape. "Boy, am I glad to see you . . ."

He leaned forward to see the face.

"Well, well, well, if it isn't the prodigal son. Come on with me and tell me all about it, comrade."

≡ 32

The screams of the butchered hogs had become part of Leo's dream, and when he awoke sitting up he did not understand why the screaming had not stopped. Men were up and throwing clothes on, starting out the door. He dressed hurriedly, not knowing if they were going toward the screams or away until he was outside. Then he, like the others, was drawn to the sound.

By the time Leo arrived at the little square, a number of men were there, some already drifting away, back to catch whatever sleep they could. He saw Mitch Castle standing near the center of the square, tall and thin, a cape wrapped around him, his big nose pointed skyward, circling the morning stars. Castle lowered his head, looked to where the women were pailing boiling water over a screaming pig, then came toward him. As he came by, his eyes distant and not seeing, Leo caught hold of his cape.

"That was some show," Castle said. He had brought Leo back to HQ. As they sat and talked, a Spaniard came in silently and fed wood into the stove, stirring the fire into blazing life. When he was satisfied, he went over to the cot and shook out the sheets and blankets and made up the bed. He put a tin of water on the stove to boil. Mitch, in his crude Spanish, instructed him to bring enough coffee and whatever else there was for his "cousin from New York" to share.

"Come over here." Castle led Leo to the window and pointed to the yard. It was still dark, but the light coming from the window made it possible to see what he pointed to. "Those empty pens? Each one of 'em had a pig in it. Each pig was so goddamned big he filled the entire pen. There was no room for him to sit down or turn around or anything. Just eat. And the more he ate the less room there was. So he just ate and ate and got fatter and bigger. I watched them feed 'em at one end and shovel away the shit at the other. I knew they were being fattened for the kill, but I never dreamed those goddamned pigs were alive all the time they were being boiled and bled." He shook his head. "I'd never believe it – people doing a thing like that."

The Spaniard came back in, lugging a number of pots and pans, which he set down on the table. He poured coffee for them and laid out bread and marmalade.

"No churros?" Castle asked.

"No, mi comandante. Todavía no hay churros. Es muy temprano. Más tarde, por seguro."

"*Bueno.* Don't forget to get them. Come on, Leo, pull up a chair and tell me all about it. You fucked off again, didn't you? What are you doing here?"

"Don't you know?" Leo stalled. "You seem to be the commander here."

"Listen, between you and me, I may be the commander of this bloody base, but I most emphatically don't know a damned thing about it, about who is here or why." Castle laughed bitterly. "I don't even know why I'm here, but if you're here too it can't be for any good reason."

"It seems to be pretty good for you now."

"What do you mean by that?"

"You have a bed, a stove, and a flunky to take care of you. Being a base *comandante* can't be all bad."

"Aaaagh, that's Gennaro. He goes in for things like that. He set this whole thing up and deposited me here. I just go along with it. But not for long. So tell me, what gives with you?"

"With me? For one thing, I sleep on the floor. I get up in the morning and I go out and dig."

"What? With the *zapadores*? Yeah, I hear they're here, somewhere. What the hell are they doing?"

"Digging."

"You said that. Digging what? Trenches? Latrines?"

"Graves."

"Graves?"

"Yes, graves. Holes in the ground to put the dead in." It seemed to Leo that Castle was still having difficulty grasping simple answers, even when, as always, they were answers to his simple questions. He remembered Castle asking for water with the rain pouring down, and what to fire at, with the fascists firing right at them. It was always something like that. Now he was in command of a base and he did not know what went on with the men in his command, or why he was in command. Leo suspected that he had been stuck away, deposited by Gennaro, whoever he was, to get him out from underfoot. Someone must have become impatient with his questions.

"Ah," Castle was saying, "that's a punishment detail. So they caught up with you, cousin?"

"It wasn't because of anything I did," Leo replied. "They were holding me in Barcelona, you know, trying to get things straightened out. I wanted to come back to the battalion or get sent home and they were working on it when one of the other guys – you remember McCall – went over the wall and they got me mixed up in it."

"McCall!" roared Castle. "So that yellow sonofabitch wound up in the can!"

"Not anymore. He's across the border by now if they haven't stopped him." Leo paused, wondering how far he could go with Mitch. "He's not digging graves, being watched, sent here and sent there, like me."

"Well you shouldn't have goofed off in the first place. Or should I say in the second place."

"Why not? Lots of guys do it and get away with it. I only panicked when Lyons shot himself in the foot to get out."

"Wait a minute. That's a crock of shit. Lyons's back. He was at Teruel. He's the commander of the battalion again. That was an accident."

"He's back? So what? It didn't look like an accident to me. Plenty of guys have bought out with a blighty."

"You've been reading too many books, comrade cousin."

Leo was surprised at the way the talk was going. The way Castle called him "cousin," and the way in which he handled him, as though attaching no significance to his desertions, and his openness about not knowing what was going on, disarmed him. Mitch had said something about "not being here for long."

"Listen, I've been in Barcelona. I could have gone over the border a million times. Do you know how many of the volunteers are going over the border? Do you know how many are in jail, how many have been shot?"

"Shot?" Castle was startled. "Don't give me that crap."

"I'm telling you. Shot. I was there."

"You saw them shot? Who? How many?"

"Yes. Every day. Two, three a day. Comrades like you and me, all nationalities. Every day they'd take them out of jail and they never came back."

"They took them out and they never came back?" Mitch repeated. "Okay, but you don't know what happened to them, do you?"

"We knew. There was talk."

"Oh, sure. There's always talk. Hell, you were taken out, right? The prisoners who remained behind, they don't know what happened to you, do they now? Some jerks like you have probably got the story out right now that Leo Rogin was shot. As Bianca would say, pure scuttlebutt." He paused and drank from his cup. "God, you don't realize how bad this coffee really is until it gets cold! Tpftui!" He wiped his lips and smiled at Leo. "You know what I think? I think they should take guys like McCall, and even you, and give them jobs in a factory or something out here. Something you can do that will be useful to the cause." He laughed. "You know, my mother thinks I'm working in a factory. How about that?"

"I think we should be allowed to go home. There's plenty to do at home."

"What are you goin' to tell the folks when you get back home?" Castle's voice was sing-song and mocking.

Leo was silent. This, of course, was what had kept him in Spain. If he could just figure what to do that would justify his leaving. McCall had come up with a million reasons, but they weren't reasons that would sit well with Leo's friends, not with Murray and Aaron dead. His father? Oh, how his father would love to hear from his son – from his own mouth, from this Communist who had been there – what terrible things went on in Spain. Oh, how he would love to hear Leo confess that the Party was all fouled up, undemocratic, inefficient. He had a picture of his father in his mind, small, neat, rotund, bald on top with a halo of grey-brown hair standing out from his head, his hands in his pockets, rocking on his heels, saying "Nuh? I told you so. You wouldn't listen to me."

"There have been men sent home."

"Well, some of them have been wounded, you know? They show 'em the wound, that's their *salvoconducto*. But it can't be too easy for them either. Five or six who were sent honorably home have come back already and I understand there are more on the way. Let's face it, Leo, it's easier being here, especially after you've showed your hand."

"Is that why you haven't gone home? You could have, I suppose, with Manny and – "

"Nick Stamos? They didn't go. They're back with the battalion." Castle looked toward the window where the sky was taking on the grey and pink of morning. "I'll tell you the truth, cousin, I just've never thought about it. It's like when I went away to the C's, you know, the CCC. Once I was there I never thought about going home. Not that I wasn't happy when I finally did get home. But I never had this great big pull on me, you know? I hear some of the guys talk about being homesick and all. Now these guys I have a certain respect for. They do want to go home. But they stay on; they don't run away or go over the border. They stay on and do what they have to do no matter how homesick they get to be."

"Well, isn't that what you're doing?"

"No, no, cousin, you're not getting the point. The point is that I don't think about it. I don't have any problem. I don't have to sweat out any decisions. It's easy for me."

He stopped as the door opened and the little Spaniard came in carrying *churros* and a can of hot milk. Castle whooped like a kid. "¡Oye, churros con leche caliente! Muy bueno, mucho bueno." He took a handful of coins and bills out of his pocket and put them on the table. The Spaniard carefully selected a few of each and departed. "He's got some family making them for the troops. He brings me the first batch. Here, help yourself."

The *churros*, like the sweetened goat milk, were warm. "You gotta eat 'em hot," Mitch said. "If you let them cool off you taste the oil. Ugh." He grimaced, his moustache outlined in white from the milk.

"I think about it," Leo said, nibbling at the *churro*. "I think about it all the time."

"That's the trouble."

"No, that isn't the trouble." Leo was determined to try out some of the things he had picked up in Barcelona from Sammy, from McCall, and from the POUMists, ultrarevolutionaries who did not trust the Popular Front and so did not support the war effort, or only halfheartedly participated.

"Listen, Mitch, if you have the time, I'd like to discuss this problem with you."

"*Hombre*, I've got nothing but time."

"If you'll get me out of detail this morning, can you?"

"Sure, cousin, I think you oughtta get it off your chest, talk it out, and then maybe we'll get you back on the track. That detail, that's the *zapadores*, right?"

"Yes, it's part of the Engineers, but the man in charge of our special group is Lieutenant Camino . . ."

"Wait a minute," Castle interrupted. "Jose!" he shouted, and the orderly came in. It seemed to Leo that he bowed slightly as he stood in front of Castle and said:

"A sus ordenes, mi comandante."

"Jose, you will go to the commander of the special company of *zapadores, Teniente* Camino, say to him that I need Comrade Rogin today. I will send him back to the company when I am through with him, you understand? Good. Comrade Rogin will say where to find the lieutenant."

Leo gave Jose the information and waited as he half backed out the door. "Things have changed a great deal since Tarazona," he said.

"We do like the Regular Army now. This is the way they operate."

"I thought this was the kind of thing we were supposed to be fighting against."

"Oh, Leo." Mitch sounded suddenly weary. "That's what everyone says. How do I know? As far as I'm concerned the thing we're supposed to be fighting against is fascism. Is that your beef? Are you going to tell me that you're all fouled up because of this military craperoo?"

"Yes, why not? They've got all these socialists and republicans and social democrats in power – Negrin, Prieto, Caballero, and the others, Miaja, that old reformists' general – working with the bourgeoisie and the landowners wherever they can find them. They're just preserving the old order, fighting the war according to old rules and regulations. Sitting on the people instead of liberating them and letting them fight a peoples' war."

"As I understand it, there ain't enough people for that."

"Yes, there are. But they don't want to fight for these characters. They want to fight for themselves, the peasants and the working class. The hell with the generals and the saluting and the flunkies and the '*a sus ordenes*.'

We should be making the revolution right now." Leo felt his recklessness heating his face, but he was in full flight now and would not draw back.

"If we were, would that make any difference to you? Would you be up there now?" Mitch was looking at him, his black eyebrows raised, zestfully munching a *churro*.

"Maybe."

"Maybe! That's it with all them nuts: maybe! I'll tell you what I think. I think not. I think they'd – you would – find something wrong with how the revolution was being made. Meanwhile, the Trotskyites, the Anarchists, are obstructing the war. Are helping the fascists, whether they know it or not. What they should be doing is fighting. Let's defeat the fascists first and then make the revolution. What's the matter with that?"

"If Lenin had gone that way, there would never have been a revolution, or a Soviet Union."

"That was different. This is a war against fascism. Everybody has a stake in it, and that means that we have to fight it on terms acceptable to everybody. 'Maybe!'" he snorted. "Maybe if you spent more time fighting Franco and less time fighting Caballero – I don't mean you, I mean the others – we'd all be home by now. Instead, we've got to fight you too. We've got to be on guard against you and the others, cutting us up, undermining – "

"All right, so don't lecture me."

"You wanted to talk . . . we're talking."

"You seem to be doing all the talking."

"Go ahead, you talk. Tell me why you're digging graves."

"It seems to me that your approach is rather a simple one." Leo shied away from the graves.

"I'm a simple guy. Get complicated, split hairs, see every side of every issue, and you wind up sitting on your ass . . . or digging graves instead of fighting."

"Being a gravedigger was not my choice."

"Oh, yes, it was."

Leo couldn't go on with it. He wouldn't go on with it because he knew Mitch was right. He was simple, perhaps even stupid, but he was right. Leo could not use McCall's arguments. As a matter of fact, he probably knew more than Castle the impact of the POUM and Anarchist tactics. After all, he had been in the middle of it. Barcelona was the stronghold of the POUM. They had been making a half-assed revolution in Catalonia while the people of Madrid and the miners in the Basque country were fighting for their lives. Whatever might be said for their position, this was one thing that no one could explain away. So he sat staring at his dim reflection in the cold coffee at the bottom of his tin mug. It was warm in the room and the sun was fully up now and he felt tired and unwashed.

"I think I'd better go back to my outfit now. I want to get cleaned up and – "

"Yeah. Well, I wasn't expecting that we'd be talking politics. I thought your problem lay elsewhere."

"I guess it does. Maybe I can come back later . . . another day . . . and we can talk about it then?"

"I don't think so, Leo. I'm going to get myself back to the battalion. I won't be around here much longer."

"You shouldn't do that." Leo wanted to hold onto Mitch. Though he had nothing specific in mind, he did feel that in some way Mitch could be his savior. "This is a job too. You don't have to be at the front all the time."

"But I do. I'm no good here. I can't function in the rear." He laughed. "You see, I have my problems too."

Leo shook his head and got up to leave, but Mitch held him back.

"Tell me, cousin," he said lightly, "how's business?"

"What?"

"I mean, are there many – do you have a lot of . . . of dead to put under?"

"Some days more than others, but always enough." He waited but Mitch was silent, looking out the window at the grey light of morning, the muscles of his jaw moving rapidly; his eyes, fastened on the window, did not blink.

"I'm sorry," he said finally, not turning around.

Leo didn't know what he was sorry about. He left him then, and as he walked across the square he thought that maybe Castle had come to the window to watch him walk up the street, but he did not look back to see if he had.

# 33

Leo walked up the street, his hands in his pockets, not knowing what to think but knowing that he would take the rest of the day off. The dead could wait, they weren't going anywhere. His talk with Castle had accomplished nothing. Reviewing it, he realized that none of his talks or escapades, those that had already happened and the ones that would – and he knew they would – would ever solve anything. Even his inability to go into a state of shock, so as to be unsuitable for front-line action, angered him. His awareness was total; he couldn't con himself one way or the other anymore, as he had when they'd carried him out at Bruneté. McCall had been able to solve the problem one way and Castle another. Neither one of them was a good example. McCall because he was just plain rotten. Even if he had not been cowardly under fire, even if he had remained a hero on the waterfront and in Spain, if he had become the Party chairman, he was still rotten, and rottenness had to come out one way or another. Castle? Castle because he was simple and naive and for some reason able to bear the rigors of Spain, the goof-ups, the flunkies, and whatever else, as he was convinced he was on the right side, doing the right thing.

No, there must be men in the battalion who were just as scared as he was and just as questioning, men who nevertheless were able to do what had to be done. Goddamn it. He must have buried more than one.

That he did not want to think about. Not today and not when he was doing it. Maybe if he could let himself go and dwell on it, he'd snap. Go to pieces. Fragment, dissolve into a gibbering, slobbering idiot. A mental case. Shell shock. Corpse shock. He shivered and forced himself to turn outward, to divert his attention to the little houses, the blank doors, the deep-set windows on either side of the street.

A woman was standing in the doorway of one of the houses. He caught sight of her white face in the deeper shadow of the doorway. If it had not been for the paleness of her face, he would not have seen her. She was dressed in black. Black dress, stockings, *alpargatas*, and a black shawl around her shoulders. Almost invisible except for the white of her face, and now he saw the light in her black eyes as she watched him. He slowed his steps.

"Salud," he said, nodding his head. He saw her lips move, but could not hear what she said. She was looking at him and it seemed to him that she would accept his stopping to talk. He smiled. His smile was small, tentative, ready to disappear or broaden.

The morning had turned grey, chill, and lonely. It had started with the screaming of the pigs getting mixed up in his dreams, and it had proceeded through a number of unfinished things. It needed an ending, this morning. And just the two of them being there, facing each other, seemed to promise that. She leaned her head forward and looked up and down the empty street, then pulled back into the darkness, moving sideways, looking at him briefly, her head turned to him. He walked past her into the darkness of the room.

In one corner there was the dirt fireplace and the orange glow of a smoldering fire. Sitting on the fire was a large black iron pot. He knew it would sit there all day, until evening came. That after a while, steam would come from the pot and the room would fill with the odor of the meal, the one real meal for that day. Over by the window there was a table and two chairs. The top of the table was bare. As his eyes grew accustomed to the light, he made out a double bed against one corner of the opposite wall. There was a baby on the bed, its head turned to the light, jamming its small hands up against its face and into its mouth, kicking up and down. It was funny about the baby, because it seemed too big for the way it was acting. Also, it made no sound.

"Sit down, please," she said in Spanish, and her clear voice was almost a command. "Would you take warm milk or wine, señor?"

"Do you not have coffee? I will pay for it."

"There has been no coffee in this house for a long time, señor."

"Do not call me señor, as a favor. I would prefer the milk."

"Good." She turned to the fireplace and poured the milk from a crock into a tin cup. "What shall I call you if not señor?"

"Comrade, *camarada, compañero*. It is different now, as you know."

She brought a cup of milk for herself and sat down with him. "I know, but I forget. Besides, 'comrade' sounds very important."

He could see that she was not young, though it was always hard to tell about country women. Her pale face had hardened – no, firmed – perhaps formed into its true self, revealing the passage of time when the skin, the muscles underneath the fat, the color of the blood, and the shape of the bones showed the person as her life had shaped her. The sheen of youth was gone and the sagging, the wrinkling, the hollowing and the puffiness, the greyness and dryness of aging had not yet begun. It was an age he could not put a number on, but he recognized it. It was not an age he had achieved, though he had seen it beginning in Castle's face even though Castle was younger than he.

He drank the milk and it was good. "What is the cost of it?" he asked, showing her the empty cup.

"Whatever you wish, señor. Wait. *Compañero*." She stood up. "Would you wish another? Or something else?"

He did not want more milk and he did not want to leave. It was pleasant in the one-room house, dark and warm. The few sausages hanging from the ceiling gave the room a smoky and meaty flavor.

"Yes, I will have another, please," he said, and when she moved away to get it, he said, "And what does the husband do?"

She crouched to pour the milk, the black dress pulling tight around her hips. "He is a prisoner, in Africa."

"A prisoner of the Moors?"

"I do not know."

"Do you not hear of him, have you no news?"

She came back to the table with the milk and set it before him. She stood there and looked down into the cup as he held it between his hands. "I have heard but once. From Madrid they informed me that he had been taken with others who did not wish to go against the government. I have asked many times before the Red Aid Society and through the *alcalde* of this village, but I have heard no more. Only now I receive a pension for myself and for the baby. I have not asked again for many months now."

She turned and walked to the window where she stood and looked out and up and down the street again. "Señor . . . comrade. It is very hard without a husband. It is very hard with so small a pension. Señor . . . I cannot say the other, forgive me, but if you wish to stay it is possible . . ."

She waited for his reply, the grey light soft on her profile, which was very regular and very firm looking. Only the shadows in the deep eye sockets edging onto the cheekbone gave some softness to the face.

"Yes. If you have it, I would now like the wine. Give the milk to the niña."

"Niño."

"Good. What do you call him?"

"Mario."

"And yourself?"

"Maria."

"I am Leo. Leonardo? I do not know how you say it in Spanish," he laughed.

"Leonardo," she smiled. "It is a good name, but of what nationality?"

"American."

"Ah, that is strange. I have heard. You have come very far."

"Yes."

She placed a water glass of red wine before him. "Taste it."

It was sour but full-bodied. He nodded his approval.

"It is not as good as once it was."

"It is satisfactory," he said and drank again. "Will you not have a glass with me?"

"Thank you, but no." She went to the window and drew the rough blind. She turned in the half-darkness and went toward the bed. "I will wait for you," she said.

He sat drinking the wine, listening to the rustle of the clothes and then the bed. He finished the wine as he undressed, leaving his underwear on.

When he came to the edge of the bed he said, "The baby?"

"He will not trouble us, Leonardo."

And later, when he was in the bed with her and with the baby, he stopped and said, "I did not make any preparation. I do not have the means."

"It is not important," she said, and he smelled garlic on her breath. "It is nothing. Come. Come."

Afterward he lay on the bed with the baby, watching her crouched over the tiny fire, poking twigs under the pot. When she lifted the lid off the pot to stir the contents, there was a good smell in the room. The baby, asleep now, did not smell good.

"I am here," he said addressing the ceiling, testing his Spanish, "and I don't know how it came to be that I am here. I am here with Maria, in her house, under the roof of her husband who is perhaps a prisoner of the Moors in Africa. Why do such things happen to me?"

"Ay, they happen to others as well. Many things happen."

"No, Maria," he said in English, "only to me. Out there they are digging graves and I am the only grave digger who is an American. I have come very far, as you say, to be the grave digger of my comrades. Though I haven't had the misfortune to have to dig the graves for Murray and Aaron, who were my best friends, who maybe died because I wouldn't stay with them. No, that can't be. It wasn't for that they died, but it's why I'm alive and digging graves . . . though I'm not now, because now I'm here and worrying about the clap."

"Clap? You are speaking American now, yes? What is it you are saying?" She laughed and it was the first time he had heard her laugh. "It is a very funny language to hear."

"Very funny."

"What did you say?" She came to the bed and picked up the baby. She took him to the table to clean him, and though he woke up he did not make a sound.

"Nothing. But I must go now." He rolled off the bed and came over to the table to put on his clothes, which she had folded and draped over a chair.

She was busy with the baby and did not look at him. "You will come back?"

"Perhaps."

"Will you not come back and take supper with me this night?"

"Is there enough?"

"It will be enough." She turned to him. "How long will you be here in the village?"

"Who knows? I will return tonight and perhaps I will be able to bring some food, though the food we have is not good. Perhaps some bread."

He put a ten peseta note on the table beside the baby. She looked at it and turned her head away.

"Be careful," she whispered because he already had the door open. There was no one on the street.

He came back that night and on other nights, and sometimes in the early morning or midafternoon, the siesta hours, when there was no one on the streets to see his comings and goings, and when he could get away from the *zapadores*. Once having gotten a piece of paper from the base *comandante* – and thinking of Mitch bearing that grandiose title was still tough for him to swallow – he had no difficulty with his commanding officer. The *teniente* was uncomfortable having an American digging graves, and all Leo had to do was wave the paper in front of him from time to time. However, he was careful not to do it too often, and he checked in to sleep every night after he came from Maria's. At first she wanted him to sleep with her, but when he explained, she made no difficulty.

The information that Mitch had left the base in the hands of a formidable major by the name of Gennaro reached the *zapadores* too late for Leo to make a last attempt to get his status changed. And now he could risk seeing Maria only in the evening, after the day's "business." He used Mitch's word all the time now; the euphemism had an ironic touch that appealed to him.

34

They came down out of the hills in single file. Against the whiteness of the snow-covered hill, the black line turning and bending was like a leafless branch fallen from a very old tree. The town sat below, and beyond were more hills, which, with luck, they would take from the fascists. It was still early in the morning and yellow light shone out of house windows onto the snow-covered street, and there was the smell of smoke in the air, though the smoke could not be seen because it was still dark.

Muffled in black and looking very small from where the *soldados* were on the hill, the villagers moved burros and sheep through the narrow streets, getting an early start in the hope of finding forage on the lee side of the hills where there was little snow covering the ground.

"Seguro de los Baños," Mitch said to Titus, who was walking in front of him. "It looks so peaceful and pretty. Like a picture postcard. Corny, huh?" He was nervous talking to Titus because Titus was a poet. Otherwise, Mitch would have gone on about how the white hills seemed like the petals of a lily cupping the yellow stamen of life that was the town. But he wouldn't risk saying that to Bill. Instead he said, "Seguro de los Baños. What does that mean? A safe place to bathe?" He was pleased to hear Bill chuckle. Titus had been moody ever since the mortars had exploded inside the convent wall. "Or maybe this is where they keep all the bathtubs in Spain under lock and key."

"No," Bill laughed, "it means 'sure of the baths.' You're right, it's pretty."

Happy to have him talking, Mitch went on, "Sure of the baths? Come here and you're sure of a bath? You go someplace else and you're not sure?"

"It depends on what you call a bath."

"Boy, I'd like to check this out. I'd like to stop in one of those houses and say, 'Negrin sent me. He said I'd be sure of a bath here.'"

"If you're going to do it, you'd better do it on our way through. Coming back, *quién sabe?*" He shrugged expressively.

They were coming into the town now and the *campesinos* stopped to look at them. They smiled when the soldiers smiled at them, they raised their arms in the clenched-fist salute when the soldiers saluted them. The troops pushed through the sheep and goats, saluting and smiling. All around them were the hills with their covering of snow, unmarked and unscarred. The houses were neat, and larger than the houses in most small villages. Mitch could see the smoke now, thin wisps of it rising from the chimneys, the women standing in the light of open doorways. There were no children; they were probably still asleep.

They went through the town and started to climb toward the hills. When they were halfway up, the battalion came to a halt. Commander Lyons and his staff pored over a map laid flat on a poncho spread over the snow. Mitch had elected to go along on the attack though he had no official standing. He had reported in at a time when staff was very busy planning the operation, and he had not given them time to wonder what he was doing back in the brigade when he was supposed to be at the Aguavivas base.

"I guess I'll go see what the Lincolns are up to," he had said, and left without waiting for a reaction. Eventually, he figured, Major Gennaro would fill in the details.

Lyons had accepted his presence without question. Lyons was in command again and they were on their way to take two hills. That was all that had to be done – two hills that had not seen any action since the early days of the war. After they had taken the hills and the Mac-Paps had taken their hill, the thinly manned enemy front would be breached, and a Spanish division would pour through to an objective kilometers beyond, diverting the fascist counterattack on Teruel. It was understood that the hills were occupied by indifferent troops who would not resist strenuously. The object was to get to them without warning in the predawn darkness. That meant no artillery or air preparation – which, in view of the lack of artillery or air support available, was not a difficult tactic to adopt.

Mitch looked anxiously at the sky for the beginning light of day. He considered joining Lyons at the maps but rejected the idea. This was Lyons's show.

"What happened to Butch?" Bill asked him. He had to think for a moment to relate the question to a happening.

"Oh, nothing. Isn't he back with the company?"

"Yes, he's back. But he isn't talking. All he says is ask Castle."

"Me? That's funny. I didn't have much to do with it."

"We thought Doran would throw the book at him. He told Doran to fuck himself."

"Yes, I know. But you don't throw the book at a guy like Butch for something like that."

"But Butch said it in front of everyone."

"Yeah, he shouldn't have."

"I might have said the same thing under the circumstances."

"Hah, not you, Bill. Not in just those words. Besides, I don't see why he, or you, should get worked up. After all, Doran is the brigade commissar. He's responsible for the morale of the brigade and that includes the brigade staff. If he has to detail men to organize a couple of bunks and other necessities for the officers of the brigade, what's wrong with that?"

"Organize? From the peasants?"

"Come on, Bill. Don't make it sound so terrible. It's just a matter of canvassing the houses asking for bedding and things like that. The people around here can spare some for the officers. Told what's wanted and for whom, they'd be willing to help."

"Maybe they would, and then again maybe they'd just be too frightened to refuse."

Titus looked back to the town. Mitch followed his gaze. In the light reflected off the snow, he could barely make out a bluish-grey column of sheep and little black figures moving out of the town, leaving a wake of trampled snow behind.

"Well, he shouldn't have cursed Doran. And having done so, he should've apologized. Which he did in the end, anyway."

"He did?"

"Yeah. I got into where they had him under lock and key and told him to apologize, and he did."

"Just because you told him to?"

"Ah, he gave me all that horseshit about the peasants and what the war was all about and all that – "

"Horseshit?"

"What else? Man, we're fighting a war. What the hell good is it if he's going to be sitting in the can defending his high principles? When we have to fight with what little we have to fight it with? That's what I told him. Sit here on your ass and rot – while the rest of us go out and do the fighting. Hell, you got plenty of time to worry about the peasants and their bedding after the war is won."

"I don't think so, Mitch. You have to live the principles for which you're fighting while you're doing the fighting."

"Yeah, but you can't live them for the next guy who is fighting the same war. Not right then."

"If you don't, right then, you never will. The war will change its character, and when you've won you'll find that you've won nothing, or only half the battle."

"All we have to do here is defeat the fascists, right? I know there's a lot of other stuff connected with it. Some comrades think we're going to make the revolution at the same time. I'm all for it. Meanwhile we have a lot of other people on our side who don't think about making a revolution. What are we supposed to do, tell them to go ahead and fight, we'll catch up later, we have a few matters of principle to settle in the rear?" Mitch swung his arm to take in the scene below. "Bill, all those peasants down there, the women and the children and their cozy homes. Like there's no war going on. In a couple of hours, or tomorrow or the next day, all hell's going to bust out right in the middle of them. That town ain't going to be safe for baths or anything else. Are you worried more about that or about Butch and his principles?"

Bill was silent, staring moodily down at the town. His eyes glistened in the half-light; there was a sadness in his voice. "I know. It's a terrible thing, but there's nothing one can do about that. And because there isn't, just because it's so tragic, is why we should insist that we be terribly, terribly dedicated and principled. Otherwise the necessities of making war will grow like cataracts in our eyes, blurring the ideals . . . blotting out the songs and slogans and banners that we carry in our hearts and in our hands into battle . . ."

He broke off. He was looking at Mitch, his expression pleading. "Don't let that happen to you."

Mitch looked away to the village, where it seemed that he could see details more clearly than he wanted to. He turned away to look to the head of the column. They were getting ready to move out.

"We're going to move," he said, "and not a moment too soon."

When the mood was upon him Mitch could philosophize to a point, or get sentimental about things like the villagers and their peaceful little town, all about to be mucked up by exploding shells, bombs, mortars, Christ knew what junk. Or he could go on about some abstract principle like egalitarianism among the troops. But he was happiest when he wasn't thinking, when he was too busy doing to stop and think.

Unfortunately, from time to time something or someone came up that forced him to think. In this case it was Bill Titus.

Before a battle, he hardly thought of the casualties that would occur, of anyone dying, much less himself. After the action was over and the dead were counted and he was confronted with the news that someone he had loved or been close to had been killed, his reaction was one of acceptance – and a bit of sadness for the loss of a comrade, not the person but the fighter, the player whose absence weakened the overall struggle. Yet, with a feeling of guilt, he would be just a little bit happy that it was someone that close and not Mitch Castle. But the guilt and sorrow were not a burden yet. He might think of the dead sometimes, speak their names, regret their loss, feel it, but not as a continuing presence . . . not yet.

He was glad they were moving out, because the conversation with Bill was getting beyond him. Also, the morning light was coming on fast over the white hills.

The fascists would see them coming. There would be a hard fight. If he had thought about it, he would not have been surprised. Even though each and every time they sat down to discuss an operation – a commander or commissar explaining just what they were supposed to do and what was supposed to happen and why – he had no doubt that everything would go as planned. It hardly ever did, except for the action at Quinto, and yet this did not surprise him or weaken his belief that the next action would indeed go as planned.

The Lincolns took the first hill without a fuss because there were only a handful of men on it. However, the prisoners said there were two companies on the other hill. *Conscriptos*, peasants and workers like themselves, but the officers – that was another matter. *Falangistas*.

The battalion headed for the hill in full daylight. A fusillade of rifle and MG fire brought it to a halt. Bill's company was chosen to lead the assault on the hill from its side. There would be some artillery, in that a gun or two had been brought up. Lyons had called them into action now that the fascists had been alerted.

After awhile the guns opened fire, a few desultory rounds that landed each one far from the one before it, down the slope, up on the crest, and finally over and below the hill. There wasn't anything hitting the gun emplacements or tearing up the barbed wire in front of the trenches.

Titus gathered his section leaders and laid out the plan of attack, which was not much of a plan: first section on the left, second one in the center, and third one on the right, pointing to the slices of the slope each was to use.

"When I give the word, we go up together. Spread out, but keep contact, keep the men firing, fix bayonets, use your grenades to cut the wire, but keep some in reserve for the trenches. I'll take the lead."

"Don't you think you ought to sit back and see how the sections go up?" Mitch said. Titus's face was chalk white, his lips bloodless, the purple of his irises so deep now as to be almost black. "If you're going to be up front, I mean, how the hell are you going to control the action?"

"Watch me," said Titus. He turned away. When the section leaders signaled that they were ready, he raised his pistol and fired toward the trenches, then brought it down, his falling arm signaling: Go.

The men came to their feet and began the assault. They reached the wire under the covering fire of the Machine Gun Company, which Lyons had brought up to support the foot soldiers. Titus was heading for the wire but Mitch hung back to see how it would all go.

The MGs stopped firing and the fascists opened up. They had one machine gun going on the first section's flank and a lot of rifle fire all along the line. The sound of a firefight came from the other side of the hill, where the First Company was attacking. The men who reached the wire first were taking casualties. The slope wasn't very steep, and Mitch had a good view of the strands of wire and trenches below the crest of the hill.

Following the action, Mitch spotted a footpath leading to a gap in the wire, presumably a supply route. He turned to point it out to Bill, but Bill was well on his way to the wire directly ahead.

Mitch started after him and then stopped. He saw that Bill was running right for the wire, but there was no way of going through it except under or over. The way Titus was running and shouting and waving his arms it was clear that he had no intention of doing anything but running right through it.

Grenades exploded all along the strings of barbed wire, rearranging their lines but leaving them largely intact. There was no way to stop Titus. The men nearest him were carried along by his rush, and they too headed for the wire. The section on the left flank stumbled onto the path that Mitch had seen, and they were going up it, getting in each other's way, scrambling and throwing grenades into the trenches whenever they got a clear field.

There were a few more shots from the fascists, and then a white flag appeared.

When Mitch got to Titus, he found him hanging on the wire. He knew Titus was dead from the way he hung there. Mitch and some of the other men picked him off the wire and laid him on the ground. Mitch looked at him briefly, furious with him for being dead, for being killed the way he'd been killed. He knelt to close the lids over the staring eyes. The irises, seen so close, were no longer violet, but grey and dulling. He got to his feet and turned away to see Doran come up the other side of the hill, accompanied by some members of brigade staff, shouting in Spanish, "We are all brothers, throw down your arms, we're all brothers."

When Mitch got to the top of the hill, he felt as though he were in a strange land. The way the enemy had left this place – the cut of the trench-es, the sandbags and gun emplacements, the articles of clothing, loose cans, abandoned guns, ammunition, scraps of paper now seen through eyes not meant to see them from this close – made it alien terrain. There was a newness to it that was unexpected, and it became fixed in his mind like a dadaist landscape. All the details were artfully meaningless. His mind re-tained the image of a strand of barbed wire, down in the lefthand corner of the panel, strung through a figure in black with sticklike arms and legs spread-eagled, two white circles in the black head, and in the middle of the circles two balls of violet holding the morning light.

The defeated soldiers were milling around outside the trenches, not knowing what to expect, and the Lincolns stood not knowing what to do with them. They were very young and poorly dressed, hardly uniformed. Some wore leather harnesses over their torsos and belts around their waists. There were leather boxes attached to the belts, and they looked like phy-lacteries that had slipped. The men were white-faced and scared-looking and small. Finally an officer appeared. He was taller than the others and in full uniform. He strode forward and, in a voice that rasped and squeaked between fear and authority, demanded that he be accorded the rights and privileges of a captured officer of an opposing army.

It seemed incongruous to Mitch that he should be acting this way amidst all the rubbish on the hill, the cruel scars in the ground, the little defeated soldiers awaiting their fate. In the space of indecision that came with the battle being so quickly over, in the sudden silence of the victory, the de-manding voice rasped along Mitch's spine.

Curses in Spanish and English exploded from his lips and the prisoners shrank back in fear. He spun the officer around and kicked his ass. The officer stumbled down the slope, sliding and falling in the snow, and Mitch followed on his heels, grabbing his uniform to pick him up, pushing him on, not wanting to be doing what he was doing because the man was not resisting, was defenseless, and yet not able to stop doing it – not until the strength and the passion went out of him. By then the others had been brought down and turned over to the *plano mayor*. And it was all over. The hills were taken. Titus was dead. Segura de los Baños looked exactly the same as it had before the battle.

35

For Leo this was a time of peace. He was not on the run; he was free of surveillance, meetings, lectures, and the threat of prison. The idea of rejoining the battalion hardly entered his mind; it was a proposal he might make in all sincerity when in danger of a worse fate, but not otherwise. True, this was not altogether an ideal situation. Obviously he could not go on digging graves until the war was over. He could not go home from a penal detail – though when he thought about it, it was not entirely impossible. If he minded his p's and q's he might be overlooked by the brigade, and when the time came he could present himself armed with papers saying he had served his time honorably in the *zapadores*. After all, there were engineers working at the front, digging trenches and stringing wire when there was wire to string, often under enemy fire.

He would be in as good shape as anyone else then. And he was now serving time easily. Maria understood that he was in the *zapadores*. He did not tell her about the graves, even though he didn't think it would make any difference. He was helping with money and food, so that things were better for her and the baby.

The baby was one reason he didn't sleep over nights. He hadn't really gotten used to sharing the bed with little Mario. Other than that, Mario was no problem. He had arrived when Maria's husband was either dead or a prisoner, maybe even fighting in the ranks of the fascists. True, she had been told that he had remained faithful to the government, but no one knew anything about these things for sure. It was a possibility that had suggested itself to her one night when they were talking about how the baby came.

It had not been her impression that her man was very political. He was a peasant. They had married and she had come to live here in his house, which was then empty because his mother and father were dead, and his brothers and sisters already married with *casas* of their own.

At any rate, when her time had come, the husband had been gone. The village doctor had been very political. Maria was not sure which party he belonged to, though he made clear that he was against the generals and the landowners. He had left the village to give his services to the front. Before he left, she had asked him what was to become of her when the baby came, and he had said it was more important for her baby's future that the Republic be defended. He had entrusted her to a midwife, who was very old and had cataracts in both eyes. It was a difficult birth, with much pain and much heat and many flies.

Mario had never cried or complained. It was only later that she discovered that the baby neither heard nor could make sounds. Perhaps when the war was over, and may God make it soon, the doctor would return to treat him. Or if not, perhaps, she could go to Barcelona where she had been told there were hospitals. It was possible if one managed to stay alive.

Leo considered taking the baby to the brigade medics, but he didn't know how they would react, and he did not want to bring himself unnecessarily to their attention. Anyway, the baby seemed okay except for not hearing or talking, and if anything could be done, which he doubted, it could wait. The war would not last forever, and one way or another Maria would manage. She was managing now. One day, after he was gone and if her husband did not return, she would be standing in the doorway and someone else would come by.

The main thing now was to keep alert and informed. He made it a point to attend any formations that involved all base personnel. He was easily lost in the mass of men, and the few Americans there would not recognize him. Castle had been the only one he had spoken to, the only one who knew about him, and he had left for the front. A crazy thing to do, but Leo supposed that that was all he knew how to do.

He had heard that Castle was already some kind of legend in the brigade. The men spoke of him as being without fear and as leading a charmed life, though it was said that it was not safe to be near him, since men had been killed or wounded standing beside him. Still, he could not be lucky forever. One day Leo might be digging a grave for him. Castle would not be the first man who had led a charmed life, only to end up in this place beside the road, wrapped in a poncho, the legend fading before the last shovel of dirt filled in the hole. Not that Leo wished it for Castle. But it was the sort of thing that happened.

As far as Leo was concerned, most of the base formations were a waste of time. They were given over to matters of discipline, new regulations, and political explanations of the current situation. Sometimes there would be a distinguished visitor, to tell them how well it was going on the outside, what a great job they were doing, how the Republic would win in the next days or next months. And about all the support they were getting from the progressive people of the world. Then Leo would go back and bury ten, twenty, or more dead antifascists. He assumed that meanwhile, the distinguished personality in question had gone back to Barcelona or to his own country; to a country that was strangling the Republic with an embargo cooked up by the League of Nations, an embargo heartily endorsed by Mussolini and Hitler, who were stuffing Franco with weapons of war.

Nevertheless, he attended the formations in the square in order not to miss any news. And that was where he was on the morning Harold Smith, who had befriended him outside of Huesca, appeared.

Major Gennaro stood erect, the sun gleaming on his polished leather and lying softly on the expensive cloth of his uniform. With his dark trimmed beard and moustache and his military bearing, he looked very heroic. He stood at attention, directing his speech to the left, to the right, and to the center, moving only his head.

"*Soldados de la Republica,*" he intoned, "we are on the eve of a great battle. The great city of Teruel, liberated by a daring *culpo de mano* delivered by the gallant armies of the Republic, is now in danger as the fascist dogs, receiving arms and men from Il Duce and Hitler, seek to recoup their loss. This they shall not do! At this very moment, courageous men of the Republic are protecting with their blood the city that was won by the blood of their brothers, their comrades . . ."

Leo knew about the blood, though the blood was all gone by the time the bodies came to the side of the road. He also knew from the way Gennaro was talking that things could not be going well at Teruel. He waited for the punch line.

"Of course, we cannot reveal the details of the blow we are about to strike, but I can tell you this: the International Brigades will share in the glory, will be in the forefront . . ."

Which is where they always are, Leo thought. *What Price Glory with Edmund Lowe and Victor McLaglen – The Stars and Stripes Forever.*

". . . we have been given an opportunity to take part in this decisive encounter that may well mean the victorious end of the war. I myself shall go to the front as soon as possible, with each and every one of you not in an indispensable position . . ."

Wait a minute. The major had Leo's full attention now. What was Gennaro saying? Was he, or was he not indispensable? Was Gennaro calling for volunteers, or telling them that it had already been decided who would go; would there be further details, appeals, evaluations?

". . . And so this is an appropriate time to introduce to you our new base commissar, who shall share with me the honor of commanding this base until we depart to join our comrades at the front. He will remain here as

the commanding officer, and you will show him the same respect and obe-
dience that you have me."

Gennaro turned his head to the new commissar and motioned him to
his side. It was Harold Smith, his arm in a sling. The major stood by his side
while Smith talked.

"You heard what Major Gennaro had to say. There is little I can add,"
Smith said. He moved around while he talked, gesturing with his good
arm. He wore a windbreaker and baggy pants tied at the ankles. On his
head he had a brown woolen cap on which a red star was sloppily attached.
Pale and hollow cheeked, his voice croaking, he looked insignificant standing next to the major, not in the same class, or in the same army. He looked
like most of the men – underfed, tired, dressed any which way to keep out
the cold.

"Unfortunately, we all can't go, though I am sure we all want to," Harold
was saying. "For those who must remain, I want to say that we will do everything we can to support Major Gennaro's efforts at the front. One job is
as important as another, and the excellent work that has been accomplished under the leadership of Major Gennaro," the Major bowed his
head slightly, "shall go forward. One final word. As commander and commissar of this base, I want you to know that the door to the *estado mayor* will
always be open. Now if there are any questions . . ."

Gennaro took Smith's good arm and pushed him gently aside. "Thank
you, Comrade Commissar," he said, facing the men. "Now will all the
commanders of the various units arrange to have your units go about their
assigned tasks under your second in command. When this is done, the
commanders will assemble in the *estado mayor* for further instructions."

Smith said something into Gennaro's ear.

"Yes, the unit commissars and clerks as well, with the roster for each detachment. It is understood? Dismissed!" He saluted smartly.

There were several attempts by the officers to return the salute, each one
different and out of sync. The men started to talk. They had a lot of questions and some of them had wanted to step forward and ask them, but
Gennaro had cut them off.

Leo had some questions, but he would not have stepped forward with
them. He would have liked for the other men to, though. More would have
become clear if they had had the chance.

Teniente Camino turned the burial detail over to his sergeant, and the
zapadores went back to their quarters to pick up their shovels and picks.

All through the morning, Leo thought of the meeting taking place in the *estado mayor*. He could visualize it almost as if he were there. Gennaro would be telling the commanders where they stood, and how many men they must volunteer. He would be instructing them how to pick the men. Call for volunteers first. If they got enough volunteers, there would be no need to go further. He would tell them, too, who could not go.

Meanwhile, Harold Smith would be going over the names with the company clerks, putting little check marks next to this name or that. This one goes. This one can't go. And so he would come to Leo's name, which he would surely recognize. Leo tried to imagine how Smith would react: disappointed, let down? Push him to volunteer for the front?

Why wait to find out? He could simply hole up at Maria's. They would assume he had taken off again, which was something else he could do. He could reestablish contacts in Barcelona. But Barcelona was where Serrota was. Maria's was better because the SIM would not look there, not knowing about him and Maria, and also because the SIM was very careful to keep a good relationship with the civilian population. They would not want to go poking into people's homes.

There was the chance that Smith was not checking lists. There was the possibility that the burial detail would remain untouched. There were only enough of them for the work they had – most mornings, anyway. And if the action was going to be stepped up, they would have more work than they could handle.

More business, he thought bitterly. "How's business?" Castle had asked. What a way to put it! He was lucky Castle had left before this happened or Castle might have been on his tail to volunteer. "This is your big chance, cousin. Now you can make it all come out right." Castle had one solution to everything: to the front and fight! Simple bastard!

Lieutenant Camino returned only to report that all was as before. The *zapadores* were, it seemed, indispensable.

"A sensible approach," Leo whispered to the man in front of him who, no matter, did not understand the language.

The next morning there were two trucks parked in the square. A group of forty men in full packs had assembled nearby. Gennaro made a speech, short for him, about how they were off to do battle. The first detachment was all volunteers. There would be others, he said. Smith shook hands with Gennaro, and Gennaro and the men boarded the trucks, *soldados* in the back and Gennaro in the cab of the lead vehicle. Those remaining behind cheered and wished them well. The men in the trucks raised clenched fists in salute.

When they had gone, Smith made a little speech about how sorry they all were that they were not among the first to join their comrades at the front.

"We all can't go. There isn't enough transportation to take everyone at once. However, we will post the names of the men who will make up the next detachment. Meanwhile, we'll carry on as before, and if there are others who wish to volunteer, they may do so. Each request will be evaluated on the basis of where the man fits in." He saluted with his good arm and turned the units over to the commanders.

Teniente Camino held his men in position and spoke to them, the first time he had ever given more than brief orders. Camino spoke slowly so that all the nationalities would understand his Spanish.

"There are no men requested from our detachment," he said. "*Pues*, if anyone of you wishes to go voluntarily, it is necessary that you give the name to the secretary now so that we may have time to find replacements. It is also to be understood that if you should decide to go to the front, it will correct your record if you may be one whose record must be repaired." It was clear that he was not a speaker, but the men understood him very well.

One man stepped forward, then two more and then another two. They stood uncomfortably in front of the others. Camino looked at them and then looked for the secretary, who was not there. He yelled something at the sergeant and the sergeant fumbled in his pockets for paper and pencil. He wrote down the names of the men while the *Teniente* looked at his shoes and the rest of the men looked up at the sky, or at the houses or the ground, but not at each other or at him or at the five who had stepped forward.

Except Leo. He tried to recall something about the men who were volunteering, but he did not know anything about them. The burial detail was not a close group. He took it all in, thinking about what to do. Each time he had made up his mind about what to do, something else had come along and he had had to rethink it.

That morning there was not much work. The men finished quickly and stood around smoking cigarettes, waiting for the lieutenant to come and take them back to town. This morning, because of the volunteering, there was some talk between the men, especially the ones who had volunteered. They formed a group with something to share, and there was a light in their faces that had not been there before. They made half-hearted attempts to convince the others to join them. Some of the men asked questions: Why? How soon did they think they would be leaving? What did they expect? And even though they had hardly gotten to know each other in all the time they were working together, they asked the volunteers to write from the front, to take care and to let them know how it was, how many fascists they killed. They asked the volunteers to send news of this one or that whom they might encounter up on the lines, a friend or brother they had lost track of.

Somehow this brought them closer together, made them conscious of being comrades once again. Those who were staying behind turned over their tobacco, cigarette paper, and cigarettes to the men who were leaving, for these things were hard to come by at the front. They passed the *vino* around and they all seemed to feel better about themselves. Or that was how Leo saw it, perhaps because that was how he felt, and it had been a long time since he had felt good about himself in that way.

 **36**

Castle did not want to stay with the battalion and he had no great desire to return to brigade.

While he stood there he became aware of a toothache starting. His tongue sought out the offending molar and tested it. He tried to evaluate the pain, to judge whether it would go away, and if it did, whether it would come back again or perhaps just grow steadily worse.

While he sucked on the tooth in the hope that he might suction the root out, Lyons arrived. Lyons wanted to know about Titus, and Castle told him what had happened.

"What do we do now?" he asked.

"Stay put until further orders. If the Spaniards succeed," Lyons waved in the direction of the fascist hinterland, "we've got nothing to worry about. They went through when the action started. Supposed to knock out their rear support positions and cut the road from Teruel."

"You going to stay on these hills?"

"Sure, we'll just turn the gun positions around where we have to."

"Well, Lyons, these hills are easy targets. The fascists know exactly where they are and will probably zero in on them pretty soon."

"Yes," Lyons said. "We're digging in in any case."

There was something about the quiet, and the way the hills showed up against the sky, and the men making tracks in the snow, that made Castle uneasy. Get the hell out of there, he wanted to shout, but he said nothing.

He went back up and watched the men go through the fascist trenches. They were laughing because it had been a good operation and because they were finding weapons and tins of fish and tobacco, and because they were alive. Bill Titus was dead, and though they would never forget him, he was no longer on their minds. Nor on Castle's, for the feeling that the operation had been too easy, the hills now too inviting a target, drove out all other thoughts.

They had breached the line and the Spaniards had gone through to cut the road between Teruel and Zaragoza. It was now noon and Castle listened for sounds of battle, but there were none.

He walked among the men, going from group to group quietly pressing them to strengthen their positions. It was a funny feeling, listening for sounds that did not come, knowing that he should be going back to brigade, doing something about the damned tooth, and yet putting it off. Most of all, it was a feeling that this hill did not belong to them. They had not dug the trenches, cut the paths, or strung the wire. The hill did not have the proper feel.

That night the Spaniards who had gone to cut the road came back. They passed between the hills and Castle heard the sound of disaster in the shuffling feet, the only sound they made. They passed by, and the night passed, and it was another day on the hill.

The chow wagon came bearing the morning meal and the story of what had happened.

The Spaniards, they said, on reaching the road, had found a fascist battery there. Their officers had tried to talk them into surrendering to the battery *comandante*.

The men had refused. But their officers had surrendered to the enemy. The men, not knowing what to do, had turned around and come back. There had been no shots exchanged, only words.

Castle looked to the west, recreating the scene in his mind. He imagined the officers who had deserted, working over the maps, pointing out the hills and one hill in particular.

"Here. Here is where the Americans are."

"Oh, yes. This is our hill. We know it well. It is a matter of dropping the range sixty-two meters. We will take care of everything."

He finished his coffee and went over to battalion HQ. "Anything new?"

he asked Lyons, who was still drinking coffee. Lyons's face was very young looking and he was smiling. "We're to stay here," said Lyons. "That's all. Hey, why don't you get over to brigade and find out what's going on?"

"They're going to be shelling these positions soon."

"You said that yesterday."

"Sí, no ayer, y tonce hoy, o mañana." Castle used his lousy Spanish to take the edge off. He was uncomfortable with Lyons, and now he thought it must be because of the way Lyons had gotten shuffled around in the scramble for battalion leadership after Bruneté. That was still in his mind. And there was the thing about Lyons shooting himself in the foot. But that was nonsense because Lyons had come back as soon as possible.

Still, it was funny how an idea like Leo's had stayed in his mind, in spite of all the evidence that it was unfounded. Most of all, the uneasiness about Lyons had set in when he had taken so long on the way to the hills, causing them to have to attack them in the early light.

"Yeah," Castle said, "I'd better get my ass back. I find out anything back there, I'll get the news up to you. Take care," he heard himself say.

On his way, he met up with the soldier he had seen in the courtyard of the convent when the mortars had come in; whom he seemed to see everywhere the action was.

"Well, there you are, comrade. How goes the war?"

"Hello, Commander Castle." The *soldado*'s blue eyes smiled up at Mitch. He was sitting against the side of the trench dabbing at his rifle with a dirty rag.

"I see you made it through another one," Mitch said.

"That's right. You too."

"What the hell is your name, anyhow, comrade?"

"Tobman. Morris Tobman, *soldado*, Commander."

They smiled a secret smile, and without fully expressing it, they knew that they were acknowledging the good work they both did, the respect for each other, the knack of staying in one piece until the war was over.

"Take care, comrade."

"You too, Commander."

Saying take care to Tobman was different than saying it to Lyons. Then, the words came to his lips as part of his general foreboding about the men on the hill. With Tobman, whom he hardly knew, the words were inspired by concern for a man who represented the ideal antifascist *soldado* – the comrade who had come to fight fascism, the uncomplaining, unquestioning Everyman in the good guys' ranks.

Castle wandered off, vaguely aware of the significance of the exchange, saying to himself, "I'm not a commander," but feeling in some way that that was the way Tobman wanted it. When he stopped thinking about Tobman and Lyons and who commanded whom, he began feeling the pain in the tooth. The throbbing ache now took over the whole right side of his face, his head, it seemed.

At brigade HQ, it was as before. He was an outsider who drifted in and out, from one group to another, from one person to another. Sometimes he would talk with Dunbar, who always seemed amused by him. But he was never able to sustain the conversation. Dunbar had been at Oxford, and Castle felt the inadequacy of his education when they talked. With the others, he simply made no attempt.

Besides, they were busy at the telephone or at the maps. It was difficult for him to relate the telephone calls and the crayon marks with what actually happened at the front. What went on in brigade seemed abstract. Moving the colored circles around was one thing, but each circle was made up of a lot of troops, some of whom walked when they moved, some of whom ran. Sometimes you had to be shooting, sometimes you were too busy to be shooting, and almost always you were being shot at; and each man reacted differently to being shot at and consequently moved differently. Then there was the thing about the enemy not always cooperating with the maneuvers you were supposed to be carrying out.

When you got off the smooth surface of the map and onto the actual terrain, there was suddenly no cover or too much, an unmarked tree or random boulder, a new feature like a shell hole or a dead mule. It never rained in the country of the maps, nor did the sun bear down nor the cold cramp. The colored circles did not have bellies that were hungry or guts that were weakened by constant diarrhea. Nor were they made up of comrades or brothers or friends. The circle that had been the Third Company of the Fifty-eighth Battalion had gone like an arrow through Seguro to the foot of the hill, and straight up the hill – which was flat on the map in spite of the scaled contour lines in ten-meter gradations, flowing one inside of another, concentrically diminishing as they conveyed an impression of rising terrain.

The Third Company circle sat on top of the hill, and it looked very much like the circle that had started out from the bottom. There was no indication that Bill Titus, who had been part of the circle, had become detached from it and was left hanging on the barbed wire just below the crest. And it seemed to Castle that Copic and Doran and the others, studying the map and taking the circle into account, were unaware of the change that had

surely come over the men who made up the unit that the circle represented. It was altogether too probable that the men themselves were unaware
of any change.

The shelling began the next day. The planes came over and bombed the
road through Seguro de los Baños, the road along which the shepherds had
moved their flocks and the women had stood in the doorways. Many of the
shells fell on the houses lining the road. The bombing and the shelling
went on together, and when the planes finished with their loads and went
away, the shelling continued.

Castle left for the hill to see how the men were faring under the shelling. He used the sheltering walls of the buildings until he got out of town
and then, in between salvos, ears cocked for the howl of incoming shells,
recalling the nonsense about not hearing the one that lands on you, he ran
crouched over to the lee side of the hill, then around to the trenches and
dugouts where the men of the Lincoln Battalion were positioned.

He found them safe, and it was comforting to discover that the fascist
gunners weren't all they were cracked up to be despite the new German
eighty-eights. The ground around them shuddered under the impact of
exploding shells, the earth giving off a burnt stink along with the stench of
cordite.

He walked along the line, checking out the positions, indifferent to the
exploding shells, holding in his mind's eye the topography of the landscape,
wondering only at the directness of the anger explicit in the rush of the
heavy shells as they smacked up against the hill, churning up snow and soil,
rudely rearranging terrain that had remained undisturbed for centuries.

The shelling continued throughout the day, stopping briefly once when
the fascists probed to see how the hills were holding up under the artillery.
The probe was easily turned back since the shelling had had little effect on
the Lincolns' fortified position.

There were not many casualties, and that night they were relieved by a
Spanish outfit and pulled back in the dark to kilometer nineteen, outside
of Teruel on the road to Valencia.

Castle's jaw ballooned overnight. *Sanidad* diagnosed an abscessed molar and shipped him off to Benicasim to have it taken care of. He was not
included in the casualty count.

37

Leo leaned on his shovel and listened to the men discuss the new developments. There was much to talk about, but Leo, who had much to think about, had nothing to say. He was relieved when the *Teniente* showed up with the happy news that they were through for the day.

After he had washed and changed one set of work clothes for another, he went off to Maria's. She and the baby were out, and he gathered from the torn-down bed that she was at the fountain with the other women doing the wash. He found the wine and poured himself a glass. He lay down on the stripped bed, propping his head on one arm, his unseeing eyes fixed on the blank wall opposite. Raising his head from time to time to drink from the glass, he thought about what he would do now. So far everything was status quo ante. Smith hadn't gotten around to him. Maybe they would get enough volunteers. If they could get five men from the *zapadores*, they must be getting more than enough from the other detachments. What was enough?

He got off the bed and refilled his glass. He went over to stand by the window. There was nothing to see except a window in the house across the narrow street. He stepped back, feeling foolish as he did so – who'd be spying on him, for Christ's sake? He went to the fireplace and took the lid off the pot. There was meat, maybe rabbit, and garbanzos and some vegetables floating around in the soup. It smelled good. He put the cover down and picked up the big wooden spoon to stir the mixture. He tasted the sauce clinging to the spoon. It tasted good. He put the cover back and poked more twigs into the embers. He and Maria were eating better now. She knew how to get scarce food items with the pesetas he gave her. It seemed to be the same here as in Barcelona, and for all he knew anywhere in Spain, probably in the world: if you had the bucks and the savvy, you could manage a fair table even if everybody else was making do with bread and water.

Maria came in, the basket of wet clothes under one arm held against her hip, the baby under her other arm. She did not smile when she saw him sitting there. She hardly ever smiled. She nodded her head and said: "Dios."

She put the basket down and put Mario into his arms. She spread the laundry around to dry. The smell of wet clothes filled the room.

"Salud," he said. "Do you want me to help you?"

"It is not right. Sit and finish your wine. Do you wish another?"

"Only with you when you are ready." She retrieved the baby.

"Later." And then, after a pause, "There are many men leaving for the front."

"You have received the news?" he laughed.

"We have seen that the important one, the tall one, has already left," she said. "And now the general."

"The important one?" Leo repeated. *This is how the people of the village rate the ranks,* he thought. So, Mitchell Castle, he was the important one! And the major rated general, on the basis of his appearance, no doubt.

"Is it your time to go?" She was standing over the pot.

"Who knows?"

"It is a thing one should know."

"In the war, one never knows anything for sure."

"You do not wish to tell me?"

"I would tell you if I knew."

"You have no control over the matter?" she persisted.

"In the army, one has no control over anything," said Leo. "One is controlled. One does not control."

"It is difficult for me to think of you as being of the army."

"I wish it were as difficult for me."

"You do not like being in the army? You would rather be here? Or perhaps in your own country? You have a woman there?"

"No. I would rather many things. Some things one would rather are not possible."

"That is the way."

"Yes." He stood up. "I will come back tonight for supper. Perhaps I shall know more when I return."

"Go with God," she said, turning to watch him leave.

"With who else?" he said in English.

When he got back to the barracks he found that he had been missed. The *sargento* in charge of quarters wanted to know where he had been. "¿Con una puta?" he suggested, gesturing salaciously.

"Oh yes." Leo went along. "But not with one. With two."

They both laughed.

"If you have strength left," the sergeant said, "go report to the *comandante*, he has a need to see you."

Teniente Camino informed him that the commissar commander himself had come to the barracks and inquired for him. Perhaps the comrade had better go to the *estado mayor* now.

Leo recalled his first talk there with Castle. Remembering brought everything since then into focus. He had become a different person, able to live with things the way they were. He had been relieved of all the scheming, planning, plotting, and shifting that had always ended back where he had started.

He was able to feel this and understand it because now, on his way to see Smith, the old feeling connected with this sort of meeting was coming back, and instead of being familiar, it was strange. He couldn't stop his mind from racing through all the things that might come out of this confrontation, and he couldn't stop himself from conjuring up all the ins and outs, the possible approaches to situations that had yet to materialize.

The first thing he noticed was the unmade bed and the unwashed mess-kit on it. It was colder than it had been last time, and the fire in the stove was not doing as well as when Castle ran the place.

Smith looked up. He was working on a pistol. He held the handle in the hand free of the sling that supported his wounded arm, working on the disassembled parts with his good hand.

"Hi, Leo. Come in, sit down. I was never any good at stripping these darn things, and with one hand tied behind my back it's even tougher. Sit down. Sit down. Boy, am I glad to see you! Where've you been? When I saw your name on the list of the *zapadores*, I really jumped."

Leo smiled. He sat down and picked up the recoil mechanism of the pistol.

"Hi. Say, this looks like an army .45."

"Yeah, it's a .38. A Spanish Astra. Look closer. It was made in Guernica."

"Yes, I see. It's built on the Colt .45 frame. You think they stole the patent?"

"Nah. Colt's probably collecting royalties from Franco on it. Do you know how the darned thing goes together? I got it apart, but I can't get it together."

"Sure. We used to have to strip 'em when I was in the National Guard. Here, give it to me. Let me do it. You're lucky you didn't shoot yourself with it like . . ."

"Like Commander Lyons?"

"Never mind." He bent over the gun, his hands and mind responding to the parts, bringing up memories of the vast cave of the armory on Park Avenue where they took turns with the pistols. They never fired them, just took them apart, learning the nomenclature, cleaning and oiling, enjoying the heavy feel of the weapon, hefting and drawing and click, click, click firing, the hammer falling on the empty chamber. Make-believe, like when they were kids playing cops and robbers. Make-believe was better. "What happened to your arm?" he asked.

"I caught one at Fuentes. Nipped a tendon. It'll be all right. Where's your guitar?"

"Oh, I got separated from it somewhere along the line. There's nothing to sing about anymore. You know how it is. You must know the story."

"Only the outline, Leo. If you don't want to talk about it, we won't."

"There." Leo slid the casement back and forth a couple of times and then let the hammer fall. He slapped the loaded clip into the handle and set the safety. "What are you going to do with it out here, with one arm yet?"

"Nothing. Maybe nothing even when the arm gets better. Comrade Castle gave it to me. He seems to collect pistols with each action. After Teruel he had this and a Luger and a Parabellum – one of those Mausers in a wooden stock-holster, you know the kind? He gave that to one of the Spaniards. He totes the Luger himself."

"Yeah, I saw it. I've been up here before talking to him." He looked around. "He had an orderly to take care of this place."

"Only one?" said Smith. "Gennaro had three. I don't need any."

"How come they did?"

"Regulations, I guess."

"You don't go along with regulations? As a Communist you reject the flunky stuff?"

"I don't know that that makes me a better Communist or not. I know I wouldn't be comfortable with orderlies. I suspect I hurt their feelings. They're probably doing something much tougher right now and cursing the bejesus out of me. Besides, the question isn't whether it makes a better Communist out of you to have 'em or not, but whether it makes you a better commander."

Leo aimed the pistol at something outside the window. "Does it?"

"What? Oh, does it make a better commander? I guess Castle's pretty good."

"When he was commanding the Machine Gun Company, he didn't have orderlies, did he? The first time he had any was here. He wasn't commanding anything here. As a matter of fact, he told me he didn't know anything about running a base and wasn't about to learn. All he wanted to do was get back up there." Leo waved the pistol in a circle.

"Oh, I'm going to have to pay attention," Harold said. "I know I'm being careless, but I go along with this all the way. We can't be doing one thing while the rest of the army is doing something else. That would put us in the same position as the Anarchists, in a way. We'd become another divisive element when the task right now is to forge one highly trained army."

"You're just going around what I'm saying, which is always the way it is in these discussions." Leo laughed again. "I'm not saying we shouldn't have a mighty, disciplined, highly trained army. What I'm asking you is, what kind of discipline? Communist discipline freely given out of conviction, or army discipline jammed down a bunch of gagging throats?"

"Neither. It has to be army discipline accepted by understanding Communists. But, of course, that's not the whole problem because most of the men in the army aren't Communists, and that goes for the International Brigades as well. It goes for the Red Army, too, I'm sure. Just because they're Russians doesn't mean they're Communists."

"Spoken like a true commissar," Leo said, fidgeting with the pistol. "Still, I maintain that it takes some of the spirit out of the troops. They learn to lean on discipline and not on conviction, and when the force of discipline breaks down in some impossible situation, what have they got to fall back on?"

"Not on each man's individual understanding of the situation. We have to achieve both objectives – political understanding plus conviction and uniform discipline. Can't you see that? Take you, for instance."

Leo had grown uneasy during this discussion. The back and forth, give and take was enjoyable for it was like being back in the Bronx or on the campus. But he knew that sooner or later the talk would come around to him. He knew it because that was what he was arguing about, trying in his attack on the orderlies, on the rules and the regulations, to find a justification for the things he had done and had not done. Now, Harold, who had been patient and had tried to handle the subject as objectively as possible, had in the end come to the particular case of Leo Rogin: the individual's decision to fight or not to fight based on his terms alone, both of them skirting the fear of the front as though it didn't exist.

"Take you, for instance."

Leo slammed the pistol down on the table. There was a loud explosion. He jerked his hand away and jumped up, his face bloodless, lips quivering.

"Oh, my God!" He reached out to touch Harold. "Are you all right? Are you hit?"

Harold stared at the pistol on the table between them, a trickle of smoke coming out of its muzzle. "Holy mackerel!" he said. "What was that? How did you do that?"

The bullet had passed to Smith's left and smacked into the far wall. There were footsteps stomping up the stairs. He got up and went to the door.

"It's nothing. An accident," Smith shouted down the stairs. "It's all right, nothing happened. Yes, it's all right." He closed the door and turned to Leo. "There you are," he laughed. "Now you see. Even an expert like you, fooling around with an unloaded gun can have an accident. Well?"

The explosion echoed in Leo's ears and his nose twitched from the smell of burnt cordite.

"So?" Harold asked. He let it hang with the smoke.

"Yeah," Leo said after a while. He sat down and put his head in his hands.

The pistol had exploded all his fine arguments. There was nothing left but the problem, and still he had no answer. What he wanted now more than anything else, more than being with Maria, was to be back with the outfit digging graves. Back by the side of the road, digging and sweating and not thinking.

As though reading his mind, Harold spoke.

"You know what my mother used to say to me when I was working for the WPA digging ditches? She used to say 'Harold that's no job for a Jewish boy.' That just popped into my head." He moved around the table and placed his good hand on Leo's shoulder. "I hate to ask anyone to do something I can't do. I can't go up with the next bunch of guys, and I don't know when I'll be able to go back to the battalion. But I'm asking you to do it."

"I'll wait for you." Leo looked up. "Get me some other assignment so I can stay here with you until you're ready . . . We can go up together." He could see that Harold was thinking about it. "Harold, you're the only one in Spain that understands. I mean about Murray and Aaron. I can make it if we stick together."

Smith returned to his side of the table and sat down. "No, Leo, it can't be done. The detail you're on now is punitive – in your case. The only decent thing to do is to volunteer for the front."

"I'm through volunteering."

"Well, I can't make you." Smith shook his head sadly. "Are you still a Party member?"

Leo was startled by the question. It was something he had not given a whole lot of thought to. Nor was it something that anyone else had raised with him. "Yes, I am," he said. Maybe some hope of release lay in that direction. "I mean, I haven't been to any meetings. As far as I know, I haven't been assigned to any unit. No one's approached me."

"But you haven't been expelled?"

"Oh, no. Not that I know of."

"Well, Leo, let me put it this way. You either go up with the next batch or I bring charges against you. We have a Party unit here and I believe it has the authority to take such an action."

"Why, what would that mean? Why would you want to do that now? Haven't I had enough shit thrown at me?"

"I don't know how come you're still in the Party after all you've done . . . not done. It seems to me you should've been kicked out a long time ago. But listen. I'm glad you haven't been. You're still a Communist and I can appeal to you on that basis."

Leo was close to tears. He sensed he had lost Harold. Party discipline came before all else. "Isn't there any limit to what goes on here? First they threaten to shoot me. Yes. What do you think of that? In Barcelona. Shoot me! For what? Then I'm thrown in jail to rot, and then shipped here to bury the dead. And now I'm about to be expelled from the Party? What for? Have any Party members been expelled back home because they didn't volunteer? So I made a mistake. I came. I volunteered. I can't make it. I can do a lot of things here that would be useful, but I can't be at the front. What kind of crime is that? And now you sit here in judgment of me. Wearing two hats, yet. Commander of the base. Then as a Communist threatening to bring charges against me. What is this?"

"Take it easy, Leo. Let's not be confused by a lot of technicalities. What do you want me to do? Go through the motions of taking off one hat and putting on another? Moving the discussion out of here when we get onto the Party angle? What I'm trying to do is knock some sense into your head . . . Make you realize what's involved. I don't think you know where you're going or what you're doing. That's all. All that other stuff is beside the point."

"Nothing I bring up, none of the questions I raise seem to mean anything," said Leo. "No one ever answers me. Suppose I just went back to being an ordinary American citizen and demanded my rights? Demanded the protection that is due an American citizen? Do you know, Harold, that I could have gone across the border a hundred times? I could have gone to the American consul a hundred times."

"Now why – "

"You're driving me to do it."

"Leo, be realistic. You're here now. Stop tormenting yourself with what you could have done. You didn't, that's all. You didn't because you're a

Communist, an antifascist, and whatever moved you to come to Spain is still very much a part of you. I know that. So why can't you function on that level?"

"I just finished telling you that that's how I've been functioning. I told you I could've skipped. Why do you suppose I haven't? In spite of everything?" All the doors were closing. He wasn't getting anywhere. "Don't you think, Harold, that I ought to be getting back? Listen, do you want me to take the pistol apart and clean it? I can do that before I leave."

"I just cleaned it."

"I know. But it's been fired. It should be cleaned and oiled after it's fired."

"Oh, yes. I didn't think of that. Forget it. I'll manage. Why don't you come to the Party meeting tonight?"

"Okay, I suppose I should. But – well – are you going to take up my case?"

"Leo, we have to. You know that."

"That means it's already been discussed?"

Harold picked up the pistol and fumbled with the clip release, then looked up. "Seven o'clock. Over at the cookhouse. Okay? Think about it, Leo. Everything can be worked out."

"Maria, are you asleep?"

"Yes." She had been in his arms and now she turned her back to him. She raised her head to see if the movement had awakened the child.

"Maria, do you think I could pass as a Spaniard? With other clothes?"

"Why not?" Her voice was muffled in the pillow.

"Perhaps we could go to Barcelona. Perhaps we can find a hospital there that will cure the child."

"We? When? How? What are you saying?" She was half sitting up now, leaning over him, her hair falling over her face, brushing against him, wide awake.

"When? It is two days until we are paid. I will have three hundred pesetas. Will you be prepared to go then?"

"I am ready now. What do I have to prepare? There is nothing."

"I will wear the clothes of your husband. We can travel as a family. It will be better, if it is necessary, that you speak for both of us. You understand. We will be a family traveling to Barcelona because the child needs care. Understand?"

"I understand," she said and snuggled down beside him. "I understand everything."

He was relieved that he did not have to go into the details or explain the reasons. He had been thinking about it while they were making love, aware that at that very moment he should have been at the meeting getting his ass kicked, his stream of thought not even interrupted by orgasm. And now his mind was still at work on the details, using Maria and Mario as cover for a visit to the American consul.

What would happen to Maria after that was something he did not want to think about. He would not leave the consulate until he was on his way out of Spain. Maria, moved by gratitude rather than love or passion, covered his body with kisses, and though his body responded, his mind was working out the logistics of the venture.

 **38**

The hospital at Benicasim was a collection of pastel villas turned to the sea and sun, and set off one from another by dark green tropical plantings. The villas had once had names like "Bon Repos," "Buena Vista," and "Vista del Mar," but now the names had been changed, and the villa to which Castle was assigned was called the Karl Marx Villa.

It was a square, beige adobe, with a roof of terra-cotta tiles cutting it off at the third floor. Castle was assigned a tiny room on the third floor all to himself. It was furnished with a wooden chair, a couple of hangers, and a cot with clean white sheets and a grey blanket. A small window looked down on the patio palms, across the road to a strip of golden sand where the waves came up gently in small irregular white lappings and the blue sun-sparkled waters swept to the horizon.

He pulled the chair over to the window and sat for a while, letting the golds and greens and blues wash into him, the silent sunlit air wash over him. A bather in black trunks came out of the water, hopping on one foot and then the other, slapping the palm of his hand against his ears to free them of water.

The bather toweled himself. He did a handstand, holding his legs straight and graceful in the air, and then, curving them down, went into a series of perfectly executed rolling handstands finished off with a one-and-a-half somersault. He picked up his towel and, still toweling himself, trotted toward the buildings.

Castle noted the muscular width of his shoulders, the narrow hips. He guessed him to be a muscle man from the beach on the Nineteenth Street side of the Steeplechase pier in Coney Island, the place they called Muscle Beach. One of those gyrating acrobatic guys he had seen go through the same stunts, whose skill he had envied, on the shores of the Atlantic. He himself was unable to manage even a handstand. And he had long since given up hope of ever developing the bulging muscles these characters sported.

The dentist's office was a sunlit room with white walls and a dental chair upholstered in black. There was a lot of chrome, the sound of running water, and the smell of antiseptics. A short, stout woman with an attractive brunette face stood smiling beside the chair. She introduced herself as Dr. Holz. While arranging him in the chair, Dr. Holz tried to find a language they could share. After a few false starts, they settled on Yiddish. She was Viennese, and her Yiddish was much more complicated than any Castle had ever heard. But they got along as she poked and probed, chattering away cheerfully. She said that all this beautiful equipment had been donated by the people of the Netherlands.

After a while she stood back and shook her head, smiling pleasantly while he rinsed. There was much work to be done, but the first thing was to extract the abscessed tooth, and for that they would need Dr. Klein, who was a specialist.

Castle was to come back after lunch. She found it amusing that he was billeted in the Karl Marx barracks, and when he asked her why, she said that that was where the VD cases were quartered. VD was the kind of thing they took care of at Benicasim, that and wounded comrades who had been treated elsewhere and then sent here for convalescence and rehabilitation.

Castle took a dim view of VD. He'd have to do something about getting moved into another villa. Who did one see about it?

She gave him the name of the American commissar, Lester Little. "See him," she said, though she did not think it would help. The hospital was full.

He found Lester Little on his way to the mess hall; Little was the man he had seen doing gymnastics on the beach.

"Hey, Comrade Little," he said, joining him on the chow line. "You're just the man I want to see."

Little's hair was combed straight back in tight blond waves. His small eyes were bright blue, close set, and his face – tanned and triangular – was

rugged in an unattractive way. Castle thought he was just the kind of guy who went in for the body-building bit. Working on the shoulders and the biceps to compensate.

"You mind if I sit down with you?" he asked. They were now inside the dining room and the tables were filling up with men talking in different languages. Little looked uneasily at the others sitting at his table, all officers of various grades. "It's all right," Castle said, "I'm a captain. Captain Castle. Mitchell Castle, here to get a tooth yanked."

"Oh," Little said, and looked more closely at his uniform.

Castle laughed and searched his pockets for the patch of cloth that had the three stripes of his rank embroidered on it; Eulalia as a seamstress left much to be desired. He held it up for Little to see, making sure the others saw it as well. "It fell off. I've never had it sewn on properly."

One of the officers sitting at the table said something in German. Little translated.

"An officer should always wear the insignia of his rank."

"Right. Listen, as soon as I get this damn tooth yanked I'll see about getting it tacked on permanently."

"You're here for dental work then?" Little eased up.

"Yes, and that's what I want to talk to you about. They've stuck me in the Karl Marx Villa and I'd like to change – "

"Why, what's wrong with the Karl Marx?"

"Nothing. Only I understand it's the VD villa. I mean all the guys in there are syphed up or something."

"Afraid of catching it?" Little laughed. He motioned Castle to sit down. "Don't worry, you can't pick it up from a toilet seat." Someone at the table had caught the drift and passed it on to the others. There was much laughter.

"Well, that isn't exactly what I had in mind. No, what I mean is that I don't want to be associated with it – that is, being in the Karl Marx and everyone knowing who's there – I mean it's like having the clap without the pleasure. I'm kidding, you know what I mean." VD was a dirty word to Castle, and though he had heard guys in the C's brag about how they had "caught the clap," he didn't think of it as some sort of merit badge. He most certainly objected to the idea that it was somehow okay or even humorous for men of the International Brigades to be clapped up. He recalled Dr. Stein's lecture on VD as a weapon of fascism. Goddamned right, he thought: a whole villa housing VD cases, men who should be at the front, casualties of careless love, so to speak. The idea that any woman of Republican Spain would be diseased and would pass it along was hard to accept.

"How come they named the clap villa after Karl Marx, anyhow?" he said.

"It was named Karl Marx long before the first VD case came here. I'll see if I can get you transferred. Dental work's pretty new around here and we stick them in wherever there's a bed. No special villa for dental work. But I'll get you moved out if you insist."

That afternoon he had the tooth pulled on schedule, Dr. Holz looking on as Dr. Klein, a tall, thin, blondish Austrian, did the job. Dr. Klein explained each step carefully in German for Dr. Holz's benefit. The overhead light glistening on his steel-rimmed glasses turned his ash-colored hair into a halo hovering over his head. There was much affection between the teacher and his pupil, and it gave Castle something to think of other than his pain. When it was over, Dr. Holz gave him a list of appointments for more work.

Looking at the schedule, Castle mumbled, "For Christ's sake, this'll take forever."

Dr. Holz caught his drift and shrugged. "It's your teeth," she said, "saved they should be."

He did not go down for dinner that evening. When he awoke, the swelling had gone down and the pain was minimal. Looking out the window, he saw Little going through his paces on the beach, his muscular body spinning in the roseate light of the setting sun through handsprings, handstands, somersaults, one-and-a-halfs, Nelsons, the whole gamut of gymnastics.

After his coffee he went to HQ to see about his transfer. There were a number of men standing around the wall board outside the building. The men were talking excitedly. The news was bad. Teruel had fallen to the fascists and so had Belchite. The front had been breached by a massive offensive; the fascists were pouring through the gap on wheels, cutting off units of the Republican army and penetrating far into the rear. All able-bodied men were urged to the front. "All to the Front." "Fortify." "Resist." Slogans added a sense of urgency.

"Well," Castle said to the men standing around talking, "Let's go. To the front. Todos. Por el Frente. A luchar. Alors, en bataille," using whatever he had of Spanish and French. He forgot about his aching jaw, the dental appointments, and the Karl Marx VD villa.

Someone said a camion was on its way, and some of the men already had their gear. He ran to his room, grabbed his things, and raced back just in time to join the men piling into the open bed of the camion. Castle saw Little standing to one side and he took him by the arm and urged him forward.

"Come on, before it gets filled up," he said.

Little resisted Castle's pull. Castle felt the mighty bicep turn rock hard in his grasp. "I can't go," Little said.

"Can't go? Why?"

"I'm sick."

"Sick?"

"I've got a hernia. I can't go."

It took Castle a minute to remember what a hernia was and try to figure out how a rupture went with the acrobatics he had witnessed. "Mierda," he said.

Getting on the truck was no easy matter because there were more men struggling to get on than there was room. Many of the men abandoned their gear, leaving it behind so that it would not hinder them in their efforts. The early boarders passed their packs back to be thrown out so that more men could get on. It seemed to Castle that everyone in Benicasim wanted to get on that truck.

Everyone but Little who, because he had a hernia, would have to be left behind to continue his calisthenics and gymnastics on the golden shores of the blue Mediterranean. It was heartbreaking.

The truck driver gunned the motor and started to edge forward. He leaned out the window, waving his free arm and hollering.

"No more! No more! You'll break the springs!"

But the men kept fighting to get on, and those already in reached for their outstretched hands and pulled them aboard, their bodies tumbling and rolling over the men already on board. Rolling slowly at first and then picking up speed, they left for the front – the ruptured front, Castle thought as he watched the standing figure of Little grow smaller and smaller.

≡ 39

Leo and Maria left Aguavivas by the main road to Belchite at an hour when the villagers would be at their late suppers and the Internationals would be in quarters getting ready for bed. If they traveled for three or four hours, they would be beyond the fields and orchards, beyond the training fields and burial ground of the Internationals. Leo carried a goatskin of milk for the baby, and cheese, bread, wine, bully-beef, and chocolate that he had saved for the trip.

Maria and the child rode on the burro Maria had borrowed from a relative of her husband's. Leo walked behind. He had convinced her that having a sick child to tend justified the arrangement. Dressed in a black suit of heavy woolen serge, a rough white shirt yellowed by time, a black serape wrapped, peasant-fashion, around his waist to keep the kidneys warm, and a matching shawl, which he used to cover his mouth and nose to cut down on the inhalations of dust, Leo looked like a *campesino.*

They walked through the night, the baby sleeping in Maria's arms, and she dozing off from time to time, catching herself and jerking awake to keep from rolling off the burro. Leo held onto the tail of the plodding animal, half-asleep on his feet. Sometimes the burro would decide that he had gone far enough and come to a stop. They would stand there until Leo came fully awake to push the animal into motion again. They made the town of Valjunquera in the early hours of morning.

The owner of the cafe where they breakfasted referred them to the *alcalde* for quarters. The story of the child and their pilgrimage to Barcelona for medical help was accepted without question.

The *alcalde* was clearly a member of the working class. His large strong hand, which he extended to Leo in welcome, was thick with callouses, but inkstained from work once reserved for civil servants and politicians.

The land had been given to the peasants and there were many details to be taken care of. There were shops and houses and offices and homes of the rich who had been part of the so-called "glorious movement" of the Falange, or Carlists or Juanistas, fascists and rightists who had fled to the Nationalists or had gone abroad when the army's initial uprising had failed. Some who had remained and opposed the elected government, land reform, and other new things had been imprisoned or killed. Their properties now belonged to the people. There were also refugees from rebel-held territory who had to be housed and assigned work.

At night Leo came to have a glass of wine in the little cafe on the square, where he heard about these things from the townspeople there. At the table with him this night was the *alcalde*: Gerardo Diego, former roofer, plasterer, and sometime builder, though there were never many houses to build in this town. Occasionally there would be a leaky roof, a cracked wall, or a wall to be taken down or put up. The *alcalde* had been moved by the child's sickness, and the need to get him to a hospital in the city.

Also at the table were the *alcalde*'s good friends, Garcia Platera, who owned the one-chair barber shop where the *campesinos* came on Saturdays for their weekly shave and exchange of news, and Jose Garzon from Lo-

grono, where he had been a cabinetmaker but which was now fascist territory. It was time for the *paseo*, and the young couples, duennas, and others
walked around the fountain in the plaza, the murmur of their voices rising
like the soft dust clouds puffed into the night air by their rope-soled shoes.
Maria and the baby were asleep in a dormitory for women and children
that had been set up in an empty stone house in back of the general store.
The men slept on the floor of a barnlike structure on the outskirts of the
town. It had been a storage shed belonging to the largest landholder in the
village, a Falangista who had preferred to live in Madrid.

Garzon, the cabinetmaker, held forth on what the "glorious movement"
had meant in Logrono. Garzon was in his fifties, a man with a big round
head, bald on top, his neck creased and reddened, his face pale, his heavy
jaw blue-shadowed. His small black eyes looked directly at the person to
whom he was speaking, the thick brows raised challengingly.

His only politics had been antifascist. Sometimes he had voted Republican, sometimes Anarchist or Socialist – for anyone who seemed to hold out
the best hope of bringing "light into the smoke-darkened rooms of my
house. I shit on the glory of the Falangistas and their black-hearted Caudil-
lo." He spat to one side. "The first thing those whores did was turn the
schools into prisons. And the second thing they did was imprison the teach-
ers in those same schoolhouses. Yes. And then they filled them up with all –
everyone, you understand – who had been for the government, all the best
minds in the town, the judge, the mayor, the engineer. Even the doctor,
who lived only to heal and to save lives, and lived as poor as the rest of us.
And not only important people. All kinds. Some member of the 'movement' says, 'this one is an enemy,' and quick, he is thrown in jail. Or your
neighbor, yes, my neighbor's son, the little fairy, Father Castillo's girl-
friend," here he minced his words, " 'Jose Garzon is anticlerical and against
the movement' he reports to the comandante. That same night five of
them – would you believe it? – five, with pistols and rifles, with ropes and
clubs, break into the house. By the grace of the Virgin Mother, I crap on
her milk, I am not yet home from work. We should all be dead now for I
swear on my mother's grave I would strangle as many as I could before they
would take me or kill me. Animals!" He rinsed his mouth with the rough
red wine as though scouring away a bad taste.

"And what happened to your woman?" the *alcalde* asked quietly.

The cabinetmaker swallowed, brooded before answering. "Ah, unspeak-
able. Unnameable. Turds!" He shuddered. "Naturally, my woman was
scared out of her wits. You can hear the beatings and the screaming in the

jail easily enough. You can smell the rot and the shit a kilometer away. We all know about the *sacas* every night. We hear the trucks taking the condemned to the cemetery and we have heard, regularly – just like the bells of the church – the firing squad do its work."

He was silent for a moment while they all drank. Leo was getting most of what he said, but he did not understand the word *saca* except that it had to do with executions.

"Yes, my woman knew why they asked for me. She kept saying she did not understand, she did not know, and other foolish things like what a good workingman I was, what fine cabinets I have made, a good father, a Christian husband, things like that. My eldest daughter told me afterward. Yes. And our heroes of the 'glorious movement?' Ay . . . They laid hands on her, they twisted her arms. They held a knife as though to cut her hair off. They stamped on her poor feet with their black boots. The *sargento* held a pistol to the head of the baby. Oh yes. It was all very glorious, very Christian. *Muy católico*, you understand. Well, she had enough sense to give in. She told them where I was at work and they left. They left to go find me, but I was on my way home. I did not meet them on the way for there is a short way to my place by a footpath through a small field that lies fallow, and they came by the main street. Believe me or no, they actually hauled off the man I was working for when they discovered I had gone! Poor bastard. I suppose they had to bring someone in for their night's work. So when I got home I wasted no time. I made off for the forest and the Republican lines."

"But what about your family?" the *alcalde* asked.

"How would they be if I was thrown in jail? I told them to say I had not come back from the job. In that way perhaps they will not be accused of collaboration with the enemy – the enemy – me – their husband and father. You see? For the crime of collaboration, one pays with one's life." He paused, his eyes far away. "Fabela, the shoemaker, would leave a little bread, cheese, and wine outside the back window of his shop at night when he closed. All day he worked on the boots and shoes of the Guardia Civil and those others, and at night he would do penance by leaving an offering on the sill of his window. He never knew for whom he was leaving it. It was just something he had heard was to be done and he did it.

"One day the patrols brought one of ours in from the forest." He looked at each of them. "No, I will not tell his name, may he rest in peace. For who knows how I would be in the same situation, who knows? And you, or any one of us?"

The *alcalde* studied his strong hands, the nails black-rimmed where they rested on the table. The barber squared his shoulders and drank deeply from his glass, the black-red wine rising and falling in slants, slopping, as he returned it to the table with force. He wiped his lips with the back of his hands. "Balls!" he spat. "A man does what has to be done."

"No," the *alcalde* said quietly. "Only what it is possible for him to do."

"What is possible is not enough." The barber finished his wine and then filled all the glasses. When he came to Leo's he raised an eyebrow. "And what do you think?"

Leo met the light brown eyes of Garcia Platero. The thought flitted through his mind that here was the first barber he had ever known, even casually, who sported a full head of hair. The plump oval of his face, neatly bisected by a nose as thin as a pencil line, his lips drawn in, his chin, thrust forward with such belligerence that the reddish bristles seemed to stand separately, demanding of Leo that he voice an opinion, or else.

"I am not sure I understand." The phrase came easily to him. "What came to pass?" he said, using another phrase that had become an early part of his Spanish.

"I will tell you," Garzon said. "In this man's pocket the patrol found a bit of cheese, a crumb of bread. They had been looking for him in the countryside for twelve days and the bread and cheese were not yet hard. So. Not content with having bagged their quarry, no, they must also know who fed him when he was on the run. Where did the cheese come from, the bread?"

They were all silent, and now Leo had caught the drift.

"Yes. They fell on him like a pack of mad dogs and they beat it out of him, more dead than alive he was when they were through. Yet it is very interesting, don't you think, that they brought him back thus and placed him in the infirmary of the jail? Of course it was not long before he was on the *saca* and executed with the rest. But they found it necessary to go through the formalities. I think that is interesting."

"It is only interesting," the *alcalde* said, his square face black and brooding under the jet-black hair, "as a technique of terror. A formula, or method if you prefer, for the control of the populace."

"That is possible," the cabinetmaker said. "Well, that is how it happened. Poor Fabela. When they confronted him with this intelligence, there in his shop surrounded by their filthy boots and shoes, he could do nothing but shrug his shoulders. Ah, but they are like vultures. 'Who instructed you to do this? How many others do you feed? What about so-and-so, and so-and-so' – rattling off the names of the others who had escaped them. In desperation, the shoemaker, knowing what was coming, could only say, 'I know nothing. I have always done this. It is for whoever has a need. Perhaps some hungry animal. Perhaps the night birds.' Can you imagine the amusement of those queers?"

"It is your fault," the barber said firmly.

"How is that?" Garzon was puzzled.

"Every last son of a whore should have been shot in the first moments of the uprising." The barber slashed his hand across the table, cutting through the streamers of blue cigarette smoke, curling and twisting them into a sudden tumult of crazy swirls.

"Perhaps," Garzon said. "But there was the election."

"And they were supposed to take it like sheep, hah?"

"Who could know?"

Before Platero spoke again, the *alcalde* cut in quietly. "We are not they. They are the criminals and they shall have to answer before the Republic."

"Ah, yes," Platero hissed, "as before, as always. A slap on the wrist. A vacation in Africa. And then what? Back again to take the lives of the same judges who spared theirs. True? Justice? There is only the people's justice. And the people's vengeance, the only way to make a revolution."

"We are not making a revolution."

"We shall see. Revolution is the only way to victory."

The *alcalde* smiled and Leo was surprised by the warmth and softness that came into his face. "Jose, Jose," he said, "if it were truly so simple. A stick of dynamite and all is solved."

"There is nothing wrong with a stick of dynamite when it is stuck up the right asshole."

Now they all laughed.

"Well," the *alcalde* smiled around the room, "it has been a good night's talk, but much too long. Come, Garcia, we are going the same way." He turned to the others. "Yes, in fact we are all going the same way, is it not true?"

40

Castle watched the British gunners lay fifty-seven-millimeter rounds into the cavalry, the small explosions breaking into the ranks, scattering horses and riders all over the slope. The gunners were dirty and unshaven. They sweated over the guns, their heads bared, grinning and shouting to one another.

"Damn it, Castle," Slater said, "Look at that lovely enfilading. Lovely. Lovely. Damn it."

Castle wanted to stay. It wasn't every day that he had the opportunity to see fascists getting killed. But he fretted about the Lincolns. Who was left? Who was commanding the battalion now? Slater didn't know. All he knew was that a shell had landed smack in the center of the Americans' battalion HQ and the entire staff had been "bloody-well wiped out. Bad bit, that." What was left of the Americans might be somewhere on the right flank. They were there the last he had seen them, but a front no longer existed and there was no telling where anyone was.

Castle found Captain Dunbar, who seemed happy to see him. The battalion had been in Reiss's command, and Dunbar was anxious to fill him in, because Reiss was dead, as was the new commissar, Parker. Perhaps some others. The rest were wounded or captured, including Sidney Rosenblatt, the battalion clerk who had stayed behind with the dying Reiss.

Though Slater, blond and thin, hadn't had a wash or shave in days, he still seemed to have everything in place, giving an appearance of being well groomed, though heavily dusted over. Dunbar, unlike Slater, had lost some of his aplomb, his uniform in disarray, the black stubble on his white skin and the redness rimming his tired eyes creating an air of debauchery.

"A noble thing to do," Dunbar said, "except if he hadn't, he'd be here with the battalion records and in a position to help bring some order out of this mess."

Castle said, "How in the hell do you expect a kid like Rosenblatt, who's all heart, to be worrying about records with the whole battalion staff dying around him?"

"It shouldn't be too difficult." Dunbar was precise.

"Who's in charge, then?"

"Al Kaufman. Temporarily, perhaps. Until Captain Lyons gets back from Barcelona. You'd better take over for now."

"Al's okay. Where'll I find him?"

"Whatever you say. We're moving out again and they will be coming by shortly."

"Moving out?"

"Moving out. Moving back. We haven't been able to establish a line. Our flanks keep giving way and we have to maneuver to avoid encirclement. And here they are."

The battalion came down through the hills, and as they came, Castle could feel the weariness in them. Kaufman was in the lead and when he saw Castle he stared, his eyes protruding, the eyeballs gritty pale blue, eyelashes coated with white dust.

"You here," he said by way of greeting, "take over."

"Just like that? No, Al," Castle said, "You can do the job . . . until Lyons takes over?"

"Yeah? Maybe. You're here now. You take over. I don't want the job." Kaufman's eyes widened as he looked up at Castle briefly, then, shifting the pack on his back, he turned around and made off toward the Machine Gun Company.

"Looks like I'm it. Where do we go from here?" Castle asked.

"Follow me," said Dunbar, "We're off for Hijar – if it's still there."

"Okay, let's go. Follow me," Castle called to the troops.

Up and down the line the weary men raised their heads. To some, the sound of Castle's voice was new, to others familiar. They followed him, and as they did, Castle wondered why. Commanders came and went, officers were killed, wounded, on leave, shifted back and forth. The troops were not consulted. Within the space of one day they had gone from Reiss to Kaufman, and in two minutes from Kaufman to Castle, who was now hollering at the top of his voice, "Follow me."

The Retreat, as it became to be called, was like a jigsaw puzzle. But for Castle it was a jigsaw puzzle with too many of the pieces missing, impossible to solve. So many pieces were missing, men who vanished, were captured, killed, scattered; towns and hills held and lost before they could be fitted in. And each man who lived knew only a small part of it, what had happened to him and those close by. Things they could see and touch and feel. But even those things were hacked up, confused and uncertain, because there was so much movement, so much noise, so much blood and dust and dirt, and above all the terrible, terrible weariness. So that after awhile they were not sure of what they had seen or heard or felt . . . except that they were tired, very, very tired all the time. Too tired to be brave and much too tired to be frightened. And afterward, they did not remember the confusion or the weariness. Each little personal happening stood out clearly like a rock thrusting up into the sunlight, the sea beating and swirling chaotically around its base. Still, for each happening there had to be a reason, and between the happenings there had to be a connection. And as they explained these things, they found causes and links, each man finding his own. So what happened to Castle and how he saw it could not be the way it was with the next fellow – for Morris Tobman for instance, who simply carried his rifle from place to place until he was captured.

Castle lived from day to day. What went on in between was not important. Or it was important but not remembered. He would flow back over the plain of that time, back across the plain until he stumbled into a hole, or climbed a hill, met a rock, not knowing if those hills and rocks and holes were the most important things, or even if they were important at all – or if he wasn't forgetting something, overlooking something, avoiding a hole or grove of trees or hill, some particularly obnoxious thing, or one that would put him in a bad light or even an embarrassingly favorable light. What happened, happened. Impressions, explanations, opinions might be valid or might not be. Might be true or half true or a reconstruction based on hindsight. Castle knew, or thought he knew, that in some instances he had behaved in such an impeccable, unimpeachable manner that afterward he found it impossible to believe.

It was all like beads on a string again . . . except here, in this case and at one time, the string broke and the beads scattered, somewhere between Gandesa and the Ebro – became men, comrades that spilled out into the valleys, rolled down the hills, sank in the river. They raced across the plain with Moorish cavalry riding them down and slicing them in half, the sun silvering the steel crescents of sabers swooping in cruel arcs out of the hard blue sky of the Aragon, of Catalonia, flat across the umbered earth and gracefully following through black with the blood of a comrade, to swing back again and again, then starting the descent, the horses prancing and galloping, the foam spurting from their inflamed muzzles, splattering the fleeing comrade now caught, raising his hand to wipe at the foam to ward off the saber, to give the clenched-fist salute, to fall on the Spanish soil like the limb of a tree lopped off by an expert woodsman. That was how it was. That was how the heart was cut out of the Abraham Lincoln Battalion. That was how Castle saw it, though afterward they would all be brave again, as brave as men could be after suffering what they had suffered.

They said their *saluds* and *hasta la vistas* and even some *adiós*-es along with the *buenas noches*, shuffling the chairs back as they came to their feet and drifted out of the cafe. Leo waited until the *alcalde* had the barber well on his way, Platero gesticulating and speaking with passion, Diego nodding his head placatingly. As he waited just outside the door, Garzon came to stand by his side.

"It would seem to me that the barber is more anxious to do battle with us than with the fascists."

"Anarchist?" Leo asked.

"It is not clear. Perhaps yes, and perhaps something of the POUM is left in him, who knows?"

"Why POUM? Why not Communist?" Leo worried about his awkward Spanish, hoping Garzon was too tired or had had enough wine or was distracted enough, or possibly all of these things. Not knowing how to break it off. Not really wanting to, because now he was talking with Spaniards and getting their various views, which he hadn't thought he would be interested in at this stage of the game, but now slowly becoming aware that it really was their war, despite the involvement of outside forces, and despite the importance of the outcome to the entire world. He shifted on his feet, dimly resenting his growing interest in the politics.

"No," Garzon said. "If he were a Communist he would be at the front. Or if not at the front, he would be working harder and talking less. That is what I think."

From Aguavivas Caliente – where the waters might have been hot but the weather was very cold – they slowly made their way from the Aragon into Catalonia. And during this time Leo, hearing only Spanish until there came a time when he often thought in the language, almost thought of himself as Leonardo Alvarez Pidal. And it seemed to him that no matter which town they put up in, there was always this spectrum of political thought. On the left, it started with the Anarchists, both the real anarchists – who wanted no part of governments or bureaucracies or army organization or discipline, who based their position on the idea that no man is able to control himself once given the responsibility of controlling another man – and those who were willing to accept a limited amount of political and military discipline because it seemed to them that there was no hope of exerting any influence without political and military participation in the war.

Also on the far left were the POUMists, who were for revolution now, the seizure of banks, plants, mines, land – which the Communist party denounced as a tactic to divide and defeat the United Front, the only alignment that could defeat fascism. The POUMists, in turn, singled out the Communist party as the main enemy, in that the CP was a tool of the bourgeoisie, a reformist party seeking only to delay the revolution, the revolution that would put guns and power in the hands of the working class and the peasantry, who would rise up to defend their land and factories, injecting a new vitality into the struggle against not only fascism but capitalism, imperialism, and that monstrosity of all monstrosities, the church. The flaw in this program was that the people apparently were not prepared to take on the fascist armies, the middle classes and petty bourgeoisie, and the rest of the capitalist world all at the same time.

And then there were the many parties of the center, which had its own left and right and center, ranging from the Socialists to the Republicans of the Left, who were on the right of the center along with the Social-Democrats. This grouping hardly called each other names except when one wing or another allied itself on a given issue with the parties of the Left or the Right. As a group, they were fighting and winning the war against fascism, and they had faith that this would be accomplished with the assistance of their fellow parties in the Democratic West. This aid was to be channeled through the legal institutions of the democratically elected government, which was the republic voted into power in the July elections of '36.

Although reforms were to be instituted in the Spanish way – which was to say some were made suddenly and with passion, and others put off to another, perhaps more convenient time – they were to be done only through legal means, by vote and referendum, through the *Cortes* and so on. They were mostly to do with such matters as education, relations between the state and the church, the liberalization of divorce laws, the liberation of Spanish women, the equal application of the laws of the land, universal conscription, and tax reform.

Hardly revolutionary enough to irritate Britain, France, or the USA.

No one asked how these countries could be driven away when they had not come near; it always seemed that they were on the verge of offering assistance "if only we do not make a mistake and do something that will support their fears of a Bolshevik turn."

Round and round like a merry-go-round.

Then there was the rightist grouping which was to the left of Franco's rightists, and the rightists who made up the Fifth Column behind the Republican lines, and those rightists who were sympathetic neither to Franco nor to the Republic and were simply waiting, along with a host of others of no political persuasion, for the outcome of the struggle. And, of course, there were the true conservatives, the legalists of the Right, who supported the government no matter how much they disapproved of it, because they believed that the law was the law, the elected government was the government, and that therefore they must support it while seeking to change its policies by legal means.

Such was the political understanding that Leo gained as he and Maria and the baby made their way from town to town, always east by north, drinking and eating in the tiny cafes and occasionally working in the fields or in some factory when called on. Leonardo, as he now thought of himself, even worked one Sunday in the fields, joining in a day of volunteer work in order to help save the crops since so many of the men were away at the front. It was a day of labor organized by the Communists, and Leo was reminded of the pictures he had seen, photos and movies of Lenin performing manual labor in and around the Kremlin. What did they call it? Sabotnik? Russians giving freely of their sweat to build communism. Spaniards now giving freely of their sweat to save the Republic . . . on a Sunday . . . holiday . . . holy day . . . the fields alive with men and women digging, hoeing, raking, weeding, irrigating . . . while in the village the church, its bells as silent as its belly empty . . . almost empty, an old woman, an old man with too much invested in immortality to give it up now, still chipping in another peseta, another prayer, lighting one more candle, fingering a final string of beads, fearful lest a lifetime of piety, paid out regularly like a life insurance premium, might be canceled just when payoff time was so near.

Mario sat on a pile of freshly turned dirt, his hands slowly working the soil, not wanting to dig or build hills or pour it or throw it or eat it the way babies do, eyes on Maria working a shovel nearby.

Leo thought how powerful the Party propaganda was to have moved Maria to this labor – Maria and virtually all the people of Corbera, where they had stopped on their journey, but especially Maria, since most of the people had worked every day of the week and every day of their lives except Sunday. But for Maria, it was an event of great importance because she had never worked in the fields before, and Sundays had been an occasion for putting her best dress on, for cooking the best meal of the week, for visiting relatives and friends and exchanging news. No one had urged her to come into the fields, certainly not Leo. But she had been in such close association with the women of the villages, and especially the refugees – the wives and daughters and mothers of men who had had to flee because of their politics – that though this had not converted her to any political party, it had nevertheless made her a Loyalist partisan. She stood knee-deep in a section of irrigation ditch, pitching small shovelfuls of dirt onto the banks, her face flushed, her black hair falling from under her shawl into her eyes, a determined, happy expression on her face; and he wondered anew at the power of an idea that was communal and selfless. Offhand, he did not know if he liked it. The dark sweat stains under her arms, the black-brown smears of soil and sweat working their way into the pores and creases on her hands and face, lessened her appeal as a woman to be made love to, but certainly made her more desirable as an ideal woman devoted to the cause, a miniature Pasionaria.

Yet, he had noticed that his initial impulse in sizing up a situation was becoming more and more one of finding the flaw, the error, the weakness on his side – it was still his side – in comrades and Party and army and the USSR and the Spanish government, and even developing a tolerance for the same faults in those outside the Party, actually being quick to find something positive in the camp of those strange and impermanent allies. Of course, if and when he sat down to reflect, and if and when he could do so with any degree of objectivity, then his contemplation of the individual and his acts, or the Party and its position, would come into focus, and he would have a definite point of reference from which to make judgments.

But now he looked upon Maria, suddenly a woman of the soil, a heroic figure, and he hoped that she would find a place to bathe, to wash the sweat and dirt out of her pores, to wash the sweetness of perfumed soap in, to soften the callouses and blisters she must be building on her palms, caressing work-roughened hands – if they were going to caress, they had better be smooth and soft. If she had chosen to sit back there in town, in the deep shadows of some room cool behind the thick adobe walls, the cool shade keeping the skin white and moist, faintly aromatic from the smell of smoke and pot over the fire slowly steaming food, he would not be proud of her as he was now, but he would bed with her sooner.

Before he lifted the pick to swing again, he examined the palms of his hands. The callouses from digging on the burial detail were still firm, and he was relieved to know that there would not be blisters under them from this one-day stint with a pick. Maria had never complained about the callouses on his hands. She had sometimes held them and fondled them and kissed the palms.

Women were different, he thought as he swung the pick into the earth with a scrunch, leaving the pick in the grasp of the earth, holding the handle, feeling the stab still throbbing up from earth inside the wood through his scaly hands to inside him. Yes, they kissed and fondled the blisters, the callouses, the hurt; they nuzzled the sweat and the stink because all these things were the wounds and the badges, the bruises and medals of hard and honest labor, of the combat for daily bread for the woman and her child. So much for the woman question, Comrade Rogin. But at least now he was thinking about things other than how to save his ass. Here he was, halfway to Barcelona and not really in a hurry to get there, because he had started out with the idea of Barcelona being the gateway to freedom from all the fucking commissars, generals, SIM bastards, and the shooting part of the war itself. He was starting to think of all kinds of things, mostly about how maybe he liked being part of all this, and it would be good if somehow he could find the will to stick with it. Well, Barcelona was a long way off. He would think some more about it.

 **42**

Castle had the battalion and he didn't. He was leading the men but he no longer knew them. He had known most of them; they had been through a great deal together. But now he did not know them because they had had something very bad happen to them that he had not shared. They had been at Belchite, and having to defend it suddenly from new positions had made everything different. And they had been commanded by Reiss, which was difficult for him to conceive of now, remembering how Reiss had been so played out after Fuentes de Ebro. Someone called Parker had been the commissar, someone he did not know. Reiss and Parker had been standing in the sun in the mouth of a cave, viewing the sudden bursts of shells, the positions erupting in smoke and flames, not knowing what was going on, trying to make sense out of the clamorous chaos enveloping them. Then one of the shells had landed just where they stood, and they were dead. Yet, for the brief time that they had commanded the battalion, their imprint on the men had been so strong that Castle seemed to feel it as a reproach. The men were strangers to him, as had been the original Lincolns, who had gone over the top at Jarama. Something had happened to them there, just as something had happened to the men when they had been forced to retreat from Belchite. They had never retreated before. It was a new experience that Castle did not understand.

Also, though he was leading, he was being led. Dunbar was leading them from a place called Abalate to a place called Hijar. The front was in shambles, and it had become impossible to know where the fascists were or where friendly troops were. Without reference points of this kind, he became totally disoriented. Not being able to locate himself on the ground, following Dunbar's sweat-soaked shirt, leading these strange men, he was without footing.

Bombers, observation planes, strafing planes, were overhead, sometimes separately, sometimes simultaneously. "Ellos!" the Spaniards pointed. "Theirs." "Nuestras" were nowhere in sight. Castle hadn't seen a Chato or a Mosca or anything else bearing the colors of the Republic in the air since Madrid and the early days of the Aragon, when they had been on the offensive.

On the way to Hijar they were caught on a road jammed with camions and troops and all sorts of gear. The strafing Stukas were on them before they had time to pull off into the groves of trees, or for the men to find shelter. Castle was up on an embankment that ran along one side of the road, and from there he could see the men scrambling for cover. He watched the planes come in, he saw the bombs detach themselves from under the fuselages and wobble free before straightening out to come slashing into the convoy – small bombs, bursting in medium-size explosions, sending up narrow columns of smoke and dust along the line of the convoy. Most of the bombs landed off to the sides of the road, missing the vehicles.

And when the Stukas had made their bombing runs, they circled around and came back with their guns hammering – kicking up puffs of dirt wide of the convoy. Castle watched them bear down, the guns sparking and crackling like bundles of tiny firecrackers, the kind they used to set off in Coney Island on the Fourth of July. The hoarse roar of the engines, the sharp chatter of the guns, and the wind howling past the wings of the planes held him transfixed. The sudden spit and thud of bullets striking the ground around him left him unmoved. He was caught up in the spectacle, the entire scene laid out before his eyes in the same way as he had seen Lister's tanks advancing under fire at Bruneté. Though he had observed that action from afar, and was now in the midst of what was coming down, his detachment was exactly the same; it was all terribly interesting – until it was over and the men came back onto the road and the convoy started off again and the men moved up along the road and they passed the wounded and the dead. Not a single vehicle, the primary targets, had been immobilized.

Later, as the column trudged along, he reviewed the situation, and a sort of fear set in, not the kind that cramps the gut, but a reasoned fear conjured in the mind. It did not last long because soon they were outside of Hijar and word came back that the fascists were already there, and there was fighting to do.

They spent a couple of days skirmishing around Hijar, sometimes inside and sometimes outside the town, and then they backtracked toward Abalate, turning off and heading for Caspe. There were many kilometers and many hills and little hope. Each step backward took something out of the men. Stragglers were lost, men would fall down exhausted and remain behind. They were harassed by enemy artillery and strafings and bombings, and each time the smoke cleared there were fewer men to get up and continue marching. They had to keep going to escape encirclement. Though they did not know it yet, nor had the word been coined, they were caught in a blitzkrieg, continually menaced by collapsing flanks, slashing motorized forays, and free-roaming fascist cavalry.

Castle was not conscious of its magnitude. He was not properly in command of the battalion because one or another member of brigade was always with them, moving them from one place to another without clear assignments or purpose or even briefing as to where they were and what the mission was. They were in constant motion without knowing why. What they wanted was a place to stand, to dig in and fight, but they could not find such a place. All around them the battle raged, and everywhere they saw troops, long black lines of men, or little clusters of men, moving across the landscape. And with the movement came the fascists to their flanks, in front of them or behind them, though it was impossible to tell the front from the rear. Complete mobility had been achieved willy-nilly. The fascists were moving from point to point, village to town to village, paying little attention to the Republican forces, only engaging them when they ran into them, and then as briefly as possible, breaking off and going around to another point or village. The fascists had control of the skies, and their observation planes tracked all movement on the ground. From what he knew of the Republic's resources, Castle figured his side, like himself, had only a worm's-eye view of what was going on. Franco, he thought, outfitted by Hitler and Mussolini, must have the latest in communication, radios and telephones to keep all units informed. Castle had no idea how, or if, Campbell or Doran or Dunbar, the men who led the column, were in touch with any higher command, nor if any higher command had any idea what was happening on the ground. The Republic had only telephones as far as he knew, and most of the time that ancient equipment – from the last war – was out of order. The enemy was on wheels, heavily armored, and unchallenged both in the sky and on the ground. The Republic, it seemed to Castle, was on foot and without artillery. Slater's antitank guns had been spiked and left behind when the ammo had run out.

That was how it was when the brigade came into contact with Luigi Longo, an Italian that Castle had been told was second to Andre Marti, the French commissar of all the international units. Longo stopped them on the road just outside of Alcaniz. He was standing there, his face drawn, a tremendous angry boil on the back of his neck reddening in the sun, asking the officers and men what unit they belonged to and directing them to their positions in the column. He shaped them up, four abreast, forming a column that Castle judged to be at least a kilometer long and led by a Mexicanski tank, and started it off for the long march to Caspe, which Longo said was still Republican territory. Or at least it had been the last time he had had word from General Walters, who was the commander of the Thirty-fifth Division.

Castle mounted the tank and positioned himself behind the turret machine gun. Things being the way they were, there was no one to question his action. The column moved slowly. He felt good being up where he could see what was going on, and where he had the familiar grip of a machine gun once again in his hands. The battalion was following Doran and Campbell, so there was no need for him to be with the outfit. He covered both sides of the road with the gun, swiveling it about, pointing it at the shut doors and blank windows of an occasional house as they went by, at bushes and clusters of trees, resisting the urge to fire a burst for fear of stampeding the column behind the tank.

They approached Caspe cautiously, saw it come into view, rising above the surrounding fields. Not knowing whether it was occupied or not, they paused. Castle came to his feet to better see a figure standing on a wall at the edge of the town who seemed to be waving them on with his hat. Castle recognized the bald head of General Walters shining in the sun. He hammered on the tank turret and shouted back to the men on foot.

"Walters. General Walters. The town's still ours!"

But Caspe wasn't entirely theirs, according to Doran, who assumed command once they got to town. Doran set up a stand-up headquarters in the main plaza, and from there he seemed to suggest, rather than order, actions the unit commanders of the Lincolns might take. He asked for opinions, for information, and for what was possible of the men under their command.

Luke Hinman, a battalion scout who had covered the rear of the column, brought word that an enemy unit had reached the outskirts of Caspe and was taking up positions on the hills just outside the town.

Doran was determined to hold Caspe as long as possible, to give the reserves of the Republican forces a chance to set up defensive lines in the rear. He asked the commanders to round up whatever men they could to mount an attack that would take the hills. Would the men be in shape for such an action?

"Christ, yes," Joe Bianca barked, impatient with all the "palavering." They were tired of retreating, they were sick at heart not knowing what had happened to almost half of the battalion that had somehow disappeared, gotten lost, or been cut off during the night of the retreat. They had wanted to make a stand, but the flanks kept giving way. They were ready to fight; they rushed into the action.

Doran led the charge up the hill, the men firing their weapons helter-skelter, yelling and cursing, hurling grenades when they neared the crest. Castle, trying to keep up with Doran, saw the fascists rise up and flee down the reverse slope of the hill and disappear into a grove of trees. From their uniforms he thought them to be of the Tercio, the foreign legion. *We must have scared the shit out of them,* he thought, *banshees howling in strange tongues charging in broad daylight.* There was no pursuit. Doran's objective was to hold Caspe.

The following day, Doran had them patrolling the streets, the men reporting back to the stand-up HQ in the plaza. Late in the afternoon, word came down that the fascists were in the streets, having infiltrated the town from its unprotected north side. They were sending patrols out, and there were brief exchanges of fire when the patrols met. The fascisti broke off contact after each encounter. The Lincoln patrols kept moving forward, while those that made no contact returned to the plaza to report to Doran. Doran kept them moving, assigning the patrols to other streets. No one, Castle thought, knew what the hell they were doing, not the fascisti, not Doran. But Doran kept them at it. All that day and into the night.

Castle, who headed a patrol of ten men, listened intently to Doran. Doran thought that his group ought to sally up the main drag, make sure it was free of the enemy for the night. He would have tanks.

"Where are they?"

"They're on their way."

"We wait for them?"

"Better start now, before the fascists get in there. The tanks will join you. Take another patrol with you."

Castle deployed the patrols, ten men on one side, ten men on the opposite side of the street, and himself in the middle leading the way. He planned to go up the street as far as it went and set up a defense position to hold it. They were well on their way when he heard the rumble of tanks coming up from a side street to their rear. It was too dark in the narrow streets for tanks to be of any use, so why were they coming up behind him? He halted the men. There was something about the sound of the tanks that seemed strange, lighter and noisier and higher in pitch than the Russkie tanks. He moved the men into the deep shadows of each side of the street and told them to stay put until the tanks arrived. There were two, possibly three or even more, but it was dark and they came up slowly, single file, so it was hard to know how many were in the column. He saw the first one and the one behind it and might have seen the third, or maybe just heard it and imagined seeing it; with the noise of the motors amplified in the narrow street and the tank tracks clanking on the pavement he had no way of knowing. Doran had not told him how many tanks he would have, and it seemed like more were crowding up behind them than he had any right to expect. The lead tank had its turret open and the torso of a tankist appeared, a shadowy figure silhouetted against the dim white of the buildings lining the street.

Castle motioned one of the men, Sam Grant, to back him up. He went forward with his arm up. "¡Alto!" he commanded. The tank came to a stop.

As he neared the tank, Castle began to feel that there was something not right about it. The paint job was too dark, but that could be the night. Still, the height was wrong. It seemed lower than it should be. By then he was standing quite close and looking up into the muzzle of a pistol and that didn't look right either. The man who was holding it on him waited for him to make the first move.

The first thing he thought of when he saw the pistol was that he himself was unarmed. He had come from Benicasim without a weapon, having left his Luger with the battalion when he had gone to have his tooth pulled. Around Hijar, he had picked up a Remington, but when he had mounted the tank for the ride to Caspe, he had given it to one of the men. The question now was how to proceed. He had Sam covering him, and though he didn't know it, Sam had brought Martinelli along with him. The tankist was now looking down at Castle and then at Grant behind him and then at Martinelli off to one side. He spoke first. "What part of Spain?"

To Castle's untrained ear it did not sound like Spanish spoken by a Spaniard. He parried the question with "And you, what part?" He kept the query to a minimum of words, not trusting his grammar or his accent.

The tankist said something he did not catch but which nevertheless convinced him that he was now facing a fascist, a fascist with a pistol aimed at his head. The tankist now reeled off a string of words among which were many that sounded like place names, none of which he recognized. During this speech, the tankist lowered his body farther into the tank. He demanded once more to know where they were from. The exchange was familiar to Castle: passwords used to distinguish friend from foe. But they had not been given any passwords before setting out on the patrol. He could only assume that there had been none.

The pistol thrust forward at him, and he ducked, shouting a warning to the others, "Fascisti."

The tankist disappeared into the turret of his tank just as Sam fired a shot at his head. Sam, Martinelli, and Castle ran for the cover of the building's shadows, and the tank's machine gun opened fire.

Even as he ran, Castle could see that the tank had had the men on one side of the road covered. There they were in a tight group and the MG fire ripped into them where they stood. Now the tank was heading straight for the group, and everybody was shooting and running. Castle and his two men moved quickly along the building toward the rest of the men, who were now crying out in pain and cursing. The tank pivoted and took off in the direction from which it had come. The other tanks could be heard grinding back down the street. He left Sam and Martinelli to look after the men and, gathering together the ten men who had been on the opposite side of the street, led them back to Doran and the command group. The rest of the battalion was converging on the same spot, coming in from various streets. He found Doran in the midst of a growing crowd of men all speaking at the same time.

Doran was trying to take it all in. When Castle told him about the tanks, he wasn't sure that Doran was listening. Doran, the muscles underlying his face trembling with the force of barely contained tension, thrust at him. "How do you know the tanks weren't ours?"

While Castle thought about that, they were distracted by the arrival of another group of men followed closely by one tank. By now the moon had come up over the hills, and in its light Castle studied the tank. It was bigger and taller than the tank he and the others had tangled with. But Doran was off on another problem before Mitch could say anything.

 **43**

Leo pushed on the pick handle, twisted, and the hard-packed earth crumbled. He brought the pick out and up over his head, feeling the sun flashing on his face for a moment before he followed the sweep of the pick back into the earth, the Spanish earth, as he thought of it: different, symbolic of the passion and bravado and drama of don Quixote, El Cid, Goya, and Torquemada, certainly not just any old Bronx dirt.

On the first Sunday of March, spring was coming to fields and villages and to the front, and spring was an easy time of the year to bear up under things. The Spanish summers and winters were real stinkers. The summers had not surprised him, for he had thought of Spain as a sunny place, but the winter in the Aragon had been bad. The cold got into his bones and sapped his will. The broiling sun of Bruneté had done some sapping as well, assisted by the chop-chop-chatter of the machine guns cutting the tall wheat overhead.

He sank the pick in deeper, tearing it out, remembrance making him swing harder and faster, little clods of dirt flying off the flailing pick, hitting his face. He paused in midswing, holding the pick above his head as the realization hit him that he had been stalling, fearful that once in Barcelona, he would fall into the same pattern of Sammy/Sebastian, the black market, passport sales, and sure as shit wind up in the arms of Serrota and the SIM. He'd be right back where he started, or worse.

He eased the pick down. There was no turning back now. They were only a couple of days' walk from the city, and only a damned fool makes the same mistake twice. He did not think of himself as any kind of fool even if the breaks had been against him – after all, that was only because of his confusion about prospects back in the States. He decided that he would tell Maria that it was up and off for Barcelona before daylight.

They came into the city on the tenth of March. The first thing Maria wanted to do was get rid of the burro, put on her other dress, make themselves look more as though they belonged.

"No, Maria," Leo instructed her, "it will go better with us at the hospital if we look like *campesinos*. It will be altogether better, the burro, the *alpargatas*, the hard-worn clothes, you understand? There is much sympathy here for the *campesinos* and workers."

"As you say." Maria's eyes, big and restless, scanned the streets: the shops, the people, the buildings with so many windows piled one on top of the other. "Still, I do not like to be so out of place."

There were fewer military men on the streets than before. The streets then had been crowded with uniformed men, and it had seemed to him that they were all looking for him. Now he wondered if there was even one who would recognize him. Maria was falling behind, her pace slackening so that she could get her fill of the sights. He took her arm.

"Come. We are not here to see the sights. We must find the hospital. We must find a place to stay. Do me the favor of asking that militiaman where is the hospital for civilians."

The soldier slouched against a corner building, an ancient Mauser carbine cradled in the crook of an arm, a crude cigarette dangling from his lips, alert only when a young woman passed. Leo watched anxiously as Maria approached and asked for directions. The soldier glanced in his direction, and Leo turned away to adjust the blankets on the burro and move Mario about as though to make him more secure. Maria, he could tell, was having a tough time following the man's directions as his arm waved stiffly in one direction and then crooked to indicate a turn, straightened again, chopped up and down to indicate the number of streets, crooked again, straightened, and then pointed to the sidewalk – there you are. But she was not there, and the militiaman knew it, and so he came over to where Leo stood fussing with the ropes and blankets and baby. Careful.

"Salud," said the militiaman.

Leo looked up briefly, touched his beret and nodded.

"Your woman has difficulty, not being familiar with the city."

"A little," Leo said.

"Well, then, I will make it as clear as possible. We are here, you understand? Good. You wish to go to the hospital which is less than a kilometer from here. So . . ." and he gave the directions again, slowly, using both arms, hitching the sliding rifle up on his shoulder from time to time.

"Yes. It is clear. Many thanks." Leo spoke sparingly into the side of the burro so that the militiaman would not detect any peculiarity in his speech. "Yes. Come, woman. It is clear. Many thanks."

"It is nothing. Salud." The militiaman watched as they moved off, and

Leo hoped that it was only to see that they went in the right direction. He called after them, "Do not forget to turn to the right on Calle Vista del Monte, you understand?"

"For sure," Leo called back, only half turning.

When they came to the intersection where they were to turn, he hesitated so that it would appear that he was not too sure, and he looked back to see the militiaman using his whole body to indicate the change in course. He nodded his head and raised his arm in a half salute before they went around the corner, shutting him from view.

"Slower, for God's sake," Maria tugged at his jacket. "You'll cause the baby to fall. What is the hurry after all this time, when we are almost there. I cannot keep up."

But his pace did not slacken, nor did the rapid beating of his heart, pounding against his ribs as his mind raced with wild and confused impressions.

Holy Moses! It had taken him about fifty seconds to realize that he had been just a few steps from freedom right there, for the building that the soldier had been lounging against so carelessly, so nonchalantly, was none other than the American consulate. All he would have had to do was to walk through that door, always open, as he fucking well knew from his last time in the city. How many times had he been tempted then! And Maria distracting the guard. Walk away from the burro, from the baby. He imagined them standing in disbelief, mouths agape, and himself inside, inside where there must be rugs and official-looking furniture, desks, files, leather-covered chairs, and cleanshaven, well-dressed Americans, white toothpasty smiles and dry handshakes and the smell of talcum powder, aftershave lotions, real coffee, white papers, typewriters, and forms offering official protection – the gateway to home. They would have been surprised by his masquerading as a Spanish peasant even down to the stink of burro sweat and shit, his own sweat permeating the one suit, the one set of underwear he had been in for almost two weeks now, smelling of half-wiped newspaper ass. He had hesitated and then the soldier had approached him to give him directions.

The grey pile of the hospital and the monastery shut out the sky, cut off his daydream of escape; he slowed his step, his heart. Hearing the soft clop of the burro's hooves, Maria breathing heavily beside him now, he eased his grim hold on the child. What difference did it make? Get the baby taken care of, get them back to Aguavivas, and himself some way back to the battalion . . . There was nothing else to do.

Their pilgrimage had turned him around again. There was such permanence to the tilled earth, the rows of twisted grapevines, the files of olive and fruit trees – lemon, orange, almond, fig – and the people. All the Spaniards they had lived with, met and talked to, drank and ate with, taking it, all in all, with calm acceptance for whatever *Dios* or the earth and sky dished out, good and bad, and with a passion at the same time for a piece of land of their own, for a voice in the government, where men had made laws that cut them off from all that was more than enough for every man, woman, and child in this Spain, a part of their lives. Their footsteps were part of the soil and the soil in the pores of their skin, along with the sun and the smoke of resined fires, moving smoothly and timelessly over the furrows, along the paths and terraces at the foot of the hills, the Ebro flowing under the bridge they had crossed, undisturbed, softly running and singing underneath. Perhaps it was fate, as the peasants sometimes said, that he had discovered the consulate too late to act, that the militiaman had come to him just then. Some things were not meant to be, Maria had said many times. It must be so, he thought, even if thinking so went against all the Marxist materialism he had absorbed in the past. Hang in there, he said, once again hearing his father saying, "It'll all come out in the wash."

 **44**

"Find positions for the night," Doran said. Again it was more like a suggestion than an order, a suggestion that turned the men loose to freelance a defense. Doran wanted to hold the town, that was clear to Castle, but no one had a plan other than just being there in any damned position they took up.

Castle fell in with Sam and Martinelli and Kaufman and Bianca and the old Maxim that Bianca and Al had carried with them all through the retreat from Belchite. They found a building that overlooked a stretch of terrain that fell away from the outer reaches of Caspe, a warehouse of some sort; it was like a replay of the mill at Belchite, only bigger and taller. They climbed three flights of wooden stairs to the top of the building and found a window that commanded a view of the lowlands beyond the town, then set up the Maxim back from the window, which was really a large opening rigged with a pulley. Sam and Al worked the hoist, pulling sacks of flour up and building a platform for the gun with the sacks, ringing it in with other sacks, leaving enough room in front so that they could get a good traverse. Working with the flour made them thirsty, so they opened one of the kegs of wine lining the lower floor walls and filled their canteens to take up to the gun position. Castle did not give any orders. They worked as a team, working out among themselves what had to be done. They worked quietly and steadily until they were satisfied with the position, and then Castle suggested that Sam go find Doran and tell him where they were and try to find out where everyone else was. As far as Castle knew, there was no battalion, and if there was, then it was functioning directly under Doran. He volunteered for the first watch, and posted himself by the window while they made pallets out of empty sacking and went to sleep along the far wall.

He sipped the wine, good strong *vino rojo del campo*, and counted stars in the night sky. A shell burst here and there, an occasional flurry of rifle fire, a roll of grenades exploding, but as the night wore on, these intrusions became less frequent, and the lonely bursts only served to accent the stillness.

Sam came back and whispered that he had found Doran. Lyons had been with him and someone called Gates. Gates, Sam said, had a big reputation on the southern front around Cordoba. Others had come back, and the situation seemed well in hand. Doran had no specific orders for the gun or for Castle.

Castle tried to sort everything out – Doran taking over the battalion, Lyons's return as nominal battalion commander, the arrival of Gates. He thought he should be thinking about where that left him and that maybe he should be back with brigade to see where he fit – in or out. He gazed out the window and thought about the tank in the dark street and the men it had nailed against the wall. He listened to the sleeping sounds of the men in the room and wondered what the morning would be like. The gun sitting on top of the white flour sacks looked like some kind of displaced monument.

Bianca, who had stood the last watch, woke them. "Come look at this," he said, motioning them to the window. Below and directly in front of their position there was a railroad station. A wooden platform, partially roofed over, with a small building at one end, and a scattering of hand trucks and wagons nearby. Several men in bright red berets appeared from behind the building. About eight hundred meters, Castle said, the words coming to his lips reflexively.

"Who wears red berets?" Sam asked.

"Navarrese. Requettes, Carlists – who knows?" Castle said.

"What'll we do?"

"We water these sacks down before we do anything."

"Right."

"Where do we get the water?"

They looked at each other. "No water, huh?" Castle said.

"Hell no," Bianca said. "I looked all over last night, the pump is dry. There ain't nothing but wine. Wine and – "

"Like in Belchite. Let's get a barrel up here and pour it on the flour. That'll do it," Castle said.

"Oh, what a fucking waste," Kaufman groaned.

"Come on, let's get it. Joe, you stay up here and keep your eye on the bastards." Castle led the men down the stairs.

"Hey, see if you can rassle up some grub," Joe hollered after them.

The hoist was out – using it would give away their position. They couldn't all get behind the barrel on the narrow stairs, so Martinelli offered to see if any chow had come up to brigade. "But don't start anything until I come back." He wouldn't leave until they promised.

"But for Christ's sake, hurry," Al said, "Joe's gotta have his breakfast."

They managed to get the keg up the stairs, and then they had a debate as to how to wet down the sacks, settling on an empty ammo carrier. They filled it from the bung hole, tipping the keg; the smell of the wine, new and bright red, filled the room as it turned the flour sacks pink. They kept at it, swigging some as they went along, gargling with it and spitting it out, rinsing out their mouths, scrubbing their teeth with the wine and the tips of their fingers.

They had been in a steady grind retreating from Belchite to Caspe, a week of fighting and running and digging and fighting and marching and running and seeing their numbers dwindle, their flanks crumble, their officers killed, but now they were spraying wine all around. The fascists in the red berets were moving up and down the railroad platform below them, and they were up here behind the thick walls of the warehouse, unseen, unsuspected with the gun ready to go. Where the hell was Martinelli? Though Castle did not feel it as much as the others, he knew what Sam meant when he said, "Man it's good to be somewhere instead of retreating all the time." After all, the Americans had come to Spain to defeat fascism. That was the whole point, as though setting that goal was the same as achieving it. As though loudly singing "We are the fighting antifascists" was training enough to do the job.

They had been shock troops in attacks, in defense, always where the going was toughest. They had been moved laterally and forward and had stood fast, but had never before retreated. They had launched attacks that had failed and they had had to come back to where they'd started, but they had never surrendered a position to the fascists. Not that they were unique in this. The Europeans were much more intensely motivated than the Americans. No matter how real fascism was to the Americans, it could never have the immediacy it had for these comrades for whom defeat meant death.

Sam and Martinelli arrived toting cold coffee and three loaves of bread, with word from Doran that they were to hold their position. Caspe was to be defended, period.

"Whatever that means," Sam said. They did not want to think about it, and besides, they were hungry. They dipped the bread in the wine and washed it down with the coffee, keeping an eye on the red berets down at the depot.

Joe was the only one drinking with any sense of decorum, taking it in small swallows with his lips pressed against the canteen.

Bianca pounded on the wine-wetted flour sacks to see if his flattened hand would raise a cloud. His palm smacked down like a wet towel. He settled himself behind the Maxim. They had a democratic discussion about the range, took a vote, and settled on seven hundred meters. Al was on one side of the gun and Martinelli on the other, Al feeding the belt and Mart pulling it through, folding the empty end into the ammo carrier that had served to spray the wine on the sacks. Sam and Castle opened up a case of ammo and prepared to refill the empty belt. They were all set to go, but when Joe fired a first short burst, Castle and Sam jumped in surprise.

There were three red berets down on the railroad platform, one talking to the other two. But the red berets just went right on, undisturbed.

Al said, "You were short."

"No, he was over," Sam argued.

"Make up your goddamned minds," Joe complained. "Look at that, now they're taking off."

One of the red berets walked off in one direction and the other went to the opposite end of the platform. The third seemed to watch first one and then the other. Whatever they were up to, it was obvious that they had not been disturbed by the initial burst. Castle could make out more details on the platform where the sunlight now slanted in under the open roof.

"You guys mind if an old gunner gives the range? Try 600, 650 is better – 650, Joe."

Bianca set the slide at 650 and waited. In a little while the one beret was joined by three more. When they had gotten into a satisfactory tight little group, Joe tried another burst. The red beret who had been talking and waving his arms stopped and looked at some point to his side. The group milled around in a tight shuffle.

Joe adjusted and fired a longer burst. The arm-waving red beret dropped. The others seemed to do a little dance.

"Another tick to the right," Castle called. Joe hit the side of the gun with the heel of his hand and fired a short burst and then another longer one. Two of the red berets went into a crouch, looking in their general direction.

"Half a tick . . . less back . . ." Castle called.

Joe tapped the magazine lightly on its side and fired a long burst. He lowered the muzzle a degree on the screw and fired another long burst. They were all down now. Joe kept firing.

"Here comes some more," Castle called. Four or five men came from behind the station building, walking fast toward the fallen men, their red berets bright in the sun.

"We see them, you don't have to yell," Al hollered. The gun hammered away. One of the original group got up and started pulling on one of the others. The men who were coming up joined in to haul the others off behind the building. They seemed to be walking between the bullets in the cone of fire, walking fast, not running, getting the men who had been hit out of there. Joe got one more before they all disappeared behind the building.

"Goddamn it, what am I firing, blanks?" Joe cursed.

"You got three or four . . . what the hell," Sam said.

"Look," Castle pointed, "There's a couple, right there next to the building. They're trying to spot us."

Joe moved the gun over and fired another burst. Two men who had come out to stand in the shadow of the building, trying to locate the gun, disappeared. Castle could see the dust chip off the building where the burst had caught it. "Good shooting, Joe."

"Did I get 'em?" Joe asked.

"Yeah," Castle said, though he wasn't sure. The men had been there and then they were gone. He was pretty sure that they would not show up again whether they had been hit or not. But he was wrong. The Navarrese – they had decided the red berets were Navarrese – had some sort of job to do there in the railroad station and they went about doing it, moving in ones and twos, moving fast but not running, up and down the platform, in and out from behind the building, across the tracks, carrying objects that he could not make out, coming back empty-handed.

Martinelli and Castle took turns spelling Joe and Sam and Al. They all operated the gun with varying degrees of success. They would fire and a man would fall. But then sometimes he would get up again, or he would lie there and when they'd shoot at someone else walking in another direction and then look back to where the first man had fallen, he'd be gone. Or sometimes one would be walking and they would let go a burst and he'd seem to jump and then run off behind the building or below the far edge of the platform, and you could score a hit but you couldn't be sure. But they kept coming and they kept moving around. Castle figured the rifling in the barrel of the gun was long gone. Anything they hit would be by pure chance.

Occasionally there would be a long time when the platform was empty. Then they quenched their thirst with the wine and nibbled on the bread left from the morning. There was no word from Doran. They heard cannonading to the north and south of them, but not much firing from the town itself or into the town, and as far as they could tell they were doing the only firing from the buildings on their street.

"Navarrese," Sam said, "dumb, brave, Roman Catholic Carlists. Sticking their asses out for some jerk who claims the crown of Spain. My God. Don't they know it's the twentieth century? What the hell do they want with a king?"

"Everybody's looking for a father," Martinelli said.

"Someone to kick 'em around. Someone to whom they can say 'yes sire, no sire' . . ." Sam went on.

"A sus ordenes mi cagen rey," Castle put in. "Let me kiss your royal highness's ass. Well, we'll defeat them and then the ones we defeat will not have the opportunity to practice fascism. Like when we took the hill at Segura de los Baños."

"Them, those miserable bastards?"

"Yeah, they didn't look very different, did they? They looked just like the Spaniards on our side. And of course they are, mostly *campesinos*, just like them. How stupid of me. What kind of fascism would they practice? I felt sort of disappointed afterward, when I saw how they looked like everyone else in Spain. I don't know what I expected a *soldado* on the other side to look like. Except that arrogant sonofabitch'n officer. For a minute I felt – here was a real fascist. A practicing believer. Not like those kids who just happened to be on the wrong side of geography. Still, when I kicked his ass down the hill, thinking of Titus, by the time I had kicked him a couple of times, it didn't mean anything to me anymore."

"Speaking of Titus – now there's a better example," Martinelli said. "Not that I'm downgrading you, Castle. But he was very intense about this. Let's face it, we all get pretty involved now that we're here, off the streets and out of the meeting halls. In struggle the involvement is staying alive, and part of that is killing the other guy, right? If you have to take a position away from them, then you gotta rout him out or he's going to drop you right on his doorstep. But with Titus it wasn't some vague 'them' as it gets to be with us once the shooting starts . . ."

"Speak for yourself, comrade. They ain't no vague 'them' to me. They're the enemy . . . they're the fascists and Nazis – "

"Why, bullshit man, you just got through telling us how at Segura – "

"That was at Segura – "

"And what about those Navarrese down there, they're just 'them.' What else? You can't call them fascists. Jerks, yes. And monarchists . . ."

"Which is the same thing as being a fascist under the circumstances. They're out there shooting at us, taking the country away from the people. Look at them. The cocky bastards."

Joe loosed a burst at a pair of red berets that came quickly into view from behind the station building and disappeared into the shadows, which had been deepening as the sun rose higher in the sky. Now it was dark under the shadow of the roof covering the platform, and the Navarrese had piled hand wagons and crates some twenty meters from the side of the building. Whatever they were up to was hidden from sight.

"Keep an eye on that space," Mitch said, unnecessarily. There wasn't anything else to do now, so they lit up and smoked, careful to shield the butts in their palms for fear the glow of the cigarettes could be seen from the depot in the dark of the room.

45

"Getting back to Bill Titus . . ." Martinelli wasn't finished with the subject Mitch had broached. "He really started to hate them with a passion at Teruel. Not with the head alone, not on the basis of a political assessment, of where they stood on class struggle, or even in terms of the United Front versus fascism, all that stuff. You see, they had dropped those mortars in on his men, you were there Castle, you saw how he was. But that was nothing. I had to live with him afterward, and the poor bastard brooded, and blamed himself for getting his men killed. And then he just had to do something for the guys that got killed, for having gotten them killed. So he had to work up a real gut hatred for the fascists, you know what I mean. You know Titus. That was something pretty hard for him to do, being a poet, and all that love for mankind he was always talking and writing about. So he began to talk about them, calling them vermin, inhumane gorillas – apes he called them. That's what he went charging up that hill against, lice and apes."

"I wonder if he could've sustained that kind of hatred had he come face to face with them?" Sam said.

"The faces aren't the important thing," Al said impatiently. "There's only one face involved here and that's the face of fascism. In my opinion," Al became thoughtful, "a guy like Titus understood why we, Yanks, pardon me, fear and hate fascism, because no other people has more to lose."

"Whoa. Wait just a bloody minute," Castle said. "Leave us not forget all the other chaps." The wine he had been sipping through all this had made him light-headed enough to imitate Dunbar and Sam Wild, especially Wild. "That's the trouble with you bloody Yanks," he chirped, "you move in and take over on the basis of some kind of moral superiority you imagine you have over everyone else. I suppose you'd prefer to have a Yank like Doran instead of a Frenchman like Marti running the IBs."

"Which might not be a bad idea," Bianca muttered.

"Why, what's wrong with the way Marti is running it?" Castle said.

"'What's wrong!' he asks. The fascists are running our asses off and he wants to know what's wrong."

"Hell, you're not saying it's Marti's fault," said Sam. "Listen, brother, if it was the other way around, he'd be getting the credit for it, so now let him take the rap."

"You're getting to be a real screwball. What difference does it make, credit or no credit. Is it Marti's fault that the fascists have all that shit to throw while we have nothing? Is it his fault that the so-called Western democracies are strangling the Republic? What kind of nonsense is that?" Castle demanded. "Listen, don't give me that bloody rot. Sure all those bigger things are . . . are the big things, but there's still the possibility of good, bad, and indifferent leadership, even here . . . And the difference, even if it doesn't mean victory, can be the difference." Castle began to lose his way again. ". . . if the leadership is good enough . . . to make the most out of what we have . . . and in the long run that can affect the bigger picture so that a change is brought about in one's favor."

With that they all fell silent. Beyond the opening all was quiet. They had talked themselves out about leadership, Castle realized, without reaching the top, the people who were running the country, running the war. There had been Prieto and Azana and Miaja and Caballero – he wasn't sure of the order in which they had served as premiers – and now Negrin. And in the military there were Rojo and Lister and Campesino, Modesto and Galan. Hell, all those names had been featured in the songs they had sung at one time or another, and Diaz and La Pasionaria of the Partido Comunista. And Durruti, who was supposed to be a good anarchist, one who fought for the Popular Front. All those figures that came and went in the Popular Front each had their agenda and that, Castle opined, watered the *vino* sure as hell.

"Well, we haven't lost the war yet," he said, and they all looked at him.

"That may be so," Sam said, "but if we don't get something to eat pretty soon, we might."

"Nothing until tonight," Martinelli said.

"What's tonight?" said Al.

"How do I know. They didn't pass out menus."

"It better be hot," Bianca growled. "A man has to get something hot in his stomach once in awhile."

"Yeah, how about a huge bowl of steaming chicken soup with matzo balls floating around," said Mitch.

"Who ever heard of matzo balls that float?"

"Ah, the way my mother made them, light as air, they float . . ."

"You mean kreplach," objected Sam.

"If I meant kreplach, I'd say kreplach. Now kreplach ain't bad either but it's getting around matzo ball time and that's what I'm ordering."

"What the hell are kreplach?" demanded Joe.

"Kreplach? Kreplach are like raviolis, just the same stuffed noodles, and now that you mentioned raviolis I'll take mine in spaghetti sauce with oregano and parmesan sprinkled on them," said Sam.

"After the matzo ball soup – no, no, before the soup I've got to have my chopped herring . . ."

"Chopped liver, you mean, dripping with chicken fat on a piece of Jewish rye . . ."

"You order what you want and I'll order what I want, all right?" said Mitch. "I want the herring with apples mixed in, and hard-boiled eggs. And then after that, and the soup, comes the roast chicken and rice pudding with prunes baked in and the sweet potato and carrot *tsimis* – wait, don't stop me, I'm not finished yet."

"I just wanted to ask you, dark meat or white?"

"Oh, you sonofabitch. This is my chicken, I get to get any part I want. The leg, the thigh, the bones so soft I can chew the joints off and suck the marrow out of them, and then for dessert thin slices of white meat with the crisp brown skin of the breast covering them. Now what?"

"How about the gravy?" said Al.

"Screw the gravy. You take the gravy."

"What do you mean, the white meat for dessert? No dessert?" said Sam.

"Of course there's dessert. The white meat is just dessert for the chicken course. Don't you know nothing? Dessert. Honey cake, brown and sweet with shelled almonds baked in. Sponge cake all yellow and gold . . ."

"Dipped in a little cherry schnapps . . ."

"Stop, you're killing me."

"Ain't there no more bread left?"

"Martinelli, why don't you go check," said Joe, "maybe they brought something up."

"If they had, they would have let us know."

"Hell, I don't think they even know we're here."

The Maxim jumped as Joe thumbed the trigger. He swept the gun from side to side in one long sweeping burst.

"What was that for?" Castle asked, seeing no movement down on the platform.

"That was to let them know we're here. Also to shut you up."

"That kind of talk is pure torture," Al said.

"Ahh, what kind of torture. You ain't never had that kind of food," said Castle.

Joe threw the bolt and pulled the rest of the belt through. He flipped the lid up and, working the bolt with one hand, he twisted the lock up and off. Wiping it with a rag he examined the head of the firing pin. "Whatta ya think? I landed on board ship right outta my mother's womb? I had a life before I met you, you know."

Al Kaufman was indignant. "It ain't been shipside hash all my life."

"I wonder if I can hit him from here with my rifle." Sam was squinting through the sights of the Remington.

"You might hit him but you'll hardly dent him at this range," said Castle.

"This thing's supposed to kill at a thousand meters or more."

"Only by accident."

Castle could see the figure that Sam was following. Wham. Sam let go a shot and the figure kept on walking.

"Not even close. How long you going to have the gun down, Joe?"

"Long enough to clean it," Joe replied, holding the barrel up to his eye and squinting at the sun through it. "There ain't much rifling left in this old barrel."

Al was already removing the spare barrel from his pack. Joe held that up and looked through it. "Not much better, but some. Here, start cleaning this one – "

"But you just said it wasn't worth it – "

"This is all we have. Clean it. It's better than nothing."

Wham. Sam fired again, and when they turned to look toward the station, they could see that a man was down and then there was a flurry around him as two or three others came out from behind the building to pull him away.

"Bueno," Sam said, stroking the rifle. "That must be the twelfth fascist I got for sure since I've been in action."

"There aren't many who can make that claim."

"And that's with the rifle . . . that's not counting the MG."

"When did you start counting?" asked Castle.

"At Fuentes. You remember Murray. Well, he went into a long speech one day about how war was nothing more than marching up and down, backward and forward, over hill and over dale. That nobody ever shot anybody else that they knew of. Just a lot of firing on both sides and maybe someone got hit and maybe they didn't and you never knew . . . except for the casualty lists. But you had no way of relating yourself to a statistic. So I went back in my mind to Bruneté and started to recall all those I was sure of because I knew he wasn't right. Maybe that was the way it was with him.

I don't think he could see much through those glasses of his anyway. So there were two I was sure of at Bruneté. And then none at Quinto and a couple at Belchite and two at Fuentes . . ."

"You mean you saw someone to shoot at, at Fuentes?" Castle asked.

"That's right."

"Where, from our trenches?" Castle really wanted to know, because that had been his great frustration at Fuentes, not seeing anything to shoot at.

"Yeah, from our trenches. In the morning. They were out digging trenches. Early in the morning. I got one one morning and one the next morning . . ."

"Hell, we were up early and late and all day, right, Joe? Did you ever see anyone? I mean a real live walking fascist to shoot at?"

"We fired at positions."

"I don't mean that. I mean like here. See one and shoot at one . . . I'm not even talking about hitting him. Just seeing him."

When Joe didn't answer, Sam went on, "Well, that's tough. That one was my twelfth."

Castle brooded over it. The sun was coming through the opening now and slanting under the roof of the platform. They could see the Navarrese had gotten two piles of whatever they had been stacking completed. There was a space between the piles, and as Castle watched the sun coming through the space, the pattern of light changed, the bottom half was cut off. "Hey, look!" he pointed, "between the piles. They just moved something in there . . . Christ! It's a tank. They brought up a tank to get at us. Look. The gun's swinging . . . see it?"

"Yeah, maybe that's the same tank . . ." Sam said softly. "Yeah."

They watched the eye of the gun looking for them.

"Al?" Castle said.

"Yeah?"

"You have any armor-piercing bullets?"

"Yeah."

"Wait," Joe turned to him. "You'll ruin the barrel for sure . . ."

"How come? They're made for the gun, aren't they?"

"They knock the shit out of the rifling . . ."

"Get them out." Castle moved to Al's side and started to slip the cartridges out of the belt. "Come on, get them out," he said to Al.

Al opened one of the cases with yellow markings on the lid, baring the boxes of shells, each shell with a dab of yellow on the point. He passed a handful to Castle. Castle pushed the shells into the belt, getting them all the way in and being careful that they went in evenly so that the gun would not jam.

"You know," he said, "This is a good place to be. High and dry. No one knows where we are. The company's good, the conversation's interesting, and the fascists're right down there where we want them." He moved behind the gun, Joe vacating the position without a word. He settled down behind the Maxim. The grips felt big and hard in his hand. He knew they were all thinking that if he fired now, the tank men would spot their location from the muzzle flash and their cannon would have no trouble zeroing in. But he had always been curious about the armor-piercing bullets. They were supposed to punch a hole in the tank and then the punched-out metal and the special steel of the bullet were supposed to bounce around, ricocheting off the walls of the tank, stabbing holes into the crew as it twanged off the walls. Maybe it was the same tank that had cornered them on that dark street. He lifted the safety with his left thumb, as he sighted in on where he thought the tank driver might be, just below the turret. He tapped the trigger once. One round.

The whole world seemed to stop dead. There was no way of telling whether he had hit the tank. In the stillness that followed, the scene became a part of Castle's life, entering his head, and he knew it would stay there as long as he had a head. The moment detached itself from time and place. Himself behind the gun in a cube suspended in midair, a cube of sunlight and shadows, from which a narrow shaft of vision went directly to the tank, and that was all there was in the whole world. He waited for some movement to clue him in to the next step. The tank remained fixed, its gun motionless. And then there was a change in the shadow behind and above the tank. Another tank was coming up behind the one he had fired at. Then there were men between the tanks and all at once they knew that the second tank had come to pull the first one out. Castle thumbed the safety and fired a burst and then another. The men around the tanks scrambled and dropped from view.

He held his fire and waited. He was being sparing, hoping that they would not be able to zero in on the short bursts. Neither tank moved. "I'll be goddamned," he said. "Those things really work."

"Yeah," Sam said, "give them another burst. Go ahead."

"What for?" Bianca said, "He's nailed them. Don't forget that's the gun's last barrel that's halfway any good."

The sun had just touched the top of the hills facing them in the west, and shadows were filling the valley below, the railroad station, and the room they were in. "I think that's it for the day. Unless they move."

"They ain't going to move," Joe said. "Hey Martinelli, why don't you get your ass over to see if chow's come up."

Then Joe urged Castle away from behind the gun. He cleared the chamber as before, and, as before, started to strip the gun in preparation for cleaning it. "Reload the belts. Change 'em to one antitank every five slots," he said to Al.

Castle got out of his way and Martinelli came over and gave him his rifle. "Here. I'm going to see what the chow situation is like."

"Yeah. Get it back before it gets cold, huh?"

"I'll run all the way."

Castle thought it was peculiar how one guy got associated with food so that when you thought of him you thought of food. And he, in turn, accepted it without complaint.

Kaufman and Joe worked over the gun silently, Al's face a bluish-grey in the fading light, Joe's a bluish-black. They were unshaven and dirty because there was no water to wash with, just the wine, and you couldn't do more with that than drink it, or use it in the water jacket of the gun, or keep the dust wetted down. They were dirty looking, yet everything around them looked clean and tidy. They had spread empty sacking, and one of the MG barrels was laid out on the sacking while Al worked a patch through on the other one. Joe had the bolt taken down and spread out before him. He picked up each part separately and cleaned and oiled it. Then he reassembled and wrapped it in an oily rag and put it to one side. He went to work on the back plate and trigger assembly.

Al looked through the barrel he had been cleaning and put it down. He picked up the spare and ran a rag through it, held it to his eye and put it back. He opened a belt carrier and began unlapping the belt, carefully checking each round as he did so. Over in a corner Sam had settled on the floor, his back against the wall, his head resting on his arms, folded on his drawn-up knees. He slept that way, his rifle between his legs, the barrel protruding somehow past his right ear, in one tight little package so that his hunger would not be awake and bothersome. Joe would not sleep, or eat, until the gun was cleaned. It was getting dark fast, now that the sun had dropped below the hill. The sounds of motors and grinding gears and clanking tracks came distantly to them. The tanks would not be looking for them again. But to the north and south, the cannonading was closing in.

In the morning they got everything ready to leave. They left the gun for last. It sat poised on the flour bags, now a dull red from successive wettings, like a green-patinated monument on a red granite pedestal, stolid, silent, and imposing, as they moved around it packing their gear. Martinelli had come back with word the night before that they would be pulling out just as soon as the lines behind them were set up, before morning. But now it was morning and the word had not come. Down at the station the tanks had not made an appearance, nor had the Navarrese in their red berets. Martinelli was leaving to see if any coffee had been brought up, and also what the latest was. Sam went with him to double-check. It was awfully quiet, and the absence of gunfire made them nervous. Castle found a ladder leading to a trapdoor that opened on the roof of the building. He scaled the ladder and lifted the door just far enough to see that the hills surrounding the town were quiet and seemed unoccupied. There was no sign of action anywhere. The sky was remote, a pale blue. The feeling of being suspended in the middle of nothing overcame him again. He returned to the room to find Joe and Al breaking the gun down.

"Can't see anything from there," Castle said.

"We're pulling out," Joe said. "Nobody's come back and it's too fucking quiet. They must've gone by now. This town sounds empty. Bring Martinelli's rifle."

"I'll cover you," Castle said, not questioning his decision – they were all in the same boat, no rank here. "I'll cover," he said, crouching at the opening, Martinelli's rifle held at the ready.

"We don't need no cover," Al said.

Castle nodded but did not move. He heard them grunting under the weight of the gun, and then bumping down the stairs.

It had been a hell of a good position. They had been able to fire from there, keeping the red berets hopping and not knowing where the shooting was coming from. It was the best position he had ever been in. And he didn't want to leave it. But after awhile the quiet, the passage of time, the empty daylight, the lifeless buildings had begun to weigh on him. He backed away from the opening, picked up his blanket roll, and looked around the room. He kicked one of the sacks of flour, his boot making a slight impression in the wine-dampened sack. He stopped at the wine barrel and tilted it, filling his canteen. He drank deeply and refilled it. Then he went down the stairs.

The streets were deserted. He walked through the town going down the streets that led toward the plaza. The plaza was empty, a large paved-over square with silent buildings on all sides, windows, doors, shell holes all

looking down on the empty square and on himself. He felt goose pimples across his body. He made a hasty check of which way the shadows leaned and headed east.

He hurried along, hugging the sides of the buildings, dashing across the empty *calles*, until he came to the outskirts of the town. There were Johnny Gates and two other commissars, red stars on their berets, moving along behind a Russkie tank that was slowly rolling down the road away from the town, its gun pointed backward.

"Where'd you come from, any more with you?" Gates asked him.

"No. At least I didn't see anyone else."

"Well, let's go then, we have to catch up with the battalion."

They followed the tank, which was steadily pulling away from them.

"It's really too good a position to be pulling out of," Castle said.

"We'll be back." Gates said.

≡ 46

The lobby of the hospital was cool after their climb, cool and clean and quiet. Leo was impressed by the quietness since he did not expect it, having anticipated a great deal of hustling and bustling, of doctors and nurses overwhelmed by countless wounded packed into the wards, rooms, and corridors, summoned to blood-stained beds by the moans and groans and shouts of pain emanating from mouths barely visible beneath blood-soaked bandages. It had been that way in Madrid.

But the young woman to whom they first spoke appeared calm and unhurried, even interested. Leo's reaction to her unhurried manner had been "business is slow," thinking of how Castle would put it: "How's business?" "Slow."

But it wasn't that slow, it turned out, not in the children's ward, at least. There, all the beds were taken, and not only by the usual infant disease cases but also by wounded children. It was difficult for him to shift his thinking from wounded infantrymen to kids who neither moaned nor groaned nor screamed, but whose little bodies were just as torn, pierced, and broken.

Back in the Bronx – and he did not think back home – the kids laughed and shrilled in the thin spring sun, soaring and swirling in wagons, on skates, on scooters, the March wind blowing them along cement sidewalks, macadam streets, while the sky remained remote and unheeded – for never had there been a thing in the sky, no warning throb of danger, of screaming speeding bombs terminating in explosive DON'Ts . . . don't play or laugh or run . . . walk to the nearest hole and crawl in and wait for the DON'T-DON'T-DON'T to find you there and turn you, toss and tear at you, burn you and deafen you with DON'T . . . the sky suddenly becoming close and menacing with the first sound of sirens and then the motors of the planes pressing the sky down on them – but not in the Bronx.

Now Mario, in white gown on the white-sheeted cot, his wide-open black eyes following them out: what are you doing, why are you leaving me, what will happen to me? Maria was crying softly and Leo tasted salt on his lips. So many children.

But back in the lobby there were forms to fill out. Where were they staying?

Remembering the Socorro Rojo – "You will be able to reach us there. We will be in contact with them every day."

Maria interjecting, "Many times each day."

"When we have found a place we will inform you," he said. "How long will it be with the child?"

"The doctors must first examine him and see what is to be done, and," the nurse added with a warm smile, "for sure it will be done. But do not fail to come back as soon as possible and let us know where you are. Salud, Viva la Republica."

Leo could see that she meant it and he felt edgy saying *Salud y Viva* in response.

"The poor little ones," Maria cried, "how is it the bombs found them? What have they done? Where will they be safe? Tell me, Leonardo, will Mario be safe in the hospital? It looks so big and strong, so well constructed, no? Mario will be safe there, true?"

"It is possible. The fascists have bombed around the docks, also in other places. They have bombed everywhere, especially among the homes of the workers, also a church here and there, and – "

"And what?"

"Well, sometimes a hospital, but not here," he hastened to assure her, "it is quite far from the center of town and at least three kilometers from the docks."

"Ay, are they so careful then?"

"Careful? No. What they are careful for is their skins – they will only go where it is safe."

"Yes, and is that not true of ours as well?"

He looked at Maria and wondered how she had thought to ask such a question when her main concern was for those who were under the bombs. But she was full of curiosity, and it was natural she should ask was it not so for all pilots, Republican as well as fascist.

"No," he replied, "for we do not have as many and ours go where they must, when there is enough gasoline and ammunition; they must go without regard for danger. Yes, simply because they cannot choose. That is it." That was the best he could manage with the language and so he repeated himself. "They cannot choose and yet they must do, and therefore they do without regard."

She thought for a little while before she spoke again. "Then they are heroes and the others are cowards, murderers of babies."

"You have said it," he said.

"And where will we be safe? For we must be safe if only not to abandon Mario."

"We will not have much choice, but we will choose a place – if it is possible – as far from the docks and as near to the hospital as possible."

"We must insist on it," she said.

"Very well, we will insist."

"Still," she said after a silence, "if it should be me, you understand, then you must see to him, take care of him. Do not leave him alone." It was a question.

He did not answer right away. He with the baby? Alone? In Spain?

She sharpened the question. "You must say yes. Or I will go no farther."

"Why, what will you do?"

She stopped, bringing the burro to a halt. He turned to look at her. She stood looking first at her feet and then straight into his eyes. "I will return to the hospital now, I will sleep on the floor next to Mario, I can wash the floors, the walls, work, do anything so that I might remain with him. You have not answered."

"Well, it is a foolish question, we are together. Whatever happens to one will happen to the other."

"It is not an answer."

"Nothing is going to happen to you."

"Very well, then, I shall go back now."

He watched her turn and start up the hill leading the burro, and he thought, let her go. He would be on his own, have only himself to worry about. But then he went after her and turned her around. Laughingly he said, "I promise. Like my own son."

"In which case," she said with a great deal of gravity, "let us go."

It was easier going downhill.

"It is a grave problem," the man said. He was short and running to the kind of unhealthy grey fat that once-active men acquire when they switch from muscle power to brain power. He fingered the grey stubble on his chin as he alternately looked down at the papers and ledgers that he pushed about on the desk, and up at Leo and Maria. "There is so little room except perhaps in one of the seaman's hotels on the Ramblas."

Maria interrupted him. "We would prefer to be close to the hospital."

"No, you are right. Also it is no good down there because of the bombing." He scanned the papers before him again.

Watching his hands shuffling the papers about, Leo recalled the logo that appeared on the Socorro Rojo membership book and on all their posters. It was a rendering of a narrow oblong window, heavily barred and at street level, with one hand of the subterranean prisoner reaching through the bars, the fingers outstretched, angrily imploring, the other hand gripping one of the bars. Was it possible that this man had been the model? Had he actually been imprisoned himself? Was that why he was now one of the few officials of the organization in Barcelona?

"There is nothing up on the hills, of course. Perhaps with a family." The man spoke as though to himself. When at last he got up to direct Leo to an address, he walked them to the door, clumsily maneuvering an artificial leg as though practicing strokes with a heavy hockey stick.

"Perhaps," Leo said, "you had better give us the name of one of the hotels as well; it is possible that we would be an inconvenience." The man looked back all the way to the desk and Leo could see that the effort would be great. "Never mind, there are, as you have said, many down on the Ramblas. I am sure we will have no difficulty."

"As you will," the tired man said. "As you will. But do not worry about the inconvenience, for now there are no conveniences, no comforts. Never has there been such an animalistic destruction visited on a city as Barcelona now experiences." And he marshaled what little strength he had left to say in parting, "Now we are all *soldados*, we all must make sacrifices." And "Salud y Victoria."

Outside on the street Maria wanted to know why Leo had asked for the names of possible hotels.

"Because it may not be wise to live in such close quarters with others."

"But that is what we have been doing all the way here."

"Yes, but these people will most likely be Communists."

"Yes? What difference does it make. They are Spaniards like the others."

"They are more familiar with the Internationals. The possibility that I am one might more easily suggest itself."

"Then you must be more careful, for I will not go to where the bombs fall, not that I fear for myself, but it is as I have said before, my concern for the child."

So they started out for the place, while Leo wondered at the softness that had come over him. He was letting her have her way in so many things now . . . or she had found her strength during the journey, while he was as he had always been.

The door to the apartment did not respond to his knock but opened easily when he tried the knob. He went in calling "Oye!" but the rooms, three of them, though crowded with bedding, books, papers and articles of clothing, battered luggage and canvas bundles, were empty of people. He went out to fetch Maria and their belongings and brought them back into the apartment.

"It seems they are all out working," he said. "You wait for me while I go to see what may be done with the burro."

"There is not room here for another," Maria said, walking through the apartment. "Though perhaps there are one or two who are away for a time or who will not return. I think it best we wait and see now that we are here. Unless we try one of the hotels. No, I will wait. You go and see to the animal."

"Getting you put up or getting rid of you in Barcelona is going to be a problem," he said to the burro, who paid no attention to him, head down, snuffing the unfamiliar dust on the hard street, his soft eyes looking for a tuft of greenery, his long ears moving to the sounds above, tail flagging the congress of gathering flies. "Well, let us try the first shopkeeper, perhaps he will have an idea."

He did.

"There was a stable once not too far away," said the tailor, peering over metal-rimmed glasses, "but now it is in the possession of the army and you must understand that the army needs burros, but on the other hand they only pay the fixed price. Also it is not likely that they will hold the animal for you. There is always the danger that the poor beast will end up in the pot. All the more so when there is no meat in the city. *Pues*, perhaps the butcher would be a better place, for he at least will be more realistic about the price and even return to you a portion of the meat. What do you think?"

"Maybe there is another stable, perhaps farther from here?"

"It will be the same since the entire city is under the same cloud of hunger and not a cat, goat, burro, or any other four-legged animal is safe in the streets anywhere. We all suffer equally."

"For sure, but aren't these animals necessary for labor as well?"

He shrugged his shoulders. "It is always possible to find a man or a woman to perform the labor, but these are not suitable for the table – not yet. Well, you understand?"

"Nevertheless, I will look."

The tailor accompanied Leo to the door to have a look at the burro. "Do not look too much," he said, "for the burro is already skin and bones, and moving him from place to place will only worsen his condition and thus in the end you will get less return for your effort."

"It is a thought," Leo said.

And in the end that was what he had to do, and though he would have preferred the two kilograms of meat that the butcher offered him rather than the two hundred pesetas, he took the pesetas, for he could not bear the idea of eating burro meat, especially burro meat that had so recently been the faithful companion of their journey, even though he knew beforehand that Maria would prefer the meat and would not be as sensitive as he was. No matter what taboos and superstitions she might be saddled with, they were nothing compared with the dietary laws foisted on a Jewish boy raised in the Bronx.

"Farewell, then, o loyal beast. At least they'll fatten you up before the cleaver falls. You'll die happy, which is rarely the case with us humans."

Returning to the apartment where he had left Maria, Leo now felt singularly unencumbered. The child was in a hospital, Maria was housed, and the burro was disposed of. Whatever he needed he had on his person – money and . . . well, that was all. He might want to return to the apartment to get toilet articles, uniform, boots, and so on, but the idea did not appeal to him, for once there, he would be exposed to a different type of Spaniard than he had hitherto consorted with, not peasants and shoemakers, but city dwellers, political activists, people more sophisticated than those of the countryside and therefore more suspicious. Also, he did not know how and when he could arrange for the necessary separation from Maria.

But more than these things, he just felt free of Spain. His promise to Maria was the kind one made in wartime, to be kept only if convenient. Having cleared himself of a sense of obligation, he felt free to go whichever way he chose to go. It was a matter of where and when and how.

Just so long as it was not back to the Ramblas, where he would be recognized, or to Sebastian's place, if it was still in business – and he did not doubt that it was. To IB headquarters? Oh, yes, and where are your papers, Comrade Rogin, where is your *salvoconducto* for Barcelona? Tell all and plead guilty, throw himself on their mercy, and it'd be back to the front at the very best.

To the front at best. And at worst? The worst being something not to be contemplated, he left off the tiresome business of working out a course, only to find that he had arrived at the doorway of the house. Without thinking, he walked into the dark hallway. The door of the apartment was closed but still unlocked, and when he went in without knocking, there was Maria with people who looked up at his entrance, obviously breaking off a discussion that had been in progress, perhaps a comradely inquisition as to who and what they were.

"Here is my man," Maria said. And Leo, feeling very much the kid from the Bronx, and not seeing how this could not be apparent to one and all, squirmed in embarrassment. "They have been asking about the front in Aragon," she said.

"Yes," the man addressed him. "We have news that the fascists have launched an offensive on the Aragon, but it is not known if we are holding our positions. You have been there recently. Perhaps you have heard."

Before he could answer, the woman said, "Of course we will hold them. And throw them back as well."

"Yes," the man said. "If the positions have been well prepared."

"Of course," said the woman, "they have been well prepared since this has been the main program of the Party for the front, ¡Fortificar es Vencer! No?"

"What else?" said the man, "but you surely do not object to my asking *compañero* . . ."

"Leonardo," Leo said with heart in full depth plunge, recognizing the enemy.

". . . Leonardo if the work has been carried out, if he has any knowledge of what is likely to be the result."

"Well, you may ask," replied the lady, "if you wish. Perhaps he will also agree to speak to the group tonight, yes?"

"Excuse me," Leo said, "no. There is nothing I can tell since there is nothing I know."

"You were not then among those working on the fortification of the front?" The woman sounded incredulous.

"You did not volunteer for making the fortifications?" the man asked, looking at him curiously. "Perhaps," he said to the woman, "he has an injury."

"What else?" the woman said, "he certainly looks young enough and to the eye without infirmities."

"We had our work to do in the fields," Maria said, and Leo looked at her with relief and admiration. "After all, the villages must have food, the soldiers as well."

"Yes," said the man, "everyone must do his own work, but certainly you knew of others working on the defenses."

"Ah," said the woman impatiently, "the Party has seen to it and lines will hold. Surely we will hear of it tomorrow. But if the comrade will agree, we would very much like to hear how it is in the countryside and in particular so close to the front."

"Wait," the man said, "is it not on that front that the Internationals are in position?"

"Yes, but yes," put in Maria before Leo could stop her, "that is so – *Americanos*."

"*Americanos?*" repeated the woman, and looked at Leo. "Why did you not mention it?"

"I have had very little opportunity to speak."

"They are very brave, no?"

"I have heard it." Leo said.

"Do you not know?" the woman asked.

"Well, in truth, I have only heard it, as I have said." He stalled for time.

"No, but at Belchite and Fuentes del Ebro, almost to Zaragoza. It is not far?"

"It is far enough," and Leo was sorry that he said it, because the man then looked at him more closely, as though the phrase had been enough to move a doubt in the back of his mind to the front. Seeing this, Leo agreed when the woman proposed that they should come to the meeting even if he did not speak, in order to meet the other comrades, one of whom was a doctor who, while he did not work at the hospital, might still be of some assistance with the child.

Not that Leo intended to be there, but he hoped that it would change the conversation, which it did. They talked of other things, mostly about

what the dinner was going to be that night. There was not much in the house, just bread and wine and some garbanzos and some greens, and it was doubtful if there would be enough for all. Leo, who had kept quiet, offered to buy food, since he had two hundred pesetas and some change in his pocket for he had just sold their burro.

"To whom?" the lady wanted to know.

Leo looked at Maria and away. "To the butcher."

"By god," said the man, "and you took money instead of meat?"

"It was a foolish thing to do," said the woman, "for money is not difficult to come by, but meat! And more, he has cheated you."

"He did not know," said Maria, "we are new here."

"Of course," said the man, "in the country it is always easier in the matter of food."

"Perhaps," Maria said in a general sort of way, and to Leo. "Leonardo, we will be able to buy another burro when it is time to return, no?"

"Ho," the man laughed, "and where will you find one to buy?"

"We will see," said Leo.

"Aha," the man said, light coming into his eyes, "that is it! You sound like an American with the Spanish and you even look somewhat like one. Surely you are not Aragonese, perhaps from the north, or even from the south, must I guess?" And he cocked his head to one side and smiled politely.

"Yes and no," Leo said, hoping to create enough confusion so as to be able to evade the questioning, but it was not necessary, for Maria came to his rescue once again.

"Never mind about the burros for now," she said. "It would be better if we went out to see if there is anything we can buy to add to the table. Perhaps you will be so kind as to direct us."

And when the woman had done so, the man kept his peace. They thanked her and left. "We will soon be back."

Outside, Leo muttered in English, "Not me."

"What is it you say?" Maria wanted to know.

"Nothing of importance," Leo said. "It is best if you stay here."

47

Twenty miles or so to the southeast of Caspe, brigade came to rest in a place called Corbera. They were not to rest there for long. About a hundred men had been on the march from Caspe. A few more joined them, men who had been lost since Belchite, men who hadn't stopped retreating until they had been stopped in the rear by brigade, or farther back by division. Some of them had gone all the way to Barcelona, and still others to the Pyrenees. It had looked like the end of the war. And there were those who knew what the situation was, who knew the outlook was not promising, and who in spite of this had continued as fighting antifascist volunteers, suppressing their forebodings and radiating, if not optimism, at least commitment. And then, those like Doran, who were determined to die fighting if necessary.

The idea of fighting to the last man was not firmly rooted in Mitch Castle's head. He could voice Pasionaria's slogan, write in his letters that "It is better to die on one's feet than to live on one's knees." But it never registered in that most sensitive seat of fear, his gut. Perhaps there was a wall in his mind that the thought of death or slavery could not penetrate, or a door that locked it away in his head, out of reach. Maybe it was just stupidity. Somewhere he had secreted away the unheroic notion that it was better to live, that under the worst form of government and the most brutal of slave systems, he would survive and probably find some way of accommodating himself. He had found ways to live under a tyrannical father, the militarized CCC, a son-of-a-bitching, slave-driving boss in the garment center; and not merely live, but get the best of them. So that if it became a choice between living enslaved or dying fighting, it would be a toss-up. If he chose to go down fighting, it would not be because he feared enslavement, but for another reason, something having to do with shame and guilt.

One thing was certain: he had very little time to think about possibilities, even though the way things were going they seemed more like probabilities. He was battalion commander again, Doran having resumed duties as brigade commissar. Besides the hundred or so men who had made it back from Belchite through Caspe more or less as a unit, there were the men who had retreated too far to the rear, who when stopped and told that the battalion still existed, returned on their own. The ranks were further augmented by about a hundred Spanish recruits, by volunteers who had recently arrived from the States, by the newly healed wounded and by

wounded who were not completely healed; by the sick and the maimed, by all those who were willing and could walk. Some of the men were in such bad shape that Castle refused to have them in the battalion and insisted on their returning to hospitals in the rear. But they had come all this way to get back into action, and so determined were they that they went from battalion to battalion until they found one that would take them. Many badly wounded and poorly healed volunteers, formerly of the Lincolns or Washingtons, or both, ended up in the Mac-Paps or the almost all-Spanish Twenty-fourth Battalion.

These men, who had been in action before, did not question the veterans of the retreat. But one or two of the new volunteers, fresh from the homeland, questioned them sharply. They were not only critical of the fact that the Lincolns had been forced to give up position after position, but of how many of them had abandoned their weapons in the process. There was much resentment among the veterans toward this attitude, and the usual predictions that these greenhorns were all mouth and no guts. "Just wait until they come under fire."

It was true that some of the men had thrown their firearms away as an impediment to flight. It was a hard thing to excuse or to accept. The fact that they were good men and had stayed with the battalion all the way through made it no easier.

There were men who had gotten as far as the border and had been picked up and sent back under guard, and loosely labeled deserters. These men were being given another chance, and as far as Castle was concerned their status in the battalion was no different from those who had abandoned their weapons but stayed with the outfit, and no different from the heroes who had carried and used their weapons all the way.

But not everybody thought the way Castle did, as the problem of Vernon Selby demonstrated. Selby had been a battalion scout, along with Luke Hinman. But when the breakthrough had occurred, he had gone all the way to the Pyrenees before he was stopped. To make matters worse, he had taken several men along with him.

He was one of the far too few volunteers who had had army training back home. He was a good-looking man, older by six or eight years than the average volunteer. Why, what, and how he had come to Spain was unclear. He was one of those who thought that, having come of his own free will, he was free to leave when he chose. Now, Castle had to deal with him.

"Well, what'll we do with you now?" he began, looking for ideas.

The battalion was bivouacked in an olive orchard and Castle held court, sitting on the ground, his back against a tree. Vernon squatted before him, back erect, head partially turned aside.

"I don't see how I can put you back in scouts. We depend heavily on them." Castle turned first to Johnny Gates, now officially battalion commissar, and then to the newly appointed Party organizer, Joe Brandt. Luke Hinman remained standing, smoking a cigarette. He had come calmly through the retreats complete with rifle and cartridge belt. Luke was a loosely put-together character. He seemed to be made up of thin, copper-red slabs, joined together at odd angles. It was hard to tell just how tall he would measure out if he ever straightened up. Castle passed the buck to him. "You wouldn't want a deserter in reconnaissance, would you, Luke?"

Luke thought about it. "We all make mistakes," he said.

"Was it a mistake?" Castle asked Vernon.

"Yes, it was, sir," Vernon said firmly.

"Well, hell, don't call me sir," Castle said uncomfortably. And then, to Luke, "That means you would be willing to have him? Would be responsible for him?"

"Yeah," Luke said.

"Okay, comrade. That settles it." Castle said.

After Luke had gone off with Vernon, Joe Brandt spoke up. Joe was short and chunkily built. His head was big and square, and his nose had been rearranged by a blow, giving him a tough-guy appearance, but his brown eyes were soft and large. "I think you handled that very well, comrade," he said, the flattened nose nasalizing an Irish-tenor twang to his words. "But I don't think these kinds of decisions should be made by the commander alone. We're all responsible for the men in the battalion, and the Party should have a voice in these decisions. Also the political commissar – "

"If I had had anything to say, I would have said it," Gates interrupted him. His scalp crawled with reddish curls, over a finely boned pale pink face, his nose as sharp as the prow of a Yankee clipper. His eyes were round, glassy, and most often red-rimmed.

"That's beside the point. You should have been consulted."

"I don't see why it was necessary. It was up to Luke," Castle said.

"On what basis do you rely on Comrade Hinman's opinion? Especially when you have sitting next to you the Party *Responsable* and the political commissar?" Brandt wanted to know.

"You heard Johnny. He passed, right?" Castle was annoyed at the defensiveness in his tone. What the hell. Was he supposed to call a meeting on every point that came up? Commissars and Party organizers were just *sol-*

dados like the rest of them. He knew they were important, but he did not concern himself with their role or their duties. He just hoped they got the chow up in time, the mail delivered, and the political situation explained. As far as the Party man was concerned, well, he just hoped that he did his job of making sure all the Party members in the outfit supported the commanding officer. What else was there? "You know goddamned well that Hinman ain't going to stick his neck out for a man he has any doubts about. That guy has been tramping up and down these goddamned hills, scouting for this outfit, day in and day out, until he's ready to drop."

That day-in, day-out routine. *Christ. That's my father talking, I even sound like him,* Castle thought. He shifted on his can, momentarily dismayed by the intrusion of his father into the matter at hand.

"Like I said already, you handled it very well. What I'm talking about now is the procedure to be followed henceforth," said Brandt.

"Henceforth?" Castle was amused. "Henceforth and hereinafter we'll see how it comes up before we decide on how it comes out, okay?"

Brandt looked to Johnny Gates for help. Castle saw Johnny make a tight little gesture with his head which he took as a signal to knock it off. While Joe turned this over in his mind, Castle had time to think about his move now that doubts were sown. He would have to tell Luke not to lose sight of Vernon.

The shipment of rifles that they had been waiting for arrived. Beautiful new Czech Mausers. They looked much more formidable than the ancient Remingtons that had been standard issue. Castle stood beside the long wooden crates, their lids pried open, fondling one of the Kosmolin-coated rifles. As the men came by picking up their weapons, he told them, "Now you've got the best. These are the McCoy. Get them cleaned and oiled. We're going out to find a place where you can get some rounds off." Holding the Mauser in his hands, he forgot about the tanks, planes, artillery against which the Mausers would be little better than the old Remingtons. The heft of the rifle in his hands was reassuring.

The drone of aircraft distracted him. Looking past the branches of the olive trees, he spotted a single plane, its small fuselage a silver fish against the pale sky. There were no markings that he could see, but, as it circled lazily overhead, its mission became clear: it was an observation plane seeking out targets, and spotting for artillery batteries.

Castle hoped the men had camouflaged their *chabolas.* The plane made one last circular pass, then flew off in a beeline for home base. Well, Castle thought, if not camouflaged, then at least deep enough to keep safe through the bombing runs. "I better see to it," he said to no one in particular. He leaned the Mauser against a tree. "Looks to me like the quiet times are about to be over."

48

The fascist planes came over in due time and dropped their bombs, wide of and to the rear of the grove where the brigade was dug in. If there was some other target back there, Castle was not aware of it. All he could think of was that the recon plane had misled the air squadrons, or the squadrons were misreading their coordinates. He preferred to think of the enemy as sometimes being as unskilled as they themselves were.

There was small satisfaction that none of the other units was doing very well under the massive attacks. Word came through that Barcelona had come under heavy air attack. The papers were full of pictures of bombed-out buildings and bodies laid out in rows . . . as evidence of the barbarity of the fascists.

A party of reporters from back home came to see how the Americans were doing – or *if* they were doing. Rumors had spread in Madrid and Barcelona that the Lincoln Battalion had been wiped out.

Hemingway seemed to be leading the press corps. He introduced Mitch, calling him Commander Castle, to Herb Matthews, a lanky, lantern-jawed man from the *New York Times*. Matthews was as tall as Mitch but as fair as Mitch was dark, with a mournful expression that seemed permanent.

"Commander Castle." Matthews shook his hand, offered him a cigarette, and asked, "How many Americans do you have left?"

"Oh, enough. A battalion, actually." Castle wasn't giving this guy numbers.

"How many men have you lost since the tenth of March?" Matthews kept angling. "Can you give me some names of those who are missing in action? We are getting a number of anxious inquiries from relatives."

"Well, no, I can't," Castle said, an edge to his voice. "You'll have to get that kind of information from base HQ."

Matthews changed his approach. "What do you think of the Loyalists' chances of holding on?"

"*Por seguro*, we will," said Castle. He thought of Matthews as a represen-

tative of the capitalist press, a label that included all the papers but the *Daily Worker*. He was not going to let pass an opportunity to get a message across. "This is a People's Army," he said in a large voice. "A United Front of democratic, progressive men and women, an army backed by the whole people of Spain. Such an army and people will win out."

Matthews made some brief notes on a pad of paper. It did not surprise Castle that Matthews did not take down everything he'd said. Still, he was piqued.

"But the fascists have broken through south and east of Teruel," Matthews said, "and they have captured Alcorisa and Agua Caliente . . ." His eyes were sad.

"Yes, but Lister will hold them."

"With what?"

"With men, with heart, with strong convictions."

"They have taken Caspe."

"We'll be going back into the lines soon."

"They now seem to be bombing Barcelona with impunity."

"I thought they were using high explosives," said Castle.

"It is interesting that you can jest at a time like this," said Matthews.

"I always jest jest about now."

"Would you like another cigarette?" said Matthews.

"You guys always pass out butts. Don't any of you smoke cigars or a pipe?"

"Would you like me to bring you some cigars when I come back from Paris?"

"Jeez. Are you going to Paris and then coming back here?"

"Yes, we have to do that to file our stories."

"All the way to Paris? Say listen, bring me back some pipe tobacco, will you, any kind . . . and if you can pick up a cheap pipe?"

"I will do that, Commander."

"I mean, put this in your report." Mitch felt it necessary to lay on the line. "The Americans should be told that if they don't get FDR to lift the embargo and get us some arms and planes for the legitimate government of Spain, then watch out, old boy, because it's going to be your ass that'll be in a sling."

"Aren't the Russians sending enough material?" Matthews asked.

"I notice you didn't take any notes while I was talking."

"Well, that's a standard statement you made. I'll have no trouble remembering it."

"I hope so. I suppose the Russians are sending as much as they can. I don't know if all of it is getting by the French. That Socialist, Leon Blum, I don't know about him . . ."

"France is a member of the nonintervention committee," said Matthews.

"Yeah, I know. I suppose the people of France will get on his ass sooner or later. It's a sure thing that they're not going to stand by while Hitler and Mussolini secure themselves a base this side of the Pyrenees."

"I've seen a great deal of support among the people during my trips to Paris," remarked Matthews, "support for the Republic, that is."

"See what I mean?" said Castle. "Uh, could you spare another butt? It takes at least three cigarettes to fill this pipe."

"Sure. Do you think that there's enough time for the Republic to get help from the outside?"

"What d'ya mean by enough time? We're holding them, we'll hold them. We're going to win this war one way or another."

"Yes, but aren't you warning that if the democracies don't come to the aid of the Spanish people then the war will be lost and thus an opportunity to dampen Hitler's plans for world conquest would be passed over?"

"You talk like an exercise for a typewriting class," said Castle. "You know what I mean . . . now is the time for all good men to come to the aid of the party. We're not losing this war, that's the first thing. But if we should, then it'll be because you guys didn't help when you were morally obligated to."

"In other words, we're not going to lose, but we might?"

"The other words are yours, not mine."

Matthews scribbled in his notebook. Down the line, Hemingway was talking to Gates and Watt, Vincent Sheean was talking to Eddie Rolfe, and Louis Fischer was in close conversation with Brandt. Everybody was smoking cigarettes that seemed exceptionally white in their grimy hands and in contrast with the dirty grey of the poor Spanish butts. The reporters all looked bright-eyed and eager. They were shaven and clean. For Christ's sake, even their hair was combed. In a little while they would be leaving for Barcelona or Madrid or Paris where there were hotel rooms and white linen on the tables. Maybe girls. But no action. Castle felt sorry for them.

Word came from brigade that a truckload of men would be allowed to visit Cartagena for a day to swim in the Mediterranean. Castle told Gates to pick out the most deserving and to make sure he included the battalion commander. A detachment was made up and they took off early the next day. George Watt, newly returned to the battalion, his wounds partly

healed, was the new Party organizer. He was left behind to mind the store, Gates having included himself in the outing. Joe Brandt joined them at the last moment.

It was a beautiful day, the sun shining and the sea sparkling blue. Warm for March. The men hit the beach, divested themselves of their uniforms and plunged into the water. There was swimming and splashing and scrubbing with the big bars of crude soap provided for the occasion. On the beach, they dried in the sun. When the morning had gone, they went into the city to find food and drink.

Castle joined Joe Bianca and Al Kaufman in one of the bars along the waterfront, where they swallowed pickled miniature octopi drenched in their own ink, and oysters and clams and other things from the sea, washed down with Vermouth and soda water. Afterward they sipped ferkin, the raw cognac that was the only hard drink available. When they had downed a couple of these, Joe took a needle and black thread out of one of his pockets. Mitch watched him carefully thread the needle.

"Bravo," he cried. "Better than walking a straight line. What the hell are you going to do, start sewing on your clothes here?" Joe had a reputation as a tailor and was to be seen frequently mending his clothes, when he wasn't cleaning his gun or tidying his *chabola*.

"No, Comrade Castle," Joe said slowly, "What I'm going to do is pass this needle and thread through my lip."

"I suppose you think he can't do it?" Kaufman said.

"I'm sure he can do anything he damn well says he can. Only he ought to sterilize the needle beforehand." Mitch held out his glass of ferkin, "Dip it in here. This stuff will kill the hardiest of bugs."

"How much do you want to bet he can do it?" Kaufman insisted.

"I don't want to bet. I know he can do it."

"Don't you want to see him do it?" Al pressed.

"Sure. If he wants to."

"Well, what'll you bet he does it?"

"For Christ's sake, what do you want me to bet?" Mitch could see that Joe was getting impatient. Evidently it was important that the thing be done for a wager.

"How about the next round of drinks?" he said.

"Sure. The next round of drinks. Oyez, chico, más cognac." Mitch threw a couple of pesetas on the table.

"Wait until he does it. How do you know he can?"

"Okay." Mitch picked up the paper money. "So I'll wait. Go ahead."

"Aah, you're taking all the fun out of it," Joe complained.

"Listen, I know goddamned well you can do it, so go ahead already."

"I'll tell you what," Joe said. "Let's make it two rounds and I'll do it without spilling one drop of blood."

"Oh, great! Now you're making a Shylock out of me. Not one drop of blood, Portia . . . not even a smidgin. You've got a bet for two rounds but no more than that. I hear there's a cathouse in town and I want to go see what the girls are like."

"They're like any other girls," Al said. "They're all whores."

"Watch the male chauvinism," Mitch cautioned, repeating a term he had heard used at YCL meetings.

"Look who's talking," said Al. "You're going to the cathouse to exploit the women, not me."

"You're not going?" said Mitch, surprised.

"There you are," Joe mumbled suddenly. The needle and thread hung loosely from his lower lip, jerking as he formed the words. There was no blood, and Mitch could see clearly where the needle had passed through about a half inch below his lower lip. Now Joe took the needle between his fingers and slowly drew the thread through. Mitch winced and looked away. The waiter was standing by the table, his mouth open and eyes popping.

"*Seis* cognacs," Mitch held up six fingers, "and hurry, I need them more than he does."

"See," Joe said, thrusting his face at Mitch. "No blood, right?"

Mitch did not look closely. "Right, right," he agreed. "Where the hell did you learn to do that?"

"I've been all over the world," Joe said mysteriously.

"I suppose you can go to sleep on a bed of spikes," Mitch said.

"A cinch, a softer berth than the accommodations around here."

The man brought the drinks and portioned them out. Mitch added pesetas to those he had put on the table before and the man took them up, counted them without seeming to do so, smiled his *gracias*, and departed.

Castle raised his glass, "To the champ." He looked away as Joe pulled the thread through and out. Al drank, but sparingly. Joe rolled a mouthful of the ferkin back and forth, swelling his cheeks as he did so. Castle swallowed his shot, the raw drink going down easy, the first one having smoothed the way. He downed the next one fast. "Okay," he said. "If you guys aren't gonna get laid, I'm leavin'."

The line outside of the *casa de las prostitutas* was long. Men from the other battalions joined the Lincolns in hailing Castle. "Oyez," they shouted, "¡El Comandante! Por favor, go to the head of the line."

"Hey, no *comandantes* here, for Christ's sake," Castle said, taking his place at the end of the line.

"Why not," said the man in front of him, someone from the British battalion. "All the other bloody brass have led the charge, and properly so."

Some of the others chorused approval. They gathered around and pushed him forward. They nudged him through the open door, just as two of the brigade officers were exiting. They smiled, seeing him being helped forward. Castle freed himself of the men pushing him and strode forward into the darkness of a long hallway.

≡ 49

When Leo had left Maria and headed for the office of the Socorro Rojo, he had been busy dreaming up a reason to insist on a different place to stay. They could not stay where they were without his being exposed. The Spaniards in the apartment were too sophisticated, too political, too aware, and altogether too curious. It was only a matter of time before they would be reporting their suspicion to the authorities, the CP most likely.

The sirens had been going for some time, he realized, before they registered in his head. Leo searched the western sky where the planes would be appearing – though he knew from experience that he would not be seeing them until the white and black and grey puffs of exploding antiaircraft shells showed themselves, seemingly always a little above or below or behind the white and silver bomber formations, undisturbed. Occasionally one of the bombers would start to fall slowly away, gracefully trailing a wisp of white smoke that grew in density and volume as the falling plane twisted down, spinning lazily, disappearing beyond the horizon. He'd keep his eyes fixed on that spot waiting for the column of black smoke to rise, and then, after a time, hear the soft sound of the impact.

Clouds were beginning to pile up in the east, rolling in from the sea, white around the edges, dark grey, thick-looking, fast-moving clouds. It seemed to him that the urgency of the sirens was affecting the cloud formations, speeding them on, making them race and tumble into each other, overcoming each other, whipping across the patches of blue, hurrying west, away from the sea, while the planes droned in a single distant monotone that was not much louder than the sound one plane would make, but which somehow had the timbre that meant formations flying east down the Ramblas to the harbor.

But there was always a wide margin for error, and he had come some distance from the apartment, though he did not know how far because he had been so preoccupied with trying to figure out the next step. He spent a helluva lot of time trying to figure out the next step. Too damned much time.

The sirens stopped howling and the antiaircraft guns opened up. A battery that must have been only a block or two away cracked in his ears, and he headed for the nearest doorway. Cowering in the shallow entryway, he heard the bombs falling, the long whoosh that sharpened and whined and finally shrieked before the explosion, the relief at the exploding end of the shriek . . . The shriek was always the threat, the explosion was always somewhere else.

You had to know about bombs. The bomb goes through the roof – he drew diagrams in his head – right in the center of the building, and it makes a hole and goes through the floor of the top storey, makes another hole and goes through the floor of the storey below and so on through all the storeys, all the flats, all the homes, right on through to the street floor and into the basement, leaving a nice clean cylinder of blue-white light shafting down in the wake of the bomb; and then there is one split second, one caught-up breath of a breathless, soundless suspension with the hole still echoing in the stillness, before the delayed impact fuse sets off the explosion that is all the storeys and all the people and the whole inside of the building with all the beds and chairs and tables and clothing and the breakfast dishes with the cold *café con leche* filming on the cups, and the picture on the wall and the rubber nipples in the glass of water and all the things that make an apartment a place where people are, where they go to and come from . . . The explosion blows all of that right out through the hole that the bomb made, and then there is nothing left but a crazy-shaped shell with bits and pieces of painted walls and splintered floor and tilted beds trailing dirtied white sheets, and fragments of glass scattered sparkling in the sun.

But not this building.

The planes were gone. The guns were quiet. The clouds had closed out all of the blue and there would be no more sun this day.

He hurried down to the Socorro Rojo office, but the bombs had been there, all in that block of houses, and he couldn't even get near. All he could see was the smoke coming up along with the dust and the stink of the smoke and the dust. Somewhere in the middle of that smoke and dust was the Socorro Rojo, red aid, red help – who would help the helpers? And the tired, worried-looking Spaniard with the bad leg – where would he have run to?

Leo turned back.

He found Maria in the street, looking for him, looking for the hospital, looking among people hurrying to see what the bombing had changed in their streets, what it had changed in their lives. Who the bombing had reached and not reached, who it had taken and spared . . . disrupting the everyday way of their lives, which was already the normal way of living in the middle of a war. They would adapt themselves to this bombing, as they had to the last and would to the next.

Together they climbed the hill to the hospital, Maria's worry hurrying them along. The hospital had not been touched. Ambulances, trucks, cars and carts filled the courtyard with noise and dust, people going every which way. The wounded were being carried in, or assisted, or they walked, or crawled, or limped, or hobbled up the steps . . . standing aside as hospital personnel came rushing to help others in . . . or to bring out beds, cots, mattresses because by now all the rooms and wards were filled and all the halls and corridors and offices and closets were also full. The wounded lay there quietly, or softly groaning, staring up at the ceiling, or with eyes shut tight or lids limply laid over twitching eyeballs.

Leo, waiting by the window, saw a row of bodies laid out, some wrapped in blankets, others in whatever they had been wearing. *Come dressed as you are*, he thought. Some, with clothes partly blown away, yet others with their dresses or suits barely wrinkled, undisturbed. Just as there was blood and no sign of blood . . . single and multiple amputations, bodies intact, yet all equally dead, equally beyond pain . . . a young girl, a kid with her dress pulled slantingly up across her waist, white and hairless in the grey gloom, smooth, rounded, unwrinkled, innocent. The attendant who had brought her out yanked the girl's dress down. Making her, Leo mused, decently dead . . . yet by death deflowered.

Maria came out carrying Mario. "There is no room for him," she said. "Also they have too much to do with the wounded. Perhaps after the war, it is said . . ."

"Well, then you must return to the house," Leo said.

"And you?"

"I cannot, it is dangerous for me. You will find your way to your village."

"You will come . . ." Maria not finishing, not wanting to hear a false promise or, even more painful, a truthful one. She desired to spare Leonardo as well as herself, and so she turned her back on him and went away.

Leo set out for the center of the town, walking fast, holding back from breaking into a run, bringing his feet down hard on the hard pavement, desperately trying to jar the images seen at the hospital, of Maria and Mario, out of his head, his skull, his brain. He did not know where he was going or what he would do . . . and then he thought of McCall and the waterfront, the ships there, the sailors. "Pretty boy like you . . ." McCall had said. "A ticket out of this fucked-up war."

The Majestic Hotel had not been hit. There was a truck parked in front, and ten or twelve men, whom he recognized as Americans, standing nearby smoking and talking. Before he could decide whether to approach them, or turn back and take another street leading to the waterfront, one of the men looked his way and then pointed him out to the others, shouting, "Here's another one!" Laughing, they waved him forward.

"Rogin, right?, I don't remember your first name, but I remember you and Aaron and what's the other comrade's name?"

"Murray," Leo said, "not that it matters, they're both dead." Leo tried to free his hand, the guy's handshake a bit too warm, too sincere, he thought, much like the appearance of the man himself, close-cropped light brown hair, regular features, a smooth tan, looking well scrubbed, as they say.

"Yes, I know. Right, and you're Leo, now I remember." He pumped Leo's arm vigorously, "Yale, Yale Stuart; Leo, we're real happy you're coming with us. We're on our way to battalion. I'm in charge of this shipment of lost souls," he said smilingly. Still holding Leo's hand, he put his other arm around his shoulder, urging him into the center of the group of men.

The only familiar face there was Mickenberg's, everyone called him Mick, Leo remembered. "Mick, long time no see." Leo said.

"That's how it is," Mickenberg said, "people come and go, go and come, and some don't ever come around again. C'est la guerre." The tone of his voice matched the bored expression on his face. Mick, Leo recalled, was always bored – much too intelligent for the company he was forced to keep, is the way he put it. Except, of course, when he helped Murray dream up the lyrics to some of the songs the Voluntarios added to their repertoire. He was saying, "You head for the hills like some of these comrades, thinking the war was over, finished, finito?"

"Hey," Yale said, "none of that. We're all here . . . And here's our chauffeur. Mount up, comrades, we're on our way. Come on," he said to Leo, "I'll give you a boost up."

And there he was, not really knowing why or how he came to be one in a truck loaded and tearing down the Ramblas, on the way to the front, the men silent, only Yale sitting next to him on the wooden bench seeming to enjoy the ride.

Doran and Campbell seemed happy. Campbell never had much to say, but Doran enthused. "Now that we're rested and reorganized, we're going back in to relieve some of the outfits that have been holding the line. We go on the offensive as well. Captain Castle, the Lincolns are going to have the honor of going into action first. When you come into your positions and effect the relief of the Spanish battalion you will find there . . . here . . ." – he held a small map before Castle – "south of this road, between Batea and Caspe, after you take this hill and this one, that will put the road under fire. If you can, cut the road and set up positions here."

"You have a map for me?"

"Take this overlay. That's all we have right now."

"Well, where are we in relation to all this?"

Again the finger pointed, this time to Corbera. "You'll move up on trucks until you come to this point, and then you dismount and move into position on foot."

Castle brought the battalion to hills that looked more or less to be where they were supposed to be, judging from the flimsy overlay. There was no Spanish battalion, or any sign of troops ever having been within kilometers of the place. Yet he was sure that he had found the right hills. Leaving the troops, he climbed to the top of the nearest hill, taking Gates and Watt along. The hill in front of them appeared fortified. There was another series of hills behind the occupied one. There was an opening in the row of hills through which they spotted the movement of troops on what Castle surmised was the road they were supposed to cut. No one had any binocs anymore – he had left his with the battalion when he had gone to Benicasim, and they had probably been lost when Reiss was killed in the shelling outside of Quinto – so he did the best he could, using his hollow fist as a telescope. The troops on the road were too well equipped to be anything but enemy troops.

Now he knew where the fascists were and he knew where he was. But he did not know if there were any friendly forces on his flanks. The French were supposed to be on his left.

He summoned Luke Hinman and Vernon Selby and told them to find the French and report back. He didn't know who was supposed to be on his right, but assumed it would be one of the battalions of the Fifteenth. He sent scouts to find out.

"Well," he said to Watt and Gates, "our orders are to cut the road. Let's get going."

Then he posted observers and sent Watt back to set up the ammo dump. He kept his eyes on the fascists.

"Dirty bastards," he muttered, "they look like they're out for a Sunday *paseo*." Inside him was uneasiness. The enemy's casualness, the fact that they seemed to be operating without concern for Republican forces or planes or artillery; the never-ending line of troops going by less than a thousand meters from where he stood.

He realized that if he attacked across the thinness of their line, he would have no trouble breaking through and cutting the road. Except that once he was through, he'd have enemy on both his flanks . . . unless the French moved up. Once in that position, he could turn his battalion either east or west to roll the line up, except he didn't know how long a line he would have to roll. If the French came along on his flank, then he could turn east and take those fascists from the rear.

He thought hard about it, the uneasy feeling in his gut an annoying presence. The column looked like it would keep going east forever.

Castle laid out the plan of attack to the company commanders. The hills between the battalion and the road were, from what he could see, neither heavily fortified nor heavily manned. He ordered Lyons and the First Company to spearhead the attack, with the Second and Fourth on the flanks, and the Third in reserve. The machine guns would come up once they had the hill. Then, if the French advanced as well, they would go on to the next hill, from which they could at least interdict the road with MG fire.

The attack on the first hill met with immediate success. Runners came back reporting the first line of hills taken. They had caught the fascists by surprise, inflicting casualties and capturing a water truck and two prisoners. One of the prisoners was badly wounded.

The bad news arrived with Hinman and Selby.

"Can't find the French," Luke muttered and sank to the ground. He fished a cigarette from somewhere deep in his poncho. Selby held the *machero* for him and then lit up his own. He remained standing, dreamily looking off to where they had been.

"What d'ya mean, you can't find them? How far did you go?" Castle was irritated.

"Far," Luke said. "There isn't anything out there except beautiful country, like California – up north . . ." His voice trailed off. His thin face seemed thinner and bonier. It was the longest speech Castle had heard him make and it only irritated him more. Beautiful country. What the hell, were they on a scenic tour? The advance had set Castle up and he wanted to keep going.

"Listen, don't finish that smoke here. Get off your ass and go find them. Don't come back until you do." Hinman used his rifle to hoist his lanky frame erect. "When you find them, tell the commander he's got to go forward and protect our flank. Do you understand what I'm saying? He's got to maintain contact with us. Tell him that when we get through to the road we're going to turn east and take them from the rear. He'll have to protect our ass."

"How am I going to tell him all that if I don't find them? And besides, I don't have the lingo."

"Draw him a picture. You got it? Why don't you repeat it?"

Luke repeated what Castle had said. But his voice was so weary and hopeless that it made Castle's stomach flip. He should be telling Luke to forget it. To sit down and finish his butt, to rest. But he forced himself to prod Luke.

"Vernon," he turned to Selby, and pointing in the opposite direction, "no one's come back. I don't know what the hell is on our right flank. I just bloody well would like to know, okay?"

Selby nodded. "Back as soon as I have the information, sir."

Castle watched him move off, the "sir" evoking a shadow of doubt in his judgment. Was it wise to send Selby, who had once deserted, off by himself? He turned to meet the red-rimmed eyes of Gates.

"What else?" he said defensively.

Gates said nothing. He closed his bloodshot eyes and drifted off. Castle wondered about Gates's eyes and apparent desperate need for sleep. Johnny had come to the battalion from the Estremadura front where he was supposed to have performed outstanding feats of leadership. Castle did not doubt this since so many of the men who had been with Gates confirmed it. Yet they had been in action only one day since the rest-up and here Gates was bushed. Hinman was bushed. The other scouts were tired too. Perhaps they had never fully recovered from the retreat from Belchite. Only George Watt, lean and smooth of cheek, golden blond, looked youthful and fresh . . . in spite of his wounds.

"C'mon, Party organizer," he said to Watt. "Let's see what we can find out from the *prisioneros*."

The prisoners were not much help. The one who was still in one piece was a scared Spaniard in his late twenties. All he could tell them was that the fascists had been on the move since early in March, they were always moving and, it seemed to him, "If the *Señor Comandante* will forgive me . . ." that they would keep on moving until they came to the sea. He, too, was very tired. Castle sent him back to brigade under guard, along with the water truck. Maybe they could make some sense out of the names of his unit and the other units with his column.

The other prisoner was in a bad way. He lay on a stretcher, bandaged in various places, his face the color of the grey canvas and his dark eyes rolling; he chewed a twig that someone had placed between his teeth. This did not stop him from screaming and calling for his mother from time to time.

"What do we do with this?" Castle said. "Can we spare any *sanidads* to take him back?"

"That ain't the problem," one of the first-aid men said. "The problem is to take him back to where?"

"Don't you know where brigade *Sanidad* is?"

"Nope."

"Well, take him back to brigade HQ, then. They ought to know."

"He thinks we're going to kill him or let him die," George Watt said. He was squatting beside the stretcher holding the prisoner's hand and trying to talk to him.

"Tell him we're not monsters. Not like the fascists and the *moros* with whom he chose to fight."

"He says he had no choice. He's a conscript."

"Yeah, they're all conscripts. Aah, leave him here until dark. Then let's see what we have to spare in the way of bearers. Meanwhile, you," he turned to the *sanidad*, "better find out in a hurry where the brigade *Sanidad* is."

"Don't yell," George said. "You're scaring this man. He thinks you want to kill him."

"What, me? I thought I told you to give him a political speech."

"I did, but I don't think he believes me."

"In that case maybe we ought to make his fears come true." Castle laughed at the look of consternation on George's face. "Come on, back to *plano mayor*."

On the way back they came across the battalion armorer, a small sand-colored guy named Carroll.

"There you are," he said. "I have a truckload of ammunition. Where do you want me to set up the armory?"

"Didn't Gates set you up?"

"No, sir, he told me to get the stuff, but just now when I told him I had it, he told me to find you and you would – "

"Of course," Castle cut in. Gates had probably gone back to sleep. Well, what the hell to do with the ammo? That was the thing about being a battalion commander. Parts of the battalion kept surfacing that he had no idea existed, or that he had thought did not require his attention. "That house there. The one with the adobe wall around the yard. Check it out. Make sure no one is there." He pointed to a house on a flat green rise about two hundred meters to the rear of the battalion.

"In the house, Captain?" There was doubt in Carroll's voice.

"No, not in the house. This side of it. Find a secure place. We'll use the house as a reference point for the ammo carriers."

"Ah, yes. I think I see a good place. Just follow that path from the gate toward us, about fifty meters and then off to the left there's a – "

"Yeah, that's swell. Check it out and let us know." Castle could not see whatever it was that Carroll was seeing. He was happy he had gotten out of the house gaffe because that would have been the worst place for the ammo dump, the fascists loved having houses to lay artillery on. He wasn't about to admit now that his eyes weren't as keen as Carroll's. All goddamned westerners had eyes like eagles. Maybe the wide open spaces developed that kind of farsightedness. In New York all you had to be able to read was the street sign across the way.

"How does it look?" Castle asked Lyons. They stood on the hill looking north. There were no troops to be seen.

"You'd better get down," Lyons said. "They've organized a position."

"They have? How do you know? No one's firing."

"They will if you keep standing there. We've taken casualties – "

"Who? How many?"

"A couple. Wounded, not killed."

"Sonofabitch." Castle squatted beside Lyons. "What have they got out there?"

"Just riflemen so far."

"No MGs?"

"We haven't seen or heard any yet."

"Well, I think we're going to have to push on."

Castle took the overlay out of his pocket and opened it on the ground. He studied it and the hills. He turned the piece of paper this way and that. "Looks to me like we've run off this fucking thing," he muttered. "They must be pretty thin up there. They don't seem to be doing much firing." There was occasional fire along the line but it was coming from the Second Company's position. In the distance they could hear artillery, which had to be the fascists, and the droning of planes that they could not see. "Do you know if they're still moving on the road?"

"Not since we attacked. But it's possible they've detoured out of sight," Lyons said.

"Do you think you can slip a patrol through and find out? We ought to know whether we've stopped them or whether they're just going around us. Find out and let me know. I'll contact brigade and see if they know where they want us to go."

When Castle got back to *plano mayor,* he found Hinman sprawled under a tree. "Well?" Castle snapped. It was his reaction to the total weariness of the man that made him bark – to get through the fog of fatigue. "Is it still beautiful country out there or are the goddamned French lousing up the landscape?"

"There's nothing out there but a few stray IB'ers. Different nationalities. They're lost." Luke spoke softly.

"Well, that isn't possible." Castle was furious. The French had to be there because he had been told they would be. He had to keep advancing because that was the last order he had had. He couldn't advance much further if he could not find the French. What did you do with a command when you didn't know what to do? He was beginning to feel inadequate. He hadn't taken care of setting up *Sanidad.* He hadn't known fuck-all about the armory. He wasn't sure if brigade was supposed to contact him or if he should get to brigade – or did they expect him to know what to do? No one had said anything about training a battalion commander and he hadn't thought to ask.

"George, you go find Carroll. Have him take you to brigade and give them the scoop on the situation. Gates, you contact the company commanders and tell them to find out what's in front of them. Skip Lyons's company. He's doing that now. When I give the word, we'll go take that next line of hills. Tell them that. And Luke, you and me are going for a walk. I wanna see with my own eyes all that gorgeous country out there. Come on, off your ass." Well, that was something. At least they wouldn't be lying around on their butts wondering what to do next.

It was, as Luke had said, beautiful country. The ground fell away from the hills, sweeping gently in green swathes, down through parklike woods. The trees, widely spaced, were of a darker green, rising out of the lawns unmoved and stately. As they proceeded farther along, keeping the line of hills on their right, he saw that now the hills were higher. The trees grew thicker on their slopes, but the stretches of green grass and trees continued unchanged. The sound of guns, which had been dully present all day, thinned and became remote. He had the feeling that he and Luke were two very tiny figures moving through a vast park, so tiny that they were surely beyond the notice of those larger forces battling around them.

When they had gone on for some time and it had become evident that Luke would keep moving on until he dropped or until Castle was satisfied by the complete emptiness of the place, he stopped. He scanned the heights rising before them and turned to Luke.

Luke looked at Castle and then at the hills. "No. I couldn't climb one of those now if my life depended on it."

There was no sign of life on the hills. The woods in which they stood were not only empty of men but showed no signs of any troops having passed through them. "Is this where you saw the IB'ers you told me about?"

"Back through where we came. This is farther than before."

"I don't see any signs of life at all."

"There ain't none."

"How far do you think we've come?"

"A couple of kilometers."

"Far enough to have linked up with the French if they were here. They're not." Luke was silent, his head hanging loosely on his neck, his eyes studying the texture of the grass underfoot. "Let's go." Castle turned back. He heard Luke collect himself and fall in behind him. "What is this place?" he asked, by way of apologizing for having made Luke retrace his weary steps. "It sure is beautiful . . . What?" Luke had mumbled something.

"Looks like a hunting preserve," Luke repeated.

"Yeah. Fox, horse and hound kind of thing?" Castle said.

"Wild boar. Maybe deer." Luke livened up somewhat. They both looked around. "They'd be under cover now with all the troops and unfamiliar noises," he added.

"Funny. I get the feeling that everything has gone around this place. That nothing's gone through to disturb anything."

"Maybe not." Luke was agreeable.

"Well, it's beautiful, like you said. If this is the way California is, I'm going to want to see it one of these days."

When they got back to the battalion, Watt was there with the information from brigade that the French were right where they were supposed to be. Castle looked at Luke Hinman, who did not look at him. His eyes were closed and he had slumped down at the base of a tree to rest. Selby had returned as well. He had been unable to contact any forces on the right flank, he said, at least not within three or four kilometers.

Gates reported that the companies had good positions and that there was now a definite line of fascist troops facing them. The men were digging in. The prisoner was still on the stretcher under a tree nearby. The kitchen truck rolled up and Fritz Schatz jumped out smiling. Gates sent a couple of runners up to the companies to let them know so they could get the food bearers down.

"Tell the men that we're staying put for the night." That was a decision, of sorts.

The next morning the first thing Castle noticed again were the very red-rimmed eyes of Gates. He was tempted to comment on them, but he did not know Gates well enough, and he was in awe of Gates's reputation, so he did not say anything. Instead he got hold of Luke and told him to get his scouts out on the flanks again. "Who knows, the French may have appeared overnight."

The morning wore on and there was no action on their small sector of the front. The shelling and bombing could still be heard, more or less from all directions, but more distant than before. He had the distinct feeling again that they were being ignored by the fascists. And forgotten by brigade.

There had been no new orders. Castle went up to the lines. Everything was peaceful; no one was shooting at anybody.

He went back down and called his company commanders. He listened to their reports, which were not very informative. The fascists were dug in to defend the road, Lyons said; it didn't look like they were preparing to attack.

"Well, then," Castle said, "let's see if we can take a hill from which we can interdict the road. We can't go too far because we don't know where anyone else is. But we can't just sit here doing nothing. Let's see what we can do." They sketched maps and positions in the dirt and worked out an attack with two of the companies moving forward and one holding on each flank. "Keep contact," he told them.

After awhile there was more firing as the companies moved across the shallow valley between the hills. They moved slowly, using the cover afforded by trees and brush. They started up the slope of the enemy-held hills and there was not much resistance. He could see a few fascists getting up out of their holes and crouching, then disappearing over the brow of the hill. As he watched, he heard the sound of a motor and he turned to see a staff car come up, dropping off Doran and Joe Brandt. Castle was relieved to see someone from brigade, and he started down to greet them, but as he drew near he noticed something grim about the way they looked. The happiness went out of him.

"What's going on?" Doran, who had been talking to Gates, turned on him with the question.

"We're pushing them off those hills to get to the road." Castle felt that this was a very unmilitary way to put it. Doran was in full uniform, with map case, pistol, boots, and breeches. His face was white and drawn, throwing the bones of his skull into high relief.

Doran hesitated for a moment and then said, "Call it off. Hold them where they are."

"I'll have to bring them back. Where they are now ain't nowhere."

"Whatever you have to do, do it."

Castle started back up the hill. He caught up with Lyons and told him to come back and get word to the other companies. They were to retire to their original positions. Improve them and wait for further orders. Lyons asked no questions. Castle got back to battalion just as the staff car returned. Campbell got out, followed by Gregor and Jim Borne. Campbell was big and broad-shouldered. His skin was fair and his cheeks flushed.

Aside from the glasses, which made him look impossibly intelligent, his clean-cut features resembled all the clean-cut Anglo Saxon features of all the clean-cut American boys that Castle had ever read about and envied. Borne, the brigade Party organizer, was more of the same, though slightly darker, exactly the good-to-the-last-drop faithful friend to Campbell. And Gregor. A short man behind rimless glasses, sharp-trimmed beard and moustache, with a mad-scientist bulge of forehead. Who the hell was he? Gregor spoke in whispers and moved an immaculate finger across the maps spread in the center of their little circle.

Castle stood outside the circle. He was acutely aware of his thinness, his dirtiness, and the skimpiness of his uniform, which consisted of overalls over a faded shirt, and torn *alpargatas*. He felt like a small boy in the presence of important men. It seemed that Doran had been having a deep political discussion with Gates. The tenor of it had been that they should keep fighting until the very last man, since the front seemed to have broken all around them and they were about to be cut off if they hadn't been already.

Campbell rolled right over that and, working with Gregor, was weighing the various routes that might still be open.

"We'll get this battalion out. Corbera is still open. Gandesa. We've got to start moving fast. Right now." He turned to Brandt. "Get the companies assembled on the road."

Brandt started up. But of course he didn't know where the companies were. And apparently Campbell didn't know who Castle was.

"Look, what we had better do," Castle said, "is get the men back carefully. We don't want the fascists to know we're disengaging." He turned to Watt. "Tell them to leave men behind, keeping up some firing until the others get off, and then fall in behind."

The companies came off the hills and lined up on the road that Campbell had come in on. Even before they had all been assembled, Campbell moved them off, toward Gandesa, he said. Campbell stood by the side of the road to see them get started. Satisfied, he joined Doran and Gregor at the head of the column. Gates joined Watt and Castle, and they waited until they were sure everybody was off the hills and moving with the column.

Castle took a last look at the hills where they had been.

The wounded fascist still lay on the stretcher. He seemed better. He had been fed and given water and wine. His bandages had been changed. His eyes, the whites very white from the loss of blood, stared up at Castle. He looked worried. "We might as well leave him. Tell him that. Tell him his friends will be here soon. Tell him to tell them about how well we treated him." Gates said something in Spanish. Castle raised his clenched fist. "Viva la Republica." The wounded man raised his arm and let it fall back on the canvas. He hadn't spoken. The expression on his face remained the same.

Castle ordered Carroll to blow up the ammo dump. Carroll protested. "If we blow it," he said, "it'll cave the house in."

"Anyone in it?" Only the red-tiled roof was visible over the walls. It wasn't a house that belonged to a peasant. It stood in the center of a large mesa, and the road passed by it some fifty meters from the main gate. The ammo was stacked between the road and the gate.

Carroll was saying that the farmhouse was abandoned but that it would be a shame to ruin a fine building like that.

Gates spoke for the first time. "We can't let it fall into the hands of the fascists."

Carroll shrugged, and Castle too had this feeling that it didn't matter if it did.

"If I blow it, they'll know . . ."

"Well, use your own judgment. Don't waste any time catching up with us."

They were a kilometer away when they heard the explosion. Looking back, they saw Carroll trotting toward them. Behind him, a column of white smoke held as if rooted to the ground, its edges sharp against the blue sky, tall and straight. A plinth, obelisk, monument . . . An exclamation mark getting indefinite around the edges, displaying a certain softness along its spine. Farewell.

"That cleans up all the loose ends."

They came down onto the plain on the outskirts of Gandesa. There were phalanxes of troops on foot, in camions, on horseback, jamming the road to town. East of the town, beyond the buildings, the sounds of guns rose into the dust-filled air.

51

Gates, Watt, and Castle joined Campbell and the others at the head of the column. Campbell thought that the fascists had not yet taken Gandesa; the sounds of battle attested to that. Which meant that there was a way out; they should get in there before it closed. The only way in, he could see, was by the road that the fascists were so brazenly using for the same purpose. Solution: hit them from the flank with the Lincolns, take them by surprise, and join the other brigade units.

"Our people must be holding the road from Gandesa to the bridge that spans the Ebro at Mora," Campbell said wistfully.

They could clearly see the enemy columns moving into town. It seemed to Castle that they were pretty far away; they would have a long way to go over open terrain, with damned little cover to get to the road. Behind them, the hills began again. He would have preferred going up into the hills and around the town.

He thought he ought to propose this, but to whom? They were all eyes forward, grimness in the collective visage, "a *shturm* in the *punim*" as his mother would say. Campbell, Doran, and the others seemed to lust for the attack with a kind of desperation that was part ignorance, part esprit de corps, part Communist resolve, and the rest hope and a prayer. Castle felt, again, that they knew something that he did not, so he held his counsel.

Campbell gave the orders to the officers bunched around him. The battalion spread out in attack formation and moved forward, deployed, for about a hundred meters. Campbell held his hand up and they stopped, sinking down in the stubble. Watt and Gates and Castle found a slight rise. Now the fascists were more clearly visible. Officers on horseback, riding up and down the road, kept the troops moving toward Mora where black smoke, red-streaked, billowed over the roof tops, and the clamor of battle went on unceasingly.

Castle flinched when the Lincolns' machine guns opened up. Mel Offsink, who had replaced Titus as commander of the Third Company, stood up and his men came up beside him. They started forward slowly, picking up the pace gradually. Only one company? Now the Third Company was firing and receiving fire. Mitch could see that the fascists had set up positions between the road and the Third Company. Offsink went down. The men around him fell to the ground. The attack was over.

"What was that all about?" Castle heard his voice hang in the air. He felt a confusion of emotions sweep over him. Had he not wanted the attack to succeed? Was he pleased that it had failed? Zip, zap – spiteful, gloating thoughts sped through his head . . . as fast as light, zip, zap – this was Campbell, the hero of Jarama? Zip, Zap – shame, shame, Mitch – men are getting killed.

Mitch approached Campbell, who was chewing on his lip, staring out over the plain at the men dragging back the wounded. The dead remained where they had fallen, Mel Offsink among them. Rupert was holding the seat of his pants, blood dripping through his fingers.

"We ought to go up into those hills," Castle pointed. Campbell looked first at him and then at the hills, and Castle realized that Campbell had been planning another forward attack. "Maybe we can get around to the other side?"

Doran looked at the hills; Campbell looked at Gregor. Gregor shrugged. Campbell looked back to where the fascist columns were still moving into town. There seemed to be no end to them.

"They'll be coming for us and this is not a very good position to be in," Castle pressed.

Campbell looked tired. Company commanders and commissars drifted away.

Castle put it as a statement now. "Let's get up into those hills." He led off with Watt and Gates walking beside him, not waiting for Campbell to make up his mind.

The field sloped up to the hills and he began putting one foot in front of the other, feeling now the full weight of the fix they were in. The hills took shape, and Castle mechanically selected two as good defensive positions. He assigned the smaller of the two to the Spanish Company. The next one, half again as high, was where he led the rest of the battalion. Now that the enemy knew where they were, he deployed the companies in defensive positions, instructing Luke to find a way out for the battalion. The brigade staff took up positions overlooking the Spanish Company's hill. Rupert went off to *Sanidad*. They would wait for nightfall before moving.

After a while, fascist cavalry drifted into the valley. The Lincolns watched them massing, coming between them and the Spanish Fourth Company. The MG crews positioned their guns, bracing themselves for the attack. Castle passed the word to hold fire until he gave the order to open up. Rupert came back from *Sanidad* to stand at his side, and Castle joked about how he was lucky he was a fat ass. "Never passed through?" he asked, remembering Altman.

The cavalry came within range. An officer, mounted on a magnificent roan, its flanks gleaming in the sun, rode back and forth getting the troops into position. Taking the lead, he spurred the roan to a faster gait.

"Hold your fire," Castle singsonged, over and over again. He was conscious of Campbell and Doran, and he pushed his voice into authority. Brandt moved to his side as though to ally himself with Castle's taking command.

The horses zigzagged up the slope, picking their way between the trees and the brush, the men leaning forward over their necks, kicking their flanks, occasionally straightening to get off a round. Castle waited until he could see the pale faces over the grey ponchos they wore, and when he saw, or imagined he saw, the weave of the woolen ponchos, he gave the order: "Fire. Fire," he roared.

All the guns opened up. The horsemen stopped. Dismounted riders grappled with their mounts. Those still mounted headed for cover in the cut between the hills. Unmanned horses wandered about; bodies dotted the slope.

The guns stopped firing. Brandt hopped about holding his hand. A bullet had hit the flesh of his thumb. "Went through, grazed it." He smiled at Castle. He wore his wound like a flower. It pleased him.

The Spaniards, the Fourth Company of his battalion, had joined the action, pouring fire from the smaller hill into the rear of the cavalry. Now the fascists reformed their ranks into a semicircle around the Spanish Company's hill and whipped their mounts up the slope. The hill erupted in a terrific volume of fire, exploding grenades garlanding the crest.

Castle ordered the machine guns into action, laying in supporting fire. Enemy foot-troops appeared. They set up a skirmish line and moved up behind the cavalry.

"It won't be long now before they zero in artillery and bring the planes over," he said conversationally to Campbell. It was late and he hoped they would not get around to it before dark. The next morning would be something else again.

Luke came up with Vernon Selby in tow. "Vernon says he's found a way out," Luke said, "if we want it."

"Yeah?" Castle said. "A way out? Which way, to where? Around to the other side of Mora?"

"No. The town's locked in, sir. This is out to the northeast."

"To Corbera," Gregor said, hauling out his maps and unfolding them.

"Corbera's still in our hands," said Campbell.

"Well?" Castle asked.

"You know Corbera?" Campbell asked Gregor.

"Like the back of my hand," he replied.

They all looked at Vernon Selby. He had deserted once before. He was a product of American military schools. Could he be trusted?

"Check it out again," Castle ordered Vernon. "We can't move until dark, anyway."

"What about the men on the other hill?" said Rupert.

They looked to the hill, which was quiet now. As they puzzled over what to do, volleys of rifle and MG fire and grenades erupted. The attack against the Fourth Company had come from the other side of the hill this time, out of sight of the Lincolns. It went on for two or three minutes, and then there was silence. Castle worried about the Spaniards on the other hill. He had not had time to really know them. They were commanded by Angel Gomez, a good-looking Spaniard perhaps a few years older than the recruits under his command, who were in their eighteenth year. Angel was warm, friendly, anxious to do the right thing, but very much his own man, aware of his responsibilities. Angel'd be able to take care of his men, Castle assured himself. It was his hill now. He would know what to do.

"No more – " Castle caught himself. He had almost blurted out "no more stupid attacks." Instead, "The Spaniards know this area; they'll find a way out."

Easy to say? Easy. The thing was to get the Lincolns out. Vernon had disappeared into the gathering dusk. A gun barked and a shell whistled overhead. There was a soft explosion beyond one of the hills behind them.

A lone plane appeared and circled the hills. "Looking for us," Castle said. There was another attack on the Spaniards' position. A lull, and then another. And finally the entire hill seemed to come alive with shouting and shooting and exploding grenades, and then it was over. They had no way of knowing what had happened. The night had closed in.

Vernon came back in the dark. "Okay." He reported directly to Campbell. "It's okay, sir. There is a way out."

"Fine. Gregor, you work with this man." Campbell had never heard of Vernon. "We'll follow."

"Okay." Castle turned to Brandt and Watt. "Make sure you get all the men off and marching in single file. Have someone bring up the rear and keep contact, everybody keep contact. See that they pass the word along."

It struck Castle then that Doran had not said a word in all this time. He looked at him now and Dave's eyes were flat and lusterless in the dark. It was impossible to read his mind.

They got the men out of their positions and into line and started the march. "Contact, keep contact with the man in front of you and the man behind you. Don't break the line, don't lose contact." The word passed up and down the line. Quiet, quietly follow the leader, winding over the hills in the night, carrying the north star on the left shoulder. Only Gregor seemed to know, seemed to think that they would get to where they were going. He knew Corbera like the back of his hand, he had said.

It was a long, hard march in the dark, the weary men stumbling and tripping over unseen objects. It was almost morning when they came to a road. The surface reflected whatever light there was. As far as they could see, the road was empty. No carts, camions, peasants, nothing. Word was passed back to cross one by one, in a hurry. But before they were all across, a convoy of camions came slowly grinding down the road, cutting the column in two. Unaware, the lead half with Campbell and the others kept going.

It was some time before Bianca could tell what had happened. The severed half lost contact because some of the men fell asleep waiting for the convoy to pass. The fascist cavalry now caught up with them and rode them down in the light of the early dawn. Rode them down and sabered them, some where they sat or lay on the ground wearied and asleep, others as they dodged the horses.

It was an accidental diversion that covered the retreat of Campbell's contingent. It kept the fascist horsemen busy, busy slicing the sharp blades of their sabers through the hard bones of the lost Americans. And Joe Bianca, who had found cover, watched helplessly as Kaufman grappled with the reins of a horse while the rider hacked at his head, the blade coming up red.

The lead part of the column kept going, the men asleep on their feet, too weary to be concerned with keeping contact.

"Let me carry your stuff," Castle said to Rupert, who was having difficulty keeping up.

"Nah, I'm all right." Rupert was preoccupied. He kept looking ahead to Gregor and Campbell and the others. He seemed worried about them. Castle thought it was the pain of the wound, but Rupert said he was all right.

Each time they stopped for the scouts to work out ahead of them, the men fell asleep. Standing, crouching, sitting, they fell asleep. They were emptied of emotion, of strength, of direction.

Vernon came back to Castle. "We're all right now, sir," he said.

"Gregor is leading the way. He recognized the terrain. They sent me back to get some rest."

"Good work, comrade," Castle said, coming down hard on the word comrade. "Fall in and take it easy. Keep contact." And then "Thanks, Vernon, good job."

As he walked, sometimes in front of Rupert, sometimes behind him, he listened to the sound of the column moving. The rope-soled feet shuffling across the dirt fields, the hard breathing of the men, the soft metallic tick-tucks as they shifted their weapons, hoarsely whispering, "Contact . . . contact . . . Keep up, comrade . . . keep up."

Rupert developed a limp that became more pronounced with each step. Castle needed something and someone to worry about, to feel responsible for. The column was out of his hands again. It was held together front and rear by others; there was nothing for him to do but keep walking. He decided that he would see to it that Freddie Rupert got through.

"¡Alto! ¡Alto! ¡Manos arribas!" Frightened barked commands, challenges, a rifle shot, the dull explosion of a concussion grenade. It was as though the column had run into a stone wall and exploded on contact, scattering the men like debris.

"Freddie, Freddie, where the hell are you, Freddie?" Castle searched for his one charge. The firing intensified, the shouts spread away from where the head of the column had been; the night came alive with a babel of noises. Castle felt the ground drop from underneath him as though he had gone off a cliff. It was a long way down. He landed on his feet, doubled over, the breath knocked out of him. He straightened up, and took stock. He was unhurt. He was at the foot of a stone embankment that reached well over his head. The wall cut off the sounds above. He was held there by a new night geography, a paved road before him, a cluster of houses, lights going on, and the crackle of a radio, the vacuum-tube voice snapping through the air in a language he did not understand. German? There was no way back up the wall. He could hear the sounds of running feet, shouting, and the pop and crackle of dispersed firing. He waited for Rupert to drop down after him, but no one came. The door of a house opened across the road, exposing a well-lit room. There were uniformed figures in the room and the electric voice became louder, the radio going full blast.

He could not remain where he was. He moved away from the road, keeping as close to the wall as he could until he had put a little distance between where he had been, and then, bending low, he shot out at an angle across the road. Once safely across, he kept moving at a fast walk. He was alone in the night, the North Star his only companion, fading as the sky lightened.

≣52

When he came into the light of the first day it was a green light. The green of the hills was different from the midnight blue of the night; the blue-white chip of the North Star and the dotted outline of the Big Dipper were gone. The black figures of men, lost and retreating like himself, appeared against the green. All of his thoughts were formed against a background of color, of light values, dimensions perceived in aerial perspective. If he drew close to one of the figures, it became a thing in faded blues, greys, and browns, the face taking on the color of the clothes, the eyes searching him out, recognizing, averting, turning away. The figure hurrying off, urgently alone as though only in aloneness was there safety. That first green day the black figures moved, approached, crossed, and separated, strangers to one another, aliens roaming undiscovered landscapes, recognizing their strangeness in silence and in silence withdrawing. There was no exchange of news, of directions. No questions were asked, no assistance offered. Each man was intent on becoming invisible, or at least too insignificant to be noticed. Each with a secret plan for escape and survival. This was the way, then, that the lost, the defeated and the demoralized traveled. Not together, not in mutual support, but privately, furtively, each man's fate his own.

Below the rise the road was choked with fascists, clouds of yellowish dust rising, pluming behind, the slash of colored banners stabbing through, appearing and being swallowed again in the rising dust, men, horses and trucks grinding eastward, leaving the green banks of the road a dirty grey.

The night was black and he went through the blackness. When he stopped to rest, he fell asleep, and in his sleep he was awake. His dreams, as the days wore on, became more real than the colors of wakefulness.

He stood alone on the banks of a river, the water flat and unmoving, the silver-green lawns spreading away into a distant violet haze out of which fresh young men came racing toward him, reporting, "So-and-so is here, sir. And we are there. And on our right flank is our right flank just so, sir, where it's supposed to be, comrade." "Very good," he would snap. "Now you go and tell Commander So-and-So to take that hill. And don't forget to check the other flank on your way and report back to me." "Yes sir, comrade sir," Luke, Vernon, Fisher, Gates, Brandt would say – smiling, the dew of the morning on their rosy cheeks, eager to be off. Smartly, untiringly, racing away from where he stood, spiraling off like particles lighter than air, centrifuging a perimeter of mist, reappearing almost at once with more reports, to receive further orders, then away again. Castle imagined his mother watching him, her blue eyes brilliant in the sunlight, seriously approving, clucking her tongue. "My, my, how important you are. How smart you are. All those boys taking orders from you. My. My." Cluck-cluck. Click.

He had had nothing to eat since the day battalion had pulled out. Now two, three days had passed, and nights. By the light of the fourth day, he came upon a road. He no longer knew clearly when he was awake or asleep. He moved forward in his dreams, and sometimes as he plodded along, plotting his course by the stars or by the path of the sun if he moved by day, in his mind he was standing still. The edges between sleep and wakefulness had worn thin. He passed from motion to nonmotion effortlessly, hardly aware if he rested or moved. Now this road had appeared, a chalky, ocher strip empty of life. It came out of the dark hills to run down between tilled fields, the furrows black, the parallel hillocks brown, and through a scatter of houses washed white in the morning light.

He moved along the hillside as it sloped down into the fields. His feet sank into the freshly turned soil. He slanted toward the road and walked in the ditch where the ground was dry and hard packed. Then, because he was having difficulty with the side of the ditch, he went up onto the road and approached the houses. As he neared, he could see a few black-clad figures moving around. He heard the sound of voices, and the smell of baking bread came to him.

When the people saw him coming, they stopped and pointed. He smiled and hurried on. They weren't looking at him. He wasn't there – they looked through and beyond so that he had to turn to see the emptiness of the road. Behind and already well out of the hills came a black phalanx, trailing dust, colors waving, band playing. He turned back to the houses, and the people were gone. The houses stood: deaf, dumb, and blind cubes, white and lifeless.

He turned off the road and started walking across the plowed field, going vaguely toward a line of dark green that marked the edge some kilometers away. He was unhappy about going in the wrong direction, because it meant that he would have to retrace his steps. The sound of music became clearer. He thought, They're not together . . . sounds awful.

He was about forty meters from the road. The furrows, parallel to the road, looked very deep. He picked one and stretched out in it. It seemed to him that he was skinny enough to be concealed by the ridge of dirt. It was soft and warm in the rut, very restful. Now he could hear the music approaching and going by. Doppler effect. Something he knew and didn't know. Another word encounter, blurred association . . . doppler . . . sound approaching, arriving, departing. From this you were supposed to be able to determine something. Velocity qua decibility equaled distance? Voices on the road. Shouting. Doors slamming. A scream. Wailing and laughter. Barnum and Bailey come to town.

He raised his head. The houses and the road were hazed with dust through which figures darted, danced, froze for an instant, and then swirled off. On the road, scattered troops looked across to him, over him. He could not see the screams, only hear them. The figures looked his way. He noticed this without feeling. He tired of holding his head up, so he let it sink back. His face was cool now against the black dirt that had lost its heat being shadowed by his thin body. It was cool and it smelled good; he could not hear the screams or they could not reach him where he was now . . . drifting off very fast, flowing into the soil . . . into sleep. Back with his battalion, the scouts reporting and being dispatched, the grass green, the river at his back. Everything was in order, all functioning well. Winning.

The cold woke him. He pressed deeper into the earth for warmth. He felt how near to the surface his bones were, the skeleton chilled and aching. The little village showed lights, sounds, human voices, and, like water running in the background, the sound of women sobbing. The column had gone but they had left troops behind. The road was empty.

It was very painful, coming up out of the soil like an old grapevine: twisted, wracked, the limbs creaking and cracking. The night air cut through him as he walked to the road and across it. Again, the sounds became louder, separating, commingling, drifting back and away behind him . . . falling away as he moved, his head held high searching for the Dipper.

He was in an olive grove. He scrounged beneath the trees for olives. Those he found were dried and wrinkled, just skin, a little meat and pit, mostly pit. He gathered a handful and sat beneath a tree. The olives tasted of the sun and the soil, a good nutlike taste. One crumbled between his teeth. It had no pit and tasted bitter. He looked at what he had spat into his open hand. Some animal had left round pellets of shit – of droppings.

He spat and spat, and wiped his mouth as far in as he could get, gagging. He looked more carefully at the handful of olives and picked out the droppings. He wiped the olives on his sleeve and ate them.

He lost track of the days. He dug for roots, for anything that looked like a carrot or turnip or onion. They all tasted alike: dark brown.

He studied the house before him. Small, poor, but with people inside. They were alone. The house, the people, and he. He needed water, and so he approached. A man and woman came out. Their faces told him nothing except that they were poor and of the soil.

"¿Agua?" The woman went inside and fetched a tin cup of water. They waited while he drank it.

"Many have come this way," the man said.

"And where have they gone?"

"The way you are going."

The woman gave him a handful of almonds in their shells.

"Gracias."

"De nada."

"Salud."

"Salud."

He turned to go. It would go badly with them if the fascists came upon them together. It would go badly anyhow. No matter. Give them a fighting chance.

"Wait," she called.

"Yes?"

"We will win?" she asked, looking into his eyes.

"Yes, we will win."

"Good." She raised her clenched fist shoulder high. "We must," she said.

"Yes, we must. *Salud y victoria.*"

They smiled.

Now, when he slept, he was spending more time among his scouts and the battalion down by the riverside. Lehan Larner, smooth-faced Negro, small, young, tight Lehan, singing "Down by the riverside, down by the riverside and . . ." What? How did it go? "I'm going to practice war some more." Now he preferred the dream state to the real thing. He couldn't wait until he slipped off into that green esplanade. Luke Hinman had said it was just like California. California. Way out west . . . an end to a tail of a dog, and the dog was what counted . . . you couldn't picture California . . . you had no thought at all of ever being there. How come Hinman was from

California? He thought everyone here was from Brooklyn or the East Side. These other guys weren't for real. Places like California, Texas, Montana, Virginia . . . No one alive came from there. All these outsiders . . . outlanders? He liked the sound of their names. He liked the way they smiled at him and ran off to find where the flank was and then came racing back with information. It was real useful having them around.

Was this the same house? Another? How many days had gone by? No matter, he wasn't counting. He was tied to the North Star. He had been carrying it on his left shoulder forever and it sat lightly there. It seemed to him to be very much the same house, and so from it he expected the same things. Every little house in Spain had a black-clothed woman and a black-clothed man, and sometimes there were children and sometimes there were none. They had olives and almonds and goat's milk. They wanted tobacco. Why not? He wanted tobacco too.

The river was here. The Ebro. Across the river was what the star had promised.

"Señor . . ."

"No, comrade." Fool, why insist on protocol now? A million years of *señor* . . . Forty years of wandering in this wasteland . . . Comrade . . . *Señor*. Okay. *Señor*. "Where are the *rojos?*" He does not know? "On the other side of the river?" He doesn't know.

"Not here, for sure. Perhaps farther down . . . more down . . . you understand?"

"Yes, yes. Where more down?"

He doesn't know . . . perhaps at Flix.

"Yes, how far is Flix?"

"It makes no difference. You cannot cross the river. The bridges are destroyed."

He could swim it.

"No *señor*, not at this time of the year. The river is very high, very swift."

"Yes. Then do you have a little food for me?"

Almonds and olives.

"Salud . . . y gracias, señor."

"Salud. Vaya con dios."

Cojónes. Everything was mixed up. *Salud* with God and *señor* with thanks.

Down a rough path, down, down in the darkness. Buildings, street. Everything shut up tight. Footsteps. Into a doorway. Press back, back. An armed patrol passes by. Ours or theirs? This side of the river I must assume, sir, that everything is theirs. Down this street and turn this corner. Not a light, not a sound. The walls of all the houses fortresses against the crawling, slimy dark. Suddenly the river. Rio Ebro! Mi cagen los dios. The star had brought him to the river. But on the other side were the fascisti . . . so he'd been told. Well, he must get round the town. The best way – and he had to go around now to set his course southeast to Flix instead of northeast to where? – was to swim around. No problem that. The gang had called him Tarzan in Coney Island. What the hell was a lousy river compared to the whole Atlantic Ocean? Hah! Into the water, the village a blue and black smudge to his right. Portside. When he was past the village, he took counsel with himself. He could go across the river and proceed on the other bank, but if the fascists were there, that was where they would have their combat units. More alert, more hair-trigger. If they were not there and he insisted on coming out on the west bank, then he would have to cross again. The water was cool and he drifted to exit on the same bank. He would wait for daylight to discover what was what.

He found a good place to hole up ten or fifteen meters from the river. A dead tree stump, hollow, shoulder-high. He crawled in and slumped against the sides. The stump squeezed him in, pressed the water out of his clothes. There was a V-shaped opening at the top of the stump that faced the river. It was a good place to be, and he drifted off. This night was without dreams. Perhaps the river had washed everything away.

In the morning when he awoke, the sun was well up. The village was awake, full of the sounds of people. There was rifle fire across the river, and from his side as well. *Mierda!* If he had made the other choice he would now have been among his own. He squirmed and twisted inside the bole, angry with himself. Everything came into clear focus. The hunger was real now, as was a sense of danger. Not fear, but the knowledge that he must survive the day, swim the river at night, and make himself known without getting killed in the process. Up till now he had been drifting, the only reality a star. He had had no plan, no prospects. Therefore there had not only been no fear but not even a sense of danger. When he had lain in the plowed field watching the fascists point toward him, he had not considered the possibilities. He had seen them see him . . . or so he had thought . . . and he had put his head in the dirt and drifted off. The event registered fully in his mind now, and he tried to remember how many days had passed. But now, remembering the field and the fascisti, a thrill of apprehension ran through him.

Carefully, after scanning the surrounding area, he crept out of the tree stump. He had chosen his hiding place well. The stump was hard up against a large rock that in turn was the beginning of a shrub-covered embankment. He could not be seen from above and there was room between the stump and the rock so that when he crouched he could not be seen at all unless someone came right up and looked in that one place.

A patrol came out of the town by a path that ran along the river's edge. There were six men in the patrol, their rifles slung. Their uniforms were blue – bagged trousers tucked into high leather shoes, leather bandoleers, white shirts, red tassels swinging from blue, tilted kepis. They moved purposefully along the path, pointing across the river and to the rise behind him, gesticulating. They were particularly interested in the outcropping of rock and his tree stump. It was clear that they were studying the terrain in order to occupy it. They went past his position for a hundred meters or so and then came back, stopping again to make note of his stump and rock and then, lighting cigarettes, continued into the town.

He had to get away, but he dared not chance swimming the river in daylight. Nor could he see any covered route from where he was, going away from town or up away from the river. He must think about what to do if he was discovered. For the first time since he had dropped off what must have been a terrace, a sense of reality returned. He saw objects in a new dimension; there was shape and light and shade. The colors, more real now, were less interesting and did not intrude. Through this long day, waiting for the fascist patrols to find him – at the same time waiting for the dark, hoping it would arrive first so that he might try the river – he had no illusions, no fantasies, no escapes into dream. If he dozed off, he did so uneasily and he came awake with his muscles bunched, stomach knotted. It seemed to him that if he was touched he would spring straight up into space.

From time to time, groups of fascist soldiers, some officers, came along the path below him. They did not seem to be in a hurry. Some went past, others stopped short, sat down for a smoke, killed time, and then returned to town, cheating on their patrol coverage. No civilians came along the path.

He took his few papers and little money and spread them to dry, out of sight. He spent some time taking his pistol apart and wiping it dry with dead leaves and grass. He removed the seven cartridges from the clip and dried each one. He frayed the end of a twig and used it to get inside the clip, forcing the spring down. It took more than one twig since they kept breaking, and then he had trouble getting the broken remnant out of the spring mechanism. The papers were almost dry. His military carnet. The ink had run and blurred the writing. Still, it was quite clear that Mitchell Castle was a Captain of the Fifteenth International Brigade, *Norteamericano* and Antifascist.

His party card had the same information, plus the data that he was a paid-up member of the Spanish Communist Party. It had been, he had thought at the time, like moving in with Dolores Ibarurri, La Pasionaria. A very satisfying feeling. Then there was the Socorro Rojo booklet, which showed that he had contributed twenty percent of his pay to that organization. Red Aid. The widows and families of men who had been killed by the fascists, or imprisoned . . . yes. The thirty or forty pesetas in paper money . . . the ink had not run on that. Still, it was of no use.

He put himself in the fascists' position. They would see that they had a captain of the Fifteenth Brigade in their hands (the book had not been brought up to date and so did not list him as battalion commander), a member of the Communist Party of Spain, and so on. A great prize, worthy of a firing squad . . . at the very least. Torture? He could think it but could not imagine the details. In any case, with the papers or without, execution was certain. He had not heard of them taking prisoners from among the IB'ers. Well, then, let them kill him without a name and without rank. Certainly without a party. He wrapped the cards and carnets in the paper pesetas and scraped a depression in the compost at the base of the tree trunk. He covered it over carefully and studied the place so that he would know where it was.

Later on this would cause a crisis of spirit within him. The honorable thing to do was to preserve one's military and party identity so that one might demonstrate to one's executioners one's integrity and commitment. As an instruction to them. As an example to others. Dying anonymously was a cancellation of everything – of every battle, of every moral decision, of every politic, all conviction. Of life and the struggles of life.

Something of this went through his mind before he concealed the papers, and it lingered there afterward. He would come to think of it as a test he had failed, for in the end the papers remained buried beneath the crumbled bits of dead leaves, the rotting wood and pieces of bark. He took only his pistol across the river with him.

It was not until dark, when he was already in the river and some way from its western bank, that he began to have other doubts. It was then that he remembered that there had been no firing that day from the opposite bank where the Republican forces were supposed to be. He had spent the day watching the fascist patrols walk along the bank in full sight of the other side, and they had not been fired upon. It was possible that the fascists had a bridgehead on the other side. He allowed the current to take him downstream as he pondered the problem. He entertained the idea of floating downstream all night with the thought that the further south-by-east he went the better chance he had of reaching Flix.

The water was not cold, and it was an easier way of traveling than by foot; also less dangerous. But now he saw that the current was taking him toward the far bank. Only a few strokes and he reached the shore. Carefully he left the river and listened for sounds. There were none. He started away from the river, going east. He came to a road and heard the clop-clop of horses. It was very dark as he waited beside the road. A squad of cavalry came by, heading toward the river.

Over the sound of the horses he could hear voices joined in song. It was a song he knew, that they had sung in Tarazona a hundred years ago, an antifascist hymn sung in French. He waited until the main body of horsemen had passed. Then he came up on the road behind them, arm raised in the clenched fist salute, calling softly to the last rider, "Camarada, camarada."

≡ 53

The Spanish captain was a real honest-to-goodness army officer, the first Castle had encountered. When he had made it across the Ebro and made contact with the French cavalry and identified himself as an American of the Fifty-eighth Battalion, they had led him into the presence of the captain because the captain and his company were of the Lincoln Battalion.

The captain had been at supper, flanked by his lieutenants, served by orderlies, eating off real china. The captain had looked at him, and Mitch supposed he had not been much to look at, wearing nothing but a thin shirt, faded too-short overalls, and wet *alpargatas* . . . a ten-or-more-days' beard on his gaunt face, no papers, no insignia, just another American that the fascists had pushed into the Rio Ebro.

With a wave of his hand the captain had assigned Castle a corner of the floor. An orderly had brought a tin cup filled with *bacalao* stew, and a chunk of bread and a mug of wine.

"In the morning," the captain had said, "the food camion will arrive from battalion and you may go with it."

Fritz Schatz had arrived with the chow truck. When he saw Castle, he threw his arms around him and shouted with joy. To the captain, who had watched the reunion with tolerant good humor, Schatz had proclaimed in a mixture of Spanish, German, and English, "Here is the *comandante* of the battalion, Commander Castle." A worried look had replaced the smile on the captain's fat face. He had become instantly deferential and solicitous.

Castle's one-room *plano mayor* was at the foot of a hill on the outskirts of Mora del Ebro. He had two orderlies now, just like the captain, one called Negro because he was dark – his eyes and straight black hair as black as midnight – and the other called Rubio, a pale pink, blue-eyed, red-haired, buck-toothed smiling giant. He was uncomfortable with the orderlies, who soon made it clear that they knew their job better than the *comandante* knew what it was supposed to be.

Nearby, a single railroad track ran through a tunnel in the hill, down to the town beside the river. Inside, the *marineros* had a small donkey engine lined up behind a couple of flatbeds. There was a twelve or sixteen inch – Mitch couldn't tell the difference – mounted on the forward flatbed; the rear car was for crew and ammo. Two or three times a day, just before and just after siesta, the donkey engine would propel the cars into the open. The crew would swivel the cannon, which had been taken from a warship no longer in service for lack of fuel, and fire a round across the river into Mora la Nueva.

It was something to see. Castle would follow the shallow, lumbering trajectory of the shell, note its landing on the empty main street of the village, and hold his breath for the explosion. There would be a flash of orange flame caught in a fat black cloud, a pause, and then a flat dull boom. Occasionally a shell would clumsily tumble up the street, a dud. It all seemed to take place in slow motion. When the smoke dispersed, the street looked no worse off than before.

There was a rough wooden bench set into the south side of the *casa*, and Castle would spend his siesta time there reading. Jimmy Sheean had been one of the first reporters to reach the battalion after the retreats, the first to report the safe return of Mitchell Castle and others. "I'm off to Paris to file this report," Sheean had said. "Is there anything I can bring back for you?" And Castle's instant reply had been "Hey, if you can, pick up two and three of Mann's *Joseph in Egypt*. I got through number one of the trilogy before I left the States, I'm dying to see how it all comes out." Sheean had been astonished by the request, but had gotten the second volume to him.

On alternate days, Castle marched the battalion about a kilometer upstream to practice river crossings on a dry streambed that ran down to the Ebro. The men shaped up in teams of eight or ten, ran down to the "riverbank" laughing, embarked in imaginary boats, and rowed across plying imaginary oars. Reaching the opposite bank, the crews deployed to storm enemy positions as they had at Figueras long ago. There were no casualties.

On the days they were not crossing the "river," there was not much else to do. Castle used the time to get to know some of the men who had just come into the battalion, or who had come back from officer training.

Yale Stuart, a veteran of Jarama, had been wounded when the fascists broke through at Belchite. He had been Dave Reiss's *Jefe de Plano Mayor*, and Castle gave him the job of organizing the new *plano mayor* company: orderlies, observers, scouts, and wire men.

Castle was content to leave these choices to Yale, who seemed bright and energetic. Brandt, however, questioned the wisdom of including Morris Mickenberg as a scout. Mickenberg, Brandt the Party *Responsable* said, was politically unreliable. But Yale vouched for him and that was good enough for Castle. It was the second time Castle had overridden a Party personnel decision. When Brandt had tried to replace Gabby Klein as the Party *Responsable* of the Third Company, Castle had said "no dice," and the Party had had to accept his decision. Gabby was one of the few *soldados* who had served exceptionally well in every action and yet remained unscathed.

Nick and Manny were back, Nick to the MG Company and Manny to staff, along with Joe Gordon, who had lost an eye at Jarama and had been sent home. He and six other wounded and repatriated Lincolns had opted to return to the battalion after hearing of the fascist breakthrough. "When I volunteered," Castle had written to Irene, "I knew nothing of what it would be like to be in a war where the bullets are real and people shoot to kill. Bombs, shells, etc., mean business. Then there's the rotten food, the thirst, dirt, and so on . . . So these comrades who have been here before, who have been wounded, been through it all, come back knowing, unlike such as me, what they are coming back to, what they are getting into. They are special, they have a special place in my heart." When he reread what he'd written, he'd been embarrassed. "Purple prose," he muttered. But he had not fully grasped the meaning of their return to war until he began to describe it, and then he had felt it so deeply that it had to come out the way it did.

There wasn't much light in the small, low-ceilinged room, and Castle wondered if Gates had arranged it that way to heighten the effect, or if it was because there was not much power available. The two small bulbs were arranged so that the dull orange light fell mostly on Leo, leaving the others in shadow. Gates leaned back into the dark, across the table from Leo, his sharp beak coming in and out of the light like a hen pecking scattered corn. . Joe Brandt and Jim Bourne sat up against the wall by the darkened window, representing the Party but not speaking. Castle and George Watt sat against the opposite wall. Charlie Abrams, the interpreter Yale had scared up for Castle, sat next to Gates, translating for Jose Valledor, the brigade commander who had replaced the repatriated Copic, and Juan Abad, who had replaced the fat captain, who had found Castle's training regime too strenuous to tolerate and had gotten himself transferred to Barcelona. Abad was Mitch Castle's *hermano de sangre* – his blood brother, his equal – to replace Castle should Castle fall by the wayside or be sent home. And Leo Rogin, not much of anything at the moment, was the center of attention.

Castle had told Gates that he would not have Leo Rogin in the battalion. He was the battalion commander and he ought to be able to say who he wanted and who he didn't – and he didn't want Leo. He had accepted the others Yale had brought back to the battalion. He didn't know them, or know whether some were better or worse than Leo. What he had felt when he saw Leo was that it would be impossible to deal with him, to fit him in. It wasn't the desertion, or the fact that Leo had deserted so often, or even that he might have been involved in other things inimical to the cause. It was remembering that Leo had lain out there in the wheat field at Villa de la Cañada until the stretcher bearers had come to carry him out. That he had let them carry him out while there had been wounded men bleeding and hurting and dying under the blazing sun, the flies on their wounds, Butch nearly getting killed carrying him out.

It had not seemed of great importance to Castle before, but now, after the retreats, with so many men dead or hacked up and still coming back for more, he had told Gates, "I can't stand the sight of Rogin. I don't want him in the battalion. He'll only fuck off again."

Nevertheless, Gates had set up this meeting and Castle watched him as he pecked away at Leo. Peck, peck, peck . . . The same old shit, Mitch thought, collaboration with the POUM, the anarchists, blackmarketeering, desertion. Gates went at him in short bursts, each word hard and perfectly formed, like an impersonal voice on the radio. Sometimes the voice came from the shadow, soft in the shadow, suggestive of omniscience, then hard and loud and accusatory when his head bobbed into the light.

"The POUMists are part of the Fifth Column. Fascists, agents-provocateurs, spies, assassins. You knew that."

"No. Yes," Leo shifted. "Maybe. But not the people I was with. Maybe the leaders . . ."

"All of them, whether they know it or not. You knew that."

"No. But I wasn't helping them. I wasn't part of what they were doing – whatever they were doing."

"You used them to get out. They used you in the process. You and the others. You were exploited as an example of the alleged demoralization in the brigade. A proof of disintegration and mass desertion. Because of you and the others, they were able to spread the rumor that the 'Communist rats' were deserting the sinking ship."

"I couldn't control what they were saying. I wasn't interested. The way things looked, it didn't seem to matter."

"All he was interested in," Castle put in, "was getting out. That's all he's ever been interested in. And he doesn't care how . . . even if he's carried out while his pals are bleeding to death."

"That's not true. This time there was a good reason for going to Barcelona. I had to take this kid to the hospital. And then I was coming back to Agua Caliente and then, well, I met these Americans. They said the war was over. Everyone's been killed or captured, they said. There's nothing between Barcelona and the fascists. It's every man for himself, they said . . ."

"'They said, they said,'" Gates barked. "Who said? Who were they? Fascists, Trotskyites?"

"No. No. I knew some of these guys. Walter Cox, Tony Shaker, Steve Tsanakas, lots of others, Communists, comrades. They said that the battalion HQ was wiped out at Belchite, the brigade HQ at Corbera . . . Campbell, Doran, Reiss, and a lot of other guys. Jeez . . . you too," he turned to Castle. "They said you had had it."

"You mean I've become a Trotskyite rumor," Castle laughed, pleased to hear that someone in the rear had noted his absence.

Leo started to say something and thought better of it. There was a moment of silence during which Castle could hear what he had just said echoing, and they were all quiet thinking that all the others were indeed dead while he himself had been missing for nine days. It was quite possible that "they" had legitimately thought him dead.

"Yeah, well," Mitch broke in. "We've been through this before, so I want you to know one thing for sure. I don't care what you do with him, but we" – Mitch put the weight of the battalion behind the word – "we ain't taking this guy back."

"But that's where he's going," Gates laughed. "And that's what this is all about." He leaned back into the shadows. "Captain Castle," he said quietly, "you'll know how to handle him."

Castle knew it was a lost cause but he tried again. "We have better things to do than . . . what the hell am I going to do with him?"

"You'll think of something."

So much for being battalion commander. It was clear that a decision had been made over his head, behind his back, around the corner. Gates, or someone from SIM, had already assigned someone to do something over which he would have no control. But this was Gates, and Gates was brigade and more than brigade. He was the Party and it was obviously a Party matter – Jose Valledor had remained silent throughout – and Castle had enough respect for the Party not only to acquiesce, but having exhausted his objections, to become part of the decision.

"Okay, so that's it."

Leo did not get up right away. He sat thinking, *that's it*. He looked around the room at the faces in the shadow. How many times had he been here? What was "it"? He was weary of the running, of the effort required both to run and to stay. To run for his life or to stay for his convictions. The convictions had somehow become a part of him, and he had them to the extent that he could not face abandoning them. Needing approval, he looked for it only among his comrades. It was not now important to him that his father or his political enemies or the guy next door understand and accept him. Somewhere along the line he had become both ideologically and socially committed. He resented all the comrades back home who were not being tested, all the guys in Spain who were assigned to safe rear positions and not being tested. He resented having been relegated to the ranks at the very beginning, because he now thought that if he had been given a position of leadership or responsibility . . . In fact, everything had tested his convictions, and though they had been shaken they had held firm, because he had not escaped from Spain; he was always stopped by the prospect of the scorn and ostracism of his comrades. Of Aaron Adler and Murray Arnov, dead or alive; alive and dead; they were still a heavy presence in his heart.

They came into his mind's eye without effort just as they had been: Murray, rosy cheeked, sweet and gentle, a happy string of words and music . . . fat Murray. And beetle-browed Aaron, who was fat and soft and looked hard and scowling, but who was smart and gentle, too. Loving Murray finding the hooks, the twists in lines and words that made the songs different, the songs of protest changing in his hands from a blunt-edged axe to a slender bright shaft of shining steel, a flashing, darting needle. Murray and Aaron loving each other and loving music and the movement, and holding him between them by their love of each other and not of him, and not loving him, loving each other the more . . . needing him and not loving him making their love more real, and he needing their love and not having it, but having the love they had for each other and the music between them and the joy of their brilliance . . . reflecting. He could not run away, because he could not bring them with him. In the end he had been picked up along with the men who had thought the war was over. Fortified by their reasoning, he concluded that the war was indeed over, and he was in one piece – safe.

"Okay, *venga, adelante* . . . let's go, comrade." Castle's big voice swept over him and he stood up.

"You won't be sorry, comrades," Leo heard himself saying. It was part of the formula, more a vague hope than a promise. But as always, he felt better for having said it. He smiled at Castle. "Yeah, let's go, *comandante*."

Castle's answering grin, white and wickedly squared at the ends of his stretched lips, came on and switched off and told him nothing.

When they were outside, where the dark of night was less menacing than the dark corners of the room they had left, and the starlit sky more friendly than the naked bulb, Leo said, "I'm sorry." And he was. He felt bad for Castle, who had become the battalion commander in a way that neither Leo nor, he sensed, Castle himself could understand; who now had the problem of worrying about other people's lives when it was quite clear to Leo that Castle had never learned to worry about his own. Castle, his thin figure wrapped in a flapping black poncho, the heavy Luger bouncing against the bones of his hip, hurried on ahead. Leo felt sorry, real bad, to have become an additional burden. . . to be "handled," how? he wondered.

But he was as much a prisoner of the decision as was Castle. There was nothing he could do about it, not now.

"Don't worry about me," he said. "I won't be any trouble."

They had come to the edge of the village. Castle halted and turned to face him. Leo tried to hold his gaze steady as Castle's eyes searched his face, but he could not. He looked up the road to the battalion bivouac, off to the side where the tilled field came right up to the edge of the village, and across the thin dark face whose black and glittering eyes probed him, and then he looked off again into space. Inwardly he cursed the uncontrollable shiftiness of his eyes.

"No," Castle said, "you won't be any trouble."

Castle leaned against the wall of the adobe hut that was battalion headquarters. The night was clear and soft, and tomorrow was May Day. There would be games and celebrations, competitions in marksmanship and the handling of weapons, and speeches. He didn't know much about the program because it was in the hands of the commissars and the Spaniards. He was grateful because it would be a break in the training program.

He puffed on his pipe, enjoying the tobacco that had been sent from home, savoring the smoke and thinking about May Day in order to take his mind off the new problem Gates had saddled him with. "You'll take care of it." All he had done so far was to assign Leo Rogin to the Third Company and send him down the hill in Charlie Abrams's custody to make sure he got there.

He jerked himself off the wall. The Third . . . Morris Tobman's company. Tobman, his ever-present, smiling, fighting, antifascist good-luck talisman, had been lost in the retreats. "Shit," he said, "Rogin's no kind of replacement – "

"What d'ja say?" Watt called from inside the hut.

"Nothing, nothing." *Goddamn, he's got me talking to myself.*

Castle heard the guard's challenge and Abrams's response.

"Por la Victoria."

"Fortificar."

To win . . . dig in. All they had to do was dig and dig and so thwart the fascist juggernaut, hold the line, stop time, and everything would be all right, which didn't make sense from a military standpoint, but you had to know as a developed comrade that war was politics as well as battles, and if they held and won time, somehow the political situation would change in favor of the Republic. Roosevelt would quarantine the aggressors. Blum would open the border, and the mighty British navy would stop the flow of arms to the fascists. Then the Loyalists could come out of the holes they were digging and smite the enemy hip and flank all the way back to Morocco, Rome, and Berlin.

"Fortificar," Abrams said and came up the path to him.

Watt came out to stand with him. "Everything okay?"

"Yes," Abrams said, "if you mean by okay did I deliver him to the Third. I did. Harold wasn't too happy about it."

"No?" Watt laughed. "What'd my fellow commissar have to say?"

"Nothing much. Something like, we'll make it work this time, right Leo? Rah, rah, rah."

"Always the optimist. That's our job." Watt was cheerful. "I'm going down to the First Company, Castle. See how they're making out for tomorrow."

"You do that, George," Castle said.

"Right." And George Watt, cheerful, optimistic, golden-haired commissar, limped down the path. He had been sent to the hospital but had returned after a couple of days because, as he put it, "There were guys there in worse shape than me." George had brought a lot of guys back with him, some of whom Castle had to return forcibly, they being in no condition to walk, much less train or fight. Everybody, it seemed to Castle, wanted to do his share. Everyone except Leo.

"He's a happy kid," Abrams said. And after awhile, "What are you going to do about him?"

"About George?" Castle knew he didn't mean George.

Abrams blew gently on his *machero*, firing the orange rope into a bright ember that flared ever brighter as he lit his cigarette, sucking the smoldering rope smoke in, mixing with the fragrance of the American tobacco, producing a pungent cloud that hid his face for an instant. And then Castle found himself looking into Abrams's bright blue eyes that seemed lit up from inside, shining through milk-glass, waiting for Castle to say what he had to say, what he expected him to say.

"We'll have to take care of him," Castle said. "Get a couple of Spanish comrades and dig a slit trench. Out there near the river. Big enough. Let me know."

Abrams came off the wall, eager and ready. "What'll I tell them about the hole?"

"Slit trench. Tell them it's part of the defenses. Mucho necessary right now. *Fortificar. Mucho fortificar.*"

Abrams spoke Spanish like a native. He was one of those middle Europeans who spoke four or five languages. He had come back into the battalion from some rear base where he had served as an interpreter. Russian, Rumanian, and French, as well as the Spanish. His perfect English sounded only a tick or two foreign. Castle had found him useful, though it wasn't always clear who was using whom. As Castle watched him hustle along the path to get the job done he wondered whose idea it had been . . . his or Abrams's.

"Like you said, Harold," Leo laughed nervously, "digging graves is no work for a Jewish boy. So I quit. I quit and I was going to take care of this one thing, this sick village kid, and then come back and get back with the battalion and all that." He sipped wine from a tin cup, put it down, picked it up and sipped again, not because he wanted the wine, but because he was uneasy. Harold hadn't been nearly as happy to see him this time as he had the last, still he sat quietly and listened, occasionally refilling his cup. Leo figured that Harold was curious about people, especially people who acted differently than he did. Harold didn't seem quite able to grasp the fact that people, or more exactly fellow revolutionaries, could or would act differently. Trying to satisfy Harold's curiosity wore him down.

He sipped and looked around. They were seated in a depression scooped out of the soil long enough ago that the smell of wine and tobacco and unwashed men masked the smell of newly dug earth and the smell of the green branches that formed the roof. A candle stuck in an empty wine bottle gave them barely enough light to see each other, but not enough light to disturb the company commander, who snored gently in the far corner, his head pillowed on a holstered Parabellum. Books and newspapers, mess tins, cartridge belts, a rifle, blankets were barely visible stacked against the sides of the *chabola*. It was warm, almost too warm in the *chabola*, as the candle consumed the oxygen locked in by the poncho draped over the entrance to keep the light from filtering out. Aside from the quiet snoring and the soft sound of their voices, the night outside, which he felt as a thing dark and solid bearing down on him, was very quiet.

"It's awfully quiet," he said. "Is it always this quiet?"

"Just about," Harold replied. "Things have settled down on this section of the front. An occasional shell across the river one way or the other. That's about it. Except down there." He waved his hand. "They yell across the river and our Spaniards yell back. Keeps 'em awake through the night."

"Doesn't that give away our positions?"

"I suppose so. But the fascists taunt them yelling, 'We know your *comandante* Castillo, who will be one fallen castle when we get through with him,' and insults like that. Our kids just have to give it back to 'em."

"What kind of commander is he, anyway?"

"Okay."

"I mean, I know him. We came over together. After all, he's only from Brooklyn."

"You must be a Giant-fan-type chauvinist," Harold laughed.

"You know what I mean." Leo was encouraged because Harold wasn't responding with the standard political-consciousness lecture. "How's the arm?"

Harold held up his right arm awkwardly, a decided angular crook in the gesture. "Two different times in almost the same place. The bastards have a thing about this arm."

Leo shook his head. "Jeez." What could you say about a man who had been wounded two times, same place or no, coming back for more.

The carelessness that came from the wine pushed Leo on. "A Dodger fan has to be a loser. A handball player. A green YCL'er. You wouldn't believe the discussions we had when we were cooped up in France, waiting to come over. He as much as admitted he'd never read any Marxist literature other than the *Daily Worker.* And you can bet your bottom dollar he's never read an army training manual." A thought struck him. "Can he read a map?"

"You're hopeless," Harold said. "You've read Marx, you've had military training, and I'm sure you can read a map, but you're hopeless. Right now you're sitting here talking yourself into another one of your grand retreats. You get another chance and here you are, working yourself up with a lot of irrelevant nonsense." Harold started up.

"No, wait." Leo didn't want to let go of Harold even though he seemed to have provoked him. He needed at least one friend in the battalion. "I'm not pitting myself against Mitch . . . Castle. I know he's been in the thick of it all the time I – well, all the time. He probably learned a lot in the field."

"You betcha life he did. We all did."

"Yes, that's what I mean. I was just asking . . . never mind." And, as

Harold started up again, "Wait. Please talk with me a little bit longer." Harold sat down, his movement making the candle flame dance. The company commander broke off his snoring, turned and grunted. "It's just that it's so quiet here. It makes me nervous."

"Oh. I thought the shooting made you nervous."

"This is almost worse . . . waiting for it."

"You just got here and you're nervous already?"

"Well, how soon before it starts up?"

"We're not quite ready to go on the offensive yet but we're getting there."

"We? I didn't mean we. For Chrissakes, how can we go on the offensive after what's happened? You know most of the guys going through Barcelona, headed for the border, thought the war was over. Jeez. I thought that they were all that were left alive . . . you should've seen them. So how can we – "

"How many?"

"How many what?"

"How many did you actually meet who were running away? Who thought the Republic was finished?"

"You don't know, Harold. You wouldn't believe it. There were hundreds."

"No, I don't believe it. And I'll tell you why." Harold leaned toward him, suddenly a hostile presence, the candlelight carving his face into dark hollows and yellow ridges. "Because while you were running, looking for an excuse to desert, our guys were being sabered down by the Moors, drowning in the river. Yes . . . by the hundreds you say you saw running. And the rest were fighting and making their way across to right here. To make a stand. To come together. We're here, you understand? Getting ready to go back. That's the way it's always been. But you, the way you are . . ." He paused. ". . . Isn't a good way to be."

"Good Christ." The company commander sat up. "What the hell are you shouting about? Can't you let a comrade sleep? What's going on?" He turned on Leo. "You still here? Hell, Harold, aren't you through giving this . . . ah . . . haven't you converted him into a class-conscious hero yet? C'mon. Let's get some sleep." He rearranged the Parabellum, laid his head on it, and drew his poncho over his head, muttering.

In the dark, the space seemed no bigger than it had in the *chabola*. Maybe less, without the poor light of the candle, for though the sky had a full complement of stars, they seemed to give no light at all, and the night walled him in on all sides.

"*Alto.* Who goes there?" Harold spoke suddenly into the darkness. Leo listened to the heavy breathing and the sound *alpargatas* make on dirt paths. His insides recoiled, feeling the sweet terrifying cramp of muscles tensing.

"What? No password, *camarada?*" Abrams came through the wall, his face white and shining, his eyes reflecting some unseen light, lighting the small space between them. "Ho. It's you. Don't commissars know the password for the night?" he said accusingly. And then, before Harold could answer, Abrams said "Leo . . . just the man I'm looking for. Commander Castle has a job for you."

"I'm taking him to his assigned section," Harold said.

"No, he's coming with me."

"What for?"

"Sentry duty. Come on." Abrams took his arm but Leo held back. He pulled his arm away gently because, though he wanted to struggle, he didn't know why.

"What?" Harold sounded surprised. "Our company has posted its guards already. What's this?"

"Battalion guard. Tomorrow's a big day and we're using the men who won't be in the festivities. The rest of us have to get our sleep."

"But he hasn't been issued a firearm yet."

"We'll take care of that. What the hell is all the fuss about, anyhow? There isn't going to be any shooting. He'll be back in a couple of hours."

"Well, you ought to go through the company commander."

"For Christ's sake, you don't even know the password and you're citing rules. Go ahead. Tell him it's an order from Castle. What are you waiting for?"

"He's asleep."

"Well, wake him up."

"Oh. Never mind. It's okay, I guess. Go ahead, Leo. I'll see you in the morning."

55

Castle leaned against the wall smoking his third pipe, waiting for Abrams and Leo, his thoughts elsewhere. He looked up at the stars and thought of Cyrano lying in the gutter reaching for a star for his love and how he and Irene had read it aloud to each other. He thought he should be able to say something wonderful about the stars that hadn't been said before. The young Joseph tending the flocks and gazing up into the firmament, noting the progression of the constellations. But all he could come up with was that night on the beach when he had carried on for . . . what was her name? No matter. He had gone on about the stars and the galaxies and the enormity of space and how small their earth was and of how little importance or significance they were as human beings and how transient their stay, and so what was a little maidenhead after all when measured against the infinities. Thinking he was making a great impression on this pretty little girl from Newark, New Jersey, whose name he could no longer remember. But when he had bent over to spread his jacket on the sand he had farted loud and clear and then the stars and the night and the girl and the romance had all gone up in fart-smoke.

Somewhere in the night a shot sounded far off. He waited for the flurry that would follow, one shot setting off a hundred nervous riflemen. But that was all. The one shot, and then the stillness swallowed it up. Irene. Damn her. He shifted against the wall. She had sent the tobacco he was smoking; it had been waiting for him when he got back across the river. And later her letters had caught up with him. The last one was too much. Goddamn her and her stars and her Roxanne and all that crap. The last letter had enclosed a clipping from the *New York Times* giving the names, his among them, of the men who were still missing in the retreat. And a copy of a letter she had sent to Franco. No. He shuffled his feet, feeling now the same embarrassment and anger he had felt when he had read it. To Franco! All about how she was a Catholic and praying for Franco and praying for Mitch and how Franco should, if he captured Mitch, take good Christian care of him. Reminding him of the Christian virtues of charity, forgiveness, mercy, and all that shit. And praying for him. To Franco! Too much.

He heard the sentry's challenge and Abrams's "Fortificar." He knocked his pipe against the wall and shoved it into his pocket. It was hot against his thigh and he came off the wall pulling his flesh away from it. He took the Luger out of its holster and shifted a cartridge into the chamber. He checked to see that the safety was off and returned it to the holster, then started down the path to meet them.

"Hello, Mitch," Leo giggled. "Captain Castle, I mean." He hated to hear himself giggle but he couldn't control himself. The dread he had felt all night, which had increased when Abrams came to get him and which had dragged on as he silently followed Abrams in the dark, staying close on his heels, not wanting to follow him and not wanting to be left alone in the night, suddenly found nervous release when Castle appeared. "Fortificar," he said. "That's the password."

"Yeah," Castle said. "Let's go."

It was funny the way Abrams, who had chattered all the way over, wasn't talking now. Leo couldn't stop himself from talking. "Hey, Commander," he called over his shoulder. "Where you putting me? How come you're personally conducting me to my post?"

"This is a battalion post." Castle's voice was quiet and unhesitating.

Taking his eyes off Abrams, who was leading the way, Leo looked back to smile at Castle. To indicate that he believed him, that he believed in him. And he did, though the whole thing seemed unreal; as fantastic as the dry runs across a nonexistent river he had heard about. Maybe it was SOP in this egalitarian outfit for a battalion commander to personally escort a new man to his post.

"I suppose I'll get a rifle from the comrade I'm relieving." Neither Abrams nor Castle carried rifles, only the holstered pistols slapping at their sides.

Leo had heard about the shortage of arms that had come about because so many of the men had abandoned their weapons during the retreats. That was one thing he never would have done had he been there. It all depended on his having been there, of course, but supposing he had . . . He was too much of a soldier to part with his weapon, under any circumstances. *Your firearm is precious . . . guard it with your life and never, never leave it because that might cost you your life.* That was military training, apart from being a Communist and not throwing away something so precious, something bought with the sweat and blood of the working class, something shipped through great difficulties to be put into your hands to protect the antifascist front. He had forgotten Bruneté. Well, that was different, he reasoned.

Apparently Castle had not heard his question.

"Don't worry, I'll take good care of it," he said. "The rifle, I mean. I know how scarce they are now."

"Where is it?" Castle spoke past him to Abrams.

Abrams seemed to be slowing down, looking around. Even in the dark Leo was able to see that they had come up on a strip of land that was higher, like a raised road running along the bottom of a shallow depression in the land. It wasn't high enough to command any sort of extended field of vision, the night seeming blacker and denser all around as though closed in by higher ground than the strip, which he knew now wasn't a road because the dirt was soft underfoot.

Abrams drew up in front of him. "We're here," he said.

Leo searched to see where "here" was. He barely made out a hole cut like a slit trench in the center of the strip. It had the familiar smell of freshly turned earth that he had smelled so many times before digging graves with the *zapadores*. He could smell the size and depth of it, even the shape.

"But there's no one here . . ." He hated the sound of the nervous giggle he couldn't suppress. "It's like a – " He turned to Castle, and as he turned, a smile on his face, he caught sight of the dull gleam of metal against the blackness of the night. A *pistol*, he thought, *why a pistol for . . . how stupid . . .*

He was smiling at the foolishness of a pistol for guard duty when everything lit up. He was still believing in everything, even though it made no sense and it wasn't happening at all, but he wasn't trusting his judgment anymore. He had to trust –

Castle's face appeared in a flash of exploding flame, and then it was gone with everything else in the sudden rush of blackness that swept him away.

56

May Day was bright and sunny. The companies were drawn up in parade formation, looking ragged because no matter how straight they stood and how precisely aligned were the ranks, still the odd uniforms, patched and unpressed, the shaven and unshaven faces, the long and short hair, the berets, wool hats, and peaked caps, all gave an impression of disorder that the geometry of squares could not overcome.

The section commanders called out the men's names and reported to the company commanders, and the company commanders made their way across the dirt field to where Castle stood with Abrams and Watt. First Company, all present, Second Company all present, Third Company, one man absent, Leo Rogin. Fourth Company, all men present.

"All right," Castle turned to Watt. "So what else is new? Let's see what kind of show you've got here." He wanted very much for the festivities to get under way. He was, he felt, putting on a good front, but the sooner the men got into the program the less time they would have to wonder about Rogin's disappearance so soon after he had rejoined the battalion.

He had had a bad night haunted by the sound Leo had made when Abrams shoved him into the slit trench, the whoosh forced out of his lungs when his body hit bottom. And when he tried to go to sleep later, he remembered his melancholy cousin Sarah, the old maid who was always threatening to kill herself because she wanted to make sure she was dead, so as not to be buried alive; there were, she said, "poor souls found in crazy positions when their coffins were opened later, with signs of torturous struggle etched on their faces, their fingers curled, nails broken and bleeding." It had kept him awake. The groan coming from the black grave.

"Sonofabitching deserter . . . took off like I said he would," said Abrams the actor.

"Oh, well," Watt said. "Let's not have it spoil the day."

"Yes," Castle said. "Let's get on with it. What's first, George?"

"The drill contest, then the races and marksmanship, and then the games, tug of war and so on. Shall we begin?" And when Castle nodded, he announced, "It's the Spanish Company first, ¡Compañía Los Quatro! ¡Comenzar!" His voice started down as low as he could get it and still be loud enough to carry, and then grew shrill with the effort, finally cracking at the end. He turned red-faced to Castle. "I wish I had your voice, damn it."

The Fourth Company came to attention, Juan Abad barking out orders in Spanish. As the company swung into action, Castle thought: Spaniards would come into the battalion in greater numbers, cadres of the future, *hermanos de sangre*; one Spaniard for each American volunteer, side by side. Castle had spelled it out to the troops. Train these comrades to take your place someday. *Soldado, sargento, teniente, capitán*, whatever. Not knowing that though they were only words to him – like "someday the revolution," only a slogan to give some long-range perspective to the day-to-day fighting – the words were a promise not only for Abad and the cadres but for some of the Americans for whom the question now was not would they go home, but when?

This was a problem that Gates had to deal with now that he was brigade commissar. "Not until we're through here," he told the men who raised the question. "Not until we're through, and any cocksucker who says otherwise is an agent provocateur."

The men had not liked being called cocksuckers. It had not done much for Gates's popularity, and commissars were supposed to be popular with the troops.

Now Juan Abad, small, thin, dark, the smooth skin of his face tightly stretched over small bones, disappeared in a cloud of dust as the troops marched off, replaced by the First Company.

They marched on a flat place with the river west of them and a great big rock of a single mountain to the east with white clouds sitting on top of it, the sun everywhere else. All over Spain probably. One sun for a Spain cut in two. Cut across to the shores of the Mediterranean. It wasn't, Castle thought, as though it was severed by a meat axe into two unrelated sections. Spain was one, and division achieved in battle mattered only for the moment.

It also mattered that Madrid was out if he got leave again. Eulalia was in Madrid, and he was thinking about Eulalia; he would love to be with Eulalia right now. He needed her. He turned his back on the marching companies. He thought hard about Eulalia so he would not be thinking about . . .

Irene. The letter from Irene. The copy of the letter she had written to Franco, and one to some bishop in Salamanca, pleading for Mitchell Castle's life. Now she'd be sure her prayers had saved him from some sort of horrible fate.

Eulalia. Well, Eulalia was out of reach. There was a line drawn on the map of Spain, and that line was a barrier. Come to think of it, the lines on the map had been changing ever since he arrived in Spain. The changes he remembered best were the ones effected by the Loyalist offensives in Estremadura and the Aragon. They looked much bigger to him than the changes wrought by the fascists' offensives, which had wiped out most of the southern coastline and the northern provinces and all of the Aragon and down to the sea at Tortosa. That was how it was with lines on a map. They kept changing and one day, who knew, Madrid might be just around the corner. He turned back to view the troops.

A bus and a truckload of civilians arrived from Barcelona. They spilled out of the vehicles onto the ocher field, bright splashes of color like flower petals, spinning in a breeze. There were shop girls, seamstresses from the city in gay colors to cheer the *soldados* at the front, the men accompanying them in black or dark blue suits, with white shirts and no ties . . . red armbands, and along one side of the truck, a white banner with large red letters, *¡FORTIFICAR ES VENCER!*

Castle shook hands with the men and women, and they were smiling and laughing with the names flying back and forth over his head along with the rapidly spoken Spanish and Catalan, Abrams pausing now and then to tell him what they were saying. It mostly had to do with how they dedicated all their work to the Fifty-eighth Battalion, to the *voluntarios*, and how proud they were, and how, united, they were going to win the war. They presented the battalion with a banner that they had made in the shop: broad bands of red, gold, and purple, the colors of the Republic, on a field of tightly woven linen with "58th Bn XV Brigade" embroidered in white silk thread.

The Lincolns, officially the Fifty-eighth, had never had a flag. Somehow, seeing this new banner raised over the troops made him think of Bart Van der Schelling, the great baritone who had led them in singing "We are the fighting antifascists" when they were training in Tarazona. Now Bart was in the hospital with a bullet in his neck. Bart would have loved carrying this new banner, singing, leading the troops. Castle wondered if Bart would be coming back, and if so, whether he would be able to sing.

"We shall do everything in our power to bring honor to this banner," Castle said, Abrams translating. Castle saluted, and everyone raised clenched fists to their foreheads. Then they all turned to watch the games. The contests went on and on, the men running and cheering and horsing around, *Americanos* and their *hermanos de sangre*. The day, which had started out bright and sunny, seemed to get brighter and sunnier. After awhile they took a break to eat and drink wine and award prizes to those who had won the events: cigarettes, tobacco, handkerchiefs, socks, books, candy, hard salami. Things that had been sent from home to men who were dead somewhere on the other side of the river, or who had drowned in the river. But Castle did not think of that as he helped Watt hand out the prizes, enjoying the wide grins of the sweating men, the applause of the civilians; and the part of Spain that was here where they were celebrating May first seemed to have more heart, more courage, than all the rest of Spain . . . except perhaps Madrid, which though cut off was still the beating, indestructible heart that would go on beating to the Moorish flamencos. *No Pas-er-an* . . . forever.

It was time, he thought, to stop the *fortificar* and start winning.

57

There were a lot of things to chew over, and Castle was sure that he would remember everything that had happened: May Day before crossing the river, October in Barcelona. One hundred and fifty days, more or less, between the Ebro and the Hotel Majestic. Nothing more to do but go back in time.

Having gone over everything and satisfied himself that he had it all, it came as a shock when he realized he had hardly thought about Leo Rogin in all that time. He would not have thought of Leo at all if he hadn't just been remembering the clear blue wonderment in Abrams's eyes as he looked up from the stretcher, asking, "Am I going to die, Mitch?" Mitch Castle was now alone with what had happened that night, the night before May Day. He had not thought of it since the day after, when he had agonized over the sound coming from the grave.

Right now he was getting a headache, and he didn't know whether it was from all the *vino* he had drunk the night before, or from the pounding his head was taking from Jo Davidson. He watched out of the corner of his eye as Davidson worked the clay over with a wooden mallet. The sculptor moved around the pedestal on which the lump of clay was mounted, and struck with short, powerful blows at what was beginning to take the shape of a head, half the size of the bearded, shaggy head of the sculptor himself. Castle's head felt each mallet stroke.

Davidson looked up quickly at him from time to time, danced around and pounded away, and it was a relief when Jo put the mallet down and started to massage the clay with small thick fingers, feeling for hollows and smoothing over rises, pinching a bit of clay from a structural sinus and working it into the spring of the jawline.

Castle could see the hills of Barcelona to the west, still green in the October sun. It was his birthday. He was twenty-three, a major in the army of the Spanish Republic, and he was in the Hotel Majestic sitting for a famous sculptor. Careless of fame, he was unimpressed both by Davidson's reputation and the fact that his likeness was being shaped for posterity.

What did impress him, he thought, was that he was alive. He fixed his eyes on a spot on the wall just above Davidson's head while the artist growled at him to stop moving. Abrams was dead and Abad was dead and Bianca was dead, along with a hell of a lot of other guys who were all dead, dead, dead. And he was sitting here alive getting his head made into a

tombstone, and according to Negrin and the League of Nations and everybody else, he would be going home; all those others were now part of the
Spanish earth and would not be going anywhere. It was a funny thing, because so many of them had thought in terms of going home someday; not
that they had hedged their bets or taken special precautions or ducked any
risks, but it was in the back of their minds and in the strings of talk that spun
out of them between the battles and the bombings and shellings and the
immediate concern for *chabolas* and functioning weapons and water and
hot food, and making sure that the wine was kept in the shade so that it
would not go sour up there on the hot, hard rocks of the Sierra Caballs;
when they were not preoccupied with those things, they would sit and talk
of food steaming from fragrant kitchens, of soft beds and scented women,
of parlors with mohair easy chairs and Caruso's voice soaring out of the
Victrola, filling a warm secure place. They had not talked of these things
as things lost, but as promises to be kept even if only promises made to
themselves. Castle had not made any promises.

The end of September had meant the end of the war for the International Brigades; it had meant Munich for the rest of the world. For Castle it was
an unsatisfactory ending. In the first place, their last battle had been a defeat, and in the second place, the war wasn't over. When you put those two
things together it made it pretty difficult to be happy about walking away.

"What are you going to do when you get home?" Davidson's eyes shifted
from Castle to the clay, back and forth, quickly.

"Ohhh . . ." Castle drew it out so he could think what to say. "Get a job,
I guess." Everyone had to have a job.

"Doing what?"

"Who knows? Whatever I can get." But not back to delivering hat bodies,
if they'd have him back, that was. Should have a more glamorous occupation,
after being sculpted by this guy who was supposed to be something in the art
world. Couldn't have him wasting clay on the head of a garment-center errand boy – man – after all, twenty-three today, the youngest major, youngest
commander . . . fame was fleeting, but this clay head, which would be cast
in bronze, would be forever. After a little while it would be just the head of a
boy-man, done by the famous sculptor Jo Davidson.

"A job to live on," Castle added, "while carrying on the good fight. After
all, it could happen in America, too."

"Sure," Davidson said.

Of course, he didn't have to tell Davidson that; fascism, spawning anti-
Semitism, could happen anywhere. They all knew it. It was the one thing

they all agreed on. Fascism had to be stopped. That was why they were all here in Spain: the reporters and artists; Hemingway, Matthews, Sheean, Fischer, Davidson, Nehru and his daughter, the scientist Haldane and the singer Robeson and Bob Minor and Robert Capa. Now they were all here in this hotel, the Majestic.

Hitler, given the green light at Munich, was gearing up the Germans to roll over Europe. Mussolini was having a ball in Eritrea and Ethiopia, bombing the shit out of the natives. Hirohito was chewing up China like it was some kind of sushi dish. Only the Spanish people were resisting. Madrid, the Tomb of Fascism. Against all odds, Castle believed it still possible.

"Hey, that Nehru's daughter was something coming down the ballroom stairs in those long silken scarves," he said to change the subject.

"Saris," Davidson said.

"You going to do a head of her?"

"What'd she ever do?"

"Well . . . I mean just because she's so beautiful, just as a beautiful piece."

"The idea is to make a thing of beauty out of a head that has its own significance. Anyhow, she's not my type. If I was in the business of doing that kind of thing, I'd do the blonde."

"Christ, yes. She's gorgeous . . . but then she ain't someone's daughter."

When Davidson laughed, the cigarette stuck to his lower lip, danced around spraying ashes over his beard and the soft clay of the forming head. "She may not be anyone's daughter but she's a damned good writer besides being beautiful. Also, doing her might be more profitable." His eyes caught the light and gleamed up at Mitch.

"Not a chance," Castle said. "Hemingway has her locked up."

"Yes? How do you know that?"

"Well, Matthews has been trying and he hasn't got to first base." To himself, he added, *how could a little bearded runt like you make it with her?* Looking at Davidson, he could see that Jo knew what he meant, because the knowing smile shifted the bearded face into a "that's what you think" expression. Davidson picked up the mallet and started pounding on the clay again.

How had that last offensive started, or why had it started? Nothing had changed in the balance of forces, unless in favor of the fascists, who were receiving more and more supplies from Hitler and Mussolini, encouraged by the huge chunks of territory captured and by the deepening mood of appeasement evinced by England, France, and the USA. A few French seventy-fives and Soviet planes had recently gotten through to the Loyalists, and they had dreamed this trickle into a huge arsenal. But not enough had gotten through to make a difference, and while Castle hadn't known this, the men who'd planned the operation must have.

It was always possible that men starting with a reasonable assessment of a given situation would, in the process of developing an operation, get carried away. Their plans take shape on memo pads, in staff discussions, and with sweeping arrows advancing on maps. A lightheadedness sets in, as Castle knew from his own experience, as when he gave the speech the day before they recrossed the Ebro.

He had gathered the men a couple hundred yards from the river – it must have been the twenty-fourth of July – to tell them that they were going over. It had not been news to them, since they had been making mock crossings of the river for a month. Nor could it have been news to the fascisti, even though when they did attack they had not met with much initial resistance.

When he had said all that he had intended to say, it still hadn't seemed enough. Standing there on the terrace with the battalion spread out before him, saying, "This is it, this is what we've been training for and we're going across and for a change there'll be artillery and air support." The morning sun on their faces, lighting their eyes, quietly hanging on his words, a matter of life and death. So he went on longer than he had wanted to, sensing a need for assurance that what they were being asked to do had purpose.

"There are no limits. We go in just as far and as fast as we can, which means that we will be retaking the ground where Campbell and Doran and Kaufman and Connors fell. And on beyond that, to slash through the wall of fascists that has cut Spain in two, that separates us from the beating heart of Spain, Madrid . . . to unite Spain again. To victory!"

Of course, he didn't remember now exactly what he had said, but it had been something like that, something that would put spirit and muscle into the *Vivas* that came afterward. And something that raised him up higher than the terrace he was standing on, higher than the mountain at his back, high and tall and out of himself so that when Mickenberg, sitting slouched and cynical, the dull brown slants of his face unmoved, asked, "How are we going to get back across the river if we have to?" Castle had said "We're not coming back." And the men had cheered. They would sweep all the way to victory. Afterward only the dead would not come back.

58

Remembering how well the crossing had started out, remembering Faterella, Mitchell Castle smiled. Davidson scowled.

He had been on a high hill looking down at the town of Faterella and it looked like all the other towns he had seen in Aragon. Fatarella had been in their part of Spain, part of the Republic, his side. Now it was enemy territory. He had to adjust to that, because looking down at the red tiled roofs, the quietness of the houses and streets all perfect and intact, with not even a bullet scar on the pale adobe walls, it seemed indifferent to sides.

"Well, do we go down and take it?" Lyons broke the silence.

Castle looked from the town to Lyons. Lyons's small brown eyes burned black with excitement. He wanted to go down there. He'd been a winner all the way. First company across the river. First skirmish with the enemy. First capture of prisoners, two hundred or more. First to take the hill where they now stood.

"Goddamn it," Castle said, "hold your water. This is as far as we're supposed to go." He held the map for Lyons and pointed to the circle that represented the hill they had occupied. "The Third Division is supposed to take the town."

"And what are we supposed to do?" Lyons wanted to go down there very bad.

"That's just what we're trying to find out." Watt said. "As soon as we get word from brigade we'll know."

"You mean, if we get word," Abrams said. "Why don't I go back and see if I can get through?"

"No," Castle said. He turned away and looked back over the way they had come. There was nothing to see. More hills. Into those hills he had already sent four separate parties of men to get word to brigade of where they were and to bring back orders for the next move – and ammunition, because they had used a lot shooting at the observation plane that had plotted their crossing of the river, and then more when they had had a night firing incident.

There was no sign of life on the hills behind them. "No," he repeated, "I don't know what's happened to Yale and the others. I don't know where brigade is. I don't know if they've found it and can't get back, or never got there and can't find it, or . . ."

He did not want to send Abrams because Abrams spoke the best Spanish, and if they ever made contact with the Third, they would need him. "Get Harry to send two of his men back to Mora." Harry Fisher and Marty Sullivan, his telephone men, had come through the retreats, as they came through everything. "Maybe brigade is still back where we started from. Anyhow, I won't miss 'em." He nodded toward the group of communications men sitting on the ground a little way below with their spools of wire and telephones in wooden and leather cases left over from the war to end all wars. "Made in the USA 1916" was piled around them, equipment useful only as backrests and pillows now since there was no getting a wire strung to brigade. It was at least ten or fifteen kilometers to the rear if it was where it had been at the start of the offensive.

When Abrams started off to carry out his order, Castle called out to stop him, but then changed his mind. "Never mind, go ahead." He didn't want to send any more men away only to have them not come back. On the other hand, some effort had to be made to establish contact with brigade, because he didn't know what to do next. They were as far as he had been ordered to go, and while he didn't dislike the idea of moving down into the town, that in itself would not solve the problem because they would still be in more or less the same place on the map and still not know what the next move was.

"I thought we weren't supposed to worry about contact," Lyons said.

Castle turned to watch as Abrams spoke to Harry. Harry got up and picked two men out of his group. The men hitched their spools of wire onto their backs, slung the useless telephones at their sides. Harry and Abrams pointed back into the hills, the men listening and nodding. He watched them go down the saddle of the hill and up the rise of the next and then out of sight. He watched for them to come up the next hill, growing smaller against the green and then taller on the skyline of the far ridge and over and gone, and he felt right away that that was the last he would see of them. He wondered briefly who they were. There were a lot of new men in the battalion.

"Well, what about this contact crap?"

"Listen, Lyons," Watt said, "It was no contact up to here . . . up to our objective. Not forever, you know."

"Yeah," Castle said. "Nevertheless it's getting late in the morning, isn't it? Ten-twenty. That's more'n twenty-four hours since we kicked off, right? If we can't locate brigade, then they ought to fucking-well locate us." He looked around, waiting for one of them to speak. "They haven't," he went on. "So we'll take the town. We might just as well wait down there as spend the day up here. Go ahead," he stopped Lyons as he turned to go, "but be careful. We'll cover you with the MG Company and hold the others in reserve if you need them."

Lyons trotted off, happy to have his way. Castle turned to the other company commanders. "Manny, set up two sections to give him cover if he needs it, and set out the other section to hold this hill if we need it. Bill, you take your company down behind him, but stay behind unless Lyons needs you. We'll keep the Spanish Company in reserve and the Third Company up here deployed in defensive positions." Now he felt better, seeing the men moving out to take up positions.

He had forgotten the name of the commander of the Third, and didn't want to ask. He would ask Abrams later. All these new men. That's how it was, he thought, you got to know a man and he was wounded, or killed, or captured, or sent away. Some came back, as had Watt and Abrams, neither of whom he had known before, or like Manny Spear and Nick Stamos, who'd come back for the hell of it. And Joe and the others who had been home and had come back. Yale had come back with Mickenberg, who had surprised Castle by wondering about getting back across the river.

Yale had been very good at running the HQ company. Castle had been well taken care of, and now he was sorry that he had accepted Yale's offer to try to contact brigade after Joe Gordon and Mickenberg had not returned.

"Juan Abad." Castle swept his arm up over the town to where the hills on the other side ran down and away in the clear morning air. "There isn't a goddamned thing between us and Burgos, do you realize that?" he spoke in English. Abad would understand, he could appraise the situation as well as anybody. "Nada, not a thing. There's nothing to stop us from going clear through to Portugal except kilometers, mucho fucking kilometers and hills and nothing to cross them with. Ni camions, ni tanques, ni avións, and not even a goddamned piece of wire through which I can say hello-how-are-you to our esteemed brigade comandante Jose Valledor."

There was another newcomer, Valledor. What the hell happened to Copic, he wondered. Not that he really cared; it was just this damned impermanence of personalities that left him with a feeling of being unconnected – especially now with Doran and Campbell gone, dead or captured.

He yearned toward all the empty space to the west, wanting to fly off the hill as he did sometimes in his dreams, taking off and soaring up above the buildings and telephone poles and wires across the backyards of Brooklyn, up with the sparrows and pigeons, flying free and effortlessly. "We could win the war right here . . . right through this gap even if we only had horses."

"Do you think it's this wide open all along the line?" George Watt asked, his eyes, seeing what Castle saw, sweeping the western horizon. "Listen. I hear small arms fire back there."

"Not much." Castle weighed the sound.

"Maybe that's what happened to brigade. Maybe they're all rushing right through and that's why we can't find them." Brandt had been caught up in the idea of a breakthrough. "They may be halfway to Burgos while we're standing here talking about it."

It was a possibility. Not halfway, of course, but on their way, and if that was the case they had better get the battalion moving.

"Okay, let's pick up Williams's company and go down and help Lyons clean this town out and get on our way. It looks to me like the Third Division is never going to get here. Watt, you stay here with Abad and the rest of the battalion until we give the all clear."

Abad was standing where Castle had left him, looking west across all that unoccupied territory. Without knowing why he did it, Castle gripped Abad's shoulder briefly before taking leave of the hill.

"Will you tell the general to stop waving his pistol under my nose?"

"He's mad at us for taking *his* town," Abrams said. He spoke very carefully in Spanish to the general. "We waited for you, but it was getting late, General. There is no need for the pistol. We should discuss this as comrades."

"Do not 'comrade' me, señor." The general's pale face had seemed to Castle to be coming apart in little puffs and flying off in all directions, an impression increased by the beads of sweat and spittle that sprayed from him as he jerked his head violently about. He was generating a lot of heat even though it was cool where they were, in the shadow of the stone arch that served as the gateway to the center of the town. The Lincolns occupied the main square, laughing, talking, and eating out of the cans they had taken from the fascist garrison, swapping articles of clothing that had come from the Guardia Civil wardroom, examining the rifles and pistols that Lyons had liberated along with the town. The general's division, strung out on the other side of the archway, stamped and chomped at the bit. The general holstered his pistol and pulled a sheet of paper from his map case. He waved the paper under Abrams's nose. "Here it is, sir. Read, if you please, the orders. I will read for you. 'You are to proceed to Faterella, take and secure the town . . .' See for yourself."

"Tell him we know that." Castle caught the drift. "But he was supposed to be here last night."

"Ah, yes," the general said when Abrams had finished. "All very well, but we met with much resistance at Flix."

"You were not supposed to stop at Flix." Castle ignored Abrams, finding that in the rapid exchange he could carry on in Spanish without help.

"You do not tell me what I was supposed to do," the General fumed. "We have taken Flix and we are now going to take Faterella, and when we have done so we shall proceed to Villalba. You will remove from the town at once, *por favor*."

"Okay, okay," Castle reverted to English. "If he wants to take Faterella, let him take it. We're going." Then, smilingly, in Spanish, "Very good. Very good. We leave at once. And in what direction is Villalba?"

The general jammed his orders back into the map case and withdrew a map, which he flattened against the rough stones. He jabbed at it. "Here is Faterella and here is Villalba and this is the road we shall take."

Villalba, Castle could see, was about ten kilometers west by south of where they were. Further south was Corbera where Campbell and Doran had been lost, where they had run into the enemy army that had all but destroyed them.

"Very good," he said. "And then we shall proceed to Corbera on . . ." he came back to the English, "on his left flank. Tell him we ought to keep our flanks in contact for the rest of the way."

"It will not be necessary," the general said to Abrams. "We shall move on Villalba from three sides. See." He went back to the map. "From here and here and here. It will not be a problem." The general had cooled down considerably and Castle thought that while he was taking Villalba from three sides on the map, it would be a good time for the Lincolns to withdraw, so he wished the general well and gave the necessary orders.

He took his staff back up the hill, and they all sat around with the company commanders while Castle, who had more or less committed himself to Corbera, studied the map and stalled for time hoping that someone would yet come back from brigade. He looked up from his map, and the others looked at him expectantly. He raised his hand for silence and then pointed. They all turned and listened. There were new sounds in the air. A humming of planes, shells bursting, small arms fire growing heavy, even heavier to the south.

"Someone's got a fight on their hands," Lyons said.

"How far?" Abrams stood up.

Castle got to his feet and after listening said, "Two or three kilometers. It has to be our brigade." He looked around. "You! Hey you, with the compass. What's your name, comrade?"

"Clem Market, battalion observer."

Battalion observer. No doubt one of Yale's creations. "Comrade Clem," Castle said, and liked it well enough to repeat it. "Comrade Clem, or Clem Comrade Market, observer. Get me a fix on that." He pointed in the direction of the battle sounds. "That's where we're going. Bill Williams's company, lead off. Lyons, take it easy in the middle, and Lopoff" – the name of the commander of the Third came to him – "leave a section here to pick up any parties returning from brigade. The rest of your company, bring up the rear."

While the companies formed up and started off, he lingered on the hill. He could see the streets of Faterella crowded with people as the Third Division fraternized with the populace, and he hoped that they would not spend too much time before getting on to Villalba. As he turned to join the troops, he had this feeling that the great big hole that had opened up, laying clear the road to Burgos, Salamanca, and Franco's rear, was closing down fast.

The only thing he was sure of was that he had done everything he could think of to protect the battalion and at the same time get a fix on the situation. He had ordered a halt in their march and had sent scouts toward the firefight. The sounds were louder now, perhaps a kilometer ahead. Market had been dispatched to determine whether the file of troops moving forward on their right flank, silhouetted on a ridge against a graying sky, was an advance unit of the Third Division.

The file on the ridge seemed endless, moving slowly, the men well spaced. They were coming from the wrong direction to be part of the Third, and there weren't supposed to be any other *nuestros* between him and the Third. So he had to wait and see, though he did not want to wait because the road to Corbera might be filling up with fascists while they waited. Studying his map, he recalled how in the dark of the night, three or four months earlier, after the column had been shattered, he had crouched against the embankment while across that road, the road to Corbera, lights had come on and a radio had squawked excited German voices into the night.

The look of disbelief on Clem Market's face, when he had returned to report, made his head seem even bigger than it was. The absolute blankness in the wide-open eyes, the thin eyebrows fully elevated yet using hardly a fraction of the available space on his huge round forehead, his nose seeming to disappear as his mouth gaped an elongated O.

"They're drunk." The words whooshed out.

"Who's they?" It was funny, Castle thought, how all their scouts and observers were people named Clem and Luke and Vernon. Vernon was gone now; hadn't made it across the Ebro. Clem waved his arms limply in the direction of a few figures remaining on the ridge. "They, the French. Why, they're positively staggering about."

Such diction, even in moments of great stress. Undoubtedly out of a university. "They can't be the French because if I got the briefing right, the French Fourteenth is the left flank of this entire operation and that's down around Tortosa somewhere. Like thirty kilometers from here. Right, George?"

"Gee. That's what they told us at the staff meeting." Watt tried to knit his brow, but succeeded only in wrinkling his nose, leaving the perennial serenity of his face unruffled.

"But Comrade Captain Castle." Clem was earnest. "I spoke to the men. I spoke with the commander. They reek of wine and they *are* French."

"Well, what are they doing here?" Abrams said. "Where are they headed?"

"I don't know." The look of astonishment had been replaced by one of dejection. "And I don't think they know either." Without asking to be dismissed, he turned and walked away.

"Well, they're gone now. Let's move out. Lopoff, you keep an eye out for them. Williams. I was just going to send for you. What's up?"

"Luke says it's the Twenty-fourth over there. Catching hell trying to cut the road," Williams said, coming up to them.

"Good," Castle said. "Get your company onto their right flank. Let 'em know we're coming, and as soon as we get there we're going for those hills. The road must be just on the other side. Let's all go at the same time. Come on, let's get moving."

Goddamn it, they'd made contact with one of their battalions and that was good. Castle felt better, though he was haunted by the presence of the staggering French wandering off toward Villalba, and he wondered about the Third Division headed in the same direction. But he couldn't afford to sit and wonder. The Twenty-fourth and the road were waiting.

"What the hell is it now, Joe? You sonofabitch. Where've you been? Did you find brigade?"

"Yeah. I gotta truckload of ammo and food and mail back down there. Can't get it up here." Joe Gordon grinned, one glass blue eye shining up at the sun, the good eye fixed on him. "Brigade sure is pissed off with you. All kinds of complaints from the commander of the Third about us being in their bailiwick and Johnny hopping up and down about how we ought to be helping the Twenty-fourth instead of roaming all around. And Yale got hit in the arm. We had to take him back over the river but that was okay because we picked up this truck, 'n' they got a great pontoon bridge across the river . . . 'n' ammo and stuff . . . Valledor says to make contact with Millman of the Twenty-fourth Spanish Battalion." The words poured out.

"How bad is Yale?" Castle asked. Yale, the kid with the perfect body and good-looking head, the Camp Unity lifeguard. Bronzed, healthy, happy Yale, who took care of all the little things that had to be taken care of around headquarters. Who'd challenged Castle to a boxing match boasting he could beat him with one arm tied behind his back . . . and almost had.

"Pretty bad," Mickenberg said. "He'll probably lose it."

There were an awful lot of things to think about. Right there. Right now. Yale had picked Mick and Joe Gordon to go back with him to find brigade and bring the ammo up. Mick and Joe, because they had been with Yale at Jarama. So that was natural. Joe had had an eye shot out at Bruneté, and when both of his brothers had been killed they had sent Joe home, but he couldn't sit on his ass and drink beer while the war was on, so he had come back. All those in the last group of volunteers. There was always a last group – or when they thought the last had come there was just one more last – only this one had turned out to be really the last. Castle hadn't known it, but up top they had already known that the days of the IBs were numbered.

So among all the walking wounded there was Joe, and among the newly arrived volunteers there was Jimmy Lardner, and among the sweepings from rearguard jobs there was Mickenberg. And Yale protected Mickenberg. Mick needed protection, because the closer he got to the front, the more he carped – about the food, the "comic stars," the party activists, the military strategy. In the rear, where he had found refuge in the brigade bureau of information and propaganda after Jarama, he had been as enthusiastic about the war and the way it was being conducted as the next guy.

Yale protected Mick from himself and to some extent – by getting Castle to intervene on occasion – from the Party. Castle agreed with Brandt that Mick was a troublemaker. He could even become a demoralizing element, Castle thought, like corrosive acid dropped into something solid but susceptible, softening the mass into an unresisting pulp.

Maybe that drop of acid was the ditty Mickenberg had cooked up:

> My name's Joe Brandt
> I own a herring stand
> I am the Party organizer
> Activist and womanizer
> I'll be a *soldado* when the masses get wiser
> Workers of the world unite
> Workers of the world don't fight.

Hardly the kind of thing Aaron and Murray composed, the funny, fighting antifascist songs laden with social significance. Aaron and Murray. Leo demanded inclusion in spite of Castle's resistance. But Leo, he assured himself, had had more in common with Mick, or the other way around.

Castle had figured only one hill between him and the road. But when they had driven off the defenders, *conscriptos* unwilling to stand and fight, there was the inevitable next hill. This hill, for a change, was somewhat smaller. It was easier going, and though the fascists' machine guns held them up, they were able to break through and drive them off.

The good feeling – Yale, ever the cheerleader, had called it high morale – that had pervaded the outfit while they were rebuilding the shattered battalion and training for the river crossing had set them forward from the moment they had taken the opposite bank of the Ebro. It had been reinforced by the taking of Faterella, and the momentum had carried them over these hills.

Even without binoculars, he could see riders dismounting and running into position. He focused on the rugged terrain of the chopped-up valley below them, a densely wooded hill to one side. The level line beyond that had to be the road. The enemy was pouring in troops and Tercio cavalry. Professionals again, and damned good. He had to move fast before they got set. He gave the companies the line of battle and sent them in. He sent a runner to the Twenty-fourth to ask them to join in the attack, but did not wait for them to get the message.

The men went down into the valley and across most of it before they were stopped by enfilading fire. There was no place to set up a line, and there was no way for them to get by, so they were getting hit and hit and hit. It was already too late.

It was too late but Castle sent them down into the valley twice more in rapid succession – three times in all trying to beat the buildup. He could hear the Twenty-fourth trying on his flank. Each time before the men went down, he tried to find the Tercio gunners in the wooded hill, but he could not. Each time he had Nick pour heavy MG fire into the hill, but they could not silence guns they could not see. Guns that he could not see. But that wasn't the only trouble he had with the MGs.

Just as the men reached the floor of the valley, he became aware of the MGs letting up. He could hear fascist guns firing somewhere on the hill, but his own guns were quiet. He was alone in the command post with his telephone man, who kept checking to see if they had gotten a line through to brigade or the Twenty-fourth or both. And they had not. Abad and Abrams had gone into the valley to see if they could find a way to get through or to set up a line. Watt had gone with Harold of the Third. And so he went over to the MGs himself to see why the guns were quiet.

"No. We have plenty of ammo. I ordered the firing stopped," Stamos said.

"But you were supposed to give the covering fire." Castle was pleasant about it because Nick was an experienced hand and there must be a good reason. "If you have ammo and the guns are working . . . they are working? Well, then why?"

"Because our guys are down there." Nick leaned his face toward Castle.

"So they're down there. So cover them," Castle was getting testy.

"Not me." A disturbed look came over Nick's face, crooked lines across his square forehead and a haunted look in his eyes. "I'm not going to be responsible for shooting our guys in the back." He stamped around in a tight circle. "Close your mouth, Castle, I know what I'm talking about. I've seen too many of them get it that way. Cover fire, my ass. You know what the cone of fire is on these old guns? I'm not killing any of our guys."

"They're getting chewed up from that tree-covered hill. All I asked was that you keep that hill under fire. I want you to do that now. Get that hill under fire."

Nick started up again about cover fire and Jarama and the wheat field at Bruneté and guys getting shot in the back, and the anger in Castle rose, so when Nick kept it up instead of giving the order to fire, Castle went over to the guns himself. The crews were made up of old-timers like Bianca, who'd outwardly, at least, recovered from the loss of Kaufman. They responded readily to his orders. He gave them the target, which was the hill in general – unless they could spot the fascist guns – until the companies moved up. He stayed until they got the guns going.

Afterward, he would send Nick to the rear for a rest. Afterward, too, he wondered if his rage at Nick had had anything to do with the MGs firing over the wheat field at Bruneté, where he and Gus had fired the gun longest without the slightest thought for the men lying in the fields. But that was bullshit, because he had seen the bullets kicking up white puffs of adobe where the enemy had been entrenched in the houses lining the end of the field. Still, it rankled and clouded the eyes, as Nick's had been, with the haunting suspicion that it could be the way Nick said.

When he had finally got the guns going, he thought they might make it to the road after all. He hurried back to his command post, where he found Abrams waiting for him.

"We're pinned down again," Abrams said.

"I've got the MGs giving covering. We ought to be able to move now." Castle stood on the ridge and scanned the valley with his glasses, looking for signs of movement. Seeing none, he fixed the glasses on the hill, but he could see neither the muzzle blasts from the enemy gunners nor any signs of where his MG fire was hitting. There were a lot of dust-covered shrubs and trees mantling the hill, concealing the Tercio gunners.

"You'd better get off the skyline," Abrams said.

Castle paid no attention. Goddamn it. He wanted that hill. He wanted to get back on the road to Corbera. He wanted a victory for the battalion. Maybe he even wanted to win the war.

"Come here." He motioned Abrams to his side. "See that? That's a gully full of underbrush. Get some of the men into that. Get them to use the cover to get within grenade-throwing range of those guns. Wait. Tell them that when we hear the grenades we'll lift our fire. Go ahead." Castle let his glasses drop on the strap and turned to Abrams. "What's the matter? Go ahead."

"I'm hit," Abrams said, and sat down. He stretched his legs out straight and leaned back to support himself on his arms, but they slowly angled until he was out flat at Castle's feet, his blue eyes looking up at Castle, questioning.

"*Sanidad*," Castle hollered down to the tree where the medics had set up. "*Sanidad*," he could hear himself bellowing. "Shit," he said, and knelt down to hold Abrams's hand, which was damp and cool. He saw the black hole smack in the center of the tan shirt, between the pockets. "Shit," he repeated.

Then Doc Simon, the new doctor – Stein was with brigade – was kneeling opposite him, unbuttoning the shirt, uncovering the white expanse of chest with the red-black hole nestling in the thin wisps of curled golden hairs. He met Abrams's eyes still holding the question, now giving voice to it. "Will I live, Mitch? Mitch?"

"Clean as a whistle." Castle squeezed his hand tight. "Nothing to worry about."

"I'm the doctor. I'll make the diagnosis," John Simon said in his squeaky voice.

Castle was surprised to see that he wasn't smiling, the pale eyes behind the steel-rimmed glasses not angry but serious, very serious.

"Sure, Doc," Castle laughed. "Sure." He squeezed Abrams's hand again and gently put it down. He got up, smiling down at Abrams. Doc's eyes slanted up at him, his head against the white chest, sounding the path the bullet had taken, his glasses pushed askew.

"Don't stand there. Get down, Commander." Abrams tugged at Castle's trouser leg.

Then the stretcher bearers came up and carried him off the hill down to the shade of the tree Simon had selected as his front-line first aid station. The little doctor – not properly an M.D., having dropped out of med school in his hurry to get to Spain – followed the stretcher down shaking his head.

That bad, Castle thought. He turned away and hurried off to do what he had wanted Abrams to do. That's the way it is, he said in Spanish: *Por esto es.*

≡ 60

"Hey, Castle, Commander Castle." Sullivan had called to him as he had turned away from the wounded Abrams. And, he recalled, he hadn't thought of Abrams again until word had come back that he had died before they had gotten him to a hospital.

He had hurried down to where the telephone men were working the hand generator and squawking over the field set. "Yes, yes," he'd hollered into the mouthpiece. "Castle, here. Yes." The receiver was full of crackling and buzzing and a small voice shouting, "Gates. Can you hear me, Castle? This is Gates."

The telephone men were crouching down and looking up at the sky now, and Castle could hear the planes coming over.

"There's a lotta goddamned noise on this line, and," he squinted into the sun, "Three, six, nine . . . a shithouse full of Henkles coming this way."

"Never mind that," Gates barked. "Get in there and help the Twenty-fourth. You've got to cut the road."

"That's what we've been trying to do. Now they're passing us by."

Fisher, who was working the field generator, straightened up and cranked furiously as though to make up for the strokes he had missed as the Henkles sailed in silvered grace overhead.

"Don't try. Do it." Gates said. "Colonel Valledor wants that road before it gets dark."

"Okay," Castle said. "I think those planes are – "

"Here they come," Gates said. "I'm ringing off. Get that road."

The sound of the falling bombs was like a distant wind in the trees, and then the earth under them picked up the shock, and clouds of white and black smoke started straight up back where Gates and Valledor and the brigade were, clouds that curved into baroque outlines with the thud of bombs moving the earth.

"That's the air support we were supposed to get." Fisher was tired, not complaining.

Castle had gone back to the top of the hill. The machine guns were firing sporadically now and the fascist guns were still. He saw no sign of the men in the brush covering the bottom of the valley. He listened and he thought about what to do. Get an enlace to the Twenty-fourth to tell them he would try again . . . not try, but do it . . . Intensify covering fire when they start out from the bottom of the valley. There was only one more thing that had to be done. Get down there himself to get the men moving forward. There was no one else to do it. Himself. Castle. He had given it much thought.

He could send a runner. The battalion commander was not supposed to expose himself unnecessarily. Too many commanders had been killed or wounded that way. Campbell, Carter, Detro, Bullard, Nelson . . . name them . . . all those who had gone before. Which was why he was the commander now. Attrition. The guy next to you gets hit. Not you. You move up.

And up until you are here. The only thing that matters now is, does he stay here because he's afraid to go down there and lead the men, or stay here because that is the military – prudent? – thing to do.

He was standing where Abrams had stood and bought it.

This was where they'd been standing and this was where he was standing now, and behind him the telephone men, the cooks and orderlies, Doc Simon and the stretcher bearers and the clerk, all watching him standing on the hill where they would not stand, except maybe Doc Simon, who customarily hopped around with his eyes on the ground like a preoccupied bird, too hungry and too busy to be aware of danger, which was not the same thing as being aware and appearing unconcerned. So maybe they thought he was brave. Or stupid. Or both. Or maybe they weren't even thinking about him. So he was standing there and being brave about it because even bravery had shades and degrees. And this standing exposed was a kind of passive thing. Like, okay I know you see me. I know you can hit me. But I'm not ducking, see? I'm standing here because even though I know you can kill me I don't truly believe it. So standing-still-brave was one thing, but moving forward to where the guy behind the gun sits and waits for you was another. And that was what Castle had to do if they were going to get to that road.

"If anyone wants me," he hollered over his shoulder to Sullivan, "I'll be down there."

And as he turned to go, he heard Sullivan holler, in turn, "The line to brigade's been cut."

"Well, we didn't have it very long," he muttered, and he hurried down into the valley where the shadows were thickening and there already was the faint smell of death in the trees.

Castle had found a shack hidden in the trees near the far side of the gully. The men had crowded around the candles on the table, leaning into the light while the orderlies busied themselves by the fire, and he had wondered why they were all feeling so good. They were sounding a lot better than they looked or even had a right to be. The one window had been draped with a poncho and the cracks in the door were stuffed with bits of dirty blanket. It was hot and smelled of rabbit stew – oh, those orderlies! – and tobacco smoke and iodine. Lyons wore a bandage around his neck where a bullet had gone clean through the flesh without hitting any vital parts. Harold Smith's arm was bandaged and slung and he was marveling that it was the third time he had been hit in the same arm. Wondered if there was any significance to it. The others were scratched and scabbing, everyone torn and tattered and more or less battered, the smell of iodine and alcohol coming from them all.

Except for Castle, who had moved them the fifteen or twenty meters to this point and had not been able to move farther, the men had fallen all around crying "I'm hit. *Sanidad!* First aid!" And the guns had chopped through the brush, splashing leaf and twig and bits of clothing in all directions while the men had crashed forward through the dirty green, the branches tearing at them, the bullets whistling in. Between the trees, the bullets, the dead and wounded, and the enemy pouring it on, an agreement was arrived at without deliberation. They stopped moving.

Now they were all talking at once, the held-in fear releasing itself in torrents of words. Laughing and talking the fear out of them, that day's work done and the next held at arm's length, out of mind.

"I've got to tell you this, now," Lyons was saying. "When we took Fatarella and all that stuff . . ."

Castle nodded, half listening, waiting for the telephone in the corner to squawk. Fisher and Sullivan had fixed the line to brigade but neither Gates nor Valledor had been there when they got through, though everyone had come through the bombing all right. He waited for Gates to come on, wondering what he would say to him. "What did you say? Ten thousand what?"

"Ten thousand duros. Right there in the Guardia Civil HQ." Lyons repeated. "Ben's got it on the truck and wants to know what to do with it."

"You took ten thousand duros out of Faterella? Silver?" Castle envisioned the general of the Third Division waving his pistol around, scampering through the empty quarters of the Guardia Civil, the bare shelves of the *intendencia*, the paymaster's office sacked. "Leapin' lizards!" he exclaimed, and, startled to hear himself say it, laughed with the men. "Where's Ben now?"

"With the chow detail, feeding the men."

"Go get him. No, not you. You get him, George. You're still in one piece. Why didn't you tell me about this before?"

"Well, we've been sort of busy."

"You mean you've had it on the truck all this time, back and forth between here and brigade?"

"We didn't know what else to do with it and we didn't want to do anything at all until we took it up with you."

"Is that so?"

There was an amused evasiveness in Lyons's eyes and Castle knew that he was only finding out about the duros because a lot of men had been killed or nearly killed that day and tomorrow wasn't much of a future. "There was no need to discuss it with me. You should have ordered Ben to turn it over to brigade."

Ben Holtzman started to speak – in an exaggerated accent – the moment he came through the door. "Aha, so you told him. I figgered dat's what the commissar wanted with me. Da jig is up. So vat's going to be now?" Holtzman marched up to where Castle squatted and stood before him, hat in folded hands, head bowed, prepared to be guillotined on the spot. Ben was the picture of a rosy-cheeked seraph, undismayed because he lived always in the expectation of disaster, never allowing the prospect to affect the optimism he brandished as a shield against evil.

"How's it feel to be sitting on ten thousand duros?"

"Vat ten t'ousand? Two t'ousand's more like it," Ben said indignantly, and then slyly, "I'm feeling like a capitalist."

"Oh," Lyons said, "I guess I meant ten thousand pesetas is what it amounts to."

Castle did the arithmetic in his head and it came out right, so he let it rest. "You mean you were contemplating deserting the working class?"

"Not a bad idea!" Ben positively glowed. "T'ings are pretty rough on the vorking classes, especially like here. Not only dey ain't eating so good, killed dey're getting yet. The vorking class here and the vorking class dere," he waved in the direction of the fascists. "The capitalists on both sides are werry much conspicuous by not being presently here. Elsewhere dey are living it up fat on de hog, and besides vat's two t'ousand duros to Mr. Señor John March. I ask you?"

"Señor Juan March," Lyons corrected him.

"I'm having enough trouble wit' English, Spanish you want me to speak yet?"

"Hey, Commander," the telephone man interrupted. "Gates is on."

"Gates?" Castle bellowed into the mouthpiece. "Castle here."

"I can hear you. Don't shout. What's the situation?"

Castle told him, and then listened as Gates repeated in Spanish to Valledor, and then as Valledor spoke to Gates. Ben stood, hat in hand, eyes roaming the rafters. Castle listened to the Spanish yakking back and forth in the earpiece, thinking all the time about the duros. And then Gates was saying something about airplanes.

"You mean ours?" Castle wasn't sure he had gotten it right.

"Yes. They will attack at 8:00 A.M. Our artillery will open up for ten minutes or until 8:10, and then you and the Twenty-fourth will advance to cut the road."

"Wow. That sounds great," Castle said. "We'll be ready."

"Valledor says he is confident that you will succeed," Gates said.

"Yeah." He couldn't think of anything to add. "Well, fine. Is that all?" When Gates agreed that was all, he hung up and turned to the men. "What do you know about that? We're going to have air and artillery support for tomorrow's attack."

"See," Watt smiled broadly. "The offensive has paid off. We've demonstrated our capabilities and now France is letting arms through for the Republic." That was George the commissar, reminding everyone that crossing the Ebro after the big retreats was primarily a demonstration that the heart of the Republic was still beating.

"I tell you what," he said to Ben. "You turn the money over to Gates, all but a thousand pesetas. What's that . . . two hundred duros? And you grab yourself a ride to Barcelona and buy what the hell ever you can find for the battalion commissariat."

"Hey, commander," Ben beamed. "Dat's a swell idea."

"Just don't get lost in one of those chicken factories. After we take the road we're going to celebrate, and you better be back here in time for the festivities."

≡ 61

"No," Castle said. "We didn't cut the road." He raised the cut crystal glass in the Hotel Majestic's splendid dining room, the good French wine catching the orange of the underpowered lights and powdering the full-bodied *vin rouge* with gold. "But we celebrated anyhow."

Davidson had finished for the day and insisted that Mitch join him for dinner; now they sat, with Hemingway, Herb Matthews, and a tableful of others, fighting the last battles over again.

No matter how deeply you drank, there was always this little pool of wine at the bottom of the glass to move around and look into, thinking how it came down in invisible cascades from the sides of the glass and gathered itself into a drop when it seemed you had drained the glass. And when you had too much to drink you emptied yourself into waiting ears, pouring in more than you should have but never quite all, there seeming always to be that little pool in reserve. He spun it around inside him now, the wine spinning on the bottom of his glass, the words and the wine still on his lips, the silence painful, waiting to be filled, for him to say more. But sometimes there was that to be said that couldn't be said and he didn't say it.

It had gotten to be close to noon before the air support showed, and when it did it had been two Chatos coming in very low, the stub wings flashing red, racing over the hill, over the valley, machine guns wide open, and disappearing to the west. The silence that followed had left them all surprised. It seemed to him that the battalion was present, bodily, but that the spirit had flown with the zooming Chatos, leaving a cemetery of shell casings. It was only when the telephone rang, the bell-buzz impinging on the emptiness, that he realized the planes, all two of them, had come and gone, and that the artillery had never begun. So when Gates and Valledor had finished ordering the attack, he had told them no. They were understrength, they were tired, there was no support, they had not cut the road the day before when their chances had been better, and now their chances were worse. All night long they had watched convoys winding down the roads to reinforce the fascists' positions. But there was more to his "no" than that. Because in spite of all that, the men would have tried again. They would have gotten up and gone the ten or twenty feet before they had to stop. Some would think about it one way and others another – those who lived through it – and they would talk it out and laugh and congratulate themselves because they had made it. They would take a long time before they became bitter about it . . . some of them never . . . but none of them would become hostile. No. Mitch Castle, sprawled on the rock-hard Aragonese earth, gripping the old telephone in his hand, looked over the valley. The brief appearance of the two planes was imprinted in his head, as he heard the fading buzz of their solitary pass and now the quiet breathing of the men, the quiet sunny day sweet with pine and sage and scrub oak and the rotting dead, and he knew that he did not want to try again. All the good reasons for not wanting to were there, but more than that, it was that he would have to lead the men to it and he did not want to.
He had thought of all the right reasons for resisting the order, and if brigade had insisted, he did not know what he would have done. But brigade had surprised him. After ordering him and giving all the reasons why it had

to be done, still he had said no; and when Gates had matter-of-factly replied, "All right. Valledor wants to know, can you hold where you are?" he had just managed to say "Yeah," and hear Gates hang up, the surprise bigger in him than the relief.

The question came to him now out of the whirlpool, inside the drop in the glass, spiraling the shattered light as then the valley swelling with the heat of the centered sun had swirled aromatically below him: Why had they ordered him to attack if in the end they had agreed that it was not to be done? There was nothing in what he had said that they hadn't already known, unless it was in his voice . . . in the way he said it.

He sensed that the talk around the table was about to become political, and he didn't know how to handle it.

"What you are doing is giving a completely subjective account of a great offensive." Joe North, who was a reporter for the *Daily Worker* and the *New Masses*, leaned toward him from the far side of the table, masses of black curls blacker still against the white of the tablecloth, head heavy over the fragile crystal, immense brown eyes rimmed by thick black lashes, moist and afloat on his face, too white by far in contrast to the sunburnt faces of most of the others.

"Aside from the courage flowing from the antifascist convictions of the Lincolns and the considerable achievements of the battalion, there is, more important, the fact that the Negrin government has demonstrated to the entire world the viability of the Republic. Its right to exist, its right to be accorded the support of the democracies, and, with the withdrawal of the IB'ers, who were as nothing numerically compared to the huge amount of men and equipment supplied to Franco by Hitler and Mussolini – "

"We all know that, comrade," Hemingway broke in.

"We ought not to take anything for granted." Joe North was careful when he addressed Hemingway, who was very big, and very big as a writer, and very important to the Cause.

"Don't lecture at me," Hemingway said.

"I don't mean to lecture you, Ernest, but I think we should all understand the fuller meaning . . ."

"You think I don't understand? You think perhaps I don't have the development, Comrade North?"

"I'm sure you do, but there are others . . ." North looked around the table apologetically. "I just want to give some balance to what our good Comrade Castle is saying."

"If you're worried about the *New York Times*," said Herb Matthews quietly, "don't. This is off the record as far as I'm concerned."

And Castle, seeing the solemnity on Matthews's elongated and bony face, wondered what the hell he had said to get North started.

"I think he's beautiful, don't you, Hem?" Martha Gellhorn's voice was music, like the toss of her long golden hair was music, and Castle thought how lucky Hemingway was and how sad it was for Herb, who was unlucky with Martha.

"If you think he's beautiful, Beautiful," Jo Davidson put a thick, short arm around her shoulders, caving them in, "you try doing his head. Also, he thinks you're beautiful, too."

Castle looked down into his glass, embarrassed.

"We're all beautiful," Hemingway said. "I'll drink to that." And he did, the others catching up with him and the drinking. "Comrade North," Hemingway wiped his lips, "I love you guys when you're in there fighting, but I can't stand your Holy Roller preaching."

"Well, if we didn't have the preaching, we wouldn't be such hot fighters," Castle said, feeling a need to support Joe and the whole idea of practice and theory, of which he had only a vague idea, but suspecting that Hemingway knew even less about theory, being more engrossed in practice. "There's absolutely no sense, no sense at all, in our being here in the first place and staying here in the face of all the crap that's been thrown at us, in spite of all the guys killed, from battle to battle, from front to front, killed all over the bloody country, and we would've never done it without morale . . . without savvy, if you will . . . not military savvy, of which we had none and have acquired little, but political savvy . . . an understanding why we were doing this. All that was part of the morale that kept us in there."

There was no point in trying to say it fancier than that, because he would have mispronounced half of the words. He did not want to risk that in such distinguished company, in the presence of fine French wine and pâté and English biscuits and Martha. "I mean, you gotta understand we're guys who hate war, who hate killing and hate being killed, and you gotta be crazy to tunnel into a hole like a fucking . . . oops, 'scuse," he smiled drunkenly at Martha who smiled encouragingly back. "A bloody rathole while some jerks are dropping tons of artillery and bombs on your head . . . and you just have to cower there and take it and it makes no sense at all . . . none of it does . . . none of war." He heard himself echoing McCall at Fuentes.

He paused, feeling that he had worked himself into a hole. "But that's why we were doing it, it just has to be done here because if we don't stop the fascists and war-makers here, you'll all be in the same hole sooner or later. You and your wives and your kids and your mothers just like here. The Spanish people, all of them, are in it up to their necks . . . for themselves and for us. That's what you have to understand." He drank from the glass that Hemingway had refilled with the good French wine, and wished to hell someone would say something. "That's more important than all this stuff I've been talking about, only I didn't mention it because I took it for granted that you knew that . . . that that was something we all knew, like we're all in it together . . . more or less, and that's why I was telling you about these other things . . ." He trailed off.

"Of course, you're right in that, Major Castle," Martha came to his rescue. "And as for the 'we' doing all that, it's perfectly clear that the commander isn't saying that the Spanish people, or the International volunteers, are the ones to stop this mad assault of Hitler and company by themselves. It will have to be done with the full participation of what we call the democracies, first of all by France and England, and yes, by the United States. I can't imagine why FDR is holding back – why he's joining in this self-defeating embargo of the Republic, unless, of course, it is the fear of losing the Catholic vote." She reached across the table to place her hand on Castle's wrist. "We do understand, Commander, and your Brooklynese is just wonderful. Beautiful. Isn't he beautiful, Hem?"

"Beautiful," Hemingway said. "And he has to say what he has to say."

"But that can't be all of it," Herb said sadly. "We all have the same convictions, arrived at from differing points of view and with the same goal in mind, but we don't all conduct ourselves in the same manner under fire."

"Look who's talking." Castle flinched at the loud explosion his voice made in the Majestic's near-empty dining room. He continued earnestly, but a couple of decibels lower. "This guy" he waved his glass in the direction of Matthews, "comes up to Hill 666 in the Sierra Pandalls and demands a guided tour of the front . . . in which I had to escort him, round and round, walking tall, him taller'n me on the skyline all the way, nice and slow and easy, like there ain't no fascists sixty meters away with loaded guns."

"He had to do that. He couldn't very well show fear in your presence." Martha took Matthews's hand in hers.

"I would've appreciated it if he had, I can tell you that," Castle said, wondering now why Matthews had had to do it. To show him? To show Martha? Hemingway? More like it. "Looked to me like he wanted to get himself killed." He muffled the words in the wineglass, thinking that that was too much to say but that maybe Herb really had wanted himself killed. Not making it with Martha. Like in a book, huh?

"That's just the point," North said. He seemed to be holding his liquor better than the rest of them.

"What's just the point, preacher?"

Castle did not like the way Hemingway enjoyed needling Joe.

"Well, I have something to preach about." Joe was hurt. "But I'm not out to convert anyone this afternoon. The point is just this: these men are not adventurers, and while they are brave, they do not expose themselves to danger unnecessarily . . . though you'd hardly get that impression from Commander Castle's recounting of events."

"Someone's necessarily unnecessarily done it, or is it the other way around?" Davidson growled through his beard.

"Do you see?" Joe raised his eyebrows at Castle. "That's the impression you give, that's the side of your tale that comes on strongest. Sure there may have been a few drunken French . . . they took a hell of a beating at Tortosa. Sure you had trouble with the MG commander. And there are Mickenbergs in all armies. The general of the Third Division was not typical. But all that put together isn't a drop in the bucket when measured against the heroism and devotion of the Listers and Campesinos and the other Spanish division, or against the sacrifice and heroism of the Thaelmanns, the Rakosis, the British, not to mention the countless good comrades dead and alive. Why don't we hear more 'bout that and them, Comrade Commander? Oh, don't get me wrong," Joe took in the whole table. "I don't mean to imply that Major Castle is lying or that he isn't a good antifascist comrade. I know better than that. It's just that he's young, and the things that he remembers and the things he talks about here are those things that stand out in his mind because they were the exceptions. The rest, the men who did their jobs well and quietly every day over and over again . . . to him all that is routine. Or as he says, taken for granted . . . not to be talked about." He turned full on Castle. "Well, you're wrong, because it is what must be talked of most by our best fighters, written of most by the best writers . . ."

"Aha!" Hemingway roared, "here comes the lecture on how to write for the cause."

"No one is telling you how to write," Joe was being persuasive, "only how I would like to see you treat the subject. If the war means as much to you, if the fight against fascism, the effort the Republic of Spain is making on behalf of the entire world, the effort it is making to come up out of the Dark

Ages, the tremendous amount of suffering and sacrifice, all these things that you know as well as I if not better – if all that means as much to you, then you have an obligation, not only to your readers but to all those who are fighting, and to the dead who died fighting and the women and children who died in the streets under the bombs . . . more than that, to all of those, as Mitch has said, who will suffer and die if Hitler and Mussolini are not defeated in Spain. This is an obligation that everyone has who knows what is at stake, whether he is a writer or a combatant, a reporter, sculptor, or whatever. That, and an obligation to himself and to his art.

"If for the sake of drama . . ." – he turned to Castle – "or self-pity and a mistaken sense of humor and humility, we emphasize the negative aspects, I repeat, if we allow these occasional weaknesses to upstage the main drama, then, and I must say I am putting it as strongly as possible because we are dealing with not a few lives here, but millions, then we are aiding and abetting the murderers of mankind."

"Bravo," Martha drummed on the table.

"You cannot be dishonest whatever the stakes." Herb was solemn. "A reporter has to be objective and truthful."

"An artist is partisan in his choice of subject matter and his treatment, sympathetic or otherwise," Jo Davidson intoned.

Hemingway leaned across the table to North, elbowing plates of tinned food, teetering glasses aside. "An artist has only one obligation, and that is to be true to his art, to be a craftsman and to tell it truly. When it comes to the fighting, you fight to win . . . any damned way you can. Dirty, dishonest, mean. That's fighting the war, and I know as much about that as anyone here. I'm as much of a *compañero* as anyone here or anywhere else, comrade, and don't you forget it, Comrade Preacher. We weren't sitting on our backsides in Madrid fighting the war in the pages of the *Daily Worker*."

"Or in the featherbeds of the Florida, either." Davidson raised his glass to Martha, who did not blush, though Castle did for her and worried about how Hemingway would take it, but Hemingway was not to be diverted.

"And if you're implying, Comrade Preacher, that I have in any way, or am, or will ever be, aiding and abetting, I say shit on you."

Joe held up his hands to protest.

"That's what you said. And I'm asking you just one question, Comrade Marx, how many fascists did you kill?"

"That seems to end the discussion," Martha said.

"The hell with the discussion." Hemingway was getting florid. "Talk is endless. Being in there is what matters. What counts . . . subtracting the bad guys from the ranks . . ."

"Boom. Boom. Boom," Davidson pointed a thick muscular finger, a thin black crescent of clay under the nail, and shot each of them in turn, "All dead except you and me, sweetheart." He hugged Martha to him.

"I'm not calling into question the contribution you've made to the Loyalist cause thus far," Joe North said, as diplomatic as he possibly could be, yet obviously determined to make the point. "But the war isn't over yet, not this one or the one that was incubated at Munich last month, which is sure to hatch a bigger and more terrible war than anything that has ever happened before. Wait just a minute please, let me finish. Herb here watched and applauded Mussolini's son-in-law when he dropped bombs on "little brown beggars" in Ethiopia, bringing to them, via the bombs that blossomed like roses, according to Benito, Jr., Roman civilization . . . little dreaming that a few bombs on a defenseless village occupied by black Africans was the prelude to a bigger bombing of an open city occupied by white Christians . . . but now I'm sure that he knows as I know and you know that the bombing of Madrid and Barcelona and Guernica are but the prelude to the bombing of Moscow and Paris and London and yes, maybe even New York."

"New York?" Castle was incredulous and wished that Joe, who was making good points, would not overdo it.

"We haven't seen the end of Dr. Technology yet," Joe went on, "but that's not the point."

"Well, let's be getting to it, and let's not stop on the way to attack my friend for saying it the way he saw it with the wops," Hemingway said.

"That is the point." Joe tried to conceal the triumph in his voice. "Reporting it as Herb saw it was being true to himself and false to the cause of antifascism, to peace, to democracy – "

"Socialism?" Hemingway said.

"Wouldn't it have been much better if you had been there to help him understand the central issue . . . as you have helped him here . . . as you have helped all of us?" Joe was really laying it on. "Perhaps the prestigious *Times* sounding the warning when Il Duce invaded Abyssinia would have prevented war here."

"What would our war correspondents have done for laughs?" Davidson demanded. His black beard was littered with crumbs and ashes and droplets of wine, his head meshed in spirals of smoke. It was difficult for Castle to figure out how he could be following the argument, nuzzling Martha . . .

or how Martha could stand being next to him. These people were sure funny. Martha was Hemingway's girl. Herb was yearning for her, Jo was doing what he was doing, and all the time this thing went on, the eating went on, the drinking went on, and the talk went on, and all of it left Mitch Castle further bewildered and intimidated.

"Perhaps," Herb said, "I made a mistake."

"An honest one," Martha defended him.

"Listen Comrade Stalin," Hemingway said, "we've filed more stuff, good stuff, in one day, more stuff for more readers in one day, than the *Worker* has printed and had read in two years."

"And the storm troopers roll on . . . and on . . ." Jo Davidson sang hoarsely.

"Of course they cut my dispatches pretty badly," Herb said.

"Wouldn't stop 'em if they hadn't." Jo insisted.

"Well I don't know about that." Castle thought he had spoken aloud, but the others went right on talking, so he must be talking to himself, which was easier to do than getting into this round-table thing that was dizzying him along with the wine. Maybe it was better that way, as he couldn't be sure that he could compete with them. They were writers, and Joe obviously had the words to express Mitch Castle's convictions.

For instance, if Hemingway and Matthews and the rest hadn't written so passionately on behalf of Spain, he wouldn't be here. Most of the guys wouldn't be. Wouldn't be dead and buried. Buried? Had anyone stopped to bury their dead? But you couldn't dwell on the dead. What you had to remember was that they came in response to the call that the penmen had issued. Now why shouldn't he say that out loud? Afraid of sounding mawkish, right? Maybe they hadn't stopped the storm troopers yet, but they sure'n hell had slowed them . . . had given everybody a chance to see what was going on and to do something about it . . . to get ready to do something about it. Though what had been done at Munich, with Chamberlain giving away the store to Hitler, wasn't very encouraging. Did that mean that if you did the right thing and got the wrong answer, the right thing was wrong to begin with? Wait a minute. But what the hell, all you had to remember was who was doing what to whom, and then you could hardly go wrong as far as the overall strategy was concerned. Though there must be a point when the number of lives you fed into the furnace reached a point where one more or a thousand more would add not one caloric unit. And that also was from the board of directors of the Marx Corporation, Marx-Engels-Lenin and Stalin in that order. And since the laws of the corporation applied to the war in Spain just as to any other situation, all you had to do was understand them, and apply them as you understood. Which proved he could run around in a circle as well as the next guy.

But when it came to application, Joe North was doing the applying, and Hemingway didn't know his ass from a hole in the ground, which in a savvy guy like him was not understandable unless you looked at it from the corporation's point of view . . . namely, that Hemingway understood but was on Hemingway's side first and the masses' second, so he'd take his understanding, estimate the situation, and write accordingly, which was "truly," but wasn't shooting himself in the foot.

Herb, on the other hand, hadn't reached that point of sophistication, so from him you took as much of it as was good for the cause. And as far as struggle was concerned, you always had to remember this, they were all well paid, heavily insured, their families were taken care of, and they could move in and out of the conflict as they needed to. So that was the difference, right? But Castle Commonplace or Commonplace Castle was not about to inject this stream of thought into the flood, because the thoughts would never come out right and he wasn't sure he had any confidence in them. Let Joe do it. But thinking about all that had happened, and how he had been telling them about it around the round table, he had to confess that never once had he stopped to analyze the situation dialectically.

That was it. Somebody must be doing something right, had to be in command, achieving predictable results. It was too much to expect of Castle, but not more than he expected of himself.

And, lost in the spinning last drop of wine in the crystal goblet, he had not mentioned Leo Rogin. Zip. Zero.

≡ 62

Take that goddamned rock in the Pandalls they'd put a number on, 666. Nice number. Very hard rock. A very hard rock to be stuck on the top of with the Italian mountain guns slicing bits of granite and steel in flat trajectories, the Italian pilots happy that almost all their bombs would fuse satisfactorily on the granite surface and the strafing would be interestingly complex because of the intricate ricocheting off the jumbled geometries of granite angles . . . the planes stitching seams and bleeding buttonholes through the virtually shelterless men. But 666 was a nice number and it overlooked Gandesa. Jose Valledor, commander of the brigade, had sworn to hold it even if surrounded, and Brigade Commissar Gates, red-eyed and solemn, had endorsed the oath because they had not held at Belchite in March and they were fucking-well going to hold 666 in the middle of August even though only one fourth of the men remained of those who had crossed the river on the twenty-fourth of July . . . which was a short time in which to have lost so many men, but which seemed a very long time, thinking back on it.

So that was what Valledor had promised to the battalion commanders and commissars, except for Millman of the Twenty-fourth, who'd been walking along right behind Castle on the way to the meeting when a stray round went plop and big old Millman'd fallen flat on his face. Sam Wild of the English Battalion had rolled him over, and Castle had said "He's dead," and Cecil Adams of the Mac-Paps had said, "Shall we move on" and they had. They'd told Valledor they had lost Millman on the way, and it didn't mean more than it should to him, but Gates had been all torn up, Millman having been a fellow commissar, not to mention a real son-of-the-working-class and a great loss to the cause. But Castle only thought on it now because this stray bullet on its mindless course had done in Millman when it could just as easily have hit any one of them. It hadn't, and there was nothing unusual in that or in Castle's reaction, which had been offhand and unconcerned and perhaps excusable, since it had happened in his immediate vicinity so many times before. It had not changed the way he carried himself, yet it had probably softened whatever mental armor he had been clad in, just as all other drops of silent acid fear had prepared the metal for final and total vulnerability. Disintegrating when they had brought Joe Bianca off the crest, slung in a blanket, gutted like a fish, green and slimy white, dying, dead.

Then it had been a different matter, because after that each death had been more real, and all the deaths that had gone before came into focus, and the chemical reactions that had been missing before now iced his bones so that the whip of a bullet, the whistle of a shell, the scream of a bomb twanged against the chilled bone and sent his insides scurrying for shelter. But he was committed to a certain posture, a certain air. He was the commander, and so he suffered this new and strange and gelid gut sensation stoically and hoped it didn't show.

"You couldn't run a peanut stand." Joe Bianca's famous – infamous? – words. Joe Bianca, maximum rank-and-filer par excellence, had spoken thus to Major Malcolm Dunbar, officer and gentleman from patrician nose to sanitized toes. The major had insisted that Joe mount the lorry, and Joe had insisted that there was no way in the fucking world to get another man in the fucking truck even if it was only him, Joe, dirty, unshaven, grey-poncho-wrapped, his soiled black mustache quivering with affront.

"I'm running this show," the major had said, and Joe had responded with the classic line . . . his epitaph . . . "You couldn't run a peanut stand" . . . his summation of all the brass, all the organizers, sea captains, capitalists, enemies of the working class, all lumped together in his mind as a bunch of windbag bureaucrats more concerned with protocol and polish than with the welfare of the rank and file.

And why remember that? Why not, instead, "The best soldier in the battalion"?

In some way Bianca and Dunbar – the united front in the fight against fascism – had been necessary to each other, and both of them had arrived at the hill in the Sierra Pandalls called 666, and Joe had died there while Dunbar was to die somewhat later though no less the best soldier in the brigade, patrician and peanut-stand-operator notwithstanding. And whether 'twas better to have died thus than to be sitting in the splendor of the Majestic Hotel dining room trying to sort it out and relate it all to the good French wine, the crisp English biscuits, the tinned Polish ham, the pâté de fois gras (he'd never say it out loud), and the Roquefort brought in from Paris . . . not to mention the delightful disputants piling syllogisms on dialectic, flirting hither, thither, and yon, other girls having mysteriously joined the company to share in the goodies, their Spanish ears tuned to the nuances rather than the nonsense.

And miraculously one blonde, too hard of face to be beautiful, or truly blonde for that matter, leaned to Castle and said, "Poor soldier. It is not good to think overmuch on the dead. Think of me, perhaps. There is still much life and happiness in Spain."

Or maybe it was "sad soldier." His Spanish was deficient. He was sure she had said there was *mucho felicidad* in Spain, and that he doubted.

"Is true," Hemingway said earnestly, reading the doubt in his eyes.

"Did I ever tell you the story about Archie?" Castle sat up straight in his chair and leaned eagerly into the faces around the table, new life in him, suppressing the words that came to his lips about the dead . . . how could you not think of them when there were so many. To the blonde he said, "You are my savior angel," and bent over to kiss the top of her head.

"She says that to all the boys," Martha said.

"Meroww," Davidson mewed through his beard, tickling the neck of a recently arrived black-haired girl who had inserted herself between Martha and him. She laughed shrilly.

"Never trust a man . . . with another woman," Hemingway said to Martha.

"Never trust a man, is good enough," Martha said.

"What is this about Archie?" Herb poised pencil over paper. "This for the record?"

Joe North's big black eyes questioned Castle.

"There we were up on this rock with no place to hide." He was too full of the wine to consider caution. "For the men, that is. Battalion headquarters was in a cave conveniently unreachable by shell, and a bomb would have had to have eyes to find it. You were there Herb, you know the layout, for Christ's sake, like I said before, you had me stroll you all over the place before this happened. Where was I. Yeah. The crap falling thick and fast and even faster. All the lines out and Fisher and Sullivan scrambling across the hard bare rocks to find the ruptured wires, splicing them, and the shells tearing them above and below the splices, the explosions so close together you couldn't separate them or find time to breathe . . . holding your breath in . . . the stone dust blasting into your ears, your nostrils; your pores open in terror, clogging with grit until there was no more you could possibly take, and then the sudden lifting of the barrage and now the wailing, you know the sound, the howl of the Moors winding up to come over and take the pulverized rock only sixty meters away from where they came out of their sandbagged trenches, and we're dizzied with the howling of the shellfire and the Moors' battle hymns, and out of all that bedlam, risen as though from the grave, comes this baggy, fuzzy-looking little guy, this commissar Archie Brown singing . . . singing the only thing he could think of to sing . . . the Star Spangled Banner, for Christ's sake, off-key, loud and brave, and the men wiping the dirt out of their eyes, laughing and shouting and firing the guns, the machine guns, the rifles, piling the Moors up in the saddle between the hills, hanging them up on their own barbed wire, piling them up like dirty laundry, choking the Allahs in their throats and killing the song on their lips. Firing and firing. And listen to this – Spear blown clean out of his clothes, the class ring on his finger blown off, naked as the day . . . the Maxim between his naked thighs firing and firing. Whatsa matter, Joe? It was the Star Spangled Banner. That's what he was singing, I can't help it if that's what he was singing . . ." Castle slumped in the chair.

"It's our song as much as if not more than Wall Street's," Martha said, " 'o'er the land of the free and the home of the brave.' "

"Arise ye prisoners of starvation," Davidson basso-ed.

"Up thou wretched of the soil," the blonde chimed in in Spanish.

"You're not saying that for me?" Herb asked.

"That's what he did," Castle said, looking at Joe.

"Wonderful," Joe said, "I agree with Martha one hundred percent."

"Is that for my benefit?" Herb asked again.

"Oh, don't be so suspicious, darling," Martha said, "the United Front is really the United Front even at the front."

"Can't you accept that?" Joe North nodded gratefully in Martha's direction. "Our comrades believe in that, believe wholly that this is the way to stop fascism. Fascism is the first item on the order of the day. We believe it without reservation or compromise. Not only idly or speculatively or theoretically giving lip service while trying to improve the position of the Party for the Day of Revolution – which is not on the order of the day – but actually retreating, sacrificing position, holding back from taking advantage of the opportunities that arise from their devotion to the struggle against fascism . . . the fight against fascism . . . Wait a minute, please . . . Even – and this is essential, hear me out – even, I say, when they have to carry the brunt of the battle, laying down their lives within that context when – and I am not saying this is necessarily the case – even when they are excessively exposed as a result. That's what I wanted to say. That's what it means, that's what singing our national anthem at such a time means. That's the whole thing in a nutshell."

"You mean when we're not up there on the front with them?" Hemingway challenged.

"Goddamn it." Mitchell Castle, grateful for the meaning Joe had given to him, the understanding of what in fact they had been doing and dying about, moved out of his fear of polemics with these people, and spoke with great vehemence. "Don't be so goddamned subjective about it. All Joe's saying, and he's goddamned right, is that you and Herb and me and everybody else who believes in this has to do his job, whatever that may be – writing, talking, or fighting – with that in mind. To stop fascism, to prevent the next war from happening, to give the people of Spain, of Germany and Italy and everywhere else a chance – so that whatever we're up to will put a thousand antifascists on that goddamned rock instead of the hundred that were there. Singing the Star Spangled Banner, the Internationale, the Marseillaise, or whatever. Anything that discourages that from happening is bad, undermining the barricades. There." Castle settled back in his chair.

He had said it, and he believed it, even if he found it impossible to demonstrate his belief in any other way than dying for it. And at this moment he thought it unfortunate that he had not died.

"That's what I believe, and there is a contradiction between what I believe and what life forces on me, and it's a contradiction that I cannot resolve a la Marxissimo. Maybe in guys like Joe Bianca and me the only way to resolve it is to keep on fighting, cut out the talking, and finally get all wrapped up in a bloodstained poncho under a pile of bomb-quarried rocks . . . the way Joe Bianca came to the end . . ."

He had said it, and they had been quiet listening, but now they were talking again. Jo Davidson was making something obscene out of Spear naked with the gun pouring out "streams of hot lead from between his naked thighs . . . sounds like a good description of, hmn, ah, War!" he concluded triumphantly. And everybody laughing, even Martha, who he thought shouldn't be, the Spanish girls laughing as Hemingway translated for them.

"That's a swell piece of symbolism," Hemingway smiled.

But in Castle's mind, besotted with the *vino* so that he couldn't help himself, it was as though only dying had meaning, as though only the best of them had died, though he knew that death had taken all kinds, many before they had been able to do much or prove more than the willingness to put their toes in the water – they had found the cold, dark depths right then, right there in the first testing. What else was there to prove? And what had been proven by Joe Bianca, for example, who had taken the first step and all the steps after that until he had walked through the fire, the long and short miles between being alive and being dead? They had all had a reason for coming to the proving grounds, they all had a cause – some with little to lose, others with a great deal, all with their lives to lose.

It seemed to him that in the end, it was only Castle Commonplace and the others, the too few others, who had lived through it and beyond – by chance, by skill, and by some inborn survival mechanism – it was only they who could prove it worthwhile. The world would not wait, nor need proof of anything, before other men on other fields repeated the entire experience . . . not once again . . . but forever and again. There was a purity in the immediacy of battle and an innocence granted by the bullet that became diluted and tainted by those who had lived through the moment and thus were given the opportunity for reflection. Afterward you tried to figure it all out, and how you figured had something to do with how you had been, how you had performed . . . and, damn it . . . there was no end to the qualifying commentaries, where the hell you had gotten to, where you were and for whom you were doing the figuring. *Mierda*. Wasn't it better, if you had had the misfortune to live through it, to keep the sacred banners clean, the battle pure, the restless heart as innocent as the heart at rest in the black earth beneath the flowering almond tree?

"What counts is the purity, the nobility of the struggle." Now Joe seemed to have seen into his mind. "Any man who thinks in terms of saints, the pure at heart in word and in deed, is naive or, worse, a fool. The ennobling struggle for all mankind is what makes heroes. It is the struggle – the struggle to end exploitation, starvation, hunger, disease, ignorance, superstition, war – that's what counts to all of us . . . all who carry a gun, or a hammer, or a pen under the banner of socialism and communism . . . no matter how corrupt our feet of clay. 'We shall make a garden for our future innocents. And to make a garden you must dirty your hands, you must destroy the weeds and the weevils, you must ravage the earth and nourish it with the blood and sweat of good and evil alike.'"

Hemingway shook his head and pushed back from the table. Standing steadily, his feet wide apart, looking straight at Joe, he said, "You cannot make a garden for future generations. Gardens aren't made that way. You make it for yourself. To teach the young to walk with your dirty hands guiding those first uncertain steps, you have to dirty their hands. It's all a dirty business and we have to do the best with it we can, each man with another."

"Never getting any better?" Martha asked.

"Not knowing if you are." Hemingway turned to go. "Are you coming?"

"If that's the last word, and I suppose it is," Martha came to her feet, "it's been educational. No. Inspiring. Hell, that sounds silly, doesn't it? Never mind." She came around the table to plant a light, sweet-smelling kiss on Castle's cheek. "What I mean is, you're all so damned wonderful . . ."

 **63**

Castle, leaving with the blonde, looked back at Joe North sitting alone at the table, solid and square behind the ruins of their eating and drinking, his black hair alive with glistening curls, his black eyes gold-speckled, reflecting the low-hanging chandelier's dangling crystals, smiling at them all as they got up and left him, saying, as much to himself as to them, "This is only the beginning, comrades, only the beginning . . ."

Up in the room the blonde was very demanding, and Mitch Castle was very tired with the talking and the drinking he had done, so it was not very good between them. He went quickly into a restless sleep, edgy with the irritability between them, uncomfortable, the unfamiliar wines and pâtés and hams churning in his gut. The grey cells, stimulated by the long hours of talk, the recounting of actions tossing him in and out of remembered battles, finally came to rest unbidden and unwelcome, in a nightmare, on Juan Abad.

Castle saw it happening as in a dream, was a witness powerless to change anything, anything at all, no matter how hard he reached out . . .

Juan Abad flashed like a sudden bursting flare in the hollow blackness of his skull. "The fire burning in him," Castle in sleep picking up from North's poetry in the splendor of the Majestic dining room, where he remained with the multiple wine-flushed faces of Hemingway, Martha, and all the rest crowding in, hanging on every word, all the things he had not said, pouring out of him as he struggled in restless sleep to suppress them, to remain silent, to fade in oblivion.

Looking at Abad, he had had a sudden hope that the night attack would succeed. He had had no faith in it when brigade proposed it . . . they had had no training or experience with night operations, but he brought it back to the battalion and laid it before Lopoff and Abad . . . Lopoff because his company was in position and Abad . . . Abad because he was chosen – *hermano de sangre*, the blood brother of Castle . . . an extension of himself, his second in command – chosen to be first when for whatever reason Castle Commonplace no longer was. *Mi hermano de sangre.*

Like an exploding star high above the high rock in the black night. A small core of man hot with black, brown, and glowing red in the eye, holding close to him an intense heat . . . the passions and yearnings of the man aching and pulsating so that he thought he could feel it, that he'd burn his hand if he touched him. But knowing that the fire was his and him consuming . . .

Abad had seized the dare to go into the darkness . . . off the rock crest down the slope of the shallow saddle and up to the enemy wire . . . to cut through and storm the Moorish trenches sixty meters away . . .

Abad had taken the cold plan and fired it with his fire, with his "Good. Good. We shall do it. We will steal across like shadows. The wire will be as nothing and when we are upon them we shall light the sky with grenades."

"Juan Abad," Castle turned to faces surrounding him, "is for me a confirmation, one El Cid who in his multitudes made the grape-purple land that is Spain, the people inseparable from the black earth, embracing the roots of vine and olive and almond, possessed of the land though he profited not therefrom, the land and its ripe sweet juice-filled fruits the legal property of a hierarchy of churchly princes and castrated latefundia rotting in cathedrals and castles. The land immortalizing the generations of Abads who work it; the withering absentee masters doomed to extinction in the barren waste of marbled vaults."

Juan Abad sped into the night, softly on rope-soled shoes. Softly on rope-soled shoes, a monstrous pistol in one hand, the other holding down the lever of a grenade, the safety pulled. Prematurely – Castle cried out in his sleep to warn him. Abad comes to the wire of the Moors and must throw the grenade to free his hand to deal with the wire, the grenade exploding short and announcing their presence before they have a chance to cut through the wire, and then the Veri flares arcing, the machine guns, the rifles, the answering grenades . . . all catching the Second Company, which had followed him, in the open.

And there he is. Commander Castle, huddling with his aides in the too-small rock *chabola* that he has made his command post for the attack, feels the shock waves of the battle as it sweeps across the saddle. It is too soon, he knows, for Abad to have reached the enemy trenches. Too soon. He feels the others stir uneasily around him. The *chabola* becomes unbearably close though the night is cool. He clambers over yielding bodies out into the hard rock of 666 to where he can see the flashes and feel wild bullets slicing the night air. And in the dark, the stumbling, cursing men, gasping for breath, loom up on the parapet and fall into the shallow trenches, carrying the wounded and dying and dead like bedding rescued from a burning house.

Slowly the night stutters into silence. Juan Abad remains behind, blood frozen on the cold rock six hundred and sixty-six meters above the town of Gandesa, where the Italian and German trucks move through the twisting streets, headlights blazing, gears rasping across the soft Spanish night, raising a stink of burning asbestos and exhaust fumes, overwhelming the sweet smell of grapes in the wine-press and the animals sharing the houses for warmth, the Moors ululating dirges, coming toward him in ghostly grey patrols recalling the slow red and gold grace of flamenco . . .

In the grip of the nightmare, Castle abandoned his post as observer . . .

Abad was now within reach of his outstretched straining arms. Castle saw Abad labor to raise the pistol, which now seemed immensely heavy. The barbed wire snagged his sleeve, and he cursed it on the milk of the Mother of God. He brought the hand, now free of the grenade, to help with the pistol. Castle felt, Castle suffered, the pain of the rusted barbs tearing through his flesh. Abad felt nothing. Both hands clutching the pistol, he yanked himself free from the barbed strands up to the middle wire that was barely sagging under his slight weight; he waited for the patrol to come closer in the dark, the fire burning out of him, the cool sweetness of peace humming, an inaudible tuning fork deep inside, waiting until they filled his eyes and he could smell the mustiness of them.

The first shot almost tore the pistol out his grasp, but the jerk of the gun sent the hum of the tuning fork into a screaming "Viva. Viva. Viva." The pistol flamed and jumped in his hands. He screamed as bayonets grated past the slim bones of his ribs . . .

Castle jerked awake. His jaws ached, his throat was raw, his tongue thick and dry. He sat up in a tangle of damp linen, saw blue light flashing on and off on the ceiling. Sharp, hard impatient shocks shook the room. Air raid sirens were going full blast. Relieved to be where he was and not on Hill 666 with Juan Abad, he fell back onto the pillows to watch the lights flash on the ceiling. The antiaircraft guns sounded as if they were in the closet. Maybe on the roof next door. He folded his arms behind his head and listened to the guns, the sirens, and the shrapnel whistling down. No bombs had fallen yet.

The blonde was kneeling on the floor beside the bed, a rosary in her hand, her eyes tightly shut, her lips moving urgently. He turned his head to the soft sound of praying, and there was a confusion in his mind that was not unpleasant. It was as though what he had dreamt was real and this was a dream. He remembered the blonde joining in the singing of the Internationale when he had told that story about the singing on 666. He turned onto his elbow and tried to get the gist of what she was praying. For some reason he felt quite secure, and while the thought entered his head that they ought to get dressed and go down into the basement, he dismissed it, feeling somehow that they would be more vulnerable in motion than they were now.

After a while the guns stopped firing, and then bombs began sounding far away. The gunners had done their job well and the fascists, unable to get through to the sleeping city, had unloaded their bombs on its outskirts as they turned back. The blonde came into his arms shivering with the cold, demanding the warmth of fucking, of affirming the wholeness of the survival of the flesh. And it was warm and easy now with them safe in the soft bed in the dark quiet room.

"Why did you pray?" he asked her afterward.

"I have always done so," she said.

"But I have heard you sing the Internationale."

"It is a prayer, as well."

"What, the Internationale?"

"But for sure. It is a brave song and it makes a prayer when one is needed of that kind, as you yourself have told about the brave soldier. To keep up the courage. True? Just so. I say the prayer of my childhood to keep us safe. When one is with many, one may pray by singing a brave song understood by all, but when one is alone and has fear, then one prays in words God will understand."

"In spite of everything, you believe in God?"

"I do not understand, but I believe. If you want me to say I do not believe, I will say it. I will say it many times. I will say it, but in my heart, who knows? When I stand alone and naked to the bombs, I must believe and I must pray. And afterward, too, though I bleed for all who have been killed and are hurt, I must give thanks that I have been spared. I do not know why. Perhaps it is because in reality I am a coward."

"Superstitions are not easily gotten rid of."

"You do not pray?"

"Not for a long time now." He tried to remember when last, not the meaningless stuff when he was a kid and kissed the bread, but when last out of need, fear, gratitude? He couldn't remember a time.

"Perhaps someday you will."

"Perhaps someday you will not."

The offensive across the Ebro into the Aragon had been a victory. The night attack on 666, Gates had said, was also a victory.

"'We have surprised the fascists with our aggressiveness,'" he read from a communique that he and Valledor had issued, "'and have inhibited them from launching future attacks that would easily have thrown us off the height, given our decimated condition.'"

And that's the way it was with the Ebro offensive. With Abad and the offensive. All that a man could do. It was also the last of it. Afterward it was fighting to hold on to the hills they had won. They went no farther. Then it was a matter of holding on. To the last man, whatever the cost.

Which sounded better in Spanish. It was a phrase frequently used by *Comandante* Jose Valledor and seconded by *Comisario* Johnny Gates, who read on, "We have won a respite, we have upset the plans and the timetable of the fascists, we have given a demonstration to the world that proved the possibility of defeating the fascists. We have given the democratic world, the western powers, a chance to think it over and to do something about it."

And they had. Chamberlain had gone to Munich – in September, about the time the IBs were pulled out of the lines for good – to talk appeasement with Hitler, and the Western world then and there prepared the gravesites for our coffins and theirs.

64

"There's something about your head that's giving me more trouble than it's worth," Davidson jabbed at the clay.

"Maybe it's your head and not mine," Castle said. "It was quite a night, a day and a night."

"No. It's your head. You're the ugliest son-of-a-gun I've ever done but you keep coming out beautiful."

"My hidden beauty will out . . ."

"There's no hiding that nose, it's a monstrosity. The forehead is positively Neanderthal, the mouth is as crooked as Jimmy Walker, and . . . and . . ." Davidson stepped back and searched Castle's face, compared it with the forming face in the clay and shook his head. "Screw it." He pounced on the clay. "Whatever comes out has to be right. I'm never wrong. Another raid last night. Caught me with my pants down. How come we didn't see you in the shelter? You and Hemingway too immersed in your work?"

"Nah. They can't bomb the city, the guns drive 'em off."

Herb came into the room. "All right if I watch for a moment?" He sat down on the bed and lit a cigarette. "Doesn't look much like him, does it?" He cocked his long head to one side. "Or more like him than he looks. From here – "

"Save your critique for the *Times*," Jo snapped.

"He's dealing in bad heads this morning," Castle said.

"I thought the air raid would short-circuit his hangover. You looked pretty alert and clear eyed in the shelter."

"I have been informed by this natural-born military genius that there was no air raid."

"There was a raid but no bombing," said Castle. "Not here, leastwise."

"See. Exact in every detail. You can quote him even if it kills the story. I prefer you write it so: Jo Davidson, working furiously and without interruption despite the falling bombs, completed his collection of heads of Spanish Republican heroes on Thanksgiving Day, for which all give thanks, and here is Ernest." Davidson wiped his hands on his smock and went around the room collecting glasses, which he rinsed out in the basin as Hemingway came in carrying a full bottle of scotch.

"I think it's a good story, the Republican gunners being able to protect the city this way," Castle protested. "I think that's what you ought to point out," he said to Herb.

"Muchos anti-avións." Hemingway uncorked the bottle and poured three fingers for everyone. "Por suerte y cojones. There's more where this came from."

"If you have balls you are already lucky." Jo downed half the drink.

It was too early in the day for serious drinking. Castle and Matthews sipped a drop or two. Hemingway matched Jo's intake.

"There's one more thing I want to get," Hemingway addressed the clay head, "without the commissar being present. How did that last day go?"

"Yes," Herb said, "what happened to Jim Lardner that day? Was he the last American to be killed?"

"What a distinction," Jo said. "This is the kind of stuff the press lives on . . . the first man, the last man . . . the youngest major, the oldest private – "

"The biggest mouth," Hemingway put in. "No one tells you how to sculpt, though you could use help . . ."

"Thus spake Zarathustra and other frustrated artists." Jo held out his glass for a refill and Hemingway obliged, saying,

"Better a frustrated artist inflicting pain only on himself, than a mediocre one foisting banalities on the populace."

"Now that we have all that settled," Herb said with considerable gloom, "and if Major Castle has no objections, I would like to hear about that last day."

"There wasn't much to it," Castle said.

But in the telling he found that there had been more to it than he had realized.

What then was the true way, the day-to-day, minute-by-minute story of what had happened and how each comrade had behaved, how Mitch Castle had been when it was all in the day's work?

But words have a dynamic of their own. And, when powered with imagination about how things might have happened to make it all more dramatic – even more believable – there is an irresistible tendency to get carried away. Castle knew that these high-powered reporters would never believe that fighting a war could be described as baldly as "all in a day's work." But that was how it had been. For him. Perhaps he was wrong in thinking that that was how it had been for every *soldado y comandante* in the outfit.

They had been in action for two months, since the twenty-fourth of July, with but one short rest, and during that rest they had been bombed and shelled. Yes, that was when Herb and Sheean and some of the others had come up to visit, Hemingway too: "You're doing one hell of a job." But the twenty-third of September had been the last day, and as always they had been moved around the front considerably, because now the fascists were counterattacking, looking for a soft spot to break through, only this wasn't like Belchite. The men were holding, both the Spanish divisions and the IB'ers, holding all along the line. The Fifteenth Brigade moved here and there, to the Sierra Caballs after the Sierra Pandalls, from hill to hill, until they were practically beaten into the ground, nailed to twisted grapevines; and how sweet and cool the grape clusters were in the early morning with the dew on them, and the fat ears of corn in the abandoned fields, the corn that the Spaniards said was only for animals but which they roasted and ate with gusto. And the rabbits springing up from bush and burrow, hopping across the skyline in no-man's-land . . . the Spaniards shouting *conejo, conejo* in hot pursuit. Some nights it was roasted corn and *conejo* stew and red wine. No-man's-land groaned with the sagging stalks heavy with fat ears and the vines dropped swollen clusters of grapes to rot on the ground, and the rabbits swarmed over the countryside. All the good and peaceful things held between the lines of men who dug long, winding, meaningless trenches that would not produce grapes or corn or give shelter to rabbits or men . . . the shards of mindless steel hurtling across the uncomplaining green acres. No man's land.

"There's a rumor that we're being sent home," Brandt had announced.

Castle shortened his stride so that Joe would not have to run to keep up with him. "You know what you can do with shithouse rumors. You're supposed to squelch them as being demoralizing. Who started it?"

"This one comes from brigade and is very political." Brandt was puffing. His flattened nose made wheezing noises. "The news is that Negrin has informed the League of Nations that all the foreigners will be out of the lines by the twenty-fifth, and out of Spain as soon as the league commission checks us out, and that the league should insist that all the Italians and Germans on the fascist side should also get out. The Republic then moves to come to some sort of understanding with Franco about new elections."

Watt joined them. "That's a very detailed rumor."

"It's not a rumor that the men should get hold of right now," Lyons said, "whether it's true or not."

"It's too late," Brandt said. "Some of the men are talking about it already."

"Oh, just fine," Castle roared, "just great. Couldn't come at a better time. Shit. Get along the line and let's pick up the pace, and any comrade mentions anything about going home, shoot him." He strode faster. "Right now we gotta get to where we're going before dark, and I don't think there's a hell of a lot of time left. C'mon, let's get them moving faster – take their minds off rumors."

"Shoot them?" Watt asked, wide eyed.

"Not literally, for Christ's sake. Just give 'em hell. I don't know what's ahead of us, but I know it ain't good and we're going to have to concentrate on that and nothing else. Just don't pussyfoot around."

"It's been a long haul," Lyons said when the others had gone to do his bidding.

"You believe it?"

"It makes enough sense to be believable. We're pretty much shot up, the Ebro offensive's made its point, and we'll never get enough volunteers or arms, nothing like what the fascists are getting. So why not?"

"You mean, make a deal with Franco?"

"If he'll make it, why not?"

"Why not. Why not. You keep saying why not. I can think of a million reasons why not."

"Give me one," Lyons said quietly.

Me. Castle pounded it into the dirt, not answering Lyons. Thinking it, pounding his thoughts into the earth beneath his feet, bringing his big feet down hard and fast. *Me. Joe Bianca. Morris Tobman and Juan Abad,* pound, *and it's better to die on one's feet,* pound, *than live on bended knee,* pound, *and after all this how could you go back to where you started with nothing decided,* pound pound, *and have to do it all over again?* "Mierda. I could give you a million reasons."

"We're getting too far ahead of the column," Lyons pointed out.

"Fuck 'em, let 'em catch up. Get your ass back there and speed 'em up. Go ahead, why not . . . go on."

"Take it easy," Watt said, catching up with Castle as Lyons went back, "the guys are tired. They can't keep up."

"It's just a trick . . . one of those diplomatic moves."

"What? What are you talking about?"

"That rumor about Negrin. It's just a gimmick. Franco ain't about to unload his imported fascisti, and he ain't about to consent to another election. Hell, that's what this is all about. He lost the last one, didn't he? Why should he consent to an election now? Bunk, and Negrin knows it. It's a gimmick. It's saying to the USA and England and that fuck-face Blum, 'See, we're willing to do all the right things and they're not, and therefore you are morally bound to come to our aid.'"

"What's wrong with that?" Watt asked, and, when Castle kept on walking, "Don't you think there's still a chance that the democracies will come to the aid of the Republic?"

Castle slowed his pace and looked at the wide blue seriousness of Watt's eyes. "Yes," he said, "I do. I think there's a chance. I think they have to . . ." He turned away and looked to the rise on the road ahead, where the advance guard had stopped to talk with two, three, four, six and more dark silhouettes slowly coming over the rise. "If not them, we . . . the Spaniards and us . . . we'll do it without them."

Up ahead, the scouts waved them on, and when Castle, Watt, Brandt, and Lyons, who had caught up with them again when they slowed down, reached the group of men, he could see that they were the Dombrowskis – the Poles, Hungarians, and Palestinian Jews, European hard-fighting IB'ers of the Thirteenth Brigade. Slowly, painfully, they exchanged information in English, Spanish, Yiddish, French . . . separately and all together.

The Dombrowskis had been under attack for three days and finally the lines had broken. They were going back. Back to where? Just back. Back to where someone would tell them what to do, but right now they were going back because there had been too much for them to take after all. They were going back to where there would be some rest and perhaps hot food, something they had not had for three days. Afterward, they would return to the front and fight some more. But now they were going back.

So, Castle thought, we're going up to hold the line that the famed Dombrowskis couldn't hold. Goddamn it and ain't it wonderful. Goddamn it, just when I'm getting the hang of this job and we're all getting good at it, somebody comes up with the brilliant repatriation idea and maybe that's why I'm so dead set against it.

"Take it easy, comrades," he said to the Poles. "We'll hold the line."

"No. It cannot be so," one said to him, "there is too much against us here."

"Don't worry about it, we'll hold them." He smiled. "Give the men a *viva* as we go by, okay?"

"Okay." The Pole smiled and waved his hand. Everyone understood "okay."

The column was now drawn up behind him, and Castle called in the company commanders, who looked wonderingly at the exhausted Dombrowskis sprawled by the side of the road. Castle gave the C.O.'s their orders, and they went back to carry them out, no one asking any questions.

He waited and watched as the column went over the rise and strung out in battle formation, the Poles weakly cheering as they went past, calling "No paseran," shaking their heads as they did so. He turned away from the Poles, went to the center of the deployed men and signaled the line forward. And they went forward over one hill, passing more Dombrowskis, silent and bleeding. Feeling the dread building up in the men, Castle was alive with the situation, the Lincolns taking over from the Dombrowskis. He moved the men on, over that hill and into a valley where now there were dead Poles, and wounded calling softly for help. Up on the next rise the silhouettes of the fascists danced and jigged and the Lincolns moved forward, stopping to fire their rifles, moving forward again . . . firing on the run as they went up the slope, finding new strength as they moved across the burnt grass on the slope, running, charging up the hill. The fascists turned and ran down the other side into the valley where now the deepening shadows of night had fallen, and Castle and his men held the hill and fired into the retreating ranks of the fascists, who hopped about like rabbits. *Conejo. Conejo.*

The hill that the Dombrowskis had lost was now theirs.

 **65**

Castle's orderlies, Rubio and El Negro, had found a bomb shelter behind the hill, and he had made his HQ there. The shelter had been about twenty or thirty meters behind the Dombrowskis' trenches, the damnedest hole Castle had ever seen. Someone had done a major engineering job, and it was as big as a small room. He had even been able to stand up under the timbers and sandbagged roof.

Everything had been just fine. Fritz had dished out a good hot dinner for the men, and Rubio had come up with extras for the staff. They had settled in for the night.

"The situation on the ground," Castle said, being professional for Hemingway's battle-trained ears, "had the British positioned on the Lincolns' left flank across the road leading to Corbera." At the time, Castle had not known about the dry stream bed that ran parallel to the road, and that was too bad . . . "Anyhow, the battalion's line ran from the road, the Britishers' right flank, along the crest of the hill to where the hill sloped down and ended."

And then about twenty meters behind and to the right was another little hill, and he'd put the Fourth Company, the Spaniards, there to cover that flank. He had had some of the brigade heavy machine guns down there, too, to give more protection. He hadn't known what was behind them, and brigade hadn't known, so he'd sent out a patrol. And the reason he was telling them all this, to the endless boredom of Jo Davidson, who kept drinking and fiddling with the clay head, was that Hemingway was a nut about military tactics, while Herb wanted so desperately to know about Jim Lardner, and this was where Lardner came in.

Castle did not tell them how he had felt when the brigade was on the other side of the Ebro and Lardner was one of the replacements, and how excited Watt and Brandt had been when they'd told him that Lardner was the son of some famous writer. Castle had not said anything, so they'd kept explaining how wonderful it was and how great it would read in the papers back home, and Castle kept silent until he had heard it for the third time, not listening to them but to the mixed-up feelings he had about it. He had not wanted Lardner, but he couldn't figure out why. Part of it was a feeling that it would be a waste if Lardner got killed. Part of it was a feeling that it was too near the end for this kind of thing. And part of it was that they had all fought, the sons of no one famous . . . sons of the working class, who had taken everything the fascists could throw at them, not to mention all those who had died and who would not be mourned or celebrated either in life or in death . . . Somehow this famous name coming to cash in on all that sacrifice . . . it didn't seem right. It was Morris Tobman's and Bill Titus's and Joe Bianca's and all those nobodies' whose glory would fall in the shadow of Jim Lardner, son-of-the-great-author . . . And Castle's too, if he wanted to be perfectly honest, and that's what had burrowed inside of him as the others delighted in the new recruit so that finally he had shut them up by roaring, "I know. I know."

Castle had taken Watt aside and suggested that Lardner be sent packing. It was too late; he could do more good in the rear. But Watt had not agreed, and Lardner was determined.

Lardner had turned out to be a pretty good guy. He went about soldiering with a kind of quiet dedication, distributing all the extra goodies he had brought with him to the men in his squad, though not to Castle, who would have liked to have gotten one or two things, even if only a bar of Lifebuoy soap. But the men in the ranks thought the brass had everything they needed, which wasn't true, even though Castle had these two flunkies taking care of his needs, scrounging up a special meal here and there – not different, just better prepared – and washing his clothes, things like that. No shoe shining, he didn't have shoes.

Castle had become aware of how easily one could get accustomed to being served, taken care of, obeyed. Could make a real prick out of you, real easy-like. He hoped to God he hadn't succumbed.

Castle would not tell these assembled figures of the literary Popular Front that after Abad had died leading Lardner and the rest into the night attack, Lardner had come out with some slight wound, had joined the Spanish Communist Party while getting it patched up so that the trip to the rear wouldn't be a total waste of time . . . He had come back a Communist as well as a seasoned vet, so that when Castle asked for a volunteer patrol to find out what was on the right flank, he was not surprised when Lardner showed up.

It had been one of those September nights in the Aragon when it wasn't very dark, and all the hills could clearly be seen. Castle wanted to find out about the higher hills to the north, the ones more or less in line with the ridge the Lincolns were on. Brigade had assured him, as always, that a Spanish division was out there and all he had to do was contact them, but he had neither heard nor seen signs of life in that direction, so he'd told Lardner to be careful and for Christ's sake not try the hills north and west, because it would probably be fascist held.

No, Castle was sorry, but Lardner had had no last words, Herb. When you set out for a patrol, there wasn't any rah-rah. Just cautionary words about clinking mess tins and stuff like that. You didn't send 'em off with good luck or anything like. Just laid it out and they took off, because if you started that bon voyage stuff like in the movies, you'd just get the wind up. It was best to send them off as though it were an evening stroll under a starry sky.

When the men had gone, Castle went back to phone brigade, and Johnny Gates, sounding sick and irritable, repeated that the hills were occupied by a friendly Spanish division.

Brigade HQ had taken a pounding when they'd moved up behind the battalions. All day, while the Lincolns had moved onto the Dombrowskis' hill, artillery and planes had pounded the rear, and Gates had been right in the middle of that along with Valledor and the rest of the staff. It was understandable that they weren't feeling particularly good. And Gates must have known that it was the last night, and that the next day was going to be the last day, so you could see how he must have felt.

But Castle had been eminently satisfied with himself, and had addressed himself to the hot meal and mail Fritz had brought up. Irene must've spent a fortune in half the churches of Brooklyn sealing his safety in wax. There was also a package, a Christmas present arriving either nine months late or three months early.

"You won't believe this." Castle swallowed the rest of his scotch. "The present was a blanket. Practical, yes? But oh what a blanket. Soft, fine-spun wool, woven into a plaid pattern of delicate shades of pink and white, fine light-green lines marking the separations of color." He paused to make sure they were seeing with as unbelieving eyes as he had when he had unfolded it and beheld it in all its pastel glory.

Watt, Brandt, the orderlies had been beside themselves. But though it wasn't really cold in the hole with Watt and Brandt there, and with all the candles the orderlies had scratched up, Castle had wrapped himself in the blanket. It was hard to imagine why Irene had picked this blanket that must have been meant to adorn an elegant English pram wheeled about a tailored green park by a nanny. The guys had thought it was very odd, but Castle had liked the soft warm feel of it. He'd wrapped himself in it and read her letters.

Then there had been a flurry of firing and grenade bursts, and he had climbed out of the dugout to see what was going on. The flashes came from the north and in front of the right flank, so he went up to the trenches to get a better look, but by the time he got there the firing had stopped.

Williams was sitting on the sandbags outside his HQ and when he saw Castle in the blanket, he got down into the trench saying, "Now, if that thing doesn't draw fire nothing will."

"We'll find out," Castle said, sitting where Williams had sat. "Sounds like Lardner's patrol made contact."

"Definitely. Harold's gone out to pick him up on the way back."

"Alone?"

"His idea. Pulled his commissar's rank. Where'd you get the blanket?"

"My girl sent it from Brooklyn."

"In Brooklyn they must think we're fighting a clean war, and no wonder.

According to the *Daily Workers* we get in the mail, hardly anyone's gotten their hands dirty much less been killed."

"The enemy reads the papers, too."

"They can figure out the casualty figures on the battlefields."

They talked back and forth, neither one listening too closely, listening instead for the returning patrol and not hearing it. Watt came up to say that brigade wanted to know the situation as soon as the patrol got back. Then he joined them and they chatted about the blanket and about girls who would send a blanket like that, and finally Harold came back . . . alone, as he had gone out.

"I was wondering what the hell that was." Harold pointed at the blanket. "I saw this ghostly vision hovering over the top of the hill and let me tell you it gave me pause. If I hadn't heard the old familiar bullshit going on I might have exorcised the apparition with my trusty pistol."

"Can the Shakespeare. What happened?"

"Couldn't find them, but I did find a squad of ten Poles dug in."

"Where'd you look? Where were the Poles? Didn't anyone tell them they were relieved?"

"I did. I found them over there." He waved his hand forward. "We conversed in Yiddish. A minion of Polish Jews . . . all that was left of their section, of their battalion for all they knew." There was pride and awe in his voice. "A minion is a temple and the temple had made a decision to stay put and fight to the death . . . None of them expected to live beyond the next twenty-four hours . . . the next sunset – "

"Oh, come on." Castle was impatient with the tribal accents. "They didn't give you that crap about minions and temples . . . not the Dombrowskis."

Harold brought his head around, surprised at the sharpness in Castle's voice. "No . . . no . . . they didn't. It was sort of implied in the situation, that's all. It called to mind that kind of imagery."

"Yeah, like the Hamlet ghost. You're supposed to read that stuff for entertainment and not take it as a guide to living," Williams said.

"I couldn't agree with you less," Harold said. "If you had seen them, the dark, weary, but determined faces . . . yes, determined and resigned . . . faces that went back through the ages . . . the same look . . . it could have been Massada, or the Maccabees making a last stand against the Syrian legions."

"Oh, for Christ's sake . . . cut this shit out and give me a full report," Castle barked.

The men standing guard looked in his direction. He lowered his voice. "Is that as far as you went? The patrol wasn't to go that far in advance of our lines. Even with us or slightly to the rear, that's what I said . . . did you cover that area?"

"Yes . . . there was no one there and besides, the shooting had come from farther ahead and that's why . . . that's how I found the Poles. There was no sign of Lardner's patrol."

"Anything else? Enemy movement, anything like that?"

"No," Harold paused, then smiled. "When they were finally convinced that they were relieved . . . they were relieved. You should have seen the beautiful smiles that lit their faces as they slowly gathered their few things together and went off to the rear. In formation, two by two . . ."

"Yeah," Williams said. "Listen, I'm going to take Vincent and look for 'em. You're in charge till I come back."

Castle wasn't happy about Williams, who was a company commander, going out to look for the patrol, but something had to be done, so he did not object. He watched Williams and his man disappear into the night. "I'm getting back to *plano mayor*. I gotta convince brigade there's nothing on our flank but maybe fascists. I'm not waiting for Lardner to come in."

"I don't think they'll come back . . . they would have been back by now if they were coming back."

"Well damn, that's kind of iffy, isn't it? What the hell's the matter with you? A Communist giving us all that drivel about minions and temples. For Christ's sake, these were not Jews. They're Poles, but more than that, they're antifascists. They're Communists, probably. They were prepared to make a stand because they're Communists, because they're Poles and they know firsthand what pogroms and fascism are all about . . . not from reading and hearing about it like us . . . but from having it shoved down their throats in real life. They're like the Germans who made that stand outside Teruel . . . to the last man. They've been in the jails, they've been hunted. They've seen and heard the firing squads, the hangman's noose, the cossack's saber . . . if you want to compare them to Maccabees and ancient Hebrews, go ahead. But don't lose sight of the fact that these comrades aren't just fighting for the Jewish people . . . they're fighting a monster that wants to enslave the entire world . . . And when we win, we're not just going to win the right to form a minion and pray. And why the hell do I have to be standing here telling you this . . . that's not what you stopped me for."

Castle hadn't said that, not all of it. But in the retelling, the scotch adding fuel to the fire burning in his head as he relived that last night, he said the things he had wanted to say then, uttered the words as much for him-self as for Ernest and Herb and Jo. They listened quietly. Jo Davidson worked furiously, fired by the intensity of his oration. He sensed they want-ed to hear more about Lardner. But Lardner had not come back.

And Harold hadn't finished with Castle. But Castle would not tell them about that.

Harold had looked away from Castle and out into the night. "No. Leo didn't come back either."

"Leo?" Castle had been surprised not so much because Harold had brought it up, but because until he had, Castle hadn't thought about Leo . . . not since May Day, and this was September twenty-second . . . except perhaps when Abrams had gotten it on the hill.

"Rogin. The deserter," Harold had explained, "Abrams came for him to put him on battalion sentry duty. He never came back."

"So? What's new about that? He did it all the time." Castle waited, but Harold was silent, still staring into the dark. "Don't worry about that bas-tard. Worry about Lardner and the patrol getting back, if you must worry." He turned to go, then stopped. "Keep your mind on the Jewish comrades ready to die to the last man on the hill, which is more than you can say for the apostles, come to think of it," he laughed. "Don't waste the grey matter on deserters."

"A life's a life," Harold said softly.

"I don't know what you mean by that." Castle was conceding nothing. "But if you mean what I think you mean . . . A life's a life, that's one of those generalities that sounds good but defines nothing. I wouldn't give a finger-nail off of one of those Poles for a minion of Leo Rogins." But it was possi-ble that Harold did not hear the last because Castle was on his way down the hill when he thought to say it.

 **66**

"Gates?" Castle hadn't been sure, because the voice coming over the wire was tired and sick sounding. "Gates, tell Valledor I've got two of the patrol back here and Lieutenant Williams. They ran into the fascists less than a half, maybe a quarter kilometer on our right. Lardner went up to check and that's what all the shooting was about." He glanced at the two men sitting in his dugout, heads hanging in dejection. "Lardner must've gotten it. He never came back down to the other guys and he hasn't come back here. Harold Smith went out looking and found some Dombrowskis . . ."

"We know, they're here with us now."

"Okay. Williams and another man went to check and they ran into wire, they heard digging and probably Moorish talking . . . but no trace of Lardner. And no sign of any of our guys anywhere. Looks like we have no flank." As *usual*, he added to himself. He listened to Gates tell it to Valledor in Spanish, and then Gates came back on.

"You have to be wrong. According to division – "

"Yeah, according to division. I've heard that before."

"We'll move the heavy weapons company into the area."

"When?"

"Right now." Gates waited for him to say something, but there was nothing to say. "They ought to be there in half an hour. Get them set up. And Castle."

"Yes?"

"The Lincoln Battalion has to hold."

"We will."

"Tonight and tomorrow."

"As long as necessary."

"Tonight and tomorrow," repeated Gates.

"Okay."

"What did he say?" Watt asked. Williams and the two men who had been on the patrol with Lardner had waited with Lyons and Brandt and Watt, eyes on him.

"Nothing," Castle said, turning over in his mind Gates's words. "Go get a good night's sleep." He helped the men to their feet. "Get some rest. Lardner might check in."

"Well, you know he never did." Castle measured his scotch . . . hardly touched. He was dry from talking, but whiskey was not what he wanted. The iodine flavor of the scotch seemed particularly strong so early in the day. Jo Davidson had thrown a rag over the clay head sometime during the narration, and now he leaned against the wall, short, solid, and square, a cigarette curling smoke out of his shaggy beard, his eyes on a far corner. Herb sat checking his notes, and Hemingway was trying to squeeze one last drop out of an empty bottle into his empty glass. "Will you drink the rest of this?" Castle held his glass out to him. "I've had it."

"No, you finish it. I'll go get some more."

"Not for me." Castle got up and placed his glass on the stand holding his shrouded clay head. "You finished?" he asked Jo, and when Jo nodded ashes into his beard, "Then I gotta go."

"Was there a chance that Lardner was taken prisoner?" Herb asked.

"It's possible."

"Eddie Rolfe thinks it's possible. He suggested that I report him captured. If they've taken him, perhaps press notification of who he is will influence their treatment."

By the door, Castle thought about it. Thought about Jim Lardner going up the hill to find out if the Moors were Moors. If Lardner had lived through all the shooting and grenade tossing, which was possible because after all it was dark; if they had taken him alive and gone through his papers and found the Party card, red hammer and sickle, the Socorro Rojo card . . . better they had killed him in the flurry . . . better for him.

"I think it's a great idea," he said.

"I don't know why he's asking," Hemingway said, coming up to the door smelling strongly of scotch and onions, "We've all treated him as missing, probably captured. Will you join us later? I'd like to get the rest of the last day."

"I'll try, but I have a hell of a lot to do. Sitting for this damned head has thrown me way off schedule."

"Well, don't trouble yourself." Hemingway opened the door. "I understand. I'll get it from one of the other men."

"Sure," Castle was relieved. "I'll see you around. Give my love to Martha."

Hemingway waved the empty glass in acknowledgment and rolled down the carpeted hall to the stairwell. He took the stairs two at a time.

"Uh, thanks for everything," Castle said to Davidson, now washing his hands at the basin. "Will I get to see it after it's cast?"

"If it's cast," Jo huffed over his shoulder, "you'll see it."

"I'm sorry you had to listen to all that stuff but . . ."

"It was certainly worthwhile," Herb said, standing up and folding his notes into his pocket, "You needn't apologize."

"Nah," Jo straightened up and wiped his hands on a towel, "It went in one ear and out the other. Battles come and go but the hills remain, people live, not everyone dies."

"What does that mean?" Castle was scornful. How could these little clay heads of Modesto and Lister and Dolores and all the rest, of Castle himself, for Christ's sake, speak for all those comrades dead out there?

"Don't get huffy," Jo said, "I'm not taking anything away from what you guys did or why you did it. You had to. We have to believe in something, and so I believe in you. Yes, you. That's what I need to go on with. But that doesn't mean that I have to buy all the attendant rhetoric." He looked to see if Castle was understanding what he said. Castle stared blankly back at him. He looked at Herb, but Herb was studying the carpeting, his forehead deeply creased. "Aaah, you'll never understand." He went to Castle and took his arm. "Forget it."

"Right." Castle loosened the grip of Jo's small, strong hand. "I'm off, see you around . . ."

Out on the Ramblas the sun was shining, and people moved quickly along the street. A pretty girl passed and he turned and whistled, "¡Qué guapa!" She smiled briefly and hurried on. It seemed everybody in Barcelona was taking the late November sunshine, the quiet air, the time free of bombs and sirens, just as rapidly as they could, taking as much of it as they could scoop up, taking it in long quick strides and gulping mouthfuls. The night was for dark damp cellars and terror. Castle, glad he had not drunk more than he had, moved along with them, smiling and calling "salud" when someone smiled back . . . even raising his arm in the clenched-fist salute, proud of his broad gold major's bar under the red star pinned to the suede jacket that Bob Minor had given him when Castle had admired it. He remembered Bob bounding up the hill, waiting for him at the top, a mouthful of large white teeth grinning, "Not bad for a man my age, eh?" Minor had been in Spain representing the CPUSA, though Castle hadn't known it until North had mentioned it.

Castle went into the first women's wear store he came across and bought a purple silk bathrobe for his mother. She had never had silk to wear, and he couldn't remember ever seeing her in a bathrobe. By the time the family was awake, she had always been up for hours. Up and dressed and breakfast made. She had never needed a bathrobe and he did not think she would ever wear this one, but it was what he wanted for her, because that was the way he would like to see her now. In royal purple, in silk, in flowing swirls of leisure . . . He did not think to buy a gift for Blanche. He did not think of Blanche now. Or Irene.

He found a men's store and got himself measured for a suit, picking out a rich brown material, because the only other choice was black. The tailor marveled at his height and worried about all the yards it would take to fit him. He was taller, even, "than the Ingleses."

"Hey," Joe North hailed him as he came out into the street, "I've been looking for you. Have a date, remember?"

"Sure thing, Joe, just doing a little shopping in preparation for rejoining the world."

"You picked the best tailor in Catalonia, and the most expensive."

"*Muchas pesetas* and nothing else to do with them. Contribute them to the Republic and they shove them back at you in the form of back pay. Also all other working-class contributions taken care of . . ."

"Hey, I wasn't implying that you shouldn't. Nothing but the best for the working class." Joe fell in alongside and they walked down the sunny avenue.

Mutt and Jeff, Castle thought. People turned around to take in the sight. Castle wore khaki pantaloons that barely reached to his ankles, the suede jacket, no hat. Joe was in civvies, a jaunty blue beret, the shiny black curls sticking out here and there, a little bounce in his walk. Seeing him bounce along like that, Castle smiled at him. To look at him, you'd never think that things were going badly for Spain. Without deliberation, he unfailingly underestimated casualties. Their defeats were minor readjustments in the line. He multiplied the number of fascist deserters, casualties, prisoners, magnified each little advance so that it read as a decisive victory; he predicted calamity if this, that, or the other thing was not done by Roosevelt or Blum or Chamberlain. He believed everything he wrote in his *Daily Worker* dispatches, without reservations or doubts, never admitting error . . . not, at least, without detailed spelling out of all possible extenuating circumstances. He was truly a "good guy."

"How'd the head go this morning?"

"Finished. By the way, Ernest and Herb were there wanting to know about Jim Lardner and they mentioned that business about his being taken prisoner, as Ed Rolfe suggested . . ."

"You think it's a good idea?"

"Oh, sure. It can't hurt. I told them how it went."

"The last American volunteer to fall, Jim Lardner." Joe shook his head back and forth slowly in wonderment. "History has a way with coincidence."

"You mean historians have a way of juggling things around so it seems that way. He wasn't the last, not by a long shot."

"Well, maybe not precisely . . . but certainly on that last day."

"Night. I don't want to be picky about a legend in the making, and I don't think Jim would give a damn about the dubious honor, but he wasn't the last. We had one hell of a day following that night." He had never finished the story up there in Jo Davidson's room, and now it was hanging loose inside him like a string of mucus that he could neither hack up nor swallow. If he told Joe, optimistic Joe North, about how they had been run off the hill – he envisioned the headline: THE LAST HILL – then maybe, no, certainly, Joe would report the operation as heroic resistance on the part of the Lincolns.

In any case it was not something he would tell Hemingway, or any of the other reporters.

"Look, we have some time," he said. "Let's stop in here for a drink. I want to talk." There were tables set out in the shade of the building, and the dark door of the cafe looked as though eventually someone would come out to take their order.

Joe sat down on the edge of a chair. "We can't keep the Central Committee waiting. Perhaps some other time?"

"Hell, it's only a farewell party, isn't it? I mean, they're not going to give us the word, or lecture us or anything like that. Everyone's late for a party . . . and for sure everyone's late for a Party meeting. Besides, this won't take long . . . it's about that last attack . . . not about Lardner."

"I pretty much know," said Joe. "I was with brigade."

"I know, I know, and that's why I want to . . . to compare notes with you . . . you from the brigade side."

The *patron* appeared sooner than he'd expected, and Castle ordered a vermouth and spritzer and Joe said he'd have the same.

"Johnny Gates won't talk to me about it and I haven't pushed him. As a matter of fact I might not be thinking, much less talking, about it if it weren't for those characters at the Majestic stirring it all up."

The spritzers arrived and Castle sipped, giving Joe a chance to say something, but Joe was waiting for Castle to finish whatever it was he thought needed finishing so they could get on to the festivities, which had to be more interesting, or more fun, or more informative . . . something that would produce *Daily Worker* headlines.

Or maybe he was just being polite. There was no way Castle could know. "Listen, I'll itemize it by points just like a report. Then if you want to comment on any of the points you'll have reference numbers . . ."

"Come on," Joe laughed, "don't be a damned fool. And don't take me for one, either."

"I'm sorry, I can't seem to get started, that's all. Well," Castle plunged in, "number one, the morning of that last day, the fascist attack began with air strikes to our rear, then commenced shelling our lines. I don't know about any other lines, but ours got it all morning and we couldn't get any word through in either direction, and the companies weren't getting any word down to me . . . which is what I can't understand . . . We never were much for communication, but this morning was the worst of all since it seemed no one even made an effort, and even worse than that, now that I come to think of it, I wasn't too upset by it all, figuring that on such a beautiful morning with the shells and the bombing elsewhere for a change, no news was good news. So I remained in the hole that was headquarters, reading letters from home, admiring the blanket my girl had sent me, kidding around with George and finishing breakfast. But after awhile the shelling seemed to be getting closer, the hole started to jump, and when one shell exploded damned near on top of us, George and I decided to have a look. So we came out into the sunshine. It was clear and clean on the hill where the companies were supposed to be."

Castle stared at the little bubbles popping to the surface of his glass. Yeah, thinking back on it: what the hell had he been doing in all that time? He shook his head, to shake loose the question. There was no acceptable answer.

"¿Qué pasa?" Joe said. "If you're having trouble with this, we can talk about it later, but we really ought to be going."

"No, hear me out. The flanks – left and right – were getting it both ways, from the air and from heavier guns . . ." He hurried on. "Yeah, like we were in suspension while this was happening elsewhere . . . Except George and me . . . Come to think of it, we were alone in that hole . . . maybe I had sent all the others out for something . . . information . . . to establish some sort of contact? I don't seem to be able to get it straight."

≡ 67

"We'll have another," Joe said to the *patron*. "Keep talking." Joe sounded sympathetic. He was beginning to understand Castle's need.

"Yeah, it must have been hours because afterward it wasn't too long be- fore it got dark . . . or maybe I have that period of time foreshortened . . . damn it." He mustn't get ahead of himself. Take it in sequence. "Where was I? Yes. That was funny. Not only weren't there any shells hitting our lines then, but there wasn't even any sign that there *had* been . . . no smoke, no dust or anything . . . just the line of the hill in the sun. So George and I went up to the hill . . . we walked . . . just walked up, George smiling the way he always did . . . maybe we were still talking about the letters I had been reading to him. They were always full of Jesus Christ and poetry and that sort of stuff. Anyway we walked up to the lines, and when we got there there was no one there. That's right, no one. We just stood there for I don't know how long, looking around, and then Cook and some other guys came running up from our right, and Cook was ashen and shot through, but we were talking when he came up to us. I asked him where everybody was and he said they were all dead. All the guns smashed and the men in the trenches smashed . . . and now the fascists were marching into that sector behind banners and trumpets. And as he was talking, we could see them coming out of the trenches and walking along the top of the hill, looking at us, pointing at us, and we turned and walked down the hill. I could feel that Cook and the men with him wanted to run, but George and I were still – I don't know how to put it, in a daze? No. Not that. More like unable to believe what we were seeing . . . I don't know. Walking and wondering what the hell had happened. Do you understand that? I don't. When we were down the hill and on the flat, I must have been walking back to the hole that was the *plano mayor*, and pretty soon the fascists were all along the ridge dancing and jigging around, waving their arms, calling us to come back, but not shooting at us, just jeering. I tell you it was the damnedest eeriest thing, and someday I'm going to get it all straightened out. Which I suppose was what I was trying to do then, but the shelling began again, this time hitting all around us, and then we were all running, running, running. I could see George running alongside of me, and he could have run faster but I wasn't running too fast, because I didn't have the situation resolved in my mind . . . sort of cantering along and thinking in a vacuum. I had no facts . . . no information . . . nothing solid to kick around, hell, it doesn't make any sense does it?"

"It must have been bad."

"Yeah, it was bad." Castle held his glass up so that the spritzer tickled his nose, the tiny bubbles releasing the clean, cool fragrance of vermouth. "It was so bad that we ran right past my *chabola*. I wanted to go back and get the blanket and the letters. But George said 'Castle, what'll we do now?' and I'll be goddamned if he wasn't still smiling, and I guess that brought home the situation to me somewhat. Anyhow, I put the blanket out of my mind. We came up on this little rise – it wasn't a hill, just a place that was higher – and I stopped and said 'Let's make a line here. And who have we got to make it with?' We had Cook and his few men, and George and me.

We had some rifles and one light machine gun, so we spread it all out as far as it would go and still keep us in shouting distance of one another. We didn't even dig in, just took whatever cover we could, and measured out our fields of fire. Cook said it wasn't much of a position, but I thought we would stay there and if the fascists kept coming we would do what we could."

Castle sighed. "Well, they didn't. They moved laterally through our former positions instead, and from what I could see, they were beginning to turn the British Battalion's flank. Jesus Christ, it was pitiful. I tell you I felt like a first-class prick leaving the British flank open like that . . . I can't tell you how I felt about it. Sam Wild over there catching hell, what would he be thinking of his ferking friend Castle now? Ah, don't worry, I'm not the crying type, but I could have cried then." He felt the choke come into his throat and the sting to his eyes. He took the spritzer, now flat, in one swallow. "Now here comes Brandt up from brigade and says Johnny wants to know what happened. The Lincolns had come back and piled up around brigade HQ where Johnny was holding them and wanting to know who gave the order to withdraw. What order? Well, in a way it was good news to know where the men were, even if I didn't know how the hell they had gotten there, so I told Brandt to go back and bring the men up because we would be needing them. I even had an idea that we might try to recapture the hill, you know? I didn't know how it was with the men or how many there were or anything like that, but I sure as hell wanted them with me, I wanted to know what the fuck had happened." Castle spaced the words out.

"After awhile Brandt came back with about fifty guys, and there was Manny among them so I picked him out and held him while I had Cook deploy the men along the line so we could see how they looked before we did anything else. 'Spear,' I said when that was done, 'how the hell did you get all the way back to brigade . . . for Christ's sake you knew where I was . . . how come you went back to brigade?' 'Castle' he says to me . . . listen to this, Joe, he says, 'There was no time, no way. They shelled us into the ground,' he says, 'and when they came up our guns were smashed, our ammo buried, the trenches caved in . . . we had to take off.' 'But I didn't see anyone or hear anything.' So here it comes. 'Why,' he says, 'we went down into the dry riverbed or ditch or whatever that runs alongside of the road. We retreated down that.' How about that, Joe? That goddamned ditch . . . it swallowed them up, funneled them out of the lines straight to the rear, and if brigade HQ hadn't been in the ditch, Christ knows where they would have gone. To the end, wherever that was."

"Oh, no," Joe said, "I was there. They came right to us and stopped, and Manny told Johnny what happened."

"Yeah, but supposing you weren't there, supposing brigade wasn't there. That's what I keep thinking of now. Aaagh. I couldn't understand it and I kept asking him why and finally he said 'If you had been at the second Belchite you wouldn't be asking.'"

"You had too much against you," Joe said. "Shelled and bombed for hours, and nothing to reply with. There were French seventy-fives positioned around brigade, but the ammo never got to them – it's probably on the other side of the Pyrenees. They had nothing to fire, and I think the planes had them spotted to boot. I tell you, it was more pressure than the men could take. Valledor thought you did well to set up a second position."

"He did?" Castle was surprised. "How come Johnny didn't tell me?"

"Well, he thought you knew. You were promoted, Major Castle, the battalion was cited for bravery."

"Well, I thought the promotion was just a matter of bringing all the ranks into line with the Spanish army. Battalion commander, major, company *comandantes*, captains . . ."

"That, too. But you had performed the assignment given you, to hold the line for one day . . . Well, so it wasn't exactly that line. You fell back fifty meters or less . . . on the map it doesn't even show. The Fifteenth held the line from ten in the morning until three in the afternoon under terrific pressure and then fell back to secondary position, which they held until midnight when they were relieved by the Campesinos."

"Yeah, I know, that's how the citation read."

"That's how it was. You were too close, you're still too close, to appreciate the significance. Don't brood over it. The Campesinos are still there, and Campesino himself is supposed to be at this party. Come on, Major, you're a hero and you don't even know it."

"Yeah?" Castle got up. "You pick up the tab, Joe . . ."

They were the last to arrive at the party, which was thrown by the Central Committee of the Spanish Communist Party. Jose Diaz, Jesus Hernandez, and Dolores Ibarruri, Pasionaria . . . All of the faces he had seen on posters, in bad reproductions in wartime newspapers, were alive and close, looking much smaller, much more ordinary than he had imagined . . . Dark, small, and typically Spanish; it was hard for him to relate the people to the legends, except for Pasionaria, who radiated enough light and warmth to affect the entire room, which, unlike the Majestic's dining room, was unadorned.

He remembered Dolores from that July day more than a year and a half before, when she had come to speak to the troops before the Bruneté offensive. Then he had been the last man on a machine gun squad, and it seemed a hundred years ago. And yesterday he had been Major Mitchell Castle, leading the Lincoln Battalion in the parade of the international volunteers down the broad Diagonal, with the people of Barcelona paving the way with thousands of flowers, women running into the ranks to embrace the men who had come from far away to fight and die for their Spain.

Then he had noticed a young woman with a child in her arms. It was tough going for her with the weight of the child, and he had wondered why she tried so hard to keep pace with the head of the column, why she had not broken into the ranks to make her farewell as so many other women were doing. When the parade was over and the ranks broke, she had approached him.

"Please. I have a need to speak with you." Her large brown eyes held him.

"For sure," he had said. They had found a place in the shade of one of the trees lining the Diagonal.

"I must ask you," she said rapidly, and he had to slow her down to get the sense of what she was saying, "about one of you I have known, from when you were in charge, I believe – in Aguavivas, yes? – a *soldado* whose name is Leonardo Rogahn? I do not say it well."

Leo Rogin, Jesus Christ. Castle's stomach turned.

"He came with me," she went on. "To Barcelona, to bring my child to the hospital. The child cannot hear – they can do nothing for him. Leon left to find a place for us to stay. He did not return. I look for him in the parade, but he is not among the soldiers. Perhaps you have knowledge of where – "

"No," Castle broke in, "I have not . . . Wait." He thought better of what he was about to say – that she was not the only one he had deserted. "What is your name," he stalled, then, when she had told him, repeated "Maria. Yes, Maria, Leo Rogin. He returned to fight in the last battles."

Make it good and make it final, he decided. "He was killed, perhaps the last of us to die so in the war."

Maria had bowed her head, had clutched the child more closely. She had not cried.

"Have you a place now, or will you return to the village?" he asked. He did not know what he could do, but he did not want to abandon her as Leo had.

"We have a place," she had said, lifting her head to the now almost empty avenue. "A place the Socorro Rojo has found for us. They are good people and kind."

"And what will you do here?"

She studied his face for a moment before she replied. "I am now one with the people with whom I am staying." She shifted the child on her shoulder. "They will find something for me. I will do as they do, for the cause. When I came here I did not know, but they have taught me much. We must all do what we can."

When he had offered her money she had at first refused to accept it. "For the cause," he had said.

"In that case . . ."

He had folded half of his remaining pesetas into her hand. She had whispered, "Gracias."

"De nada," he had said. He watched her departing figure, the child's head resting on her shoulder, disappear down the Diagonal.

Dolores Ibarruri had stood on the reviewing stand, along with the premier of the Republic, Dr. Juan Negrin. Again, as at Bruneté, her clenched fist was raised, challenging the heavens. She spoke of the gratitude of the Spanish people, bidding the volunteers farewell, urging them to return when Spain was free and at peace, to be welcomed as her own flesh and blood. Castle had given her the clenched-fist salute as the battalion passed. The men behind raised their fists and roared "¡Viva! Long live the Republic!" and "¡Viva Pasionaria!"

And now here she was, close up. Tall for a Spanish woman, her solid figure clad in black, her eyes lively, her black hair drawn tightly back from her brow. She looked great, he thought, seeing her close up for the first time.

The room, a union hall, was large and square, low-ceilinged and full of guests, but Dolores easily dominated the place. She and other members of the Central Committee circulated among the square tables. There were blood sausages and spicy sauces and some sort of green cheese, garbanzos and parsley in olive oil, bread and red wine and water, and little wildflowers in glass vases at each table. A small space in the center of the floor was cleared for dancing, and nearby there was a black baby grand.

From time to time, Ibarruri would stop at the piano and rip off a gay Spanish tune, sometimes singing the words as well, and they all laughed and applauded and she smiled lovingly at them and applauded along with them. There were no speeches. Instead, each member of the Central Committee said what he had to say, moving from table to table, man to man, and what they had to say was very simple and had something of gratitude but more of love.

It was all balm to Mitch Castle, and he forgot about that last day and the dead. Sam Wild, who was there with the rest of the battalion officers and the brigade staffs of the IBs, never said a word about what had happened. And Mitch sang and danced a step or two with Dolores, and she hugged him and kissed him and autographed his new Party *carnet,* and then everyone was holding out their *carnets* for autographs and signing the Central Committee members' little red booklets.

All the brigades were represented: officers, commissars, rank and file . . . all the nations gathered in a feast that magically washed them clean and healed their hurts and strengthened their hearts. Here there were no questions, no soul searching, no doubts. The front, with its filth and noise and stench and boredom, disappeared, and the war itself brightened, became full of hope, fired by idealism. It became again a collective of shining courage, in which they had been highly privileged foreigners honored to participate and to share in the glory. And the glory belonged to the people of Spain and the heroic Spanish divisions, especially the Spanish Communist divisions, the Listers, Campesinos, Galans, Modestos, Durans; the famous *Quinto Regimiento,* the Fifth Regiment.

Jose Diaz, a small man in a heavy black suit, spoke quietly, saying his thanks confident of the victory of truth and justice, asking that they who were about to be reunited with their families give thought to Spain and bring the truth to their people. In the victory over Franco and fascism would lie peace and their own salvation. And if they would be so kind, he added, he and the other members of the CC would beg to leave, as there was much work to be done this day . . . as there was every day in Spain, now.

But the IB'ers were out of it. If there was work for them to do now, it would have to wait till they got home.

A week after the party, Negrin, on behalf of the government, invited selected members of the IBs to a luncheon. They came together in a banquet hall, a large, high-ceilinged room with somber shadows. The long table was of black wood, as were the chairs and sideboard; the drapes at the large windows were wine-red; and it all combined to create an atmosphere of gloom. Castle thought of it as typical of the elaborate mansions that would surround a city the size of Barcelona; dark isolation from the people whose blood had paid for it all. To dispel the gloom, Castle rejoiced that whoever had owned the joint, he was now gone; the place now belonged to the Republic.

They sat down to a spartan meal served on fine china. Though most of the government was there, Juan Negrin was unsmiling, his pale face seeming the only source of light in the room. He looked tired, drawn; he had just returned from a tour of the lines west of the Ebro, the lines the Internationals had left to the Spanish troops.

Negrin represented something different, Castle sensed. Perhaps something more of the core of Spain than Pasionaria. The Spain of letters, of art, of commerce, of a middle ground between the zeal and fanaticism of the monarchists, the church, the military, and the moguls of finance on one side – and on the other, the *campesinos*, workers, trade unionists, revolutionaries, and anarchists.

Castle thought of all the Spaniards he had known and loved: Pedro, Juan Abad, Eulalia laughing at the sight of a cripple in Madrid; the blonde kneeling for prayer as the bombs fell on the Ramblas; Jose Valledor, who had escaped after the fall of the north to come back and fight in the Aragon and now in Catalonia; the couple that had fed him before he swam the Ebro – they, in their different ways, had been Spain.

But Dr. Negrin was Spain now. Spain doomed and yet eternal, beaten but unconquerable; the soul haunting the dark places of time past, a presence in the half-light; a promise, in the bright gold of her skies and the blood-red of her people, of flamenco tomorrows.

Negrin spoke briefly. He promised to go on fighting, and asked that the volunteers be the Paul Reveres of their various countries, sounding the alarm of impending Nazi horror, rallying support for Spain to help make Madrid the tomb of fascism.

And then, in that gloomy mansion, they cheered him. They broke away from the table and surrounded Lister and Campesino, embracing them, promising a fight to the end. The end – a victory for all the democratic peoples of the world.

Castle, seeing things his own way – often so different from the way they were seen by others, and too often quite different than the truth – experienced this as certain. It was his own reality, and he had to live by it even if in the end it killed him.

That was Spain, and an end to Spain, and the end was the beginning. But the end was not to be until sometime in December, for the Lincolns had to wait in idleness while Spain struggled in agony. They had to wait for some goddamned commission from the League of Nations to make sure all the Russians left Spain, which was just so much horseshit because so few Mexicanskis had been there and they were already gone. He wondered about good old Maxim, round and boyish of face, smooth and unwrinkled, good humored, who had done what he could, teaching them the Maxims and Dicterovs and Remingtons.

And finally the commission came. Paste-white worms full of pomp and self-importance, some shining in uniforms, some stiffly attired in civilian clothes. One was clearly an American agent, fingering them over through the sheaves of paper spilling out of his gleaming black attaché case. A Persian officer, resplendent in gold braid and sky-high military cap, scornfully scanned their poor uniforms, looking down his long thin nose, disdaining to soil his black kid gloves or relinquish his gold-headed riding crop for even the pretense of counting.

Of course, Castle thought, he was the most honest of all, making no secret of his contempt, not only for them but for the entire procedure. He, at least, made no bones about the fact that Spain had been sold down the river.

The sights and sounds of the last battle were already slipping away. Castle's war was merging into a generalized mix of bravado and fear, an ending that wasn't, movement that seemed circular. In defeat, there was a promise to be kept.

AFTERWORD

CARY NELSON

For the full story of Mitch Castle's (and Milt Wolff's) life after Spain we will need to wait for the sequel to *Another Hill* that Wolff is writing. In the meantime, more detail about Wolff's postwar experience is in order. Wolff left Spain still in command of a group of Americans. In France, the men found themselves in an internment camp. Although they were released and permitted to sail home before long, many other members of the International Brigades spent much longer in those camps, as did thousands of other Spanish refugees, many of whom fled their country when Franco occupied the whole of Spain in 1939.

Back in the United States, Wolff became national commander of the Veterans of the Abraham Lincoln Brigade and devoted himself to veterans' affairs and political action. Since the Lincolns had no official status as veterans, there was no American government provision for their medical needs and no mechanism to help them gain employment. The veterans organization, named so as to include the Americans who served in a number of different battalions, would have to serve that role. Meanwhile, other Americans remained in Franco's prisons, while the fate of those Internationals from fascist countries like Germany and Italy was doubly uncertain. Wretched as the internment camps were, therefore, they were for many refugees a better option than repatriation. Loyalist supporters sent back to Spain often faced summary execution. That was exactly what was at stake when France proposed closing the camps in 1940. As a result Wolff was among several hundred people who picketed the French consulate in Manhattan. He was arrested there, and while on trial was served a subpoena that heralded the Left's public treatment over the next twenty years: he was ordered to appear before Martin Dies's House Committee for Un-American Activities. It would not be the last time Wolff had to testify in Washington to defend the Americans who fought in Spain.

Before that time, of course, other events intervened. Wolff had applied for a commission in the United States Army's Officer's Reserve Corps in March 1939. "I went to Spain," he wrote in his application letter, "sincerely believing that in fighting for Spanish Democracy I was helping preserve American Democracy. In view of recent world events and the growing threat to America, I am anxious to volunteer my experience and myself for the United States Army." He was turned down a few months later, his service in Spain explicitly cited as the reason. As World War II widened, however, other opportunities opened up. Wolff met William Donovan socially when Donovan was serving as a liaison with the British Special Services, and Wolff was subsequently recruited. Wolff then served as a recruiter for the British from 1940 to 1941, and in fact recruited several other Lincoln vets. The following year Wolff enlisted in the U.S. Army, but he found his advancement at Officer's Training School blocked. Seeking an explanation, he noted the initials "P.A." on his file and soon found out they identified him as a "premature antifascist." Prevented from finishing OTC, he was then assigned to pointless noncombatant roles. Through a complex series of maneuvers and accidents Wolff managed to get transferred to the campaign in Asia. In the fall of 1943 he was in North Africa and a few months later he joined General Joseph Stillwell in Burma. Wolff was among those who marched down through the central jungles as part of the campaign to retake the country. It was there that he was awarded a field commission, there that he received a theater ribbon with the first of his battle stars, and there as well that he came down with malaria.

Meanwhile, "Wild Bill" Donovan had been asked to form the U.S. Office of Strategic Services and he wanted Wolff on board. In August 1944, Wolff was in the OSS in Europe. He took parachute training and participated in one mission behind the lines, eventually crossing from northern Italy into southern France where he managed to connect with the Spanish resistance. In May of the following year Wolff was back in the United States.

Active again as national commander of the Lincoln vets, Wolff defended them during the long years of national anticommunism. He also participated in a number of other progressive organizations. He was political director of the Joint Anti-Fascist Refugee Committee in the late forties. He toured the South as assistant treasurer of the bail fund of the Civil Rights Congress to raise funds and build support for Willie McGee and the Martinsville Seven; in both cases African Americans were facing death sentences on framed charges. Later, Wolff helped furnish bail for those prosecuted under the Smith Act.

Meanwhile, Wolff had married Anne Gondos and raised two children in Connecticut. Eventually, Wolff was divorced and moved to California, where he married Frieda Irene Salzmann, well known as a passionate defender of the Spanish Republic. More recently, he has been active in the San Francisco Bay Area Post of the Veterans of the Abraham Lincoln Brigade. In that capacity he has helped provide ambulances and other medical aid for several Central American countries, helped establish ANC clinics in South Africa, and worked to fund Oliver Law Scholarships for African American students in Oakland. In October 1993 he went to Cuba to challenge U.S. travel restrictions and encourage normalized relations between the two countries. On his return to the United States, as on his return from Spain more than fifty years earlier, his passport was confiscated.

MILTON WOLFF was the last commander of the Abraham Lincoln Battalion, which fought in the Spanish Civil War. He served with the British Special Services before Pearl Harbor, marched with General Joseph "Vinegar Joe" Stillwell in Burma, and was with William "Wild Bill" Donovan in the OSS. Wolff has been national commander of the Veterans of the Abraham Lincoln Brigade. He continues to be active in civil rights and human rights movements here and abroad.

CARY NELSON is Jubilee Professor of Liberal Arts and Sciences at the University of Illinois, Urbana-Champaign. He is the author of a number of books, including *Repression and Recovery: Modern American Poetry and the Politics of Cultural Memory*, and is the coeditor of the *Collected Poems* of the Lincoln Battallion's poet laureate, Edwin Rolfe.

University of Illinois Press
1325 South Oak Street
Champaign, Illinois 61820-6903
www.press.uillinois.edu